Homeseeking

Homeseeking

KARISSA CHEN

G. P. Putnam's Sons
New York

PUTNAM
— EST. 1838 —

G. P. PUTNAM'S SONS
Publishers Since 1838
An imprint of Penguin Random House LLC

ISBN 9780593712993

Printed in the United States of America

Book design by Daniel Brount

This is a work of fiction. Names, characters, places, and incidents either are the product of
the author's imagination or are used fictitiously, and any resemblance to actual persons,
living or dead, businesses, companies, events, or locales is entirely coincidental.

For my grandparents,
Henry 陸海林, *Eileen* 康秋季, *Larry* 陳隆寶, *and Chi-Yen* 張笄翊,
who carried home with them wherever they loved

那些消逝了的歲月，彷彿隔著一塊積著灰塵的玻璃，看得到，抓不著。

他一直在懷念著過去的一切。如果他能衝破那塊積著灰塵的玻璃，他會走回早已消逝的歲月。

—花樣年華 (根據劉以鬯的《對倒》改編的)

As though he were looking through a dusty windowpane, those bygone years were something he could see but not grasp. He yearned for everything that had happened in the past. If only he could break through that dusty glass, he could reclaim the years that had long since vanished.

—*In the Mood for Love*
(quote adapted from Liu Yichang's "Intersection")

「世鈞，我們回不去了。」
—張愛玲《半生緣》

"Shijun, we can't go back."

—Eileen Chang, *Half a Lifelong Romance*

A Note on Languages

O NE OF THE challenges in writing an English-language story about the Chinese and Taiwanese diaspora is figuring out how to faithfully represent the different Sinitic languages spoken in different regions (and sometimes even within the same region). Because the Chinese written language uses a representational (versus phonetic) system, the same written word has many different pronunciations, depending on what language the speaker is using. This includes names. Given that my characters move within various Chinese-speaking regions of the world, I wanted to make sure to denote their code-switching in a way that would feel accurate. Therefore, each character may be referred to in a multitude of ways and may even broaden or change the way they think of themselves given a situation or over time. For this reason, chapters have not been labeled by character names, as our characters' names evolve over time.

An astute reader might also notice the novel is told in alternating points of view, with Suchi's narrative moving forward in time and Howard's moving backward in time, with only a few exceptions.

Mandarin is mostly represented in pinyin, although there are several exceptions, particularly when in Taiwan or for commonly used romanizations (e.g., "Chiang Kai-shek"). Other Sinitic languages are represented in a combination of accepted romanization systems and my own sense of how words are pronounced.

For many people in the world, learning more than one language is a necessity, either because of migration or simply because the place they live in is a global one and survival dictates it. It is a skill that requires an ability to adapt and challenge oneself, and for many immigrants, it's one of the most difficult, humbling, and uneasy parts of coming to a new country. If you, the reader, find yourself confused, I hope instead of giving up, you might take a moment to imagine what it must be like for those who have to navigate this on a daily basis, and then forge onward.

Homeseeking

Overture

APRIL 1947
Shanghai

IN THE LAST violet minutes of the disappearing night, the longtang wakes.

The neighborhood's familiar symphony opens with the night-soil man's arrival: the trundle of his cart on the uneven road, the chime of his bell. With a slurry and a swish, he empties the latrines left in front of uniform doors and sings a parting refrain. In his wake, stairs and hinges creak; women peek out into the alleyway to claim their overturned night stools. Crouching, they clean silt from the wooden buckets: bamboo sticks clock, clamshells rattle, water from back-door faucets glugs and splatters. By the time they have finished, the sugar porridge vendor has emerged, announcing her goods in repetitive singsong as she pushes her cart. Later, the others will join her: the tea egg man, the pear syrup candy peddler, the vegetable and rice sellers, each with their own seasoned melodies. But for now, it is her lone call that drifts through the lanes of Sifo Li.

She passes the Zhang family shikumen, the sixth row house along this perimeter. Inside, on the second floor, sixteen-year-old

Suchi sleeps fitfully after hours of weeping, her slender limbs twisted around the thin cotton sheet, her sweat seeping into the mattress. She is mired in a nightmare in which Haiwen no longer recognizes her. A delicate crust of dried tears rims her lashes.

Next to her is the older Zhang daughter, Sulan, who snuck back home only an hour earlier. Her skin is sticky with the smell of smoke and alcohol and sweat. She sleeps peacefully, dreaming of dancing in a beautiful dress of plum taffeta and silk, arm in arm with her best friend, Yizhen.

In the room above, her father, Li'oe, lies sleepless, troubled by uncertainties. He wonders how much his stash of fabi has depreciated overnight, how much gold he might buy off the black market with what currency he has left. He weighs the continued cost of running his bookstore, of printing the underground journals—all he is taking from his family, not to mention the danger—and for a moment guilt licks at the edge of his thoughts. He regrets now pawning that little ring he purchased the day Suchi was born, two delicate twists of gold braided into one, something he'd saved for her dowry. But Sulan had insisted she'd found the perfect secondhand cloth to make Suchi a qipao for her birthday, and he'd agreed to give Sulan the money. Now he thinks only of how valuable that loop of gold has become.

Beside him, his wife, Sieu'in, pretends to sleep, pretends to be unaware of her husband's nervous shifting. She inventories the food left in their stores—half a cup of rationed gritty red rice, a handful of dehydrated mushrooms, cabbage she pickled weeks ago, radish scraps boiled to broth, a single cut of scallion she has coaxed into regrowth in the spring sun. She can stretch these ingredients for a week, maybe a week and a half—she will make a watery yet flavorful congee, and when none of that remains, she will empty the rice powder from the bag and boil it into milky liquid offering the illusion of nourishment. After that? She won't add to her husband's worries by asking him for more money, she decides. She has a few pieces of jewelry remaining—the jade bracelet that presses coolly against her cheek now, for instance. Her mother gave it to her from her own dowry, and its color is deep, like the dark leaves of the green vegetables she so desperately craves.

A floor and a half below, in the pavilion room, Siau Zi, their boarder and employee, is dreaming of the older Zhang daughter. Sulan smiles invitingly, her lips painted red, her hair permed and clipped. He is effortlessly charming in this dream; for once he says the right things to make her adore him. *I can take care of you*, he tells her, *I'll be somebody in this new China, you'll see*, and she sighs into his embrace.

Outside Siau Zi's window, the sky is turning a violent shade of pink. The neighborhood's song shifts its layers as its inhabitants dust off their dreams and rise. Lovers murmur. Coals in stoves crackle. Oil sizzles in a pan, ready to fry breakfast. Doors groan open, metal knockers clang against heavy wood. A grandma sweeps the ground in front of her shikumen, the broom scratching a staccato beat against the cobblestone. A child cries, seized from sleep.

The porridge vendor continues her route. In vain, she calls out, remembering a time when her goods were beloved by the children of this neighborhood, a time before the wars, when she could afford to use white sugar and sticky rice, when adding lotus seed hearts and osmanthus syrup was standard instead of a great luxury. As she nears the shikumen where the Wang family lives, she pauses, recalling how the young son particularly delighted in her dessert. She bellows out twice: *Badaon tsoh! Badaon tsoh!*, deep throated, as passionate as if she were calling out to a lover—but she is met with the dim stillness of the upper windows. After a moment, she blots her sleeve against her forehead, leans into her cart, and continues on her way, the echo of her song trailing behind her.

But the Wang household is awake.

Yuping has not slept the entire night; her eyes are puffy and dark. She tries to cover her despair with makeup, but when she catches her reflection in the mirror, the tears resume. Her husband, Chongyi, pretends not to notice. He dresses quietly, parts his salt-and-pepper hair to one side with a fine-toothed comb, and slicks strays with oil. He thinks to gift his son, Haiwen, this comb. It is carved from ivory and inlaid with mother-of-pearl, a frivolous vanity he has held on to after all these years when they have sold so much else.

In the next room, their eleven-year-old daughter, Haijun, rummages through her music box, searching for a memento to gift her big brother. Onto the floor, she hurls the paper cutout dolls, the hair ribbons, the red crepe flower she palmed from a store's decorative sign. All these so-called treasures and she has nothing worth giving him. In a fury, she balls herself beneath her blanket, hoping to suffocate in the damp jungle of her breath.

In the attic room, the eldest son, Haiming, and his pregnant wife have been up since before dawn. The room is foul with the stench of bile, Ellen having vomited twice. She doesn't want to go to the train station later, she tells her husband. But Haiming only looks at her, silent and somber.

Haiwen is first to descend the stairs. In his new uniform, his armpits are already sweating through the heavy, unforgiving fabric. He steps outside, into the modest courtyard of their shikumen, and looks up at the expanse of sky. The pink is receding, giving way to a noncommittal blue. In several minutes, nothing of that brilliant color will remain, only a veil of thin cloud, like a layer of soy milk skin.

He listens to the longtang's symphony, this comfort he has grown up with. He closes his eyes and sees it all, no longer a symphony but a movie, one more vibrant than any he's attended at the cinema: The cobblestone alleys crammed with wares and possessions. The neighborhood children, laughing as they chase one another. The barber they nearly knock over, Yu yasoh, and his client, Lau Die, whose crown is sparse but beard is full. The nearby breakfast stall opened daily by Zia yasoh, and the rickshaw driver who sits slurping a bowl of soy milk on a low stool. The second-story window that opens so Mo ayi can call to a passing vendor, who stops as she lowers a basket with a few coins in exchange for three shriveled loquats. Loh konkon and Zen konkon in the middle of it all, the two men oblivious to the surrounding hubbub as they mull over their daily game of xiangqi, a ritual that continues uninterrupted as it would on any other day.

But it is not any other day.

Haiwen opens his eyes.

Today is the day he is leaving.

In another two hours he will be on the train with the other enlistees, a bulging backpack pressed against his belly, a photograph of Suchi against his breast, a tremble in his heart, waving at the receding image of his family. The longtang of his childhood, Sifo Li, will be behind him; Fourth Road, with its bustling teahouses and calligraphy stores, will be behind him; soon, Shanghai, too, will be behind him. For years afterward, he will riffle through his memories of this place he considers home, layering them on top of one another like stacks of rice paper, trying to remember what was when and never quite seeing the full picture.

For now, Haiwen closes his eyes again. His mind traces the alleyways he knows so well, the well-trod path between his house and Suchi's, cobblestones upon which he will walk one last time in the coming minutes: The four-house expanse between his shikumen and the first main lane on their left. The right turn down the lane that intersects with the one that heads toward the west gate. Another left, another main artery. The straight long distance toward the south gate's guojielou, the turn right before the arched exit. The five plain back doors until the painted bunny comes into view, its flaked white outline wringing a pang in Haiwen's chest. He will leave his violin here: he sees himself setting it down, laying it against the chipped paint as tenderly as he imagines a mother abandons a beloved baby.

He knows he will look up at the second-floor window. Suchi's window. Its vision dredges an unbearable loneliness in him.

He squeezes his eyes tighter, tries harder, and what comes next is impossible: He is peering through her window, gazing upon her as she sleeps. In another moment, he has prised open the panels and is inside her room. She is dreaming, she is talking to him in her sleep. He places a palm against her cheek, strokes a thumb across the soft velvet of her skin. He takes in the fringe of her lashes, the bud of her mouth. A mouth he wishes he had remembered to kiss one final time. He wants to remember every pore, every stray hair, wants to emblazon her into his memory, even as he is certain he will always know her, that even if he is an old man by the time he returns to her, even if she has aged and changed, he will know her. He brushes the hair sticky on her parted lips, his fingers lingering on the warmth of her breath. He is sorry for what he is about to do, what he has done; he will never stop being sorry.

Her nightmares have turned sweet. Suchi can smell sour plums on the horizon. *Is it already so late in spring?* she murmurs. Later, she will wake and remember yesterday's careless words; she will lose half a lifetime to regret. But for now: she can feel the warm heft of Haiwen's presence encircling hers, the tender touch of his hand cupping her face, and she believes he has forgiven her. Her body unclenches. Right before a deep, untroubled sleep claims her, she hears his voice in her ear, kind, reassuring. *Soon*, he promises her, *the plum rains are almost here.*

JANUARY 2008
Los Angeles

A CHORUS OF VIOLINS ushered Suchi into Howard's life for the third and final time. Mozart's Violin Concerto No. 5 in A Major, celebratory and elegant, floated out of muffled speakers in the 99 Ranch Market, its golden jubilation incongruous with Howard's mood, the blank haze of gray he'd been living in since he'd buried Linyee sixteen months earlier. He glanced up from the bananas he was inspecting to search for the source of his irritation. Instead, he saw her.

She was picking up Korean melons, their skins the color of lemon curd. He watched her knock on them with her knuckles, her head bent to listen. Howard was sure it was Suchi this time, but he had mistaken so many women for her over the last four decades. Women with cheekbones like hers, gaits like hers, but who transformed into other people when he approached. He stood transfixed. This woman's face was plump and sagging, her hair was thin and gray at the roots, but her eyes—eyes never changed, he had once heard someone say.

And hers, caramel and bright, were every bit as intense as he remembered, even in the task of selecting the ripest melon.

"Excuse me," he said hesitantly in Mandarin, and she glanced up. Her eyes widened.

"Wang Haiwen." The name came out carefully, more a statement than a question.

For a moment he couldn't respond. He was a child again, a teenager again, not in this American supermarket but in the alleyways of their youth. He gripped the handle of his shopping cart, feeling the bite of plastic where it was uneven. "So it is you," he said.

"Wang Haiwen," she said, more briskly this time, a confirmation. She smiled, revealing teeth too straight and white to be real.

He pulled his cart alongside hers. His, empty aside from three bunches of bananas; hers, already filled with various greens, tomatoes, a box of Asian pears, and a daikon radish. "You live here now?" he asked. It was a dumb question; he didn't know what else to say.

"I moved in with my son and daughter-in-law a couple years ago," she answered in Shanghainese.

A jolt ran through him. Howard had not heard his childhood language in several years, and it caused in him an aching relief, the sensation reminiscent of a sour candy his granddaughter had once given him.

"They said they needed help with the grandchildren," Suchi continued, "but to be honest, I think they worried I was getting lonely, living all alone."

Howard understood that loneliness. Each morning he woke up to an empty house and expected to hear Linyee in the kitchen, pots clanging, a mug being washed, a soap opera keening on the television set. Instead, he heard nothing but the breeze in the trees, or a lone pigeon purring, or the neighbors mowing their lawn.

"And you?" Suchi asked. "Have you lived in Los Angeles long?"

"We've been here for about thirty years," Howard responded in Shanghainese, then inwardly revised. Not *we* anymore. *I.*

Suchi's eyes grew soft. "And your wife?"

Had he become that transparent? Did every thought of Linyee paint itself across his face whether or not he wanted it to?

"Linyee passed away a little over a year ago," he said quietly.

She murmured a sound of condolence. She reached out and touched his arm. He stared down at the back of her hand, at the age spots dotting her dark blue veins. One splotch of chipped coral polish remained on her pinkie nail. He remembered she'd had beautiful hands, once.

"Pneumonia," he said in response to the question she hadn't asked. "But really, Parkinson's."

Suchi retracted her hand. "I wish I could have met her," she said.

"I would have liked that," he answered, and they both said nothing for a while, letting each of their kind lies mingle and hang in the air.

Suchi broke the silence. "You must love bananas." She looked pointedly into his shopping cart.

"They help with digestion," he said with mock defensiveness.

"I recall you having an extremely efficient digestive system."

"I don't know about you, but things don't work quite as well as when we were kids. Getting old has been a disappointment."

Suchi laughed, full bellied and open-mouthed. Her laughter sounded exactly as he recalled, like spring rain upon glass.

"It's so nice to hear you laugh," he said, and immediately regretted the sentimentality of the words.

10

"And it's nice to see you, Haiwen."

"People call me Howard now. Easier for the Americans to pronounce."

"How-wud," she pronounced slowly. "Not so easy for a Chinese person to pronounce."

"And yet even my Chinese friends know me as Howard."

"Wasn't that the name they gave you at that missionary school? I thought you hated it."

He was surprised—even he'd forgotten the origin of his English name. "I couldn't think of another one," he said. "Now I'm used to it."

"Lucky for me, my name is easy for Americans. Many people just call me Sue." She shook her head and smiled. "I must be going now," she said. She plucked a melon from the mountain before her and made a show of rapping it. "You should buy a melon. They sound promising."

Howard was pulling the car out of the lot when it occurred to him that neither of them had asked for the other's contact information. He wasn't sure if he was relieved or sorry.

AS HOWARD WAS UNPACKING THE GROCERIES, HIS CELL phone rang. It was an unwieldy black brick of an object with (preposterously) no buttons to dial and a crowded touch screen, a gift from his older daughter, Yiping, who insisted it was the coolest new technology. Aside from picking up phone calls from his daughters and occasionally hitting autodial, he hadn't figured out how to use it. He reminded his daughter what a waste of money it was each time she called and did so again this time.

"Ba, I told you, I could teach you to use it. It's not that hard. You're just being stubborn."

"I'm too old," he said. "It's too late to get used to something new. What's wrong with the regular phone?"

"I feel safer this way," Yiping said. "So I don't have to wonder where you are."

"I'm a widower, not senile," he responded.

Yiping caught him up on what the kids had been doing— Jennifer had won second place at the fifth-grade spelling bee and Charlie had been named the high school orchestra's first violin. She mentioned that her husband, Adam, an American-born Chinese of Cantonese descent she'd met in college, was away again for work and that she herself was overloaded at the hospital.

"It's not good he travels so much," he told his daughter. "Couples need to be together."

"That's the nature of consulting, Ba," Yiping said. "You go where the client is."

"I'm telling you, that's how couples fall apart."

"Well, we can't all be you and Ma, never spending a single night away from each other. Things aren't like when you two were married. It's different now."

Howard was about to point out that he had occasionally traveled for work too, but Yiping interrupted.

"Hold on, the kids want to say hi." Charlie didn't say much more beyond "Hey, Gonggong, how's it going?" in English before handing the phone to Jennifer, who chattered for several uninterrupted minutes, giving him a blow-by-blow account of the spelling bee and spelling words in English he'd never heard of. "X-E-N-O-P-H-O-B-I-A!" she exclaimed proudly.

"Great job, baobei," he said.

Before Yiping hung up, she asked him again if he would consider moving in with them. Haiwen sighed inwardly. Although both of his daughters had grown more concerned since Linyee's passing, he couldn't help but feel that his older daughter's frequent calls to update him on the children were now nothing more than thinly veiled excuses to fret over him like he was her third child. At least his younger daughter, Yijun, seemed to genuinely care about what he was thinking about and doing; she didn't nag at him the way Yiping did. But he didn't know how to point this out to his older daughter without hurting her feelings. He knew she didn't know how else to demonstrate her love.

"Maryland is too cold for an old man like me" was all he said, and Yiping sighed.

Howard cooked a simple supper of rice, string beans, and sliced pork with onions while soccer played on the television in the background. He couldn't understand a word the Spanish sportscasters were saying, but the rising inflection and rapid excitement in their voices needed no translation.

He finished dinner with a wedge of the melon Suchi had encouraged him to buy. If Linyee were alive, she would have cut each wedge into perfectly proportioned cubes and served them on a plate with toothpicks. But Howard couldn't be bothered with the extra work. Instead, he bit into the canoe-shaped slice, letting the juices slide down his chin. The flesh was soft and sweet and smelled like a day-old bouquet of lilies. He ignored the grief lapping at the edge of his skull and focused on the freedom he felt in being able to make a mess. *This is joy*, he told himself as he took another bite.

THAT NIGHT, HE DREAMED THE OLD NIGHTMARE OF Shanghai on fire, bombs bursting into crimson flames on the horizon while he stood in a boat rapidly filling, cold water sluicing across his boots. Muddy figures ran toward him, disappearing before he could touch them. It happened in perfect silence. No screams, no brick exploding, no wind or percussion of firearms. He sensed he was waiting for someone, that he was forgetting something. Before the feeling clarified, a white sea engulfed him, drowning him.

Howard woke up in the morning holding on to an empty ache. It felt as if his arms were encircled around nothing, that the cavity in his torso was more cavernous than his skin allowed.

HOWARD HAD JUST RETURNED FROM HIS WEEKLY VISIT to the cemetery when the phone rang. Normally, he ignored numbers he didn't recognize—they were usually telemarketers trying to trick him into buying vacations—but the pang of loneliness lingered in his chest, and on impulse he answered.

"Hello?" he said in English.

There was a brief static pause. He heard a shift in movement. And then: "Howard?" The voice was female, tinged with a Chinese accent. Howard didn't recognize it. His throat shuttered.

"Who is this?" he asked in Mandarin.

"Are you coming to Wei's party?" the woman asked. Howard didn't respond, confused. The woman added in English, with a touch of exasperation, "This is Yurong, you know, Wei's wife?" She switched back to Mandarin, chiding playfully, "You've really grown into an addled old man, haven't you?"

Howard had forgotten about his friend's eightieth birthday party. Linyee had been the one to organize their social calendar.

"I didn't recognize your number."

"Ah, our children bought us these phones for Christmas, the ping-guo one like your daughter buy for you," Yurong said, switching to Chinglish. "Wei think they are too mafan, but my grandchildren showed me how you take pictures with it." She giggled. "Anyway, bie wang le, Friday at Golden Phoenix. Five o'clock. Everyone will be there. It's been too long since we get together. You must come."

The last time he'd seen all of his friends was at the reception after the funeral, hazy faces pitying him, murmuring condolences. Before then? He couldn't remember. He'd been too preoccupied with Linyee's illness.

"Of course," Howard answered, scribbling down the details on a Post-it note. "I'll be there."

THE GOLDEN PHOENIX WAS ONE OF THOSE SAN GABRIEL dim sum banquet restaurants situated in a strip mall. On the weekends, families in cars circled the vast parking lot trying to be the first to zero in on a car pulling out and triumphantly claim the spot. This evening though, the lot, while still crowded, seemed far more civilized. The Hus, who were old friends of the owners' parents' cousins, had negotiated a deal to reserve the entire restaurant for Wei's party. As Howard walked in, a young woman introduced herself as their oldest granddaughter and took his coat, giving him a red card with a table number handwritten in gold.

The main hall was already festive with people. Small girls swathed in tulle and boys in gray suits and miniature checkered bow ties chased one another with balloons bouncing in their hands. Their parents slouched nearby holding heavy glasses of dark liquid—cognac, or maybe just Coke. Howard found his way to his table, near the front dais, where he assumed Wei and Yurong would sit with their family, and settled into his chair.

He was glad he wouldn't be the group's only widower—Winston's wife had passed five years ago—and then felt ugly for the selfish thought. Still, he didn't know if he could have handled sitting at a table with all couples. Although Tina and George's constant bickering drew awkward smiles from everyone and Jianfeng consistently talked over his newly immigrated forty-something-year-old wife, Howard envied them. His and Linyee's marriage had not been perfect by any means; it had survived their different backgrounds, her father's disapproval, his gambling problem, immigration to a foreign country, financial uncertainty, and more. There'd been moments when he wasn't even sure he still loved her. Yet, by the end, they were bound by their history, by the pain and laughter that could never be understood by anybody else. He missed her companionship above all.

Tina and George appeared at the table first, followed by Mary and Michael, Jianfeng and his new wife (what was her name? Howard could never remember), and Yanhua and Ted. Howard rose with the arrival of each couple, shaking hands with his old friends, dutifully answering questions about what he had been doing ("Yes, I still teach violin from time to time, to get me out of the house") and asking about their kids. George reminded Howard he was next—"Didn't you just celebrate your seventy-seventh? Three more years and you'll be joining the octogenarian club!" And though Howard made a mental note to look up the unfamiliar word, within a few moments, he couldn't recall how it was pronounced.

Despite their varying levels of English (George, who had been educated at a British school in Hong Kong, spoke nearly perfect—if slightly accented—English, while no one was sure how much Michael actually understood), over the years, it had become the language they predominantly slipped into when they got together, peppered with phrases in various Sinitic languages. Although they all understood some Mandarin, Tina and George were most comfortable with Cantonese, Mary and Michael preferred Taiwanese, and Jianfeng's Beijing accent was so thick, Ted complained it was like listening to someone with marbles in their cheeks. So they defaulted to the language of their adopted country, as difficult and slippery as it sometimes proved to be.

When they were all seated, Yanhua leaned in conspiratorially and gestured at the three empty seats at the round table. "I hear Winston has a new girlfriend," she said.

"Hai me!" Tina exclaimed in Cantonese.

"I hear it from a friend who live in Coral Sunset," Yanhua said.

"Coral Sunset?" Jianfeng's wife repeated in halting English.

"The retirement community Winston lives in," Jianfeng told her impatiently in Mandarin. He gestured at Yanhua to continue.

"She say she see Winston spending lot of time with a woman there. Someone not from the community, so she think he must have met her somewhere else."

"Somewhere else!" Tina said. "But where would Winston go to meet women!"

"He's not a cripple," George said. "There are many places to meet women in the world. The supermarket, the library, Starbucks—"

"Oh, and you know?" Tina said. "That's what you do when you say you have errands to run? Meeting women?"

"I'm not going out to meet women, I'm escaping the nagging of one."

"Ha," Tina snorted, "as if any woman would want to talk to someone as ugly as you!"

Yanhua glanced at them and rolled her eyes. "Okay, anyway, Yurong say he ask a 'plus-one' for tonight. Yurong want to know who, she is very annoyed, because it ruining her seat arrangements, but Wei tell her suanle, just let him bring who he wants. Wei's only condition is she also bring along a friend." Her gaze slid to Howard. "For you."

Howard sensed everyone's eyes turn to him. "Oh, no no," he said.

"Wah, this should be an interesting night," Tina laughed, clapping her hands.

"You take too much enjoyment in people's embarrassment," George said. He cut off any retort his wife might have had by waving down a waiter for a bottle of Tsingtao.

"Nice to see everybody is here," a deep voice bellowed. Howard swiveled around. Winston, a portly, balding man, stood by his chair, and behind him, an elegant woman with a short black bob wearing a gold-sequined shirt and cream-colored silk pants. Howard heard—and felt—a murmur ripple around him. Winston clapped him on the shoulder. "Howard," he said. "Good to see you."

Howard stood and shook his hand as he discreetly studied the woman. She was so different from Kay, Winston's wife. Kay had been matronly, someone who had sported a practical curly perm for decades. As a devout Buddhist, Kay had preferred modest clothing, and aside from her wedding band and a jade pendant Howard had never seen her without, she had rarely worn jewelry. Winston had enjoyed complaining about her austerity: "What a difficult woman! What can a man buy his wife if she doesn't like what all other women

18

like!" Everyone knew, however, that Winston had loved not having to waste the money.

This woman, in contrast, shimmered with diamonds and gold that adorned her fingers, wrists, and earlobes. Howard could tell she had once been beautiful, and even now, in what appeared to be her early seventies, she was still handsome.

"And you are . . . ?"

"You can call me Annie," she said, holding out a hand, two digits flashing with jewels. Her voice was surprisingly girlish, and she had no discernible accent to her English at all.

The rest of the table introduced themselves and began to pepper Annie with questions while the couple got settled. Winston flashed Howard a grin behind Annie's back.

"So," Mary asked, leaning atop her folded arms, "how do you and Winston meet?"

"We both live at Coral Sunset," Annie said.

"Oh! So you *do* live there," Yanhua said.

"Well, yes, we're both involved in the choir—Winston has a marvelous voice—"

"How romantic," Tina chimed in. "I wish *I* had chosen a man who could sing to me. George is tone-deaf."

"I still sing to you, my dear," George said.

"To torture me," she said, tossing him a dirty look.

"Oh, wait, no, we're not—" Annie began at the moment Winston rose and said, "Ah, here she is—"

Howard turned to see Winston reaching out to shepherd a woman closer to the table. A bubble of surprise rose in him. It was Suchi.

"Sorry I'm late," she said in Mandarin, dipping her shoulders in apology. The loose sleeves of her navy dress shifted upward as she bent, revealing a small scab above her left elbow. As she lifted her head, her eyes met Howard's. Her lips parted.

"This is Zhang Suchi," Winston introduced her in Mandarin, then switched to English. "But you can call her Sue."

The group murmured weak hellos, confused or embarrassed or maybe both.

"Sue," Annie said from her seat, reaching out to touch Suchi's arm. "I'm glad you could make it."

Winston led Suchi to her chair, three from Howard, and sat next to her. "It's so nice to have everyone together again," he said in Mandarin, patting Suchi's hand. She looked down and, after a beat, withdrew her palm into her lap.

"So *you're* Winston's new girlfriend," Tina said, switching the conversation back to English. Mary shot her a cautionary glance.

"Aren't we too old for those terms?" Winston asked. "At her age, it's a bit insulting to call her a *girl*."

"Where are you from?" Mary asked Suchi.

"I moved from New York," Suchi said. "My son lives here."

"She means laojia," Yanhua said. "Back in old country."

"Shanghai," Suchi responded.

"Oh!" Tina said. "Howard is from Shanghai too. You should see if you were neighbors!"

Again, all eyes fell on Howard. He stared down at the silver chopstick holder in front of him. Shaped like a miniature dragon, it curled in a sideways S and held a cloud aloft.

"Actually—" Suchi started to say, but she was interrupted by a woman's voice blaring, "Good evening!" in Mandarin through the speakers. Yurong, wrapped in a gold and cream lace dress, had walked to the edge of the stage with a microphone.

"Welcome, everyone!" she said. She flashed a grin, then switched to English. "Me and Wei are so happy you are here." She glanced at Wei, seated behind her in a tux. He waved, nodding and smiling. Behind them on the bright red backsplash, the gold character 壽[1] glinted from floor to ceiling. "So nice to see so many friends and family. We will make some speeches later, but I know everyone is hungry—for us old people, it is past our dinnertime!—so first course will be served."

A large platter of cold jellyfish, julienned pig's ears, sliced marinated beef, cucumbers, and wood-ear mushrooms, garnished with an impressive carrot rabbit, was placed on the lazy Susan in the center of the table. Questions were forgotten as everyone dug in.

For the next few courses, Howard tried simultaneously to dodge questions from Annie about his grieving process while straining to listen in on the conversations Suchi was having. Had she told anyone yet they'd known each other? Was she waiting for him to tell them? But the moment to bring it up seemed to have passed.

At the climax of the thirteen-course meal, right as the lobsters were served, Yurong reappeared onstage to announce several people wanted to make speeches. "Not me, though—Wei says I talk too much already." She called their son, Jack, onto the stage.

"I hear he went through a terrible divorce," Howard overheard Yanhua whispering across the table to Tina and Mary. "His wife cheat on him with a man she work with."

Jack gave a sentimental speech about how Wei had taught him how to fix the toilet when he was nine, and how he admired how his father had arrived in this country with nothing and managed to build a successful business. After Jack, Bruce, a white man who was Wei's longtime coworker, got onstage and cracked a few jokes. "Wei was

21

the first Chinese guy I'd ever met, which was lucky for all the Chinese guys I met afterward," he said, laughing nervously when no one else did. Ted made a speech too, about how he was grateful Wei had taken him and Yanhua into his fold when they'd first immigrated. "Without him and Yurong, we would never have figured out where the cheapest Chinese grocery was or how to pay our bills!" Ted's speech was followed by a performance by one of Wei's granddaughters, who strummed a guitar and sang a song she said she had written in his honor. The song was funny, if only because the lyrics described the golden rice paddies and thatched huts of Wei's youth, things Howard was certain had not factored into Wei's memory of growing up in bustling Beijing.

After the speeches, a DJ began playing music. He started off with "Goodbye My Love," a popular Teresa Teng song that played at every social event Howard attended with this group. Howard watched as Wei led Yurong to the dance floor and remembered the many times he and Linyee had slow-danced to this song. She'd loved Teresa Teng.

"Dance?" Winston asked Suchi.

"I'm too full," Suchi said in Mandarin. "You go without me."

"Well then," Winston said. "Annie?" He extended his arm to her and they wove toward the dance floor.

Howard glanced at Suchi, who was staring after the couples.

"You used to love dancing," he said in Mandarin. "Even if it was by yourself."

Suchi turned to Howard. "I have bad knees now," she said in Shanghainese, and he recalled the way they used to speak with each other, fluidly shifting between the language of their classroom and the language of their streets.

"So you and Winston," he responded. "How long has that been?"

"We're just good friends," she said.

"Do you hold hands with all your friends?"

Suchi grimaced. She focused her attention back on the swaying crowd. "I love this song."

"Have you given up singing too?" Howard asked.

"Have you given up the violin?"

"Not exactly," he said; arthritis had made it difficult for him to play much more than the simplest pieces for several years now.

"And I haven't given up singing. Some things remain the same."

"Like you," Howard said. "You look the same."

Suchi laughed and threw him a wry glance. "The same as when? Certainly not the same as when we were young. I stare in the mirror now and wonder when my face became so fat!"

"You don't look that different from my memory of when we were teenagers," Howard said. "But what I mean is you haven't aged much since I saw you last."

"Last week at the supermarket? I should hope not." She grinned. "You look well too."

Was she was intentionally misunderstanding his meaning? He recalled the night they'd spent together all those years ago, and his face warmed. If she was embarrassed, it would be impolite to press her on it. "I notice you didn't say I haven't changed," he teased.

She chuckled. "I was trying to be nice without lying."

"When have you ever tried to be nice to me? You were so mean when we were kids."

"You made it so easy!" she exclaimed. Her eyes danced as she spoke, tugging at his memory. The way she used to look at him.

"You were bossy."

"You liked that about me," she said. "Besides, how would I have gotten your attention otherwise? You were constantly listening to the music in your head."

"It's true," he conceded. He thought about all the times she would bother him while he was practicing his violin in the skywell court-yard in front of his family's shikumen, how she would perform silly dances to make him laugh and trip him up, or how she pretended to be a Peking opera singer, pinching her nose while singing in a high, irritating timbre. He'd admired her then, her confidence and vivac-ity, but had been determined not to let it show. "Without you and Sulan, I'm not sure I'd ever have emerged from my shell."

"Sulan was bossy to you, too, if I remember. You were so good to let us order you around."

"How is your sister these days?" Howard asked.

Suchi's smile disappeared. She shook her head. "She passed away in 1990."

Howard brought his hand to his mouth. "Oh, Suchi." A rash of guilt traveled up his spine as he recalled his surprise encounter with Sulan. She'd appeared older, frailer, but had still radiated poise and elegance. Had Sulan told her sister about that meeting?

Suchi was gazing off into the distance. "She had been battling a chronic disease for many decades, but in the end, she contracted a bladder infection and—" She twisted her palm in the air as if to say, *You know the rest.* "She lived a good life though. She was happy." Suchi's voice was tinged with bittersweet longing. Howard won-dered if this was what he sounded like when he talked about Linyee.

"It never gets easier, does it?" Howard asked.

Suchi looked back at him. "Has it been terrible?" she asked him in English. The words came out careful and quiet, so unlike the clipped, fast cadence of her Shanghainese or the polish of her Mandarin. She hadn't spoken to him in English before, and this alone snapped the years between them into view.

"It's hard. I miss her every day."

"It must be," she said. "I'm sorry."

"Thank you," he said. "For asking."

She nodded, a tenderness in her eyes, and Howard felt the way he had when they were young—that she could see him, that somehow he was exposed even when she insisted he was inscrutable to most people. The recognition gave him relief.

"I'm afraid." He hadn't expected to say these words, but once he heard them in the air, he knew they were true.

"I know," she said, her voice shimmering with compassion.

Howard realized Suchi had yet to mention her own husband, that at the grocery store she'd said she'd been living alone prior to moving in with her son. He wondered what had happened, if they'd separated or if he'd passed away.

"Have you felt this way too?" he asked in Shanghainese.

She paused. "It's how I felt when you left."

For a moment, Howard said nothing. He bent his head and stared at his hands, weathered and clasped in his lap. "Suchi—"

"Doudou," she said gently. No one had called him by that name in years. "What's past is past."

AUGUST–OCTOBER 1938
Shanghai

I
T WAS MIDMORNING, and the heat and humidity were already rising through the cobblestone streets. Seven-year-old Suji wandered through the arteries of the longtang, a bun M'ma had given her half-bitten in her hand. Light filtered through the clothes dangling on bamboo poles above her, offering uneven shade from the sun and casting fluttery shadows on her face. She loved exploring the alleys of the longtang she had been born in, and it was better alone, she told herself. The other girls were always so boring, interested only in marbles or dolls, looking at her strangely every time she suggested it might be more fun to explore the neighborhood. *What's so fun about it? We live here*, they said, turning up their noses. They didn't understand: every twist and turn held the possibility of a heroic adventure; behind every door or window lay a secret only she could discover. She had been shocked by a pair of lace panties hanging from Lin ayi's window, for instance, since Lin ayi seemed so cold and humorless. She still wondered about the broken figurine of a Buddha-faced baby she once found in front of Tsy

konkon's door, a diagonal crack running between the eyes and sloping down toward its ear.

On this day, she decided to get away from the perimeter, onto which the back doors of all the snack shops and businesses, including their own shikumen, opened, and weave through the narrower sublanes that branched off the main drag like a maze.

Nearly a year after the fighting with the Japanese, things in the neighborhood were finally finding an uneasy new normalcy. Though most of Shanghai was now under Japanese rule, the International Settlement, where they lived, was thankfully still protected by its British governance. Even so, the terror and uncertainty of those months were something nobody would soon forget. Suji and Sulae had spent weeks huddled in the same bed as their parents, trying to shut out the terrifying shudders and roars of planes, bombs, and gunfire. Suji had been unable to start school, since classes had been halted when bombing had damaged the building, and Apa closed the bookstore, since hardly anyone would brave the streets for the sake of some magazines. On the rare occasions Suji had been allowed to go out, she'd overheard the neighbors' breathless descriptions of department stores reduced to rubble; of train tracks destroyed and bodies flung across them like broken dolls; of the unending sea of fleeing citizens from other parts of the city. Sometimes, during a lull, the two girls had sneaked onto the terrace, where they'd watch large coils of smoke stretching out across the city, the smell of char omnipresent, ashes and scraps of burnt paper occasionally floating into the alleys.

She remembered the day in November when all of Shanghai awoke to find headlines announcing Chiang Kai-shek's withdrawal from Shanghai. The Japanese had won. Apa, usually calm, had used words Suji knew she should never repeat. He'd cracked open a bottle of rice wine and drunk until his face was red and shiny. M'ma had said nothing as he curled over their wooden dinner table with the porcelain cup in his fist, but tears had flowed down her face. "What will happen to us now?" she'd whispered, but Apa hadn't responded. The girls, afraid of their father's strange behavior, had crept into bed without dinner. Pressed side by side under the cotton-padded blankets, Sulae, whose three extra years made her more knowledgeable, had whispered to Suji that the Japanese had won the battle for Shanghai. Things about the Japanese Suji had overheard the neighbors say had swirled through her head, their horrors unnameable. Sulae must have also been thinking about them, because Suji felt her tremble, punctuated by little sniffles. A fierce red tide had filled Suji's chest, equal parts anger and love. She'd reached for Sulae's fingers and interlocked them with hers. "If a Japanese soldier comes for us," she'd whispered, "we'll jump off the roof together with our hands held like this." She'd felt her sister nod in the dark.

But Japanese soldiers hadn't come for them, and slowly life resumed. Now Suji would be starting school in a week, and while she was excited, she also knew she'd never have the same freedom to explore again. The knowledge made this morning's adventure—and every remaining adventure—extra precious to her.

Suji took another turn and passed several doors. Suddenly the shade gave way to beating sun. She looked up. There were no clothes hanging from poles over this shikumen, no old pots and pans piled up on the outside balcony. The space in front of this house was entirely uncluttered, a rarity in the neighborhood.

That's when she noticed the other peculiar thing. From inside the shikumen came a strange music she'd never heard before.

The notes reminded Suji of the erhu Koh konkon sometimes brought out, but rounder, darker, like a young woman singing. She crept closer to the shikumen's stone door frame, half afraid that if she moved too suddenly, the music would stop. The door wasn't entirely shut, and through the sliver of space between the two black-painted gates, she could peek into the courtyard.

Less than a meter away stood a little boy. He seemed younger than Suji, maybe six years old. Pressed between his chin and left shoulder was the source of the music, a gourd-shaped object with a long skinny neck, wood shining the color of a chestnut. The instrument appeared too large for him; his left arm strained to grasp the length of it. In his other hand he held something that looked similar to an erhu bow, which he drew across the top of the instrument with a fluid motion, as if he were skimming ice.

Suji didn't immediately recognize the song he was playing; she was too wrapped up in the delicacy of the notes. But after a few seconds, she realized it was the popular folk song "Jasmine," a song she'd learned before she had memories. She breathed the lyrics as the boy played. When the song finished, he repeated it. Suji wondered who the boy was, where he had gotten such an instrument, how he had learned to play. Koh konkon had tried to teach her to play his erhu once, but the motion of dragging the bow across the strings had felt jerky and awkward and she had scraped out squawks that sounded more like the gulls that flew by the creek.

The boy played the song a third time, this time faster. He wore pressed dark shorts and a white shirt. His hair was flat and straight, one strand separating from its side sweep and falling into his face, and another portion sticking up in the back. He had serious dark eyes, focused intensely on the instrument he was holding. It was the one aspect of him that seemed mature, in contrast to his chubby round face and small stature.

Halfway through the boy's fourth run, a woman's voice came from inside the double doors behind him. "Doudou," the woman called in Mandarin, "please come in and eat your breakfast."

The boy retracted the instrument from his face. Cradling its wooden frame under his armpit, he slipped into the house, out of Suji's sight.

Suji stood outside the door for a while longer, hoping the boy would come back out and start playing again, but after ten minutes or so, she became antsy. She filed the experience away in her mind to share with Sulae and ran off to explore another alley.

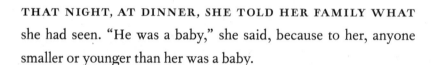

THAT NIGHT, AT DINNER, SHE TOLD HER FAMILY WHAT she had seen. "He was a baby," she said, because to her, anyone smaller or younger than her was a baby.

"Who is he, M'ma?" Sulae asked their mother, for they expected M'ma knew everybody in the neighborhood.

"He must be the Waongs' son," she said to Apa, who was putting a pickle in his mouth while he scanned a newspaper. "They moved into Den abu's shikumen a few days ago. I heard Mrs. Tsen say so." She clucked her tongue. "Poor Den abu. Dying all alone, with no knowledge of whether or not her son in Nanjing survived."

Apa didn't respond. He chewed, his eyes still on the newspaper.

"I never saw anyone play that kind of instrument before," Suji said. "It was like an erhu you play under your face. It was made of wood, a dark brown kind, and shiny. It had a funny shape . . . maybe sort of like a pipa." She frowned because that wasn't exactly it.

"It's called a violin," Suji's father said offhandedly. He reached for a piece of fish. "It's from Europe." A note of disdain entered his voice.

"The family must have money if they can afford to own a violin and give the boy lessons," Suji's mother said. "I heard the husband was educated in Britain. His father was a rich textile merchant of some sort but passed away during the fighting."

"Does that mean the boy's father is a foreigner?" Sulae asked. She turned to Suji. "Did he have gold hair?"

Suji shook her head. "He looked normal."

"Many Chinese went to the West for university," M'ma said with a slight disapproving tone. The girls knew M'ma did not like anything Western, believing foreign things could only poison and weaken China. M'ma was a traditional woman, proud of her bound feet even though the practice had gone out of fashion with the last emperor and embarrassed her daughters. Her marriage to Apa had been arranged when she was three; their fathers had been friends in the same Zhejiang village, and they had been married when she was fifteen and he was seventeen. But then Apa had gone to find work in Shanghai, and by the time M'ma had joined him in the city, he'd changed. "Your father has all sorts of ideas I don't understand now," she told the girls in confidence once.

"I want to learn violin too," Suji now said. She could already see the frown forming on her mother's face, so she turned to her father. "Can I learn?"

"The guzheng is a nice instrument for a young lady to play," M'ma said before her father could answer. "I always wished my family had the money to pay for lessons. It's the sort of instrument the ladies of the court would play."

"I don't want to learn the guzheng." Suji pouted. "I want to learn the violin."

Apa lifted his eyes from the paper and placed his chopsticks on his bowl. He regarded Suji intently. Suji shrank in her seat.

"What's wrong with the guzheng?" he asked.

"It's boring," Suji mumbled. Sulae kicked her under the table.

"What about the erhu then, or the pipa?"

"Those are boring too," she said. She knew this would get her in trouble, and she didn't know why she was digging in her heels. The truth was, she didn't have a desire to learn to play the violin, or any instrument at all, really; she just wanted to be near the sound of it.

"What about them makes them boring?" Apa asked. He had not raised his voice, but Suji felt a fist of anxiety settle in her belly.

"They're old-fashioned," she said. She hoped the word *old-fashioned* would bring her father to her side. He often derided things for being "old-fashioned."

"Hmm," Apa said. "And you don't think the violin is old-fashioned? The violin has existed since the sixteenth century."

Why had she insisted on arguing? Next to her, Sulae ate her rice in quiet bites.

"Does it seem less old-fashioned to you because it's foreign?" Apa asked.

"No," Suji answered, her voice still stubborn but much less audible.

"There's a difference between something that is old-fashioned and something that belongs to your heritage. An instrument like the guzheng is timeless; what makes it old-fashioned or contemporary is how you use it. Don't you know in some dance hall performances, musicians use traditional instruments to play popular music?"

M'ma made a sound of disapproval.

"Okay, Apa." Suji was now desperate for the conversation to end. "I'll learn to play the guzheng."

Apa shook his head. "I'm not forcing anything on you, daughter. We don't have the money to afford lessons in any case. I just want you to understand why you disdain one thing over the other."

M'ma clucked. "Those Western instruments can't possibly measure up to our Chinese instruments. I don't know why you're so interested in them."

Apa glared at M'ma, then turned back to look at the girls. "I want to tell you a story," her father said. "A long time ago, during the Ming dynasty, when China was truly the Middle Kingdom, the emperor had a trusted friend named Zheng He who wanted to explore the ocean. He told the emperor that in all that vastness out there, there must be much to see, much to learn. So the emperor gave him a ship. In Zheng He's explorations, he met many different people and saw many different places. He brought them silk and porcelain. They gave him spices and exotic animals. The kingdom learned of places they had never known of before, saw creatures they could never have imagined possible." He paused and regarded Suji. "Don't you think that's a good thing? To learn about things you didn't know before?"

Suji nodded.

"But when the emperor died, Zheng He was forbidden by the emperor's son to continue to go out to sea. The new emperor thought the outside world was dangerous and barbaric and offered no value to China. And all the emperors after him agreed. For hundreds of years, China did not explore the seas. Until one day during the Qing dynasty, a foreign man came to Emperor Qianlong bearing gifts from his country. He thought, even if China did not want to sail out, surely it might welcome visitors? He hoped their two kingdoms might become friends, that they might visit and trade and learn from each other. But the emperor laughed. *What would we possibly gain from this friendship?* he asked. *We have everything we need right here. We have delicious fruits and beautiful mountains and the most pleasing music in the world. We have wonderful machinery and useful tools and the strongest army. We have gold and fireworks and the most fragrant tea. We have no need to befriend anyone else; what can you teach us that we don't already know?* He sent the pale man away and shut the door to the rest of the world.

"But do you know what the rest of the world did, girls?"

The girls shook their heads.

Apa's face grew grim. "The rest of the world grew without us. They did it in terrible ways—they conquered other lands and enslaved the bodies of men for labor. They stole from places and used what they stole to build factories and bigger guns and ships. So that one day, when the foreign men returned to our shores, we were unprepared. We had stayed the same while they had become powerful. They wanted our tea and porcelain and they no longer wanted to be friends—they planned to take what they wanted without asking. They tricked us by poisoning us, little by little, with opium. They made us weak. And now they are everywhere, treating us like dogs in our own lands."

Suji fiddled with her chopsticks, understanding now why Apa seemed contemptuous of an instrument brought over by the foreigners.

"We became so complacent," he scoffed. "What was the Qing dynasty at its end but a soft regime, made weak by its arrogance? They allowed the Westerners to poison us, which in turn allowed the Japanese to look down upon us and believe they could bully us.

If we had been more curious, humbler, braver, this would not have happened. Perhaps we would have gone out to sea ourselves, when we were still the most advanced nation in the world—gained allies, discovered new weapons, been better, more civilized, more tolerant and magnanimous. Perhaps we could have befriended and protected those lands and people these Western nations plundered, so the imperialists would never have grown strong enough to harm us."

Apa stared hard at the girls. "I'm glad you are interested in outside things and ideas. It will help you to be strong. I'll never be against exposing you to what might seem foreign, even if some might find it odd." Here he looked at M'ma, who glanced away. "We must always be brave and meet what scares us head-on, even if it is hard. But still, you must not forget who you are. You must always remain proud."

The girls nodded. Apa returned to reading his newspaper. M'ma gave Suji a stern look. Underneath the table, Sulae pinched her thigh and Suji stifled a cry.

OVER THE NEXT FEW DAYS, SUJI TRIED TO RETRACE HER steps to the shikumen where the boy with the violin lived. She kept an ear out for the sound of his music, something to lead her back to him, but all she heard was the longtang's usual hum and chatter.

She didn't have long to dwell on her disappointment; the start of her first school year was approaching and she was jittery with nerves. The night before the term started, Suji peppered Sulae with so many anxious questions that Sulae threatened to move into their grandmother's old room. "Go to sleep so you can find out these answers yourself tomorrow!" Sulae cried, burying her face into a pillow.

The "classroom" was crowded, two years' worth of first graders crammed into the sitting room of the shikumen being used as a makeshift schoolhouse, both the ones who had missed entry into school the year before, during the fighting, and the batch of children who had newly become school age. Suji shifted nervously in her seat, sneaking glances at En'en, the girl with whom she shared a desk. She at least had the advantage of being a year older and, therefore, slightly bigger than some of the smaller kids, including En'en. She looked around at the other girls. Some of them appeared as nervous as she felt, others chatted with friends they already knew. She wondered if any of them would like her.

From the far back right of the classroom, she heard a commotion. Turning, she saw a group of boys laughing in a crowd. "Are you sure you're in first grade?" they were saying. "Surely you must belong home with your mother." The crowd parted as one boy went to his desk, and in the gap, Suji recognized the boy who had been playing the violin. He sat stoically, his hands folded on top of each other over his desk, his eyes staring straight ahead.

The teacher walked in. Everyone scrambled to their feet and greeted her, bowing. The woman introduced herself as Xie laoshi. As Xie laoshi began roll call in Mandarin, Suji took a peek at the boy. He was small, but his expression made him appear older. His brow furrowed the tiniest bit, as if he had something grave on his mind, at odds with his baby face and the cowlick standing from the back of his head.

"Wang Haiwen!" Xie laoshi called, and the boy raised his arm, straight and confident. So that was his name.

Before Suji could wonder too much about the boy, the teacher explained she expected they would all speak Mandarin while at school. "Please keep Shanghainese for home," she said. A low murmur ran through the classroom. Many students appeared worried, and in fact, several seemed completely perplexed, as if they hadn't understood. Suji was glad she'd already picked up some Mandarin from Sulae.

Xie laoshi announced they would start the day with a quiz to see who among them already knew basic Chinese characters. Suji, who had been learning to read and write with Apa, was eager to show off.

At lunchtime, after the students' lunch boxes had been reheated and distributed, the other boys gathered around Wang Haiwen's desk again. "The baby forgot his milk!" one boy called as the others laughed. Suji noticed Wang Haiwen was not eating. His family must have forgotten that on Mondays they had longer classes and were expected to bring food as opposed to returning home for lunch.

"Mandarin, boys!" Xie laoshi scolded, and the boys hushed, giggling.

Wang Haiwen continued to look straight ahead, as if he hadn't heard the boys. She wondered if the taunting bothered him. Suji was often teased too, for her mother's bound feet; for her unusually light-colored eyes, which she had inherited from her father; for asking too many questions and not being interested in what the other girls liked. But Suji was used to it. She knew how to fight back. Wang Haiwen, on the other hand, seemed so small and lonesome, even if he wasn't reacting.

Suji looked down at her tin lunch box. An egg, rice, pickled cabbage, and one precious lion's-head meatball saved from last night's dinner. It was less meat and more filler made from dried mushroom, mashed soybeans, and starch, but there was a bit of minced pork mixed in, and that made it a luxury. How her father had managed to procure meat when several months ago they'd barely had any rice was a mystery to her, but M'ma reminded them constantly not to waste it, that they were lucky.

Suji broke the meatball in half with her chopstick and watched a wisp of steam escape from its soft, fleshy insides. She stood up and walked over to Wang Haiwen's desk with the lunch box in her hand.

"Excuse me," she said to the boy hovering closest. She gave him a glare. The boy's face flushed, and he hurried back to his desk. The other boys looked at her curiously, but she ignored them. "Wang Haiwen," she said nonchalantly in Mandarin, "would you like some of my meatball?"

A couple boys tittered, exclaiming in Shanghainese, "Tsan Suji is running a charity! She probably also feeds the smelly, dirty refugees!"

One boy added, "Those refugees are probably relatives of her country-bumpkin mother!"

She turned and gave the boy who had spoken a long look up and down. It was Yongyi, a chubby boy who lived in the next lane, known for being the only child of an overprotective mother. Suji did not like him because he was always chasing the feral cats with rocks. "From the looks of it, *you* don't need any more meat," she said in Shanghainese.

The other kids laughed while Yongyi scowled at her. Suji turned her attention back to Haiwen, who had said nothing through all of this. She placed the lunch box in front of him. "It's good," she said. "My mother's recipe is famous."

For the first time, Haiwen looked at her. He unfolded his hands and pulled them into his lap. "No thank you," he said in perfect Mandarin. "I'm not hungry."

"Don't be silly," she said in Shanghainese. "It's been hours since breakfast." She began to feel resentful this boy wouldn't just accept her kindness, that now the attention of her classmates was on her.

After a few seconds, one boy made to reach for her lunch, but she slapped his hand away.

"Go away," Suji said to the other boys. "How can anyone have an appetite when you're hovering like pigeons?"

The boys grumbled but eventually went back to their desks to eat their own lunches.

"I'm Tsan—Zhang Suchi," Suji said to Haiwen. The Mandarin pronunciation of her name still sounded awkward to her ear. When Haiwen didn't react, she added, shyly, "I heard you playing the violin the other day."

At this, the boy perked up. "You did?"

Suji nodded. "It was really pretty."

"Thank you."

Suji shifted her weight on her feet, unsure of what else to say. After several seconds, she reached into the tin and plucked out the boiled egg, taking a bite out of it. "Eat the rest," she said.

At the end of the school day, while Suji was gathering her books, Haiwen placed the lunch box on her desk. "Thank you," he said, and left.

Suji cracked the tin open. He had eaten everything.

THE NEXT MORNING, HAIWEN PUT A PASTRY IN FRONT of her. It was a beautiful thing, glossy and browned on top with a sprinkle of sesame seeds, crisp, the shell separating in delicate flaky layers.

"I brought this for you, because I ate your lunch," he said. Suji could feel the eyes of the other students staring in their direction. Before she could respond, he was already returning to his desk.

Suji broke the pastry in two. Inside, thin, translucent strands of turnip glistened, dotted with bits of ham and scallion. Suji handed one half of the pastry to En'en, who took it happily.

Suji took a bite. It was still slightly warm, the inside peppery and flavorful. It was one of the most delicious things she had ever tasted.

At lunchtime, when Sulae descended from her upstairs classroom, Suji told her sister to go ahead home without her.

"M'ma will be mad if she knows I left you," Sulae said.

Suji glanced at Haiwen in the corner, still packing up. "I won't get lost," she said.

Sulae followed Suji's stare and turned back to her, grinning. "I know you won't," she said.

Suji dawdled as she stacked her books and cinched the book strap around them, still eyeing Haiwen. As he headed out to the lane, she ran after him.

"Wang Haiwen!" she called in Mandarin. He turned, his books bumping against his legs. "Thank you for the pastry. It was so crispy and flaky! I've never had a turnip pastry like that before."

"It's Cantonese style," Haiwen said. "My mother made it." He began walking, so she kept up with him.

"Is your mother from Guangdong?" she asked.

"No," he said, "but she and my father lived in Hong Kong for a short while before I was born. She learned to cook Cantonese dishes from a housekeeper they had."

This seemed incredibly exotic to Suji. She knew there was a place called Hong Kong owned by the British—her father had lectured her and Sulae about how the British had poisoned the Chinese with opium and stolen away the territory that rightfully belonged to China. Sulae had told her she'd seen pictures of Hong Kong in some magazines in Apa's store, that the city had big hotels and glamorous foreign women. But Suji had assumed those lavish places must only be for the terrifying blond men and women with big noses who lorded over the destitute Chinese slaves they had conquered.

They walked side by side on the cobblestone street. The air was comfortable, with only the slightest chill. Sifo Li was large—one of the biggest longtang communities in Shanghai, everyone said—and the shikumen that housed the school was at the northern section, the opposite end from where she lived.

After what felt like a long silence, Suji's curiosity won out.

"Did you move from Hong Kong then?"

Haiwen looked confused. "What do you mean? I was born in Shanghai."

"So you speak Shanghainese?" she asked, switching into Shanghainese.

"Of course," Haiwen responded.

Suji was relieved. She'd worried her Mandarin wouldn't be good enough for her to keep talking to him if he couldn't speak Shanghainese.

"Then how come you can speak Mandarin so well?" she asked.

"My mother speaks to us more in Mandarin. She says she spent so many years out of Shanghai when she was young, her Shanghainese isn't good anymore."

Suji tugged at her hair. She hadn't realized that could happen to a person.

"Where did you live before this? I mean, before moving to Sifo Li?"

"Oh. We used to live in a bigger house, far away from here." He looked sad.

"A bigger shikumen?" Suji asked.

Haiwen shook his head. "No, a house. Like one that had big rooms and stairs and things."

Suji wondered if he meant a grand Western-style garden house with columns and an expansive lawn, like the ones she had seen from afar during the walks she had taken with Apa when she was small, before the war. She'd always imagined those mansions housed foreign kings and queens. And yet, Haiwen was a regular boy, a Chinese child just like her. His life seemed mysterious and extraordinary to her.

"Are you rich?" she asked. "My mother says you are."

Haiwen looked at her, confusion in his eyes again. "What do you mean?"

"I don't know," she said, twisting her hair around her index finger. She was struggling to explain. She thought of everything else she'd seen during those walks with Apa. Her father had told her and Sulae he wanted them to know more than the small corner they lived in and had introduced them to the butchers, the shoe repairmen, the rice sellers. He had pointed out the shantytowns and taken them through the black market. She'd been awestruck by the wide expanse of the boulevards, by the trolleys threading through crowds, by the men in red turbans directing traffic. But her favorite part of these walks had always been the stops closer to the Bund. She'd been dazzled by the powdery cosmetics and beautiful dolls in the department store windows, had admired the elegant women emerging from sleek clubs, had salivated over the glossy sweets tiered in café windows. Although it had now been a very long time since she had left the longtang, in her mind's eye, outside of Sifo Li's walls, Shanghai remained as vibrant as always, even if she'd been told it was overrun with refugees, destroyed, burned to rubble. She wanted to know the proximity this boy had to the opulent world she'd coveted. "Like, does your house have gold lights and do you have a shiny black car and does your mother wear sparkly jewelry?"

He didn't respond immediately. "We used to have a car," he said after a moment. "We had a driver, Xiao Yang, who was nice to me and sometimes gave me sweets. I haven't seen him since we moved, though."

Suji nodded. So he was rich; the car proved it.

They passed under the floral art deco archway that unofficially marked the border of their section of the longtang and emerged into the communal space. Some residents were sitting on stools, sharing watermelon seeds they were cracking with their teeth.

"Ah, the children are home from school!" Tsen ayi greeted them in Shanghainese. "How were your classes?"

"Very well, Ayi," Haiwen answered politely.

"Waong Haeven," she said, smiling, "how are you adjusting? This must be a very different life than you're used to, eh?"

"I like it here," Haiwen said.

"Good, good." She nodded. "It seems you've already made a friend in Tsan Suji."

Suji blushed.

Tsen ayi smiled. "Run home now. I'm sure your mothers are waiting."

They headed down the main corridor. When they hit the west gate intersection, Haiwen said in Mandarin, "I turn here." Suji nodded, feeling sorry the walk had come to an end. Haiwen hadn't seemed to mind her questions, and he hadn't acted as if he thought she was strange or annoying. She watched him turn to the left, then continued straight and went home.

AT DINNER, SHE ASKED HER FATHER ABOUT HONG KONG.
"Is it true Chinese people can go there?" she asked.

"Aiya," M'ma muttered. "Why does this girl have so many questions all the time?"

Apa ignored M'ma. "The island is Chinese, after all," he said to Suji.

"But didn't the British take it over? Doesn't that mean they're keeping everyone out?"

"Not exactly," Apa said. "Chinese people can still go there. And many do. They go to study or work. The Chinese government just doesn't have control anymore and so sometimes they're not very nice to Chinese people." He paused. "It's like Shanghai. We live in the International Settlement. Technically, even though this is Chinese land, many people who live here are not Chinese. And the Chinese government isn't in charge here."

"The Japanese are," Sulae piped up.

Apa frowned. "Not quite. For now, the International Settlement is still governed by the British, just like the French Concession is under the French. The other parts are the ones the Japanese have control over. But just because all these other governments are in charge, it doesn't make Shanghai any less ours, right? We still live here."

"Oh," Suji said. She wasn't entirely clear about the different governments and what that meant, but Hong Kong was much less exotic if it was merely another Shanghai.

"Why are you asking?" Apa asked.

"Waong Haeven said his parents lived in Hong Kong before he was born," she said.

"They *must* be rich," M'ma said.

"Maybe they used to be," Apa said to her. "But you said yourself you'd heard they lost all their factories because they refused to work with the Japanese. We should pity them, not disparage them."

"I hear they have the whole shikumen to themselves. To afford that!"

"So do we," Apa said sharply. "And we aren't wealthy, just lucky."

"For how long?" M'ma sniffed. "You think I don't notice anything, but I hear things. When were you going to tell me you planned to rent out your mother's room to Siau Zi?"

"I thought you didn't like to concern yourself with finances," Apa said, an edge to his voice. M'ma stiffened. She shoveled rice into her mouth and chewed silently. Apa sighed, his demeanor softening. "You know I don't like you to gossip," he said.

"I don't think it's gossiping if someone tells me news about my own household that I'm not aware of," M'ma said, her eyes on her bowl. "It's embarrassing, that's what it is."

Apa set his chopsticks down abruptly. "I haven't decided anything yet. But the Japanese completely ravaged Siau Zi's neighborhood. How can I not help a fellow Chinese out, especially one who has worked so diligently for me? You know he doesn't have family in Shanghai—he still sends money back to that rural village he's from. He has nowhere to go. Plus, we could use some extra income. It isn't as if people are lining up to buy books these days."

"I looked a fool when Mrs. Tsen asked me about it," M'ma murmured. "What husband doesn't discuss these things with his wife first?"

"I just told you," Apa said. "I haven't decided anything yet."

"Forget it," she said. "I defer to you, great husband." Apa sighed but didn't reply.

Later, as the sisters lay in bed next to each other, Sulae teased, "You told me to go ahead so you could walk with Wang Haiwen?" She nudged Suji on the shoulder. "Do you want to marry him?"

"Ew," Suji said, shoving her back. "He's like a baby."

"I'm going to tell M'ma we should arrange your marriage with Wang Haiwen."

"No!" Suji protested. "I'm never getting married. I'm never leaving the three of you."

"We all have to get married," Sulae said. "Just hope you don't end up with an ugly man with a pockmarked face and missing teeth. That's worse than marrying Wang Haiwen."

"Never," Suji said, her voice fierce.

FOR A WEEK, SUJI IGNORED WANG HAIWEN AT SCHOOL. She didn't know why—maybe it was embarrassment from Sulae's teasing, or maybe she didn't want to appear too eager. Whatever the reason, she didn't approach him and he seemed oblivious to her.

She didn't care, she told herself. She focused on the rush of joy she got from being good at lessons. Aside from being better at speaking Mandarin than many of the other students (not including Haiwen), she was one of a handful of students who had already memorized the multiplication tables. Thanks to Apa's many lectures, she knew more about Sun Yat-sen than anyone else in class and sang the national anthem and the anti-Japanese songs they were taught in music class perfectly; she even recognized the old Tang poem her teacher wanted them to recite, one her father had taught her as a nursery rhyme. She worked hard on the homework assignments she was given, and her teacher was so impressed, she held up the brief journal entry Suji had spent hours writing in her best handwriting and told everyone they should be more like Zhang Suchi. That night at dinner, when she shyly told Apa what her teacher had said, he gave her a rare smile and patted her head tenderly, then plucked out the fish cheek, his favorite part, and placed it into her bowl.

Her academic excellence did not make her popular. While the other girls were mostly nice to her, they rarely invited her to join their circles at lunch or after school to play.

Over time, Suji noticed Haiwen had even fewer friends than she did. He seemed to live in his own solitary space, an invisible balloon around him that set him apart from others. The boys had given up on teasing him, opting instead to ignore him altogether. He said little in class, often sitting through the day without ever uttering a sound.

One afternoon, Suji had just met Sulae outside the schoolhouse when Wang Haiwen emerged from behind her, passing the sisters and walking ahead. The strap wrapped around his schoolbooks was almost as long as he was, and the books bumped as he walked.

"There goes your boyfriend," Sulae said, and Suji punched her in the chest. They walked a distance behind him as other students ran past them. "He looks lonely. We should invite him to walk with us."

"Don't," Suji said.

"Suddenly shy?" Sulae asked. "You *must* be in love with him!"

Hot irritation streaked through Suji. Impulsively, she shouted out, "Wang Haiwen!"

The boy turned around. His hair was mussed and sticking up in the front.

Now that she had his attention, Suji didn't know what to say. She could feel her sister smirking beside her. Her face burned. "We're all going in the same direction," she finally muttered. "We should walk together."

Haiwen nodded as the girls caught up to him. He squinted up at Sulae. She was already a head taller than Suji, so she towered over Haiwen.

"This is my big sister," Suji said.

"Zhang Sulan," Sulae said.

"It's nice to meet you," Haiwen said politely.

Sulae laughed. "You're so formal!" she said. As they began the walk home, she added, "My sister says you play the violin."

Haiwen nodded.

"How old are you? Six? Seven?"

"I'm seven," Haiwen said to Suji's surprise. She'd assumed he was one of the younger children.

"That seems young to play an instrument," Sulae continued.

"He's really good," Suji said, for some reason defensive on Haiwen's behalf. She turned to Haiwen. "Why don't we go to your house so you can show her?"

"Okay," Haiwen said.

He led them down the sub-lanes until they were at the shikumen Suji had crouched in front of weeks earlier. He knocked on the door. A woman's melodious voice responded, "Coming!" and a moment later, the door opened.

"Wah! Who do we have here?" The woman was beautiful, her eyebrows drawn in thin arches that lent her eyes a kind expression, one that reminded Suji of the benevolent smile painted on the porcelain Guanyin her mother kept in the dining area. The woman's hair was cut into a short, crimped bob, like that of women in advertisements, and her body was a slender silhouette in the gray silk qipao she wore, the fabric lined at the edges with rose piping.

"Mama," Haiwen said, "this is Zhang Sulan and Zhang Suchi."

Both Sulae and Suji found themselves struck dumb by Haiwen's mother. She leaned down and smiled at them. "The Zhang sisters," she said in Mandarin. "I've heard so much about you. Your father is Zhang Li'an, the man who runs the bookstore, right?"

The girls nodded.

"Come in, come in," she said. "It's always nice when Haiwen brings friends over. He spends too much time with his violin otherwise."

"Thank you, Wang ayi," the sisters chorused. They stepped into the courtyard. Several potted plants lined the edges of the modest space—a kumquat tree, a jade plant, a fragrant osmanthus bush, and other greenery Suji couldn't identify. Haiwen's mother led them into the sitting room, where a toddler was kneeling on a stool in front of a teak table, grabbing at wedges of persimmon.

"Junjun!" Wang ayi scolded. "Sit down like a good little girl." Junjun ignored her and crushed a piece of fruit in her hands. Her chubby fingers shone bright with sticky orange pulp. Wang ayi sighed and picked her up under the armpits. "I'm going to give your sister a bath," she said to Haiwen. "Doudou, make sure to offer our guests some fruit." She disappeared into the back with Junjun squirming in her arms.

"Your mom looks like a movie star!" Sulae gushed as soon as Wang ayi was out of sight. "Doesn't she, Suji?"

But Suji was busy gazing around the sitting room. Suji's family didn't have a proper sitting room, the area having been transformed into the bookstore. Even if they'd had one, Suji imagined it wouldn't be as refined or as airy as the Wangs'. There was an artful quality about the way their furniture was arranged, the way the ancestral altar in the back was set up. The lacquered panels hanging on the wall were intricately carved pieces with birds and flowers and reeds. A wooden European clock with brass embellishments and a golden face sat in the corner on a handsome half-moon side table, a silvery blue silk draped beneath it. On another wall hung a piece of calligraphy, words Suji couldn't read, its brushstrokes free and flowing like a river.

"Why does your mother call you Doudou?" asked Sulae. "It's such a strange milk name!"

Haiwen's face flushed slightly. "When I was born, I was small like a bean," he mumbled. Suji laughed. She wanted to tell him he was still beanlike.

"Well, let's see that violin of yours," Sulae said. Haiwen ran up the stairs. A moment later, he reappeared with his violin case and they moved back out to the small courtyard. Sulae and Suji crouched in front of Haiwen as he took out the violin. The glossy wood shone in the low afternoon sun.

"What should I play?" he asked uncertainly.

"I heard you doing 'Jasmine' the other day," Suji said. "You could play that."

Haiwen brought the violin under his chin and paused with the bow over the strings. Suji noticed how he closed his eyes momentarily, and when he reopened them, it was like the violin was the only thing he saw in the world. He began to play, and the sweet, comforting melody drifted around them. Suji started singing the words under her breath, and although Sulae shushed her, Haiwen didn't seem distracted, so Suji sang along until the end.

When he was done, the girls leapt to their feet and started clapping. "That was amazing!" Suji said.

"Can you play something else?" Sulae asked.

"Like what?"

"Your favorite piece," she said.

Haiwen pondered a moment. He lifted his violin again. The girls sat back down, their legs crossed beneath them.

The piece was strange and melancholy, unlike any music they'd ever heard before. Suji's body grew still as she listened to it, even as some hidden part of her was pulled along as the notes rose and fell, as the tempo slowed down or sped up or took an unexpected turn. She had the sensation of being carried down a river, but not in a scary way; more like she was floating peacefully through mountains and past willow trees on a simple boat, birds scattered overhead and around her.

A note screeched out of tune. "Sorry," Haiwen mumbled, the instrument falling to his side with his arm. "I'm still practicing this one. It's not good yet." He plucked absently at a string. "My teacher says it's too hard for me, but I like it so much, I've been trying to figure out how to play it by ear. But this part is just so high."

"No, it was wonderful!" Sulae said, jumping to her feet. Suji rose slowly, feeling a little breathless.

"What was that piece?" she asked.

"It's called 'Meditation,'" Haiwen said. "It's by a French composer named Massenet."

"French!" Sulae said incredulously. "How do you know French songs?"

"My violin teacher, he's a foreigner," Haiwen said.

"Our mother says Chinese music is superior to Western music," Sulae said in her know-it-all voice. "We don't listen to Western music." She nudged Suji. "Right?"

Suji nodded, though the truth was she thought the piece, though different, was one of the most beautiful things she'd ever heard.

Wang ayi emerged and gave them a warm yet apologetic look. "Sulan, Suchi, I'm afraid Haiwen needs to get started on his homework. But it was very nice to have you. Please feel free to come anytime."

As they walked home, Sulae said, in a mixture of Mandarin and Shanghainese, "Wang Haiwen is a strange boy."

"Yes," Suji said. She was still thinking about the piece Haiwen had played. She was trying to recall the melody, but it had evaporated from her memory, though the way it had made her feel remained.

"But he plays that European instrument well. I wonder if his mother was a musician or performer of some sort. She's so beautiful, she has to be. Did you notice her hair? And her dress? M'ma never wears anything so stylish."

Suji wondered what it was like to have such a beautiful, fashionable mother like that.

"I liked the way she said my name in Mandarin," Sulae continued. "*Sulan, Sulan.* It sounded so refined and pretty when she said it, don't you think?" She glanced at Suji. "Let's use each other's Mandarin names from now on when we're not at home—it's more sophisticated."

Suji nodded in agreement, though she rarely called Sulae by her name unless she was mad at her. Sulae was always "Tsia" to her. Suji wondered when she'd get used to being called "Suchi" by teachers and other students.

Right before they stepped in the door, Sulae stopped Suji. "Don't say anything to M'ma and Apa about visiting Haiwen's house," she said.

"Why not?"

"Just don't," Sulae said. "I don't think M'ma would like it. Remember how she got chastised by Apa, all because you brought up Hong Kong."

"Okay," Suji agreed. She hated it when Apa and M'ma argued— afterward, M'ma was always in a sour mood, snapping at them for the smallest transgressions. If staying silent about Haiwen meant fewer run-ins with M'ma's temper, Suji would be glad to do it.

~

AFTER THAT AFTERNOON, SULAE, SUJI, AND HAIWEN OF-ten walked home together after school, going to Haiwen's shikumen most days, where Sulae and Suji spent an hour or two before returning home.

Suji knew Sulae wanted to be near Haiwen's mother. She saw the way Sulae's eyes lit up whenever Wang ayi greeted them, how she became the model of a perfect young lady when she was around her. At home, Sulae would review every detail of the encounter, commenting on what Wang ayi had worn that day, if her hair or makeup looked slightly different.

Suji was also enamored with the Wang family. She found their entire existence a marvelous mystery. They were so unlike the other residents in the longtang. The other neighbors were a hodgepodge of people: small-time merchants and business owners from nearby provinces; old grandpas and grandmas who for whatever reason could not live with their grown children; factory workers and managers. While they came from differing means, they were all similarly down-to-earth, practical and hardworking.

But the Wangs were different. They were people who had access to a world Suji couldn't quite fathom, a world she'd glimpsed while walking with her father through the nicer areas of Shanghai but didn't think real people could actually *touch*. Suji wanted to know more about the secrets of this world. She wanted to understand how a boy like Haiwen could have a Western violin teacher; how his mother could have lived in Hong Kong; how his father, whom she had rarely seen, could have been educated in Britain; how they could so cavalierly leave such beautiful things like that ornate European clock lying out in the open as if they were ordinary.

Once the three arrived at the Wang house, they played games. Sulae and Suji drew boxes onto the courtyard pavement with a piece of rock, and they would take turns hopping in and out of the boxes, or they would act out animals and have the other two guess what they were. Other times they demanded Haiwen play the violin while Sulae and Suji danced in circles, their hands clasped together. When Wang ayi chided them, they'd do homework together: Suji helped Haiwen with his arithmetic and Sulae checked over all their work. Sulae teased him like he was her younger brother, joking he resembled a freshly pulled radish with his prickled-up hair and big head or that his wrinkled clothes were like the leaves of pickled cabbage, and Suji followed suit. Haiwen always smiled mildly, never appearing to take offense.

Suji enjoyed these days; it felt good to reclaim time with her sister. Although Sulae and Suji had often played together as small children, when Sulae had started school, she'd formed new friendships with her classmates. But now Sulae had found a surrogate younger brother in Haiwen, or, more accurately, a pet of some sort, and this had brought Sulae back to her side.

UNFORTUNATELY, THAT TIME WAS SHORT-LIVED. A month and a half into the school year, Sulae began spending more time with a girl in her class, Yizhen. In the afternoons, Sulae told Suji and Haiwen to go home together because she was going in the opposite direction, to Yizhen's parents' shoe shop. Suji would watch them holding hands, skipping away from her, and wonder what it was about Yizhen her sister liked so much.

Without Sulae's presence, Suji felt shy around Haiwen, and the walk home was mostly silent. Though they had spent plenty of time together by now, Suji was unsure of her relationship with Haiwen—were they really friends? After all, at school, they barely spoke to each other. They still walked from school together, but once they reached the intersection where their paths home diverged, Suji would blurt, "See you later!" and run home.

Sick of how quiet Haiwen was on their walks home, after a few days Suji grumpily complained, "Don't you ever have anything interesting to say?"

Haiwen looked surprised. "Am I supposed to?"

"I don't know," Suji said. "You're just *there*. If I don't say anything, you don't say anything either!"

"Sorry," Haiwen said. He looked stricken and a pang seized Suji. Why was she being mean?

"It's okay," she said in a much nicer voice. "I just don't like when things are so quiet all the time." She kicked at a stone in the road. "If Tsia were here, she'd think of something fun to talk about."

"Sorry," Haiwen said again.

"Stop saying *sorry*!" Immediately, she regretted her tone. She registered Haiwen's face, confused and helpless. She remembered how Haiwen sat alone in class, how everyone treated him as if he were invisible. Perhaps he was unused to talking, being talked to. Perhaps he needed practice.

In a much more subdued voice, she said, "At least tell me what you're thinking about when you're so quiet."

"Nothing," he said after a moment. "I'm not thinking about anything. I'm just listening to music."

"Music?" She had never noticed music in the streets during their walk.

"Music I want to learn to play. Or music I heard somewhere. Or even music I didn't hear anywhere but is just in my head." He paused. "Sometimes it's also the music of stuff, like the note of a pot clanging or a car honking or the tofu-skin man announcing he's here. Even you, the way you talk, your voice goes up and down like a song."

Suji glanced at Haiwen to see if he was teasing her, but his face was solemn.

"You're odd," she said, giggling. She tried to imagine what he was describing but couldn't fathom it. "Do you hear all of that now?" she asked. "Even while we're talking?"

Haiwen nodded.

Suji wondered what that was like. "Did you always hear music?"

Haiwen considered. "I don't know," he said. "I can't remember not hearing it, but I also can't remember not playing violin."

"That can't be true! You *have* to remember. Like the day you took your first lesson, you remember that, don't you?"

Haiwen shook his head. "At first, my brother was the one—"

She cut him off. "You have a brother?" She had never seen any brother.

"He doesn't live with us right now," Haiwen explained. "When we moved, they sent him away. He goes to a school in England now."

How extraordinary! thought Suji. "Oh! So he plays the violin too."

Haiwen shook his head. "No, he quit. But he was the first to take lessons with Mr. Portnoy—"

"The foreigner."

Haiwen nodded. "He's a Russian Jew. But he's lived in Shanghai for a long time and speaks Mandarin and Shanghainese. And English too, so sometimes he teaches me things in English."

This impressed Suji. Haiwen knew things in *English*! "Why didn't your parents find a Chinese teacher?" Suji asked. As the words came out of her mouth, she realized she didn't know if any other Chinese even *played* the violin. Until she had met Haiwen, she had assumed Chinese people played Chinese instruments and European people played European instruments.

"My mother thinks foreigners know their own instrument the best." He shrugged. "Anyway, Mr. Portnoy started coming to our house when my brother was eleven. My mother says I'd sit in the room and play with my toys while he was having lessons, but she didn't think I was paying attention. Then one day, she was sitting in the parlor drinking tea while my brother was supposed to be in the next room practicing, and she realized the sound of bad notes had been replaced by smooth scales. She thought to herself, *The lessons for Mingming have finally paid off!* She was so surprised when she walked in the room and saw it was me. I must have picked up his violin after he'd thrown it on the ground." He furrowed his brow. "My mother says I taught myself to play a G scale all on my own, but I don't remember any of this. I was four."

"Wow," Suji said, impressed. "Does your mother play too?"

He shook his head. "She fell in love with it while abroad. She says it reminds her of a certain time in her life."

They were nearly home and were approaching the intersection where they normally parted. "Well, okay, bye," Haiwen said, and began turning left.

"Want to come?" Suji blurted out.

Haiwen turned. "Come?"

"To my home," she said. After a moment he smiled and nodded.

Suji led him to the back door of her shikumen. "If you forget which one is ours, look for the rabbit," she said, pointing at the crude figure she and Sulan had painted in the lower corner of the door last year. She pushed it open and led Haiwen through the kitchen and into the area they'd set aside for their "sitting room," walled off from the bookstore by a thin partition. Glancing at the cramped space, nearly entirely taken up by their plain round dining table, Suji realized how shabby her home was compared to his.

"M'ma," she called, "I'm home! I brought a friend."

There was the sound of movement above them, and eventually her mother came downstairs, slowed by her bound feet. Suji was acutely aware of how plain and old-fashioned she was, nowhere near as warm and sophisticated as Haiwen's mother.

"Suji!" she said, frowning. She regarded Haiwen. "Who is this?"

"This is Waong Haeven," she said in Shanghainese—her mother's Mandarin wasn't very good. "The one who plays the violin."

58

M'ma pursed her lips. "Good afternoon, Waong Haeven."

"Good afternoon, Tsan ayi," he answered politely.

"Would you like some tea?" she asked him, and without waiting for him to answer, she told Suji, "Can you please come to the kitchen to help me make some tea for our guest?"

Suji knew she was in trouble. She could tell by the tightness of M'ma's voice. She followed M'ma into the kitchen.

"Did you even use your brain?" M'ma hissed, pulling on Suji's ear.

"Ow!" Suji complained.

"Bringing a boy like that here, unannounced. What will the neighbors think!"

"He's my friend, M'ma," she said. "We go to school together."

"How is it that you have time to make friends with boys when you're supposed to be paying attention to your lessons?"

"After school, we—" Suji realized her mistake and abruptly cut herself off.

M'ma narrowed her eyes. "What?"

"Sometimes—we share—we do—in class—"

But it was too late. M'ma jerked her ear harder and Suji yelped.

"Speak up. Don't you dare lie to me. How do you know the boy? Don't tell me it's just from school."

Suji said, in a small voice. "Sometimes we go to his house to play."

"*We?*"

"Me—me and Tsia," Suji responded miserably, realizing she had made another mistake. Sulae would be so angry with her.

M'ma yanked her ear once more, this time hard enough to bring tears to Suji's eyes. "This whole time I thought you and your sister were at En'en's house," she said. "That's what she told me."

"M'ma!" Suji started to cry, but her mother didn't release her.

"I don't like that Mrs. Waong," M'ma added. "I've seen her walking around like a . . . a . . . a cheap song girl. I don't want you going there."

"But M'ma—" she started.

"I'll talk to your father about this tonight. We'll see what he says." She released Suji. "Stop crying," she said. "Your face will turn ugly."

She led Suji out to where Haiwen was still standing in the sitting room. His books were in his arms.

"I'm sorry," M'ma said to Haiwen in a genial voice, "it turns out Suji has some chores she must be getting to. So it's best you go home."

Haiwen looked at Suji, his eyes filled with questions. She studied her feet. "Thank you for having me," he said. M'ma gave a thin smile. With mincing steps, she led him to the back door and opened it for him.

"Be careful on the road home," she said.

"I will," Haiwen responded.

THAT AFTERNOON, M'MA SPANKED BOTH SUJI AND SULAE for lying about where they'd been. The girls sobbed, clutching each other while M'ma took to their butts with the wooden handle of a feather duster.

"Do you think I am scolding you for anything but your own good?" she exclaimed as they cried. "Your father has spoiled you! You can't run around like wildings with no education, sneaking off to boys' houses, particularly one with a mother like that! What will people think! How will you ever get married off!"

"M'ma!" Sulae cried, squirming on the bed. "We won't dare do it again!" But M'ma paid her no heed.

"Your father thinks he knows best, the way all of his intellectual friends do, these men who know nothing of being a woman. Do you think I would have been able to marry your father had I had big stinky feet like the two of you do? These men have never had to worry their mother-in-law might make their lives unbearable simply because she doesn't like the way they brew a cup of tea."

Tears were streaking down M'ma's face as she continued to bring the wood down on their bare skin. Suji cried out, the humiliation more painful than the blows.

"They have the gall to ridicule us, to tear the ribbons off our feet and say they're liberating us, but when have they ever cared to ask us what *we* want? Have they ever asked how their underwear is washed, how their clothes are mended, how their dinner is hot when they come home from cavorting with god-knows-who? What do they know of being a woman? Who will teach you how to live in this world if not for me, daughters? Who? That Waong woman with her uncouth ways? Your precious father? When society decides it prefers its traditions after all, will either be able to suffer on your behalf?"

When M'ma had spent herself, she retired to her room, where they could hear her still sobbing.

Suji thought her sister would be mad at her, but instead Sulae asked quietly, "Does it hurt a lot?"

Suji, her eyes puffy with tears, shook her head and mouthed, *I'm sorry, Tsia.*

When Apa came home, they were still in their room, lying on their bellies so their tender bottoms were up in the air, arms flung over each other's backs. M'ma and Apa's conversation floated up the thin walls.

"You said it yourself, you don't trust those Chinese who get in bed with foreigners. The Waongs are exactly those sorts of people! Both foreign educated, with moneyed backgrounds. Some even say the wife is mixed blood, half European! The way she dresses, the way she walks, as if she's too good for this place—"

"I don't have time for your petty female jealousies," Apa said, cutting her off.

M'ma sputtered. "I'm not jealous," she said. "I'm only thinking of what's best for our daughters. Look at her, still so splendid during wartime, so decadent, so wasteful. Tell me, do you feel comfortable, letting our children keep company with a woman like that?"

"If we raise them well, to be proud of their Chinese heritage and proud of themselves, they'll be impervious to outside influences," Apa said. He paused. "Unless you're saying you're not confident in your ability to raise your daughters."

M'ma, flustered, responded, "Of course that's not what I mean! But you know how it is for young women, their reputations—"

Apa cut her off. "Then there should be no problem."

Either M'ma said nothing, or what she said was too quiet for the girls to hear.

"What about the boy?" Apa asked. "What was he like?"

"He was polite," M'ma answered. The girls could hear a hint of injury in her voice. "Very small. If I didn't know he was in Susu's class, I would never have guessed he was her age."

"I hear he's quite musically gifted," Apa said. There was another long pause. "I don't think there's any harm in letting the girls play with him. Especially Susu. Weren't you the one worrying she seemed lonely now that Laelae has her own friends? It will be nice for her to have a friend in the longtang."

"If you think that's best," M'ma said.

They heard Apa sigh. "Where are the girls, anyway?"

"They're in their room."

"Daughters!" Apa shouted. "Don't you know to greet your father when he returns?"

Gingerly, Sulae and Suji rose from their beds. Without speaking they both knew they would not reveal to Apa that M'ma had punished them. They did not want M'ma to get in more trouble. Gently, they lowered themselves onto the wooden chairs set around their dinner table.

Apa looked at each of them with a severe expression on his face. "In this household, we do not tolerate lying. Understand?"

"Yes, Apa," the sisters answered quietly. "We were wrong."

Apa picked up his chopsticks, signaling the end of the discussion. M'ma sniffed loudly but said nothing.

Sulae and Suji sat through dinner as still and erect as they could manage, determined not to reveal their pain.

JANUARY 2008
Los Angeles

A WEEK AFTER WEI'S party, Winston called Howard and asked if he'd like to join him for a game of ping-pong at Coral Sunset.

"I can't move like I used to," Howard responded. "It's not fair to challenge a man five years your senior when we're as old as we are."

Winston groaned. "Okay, to be honest, it's because Annie has been asking about you. She liked you, Howard. Why don't you come and spend some time with her? She's a nice woman."

"Annie?" It took Howard a moment to remember the woman with the jewels on her fingers. "Oh. I don't know. I'm not sure she's my type. I'm not really interested in dating."

"Come on, Howard, what else are you doing? I'm not asking you to marry the woman. But take it from me, companionship is important. Linyee would want you to leave the house."

Coral Sunset was down in Laguna Hills, made up of identical triplex town houses, where residents each took up an entire floor. The town houses were arranged around a main recreational center and dining hall, while luxury amenities, including a swimming pool, tennis courts, and even a hiking trail, dotted the rest of the campus. It was one of the nicest communities in the area, and it surprised Howard that Winston had splurged to live out his days here. Yiping and Yijun had taken him to visit several more modest communities shortly after Linyee had passed away, but Howard couldn't bear the thought of moving out of the home they'd shared.

Winston gave him a tour, showing him first his apartment—a one-bedroom with a balcony and a kitchenette he never used—then the "neighborhood," which they zipped through on a white golf cart as Winston pointed out various identical houses and told him who lived where. Often they were stopped by someone Winston knew, and Winston, ever the social butterfly, would talk to them at length about their day and introduce Howard as his "good friend of many years." After an hour, Winston took him to the five-story recreational hall, which featured an intimate movie theater, a game room, and a room with musical instruments, some donated, Winston said, but many others salvaged from residents who had already passed on. They went to that final space last, opening the door to reveal Annie and Suchi rehearsing a duet arrangement of a bluesy American song Howard recognized but couldn't place.

Annie had a beautiful voice, a clear, high soprano. Suchi sang the line below. She wasn't as good as Howard remembered—her voice had thickened, grown a bit raspy and less confident. But Howard noticed Suchi still sang with her features pulled wide—her eyebrows high on her forehead, her eyes enlarged, her nostrils flared—an expression of passion that had made her self-conscious the one time he'd pointed it out to her.

When they stopped, Winston applauded. Annie mimicked a

curtsy, but Suchi flushed. "We thought you would be longer," she said.

"You remember Howard," Winston said. Annie nodded and smiled. Her outfit was more subdued today—a peach blouse and loose-fitting black trousers, with only a pair of pearl earrings, a pearl necklace, and a single diamond ring to accessorize—but she still gave off a hyperpolished aura, one that made Howard vaguely uncomfortable.

"I hear you're a musician too," Annie said. "Do you still play the violin? Perhaps we could have you accompany us sometime. One of the men around here plays the piano, but he's only interested in playing American country songs."

He glanced at Suchi, who was suppressing a hint of a smile, and wondered if she was remembering the many times she'd made him accompany her while she practiced a new popular love song she'd heard on the radio. *How will I become a famous singer if I don't practice?*

"Aside from the occasional demonstration of 'Twinkle, Twinkle' for my young students, I don't perform much anymore." He waved his knobbed fingers, which cracked as he moved them.

"Too bad," Annie said, pouting.

Winston clapped a hand on Howard's shoulder. "If it hadn't been for the war, Howard would have been one of the premier violinists in China, I have no doubt."

Howard kept his face neutral. It was funny Winston liked to repeat this line to people when first introducing him. Winston had, in fact, never heard him play the violin; they had met long after the arthritis had kicked in.

"Such a shame," Annie said, shaking her head.

Winston laughed loudly, patting Howard's shoulder once more.

"Well, probably better this way. You would have been stuck playing Madame Mao's compositions, right?" He laughed again. "Come on, let's go get some lunch."

Over a nice sit-down meal in the dining room, Winston regaled them with tales about his time in the war. Howard suspected he meant to impress Suchi.

"You know I wasn't even supposed to fight in the war? None of us were! We were just a bunch of pimply, bobble-headed students on the run with our teachers. When we arrived in Penghu, we were much better at carrying our little chalkboards than rifles. I think the rifle was taller than I was!" He said this as if it were a great joke, his eyes crinkling with small tears as he laughed, but Howard knew the truth. Howard himself had arrived in Penghu after the July 13 incident, but there was nobody in the unit who didn't know how their youngest recruits had been conscripted—at the point of a bayonet. It was only much later that Howard learned several students and teachers had been executed—some immediately stabbed to death in front of the entire school and others labeled Communist spies after the fact—for daring to protest for the younger students' right to continue their studies.

If Winston had borne witness to that cruel, gruesome injustice, he never let it show, instead twisting all of his stories into comedic anecdotes: the half-bitten worms he frequently discovered in his gruel; the pranks he and his comrades played on one another involving spiders left in bedding or ghost calls during night watch; his exaggerated failures at running drills. "God, it was such horrible, terrible shit," he said, laughing. "It turned me quickly from a sniveling brat into a man, I'll say."

"You're still a sniveling brat," Annie teased. Seated next to

Winston, Suchi chuckled demurely into her napkin. So unlike her, he thought. When had the Suchi he'd known ever been demure?

"Ha," Winston said. "What about you, Howard? What was it like for you? I don't know that we've talked about it much."

Howard glanced across at Suchi, who was folding the napkin back onto her lap. Finished, she returned his gaze.

"About the same," he responded. "It was shit."

Winston laughed loudly, then moved on to his next story, something about the time he tried to steal bread from pigs.

Suchi was still staring at Howard. She shook her head. He wasn't sure what it meant. If she was disappointed, or if she was telling him she didn't want to know.

LATER, WHEN THE WOMEN WENT TO THE BATHROOM, Winston leaned over their cups of oolong and, switching to Mandarin, said, "I really like Sue. She's a remarkable woman."

"How did you meet?"

"We were short some altos, and Annie said she'd invite a woman she'd heard liked to sing, the mother-in-law of one of her daughter's friends." Winston took a long gulp from his mug, as if he were drinking whiskey and not tea. "She's kind of quiet, you know? And don't get me wrong, I like them quiet. It makes me want to tease them, to see if they'll come out of their shell. What surprised me though is that Sue's no pushover; if I tease her, she'll retaliate with a sharp retort. Like a snapping turtle. I like that about her. A quiet woman with a bite. It's a welcome challenge."

Suchi had changed so much, Howard thought. *Quiet* had never been a word he'd have associated with her. *Passionate* maybe. *Stub-*

born. He had been the quiet one of the pair, the one she'd had to tease out of his shell, the one who meditated on what things meant or what to do. She'd been the vivacious and mercurial one, excited by a fresh idea or upset by a turn of events, flying from one emotional extreme to another with shocking volatility. What had happened in the intervening years? With a pang of sadness, he realized the Suchi he remembered was perhaps not the real Suchi at all; this new version, the quiet, careful one—perhaps that was who she had always been destined to become. Perhaps if they'd stayed in touch, the progression would have seemed more natural.

"She's a divorcée, but I don't hold that against her," Winston continued, oblivious to Howard's pensiveness. "After all, at our age, everyone's either widowed or divorced. But what's interesting is her ex is the owner of a huge Hong Kong import-export business."

So that was what had happened with her husband. She was divorced. "Does she ever talk about him?" Howard asked.

Winston shook his head. "She doesn't bring him up at all." He leaned in closer to Howard. "By the way, don't mention this to her. Annie learned all this from her daughter, who heard it from a good friend of Sue's daughter-in-law."

For a moment, Howard was seized by a violent animosity toward his friend, who seemed a little too eager to share Suchi's secrets. He wondered how Suchi would feel if she knew her daughter-in-law had exposed her dirty laundry.

Winston continued in a low voice. "So apparently, Sue met this fellow at a nightclub where she was waitressing. My guess is that it was for her what it was for many women who fled to Hong Kong at the time; she was desperate and needed the work. And in swooped this man, with all of his promises of a better life."

Sourness spread in Howard's gut. He had not known she had waitressed at that kind of nightclub—decades ago, hadn't she said she was working at a noodle shop?

Winston continued. "I asked some of my Hong Kong buddies who worked in that business. He is very, very rich. And from all reports, braggadocious, the kind of guy who throws money around just to show you how little it means to him, who buys and retains favors and power. I guess that's why she eventually divorced him, despite the fact that—because all of his assets were in Hong Kong— she wouldn't receive a cent. She has principles." Winston smoothed his shirt and patted his chest. "What do you think, huh? Think she could like an old idiot like me?"

What did Howard think? Winston had used the word *braggadocious* to describe Suchi's ex, but the truth was it could have applied to Winston too. He preened too much, had too many uninformed opinions. Suchi had hated those types of boys in school. But things had clearly changed a long time ago. He never would have believed Suchi capable of being attracted to the man Winston was describing. And maybe she hadn't been—maybe it had been, like Winston said, merely about a better life.

"I thought you two were already dating seriously," Howard said. "Yanhua said you've been seeing each other for a while."

"Ai, no," Winston said, shaking his head. "She comes once a week for choir practice and I invite her to lunch afterward," he said. "But when I bring up the idea of something more serious, she tells me she's grateful for my company and changes the subject."

Before Howard could answer, Winston gestured with his chin. The women were back from the bathroom and ready to go.

THE REST OF THE AFTERNOON PASSED PLEASANTLY.
While Winston continued to regale Suchi with funny stories, Annie
told Howard about her own life, how she was a first-generation
American, born and raised in San Francisco's Chinatown. "My father was one of those 'paper sons' you might have heard about. His
parents paid someone who already had American citizenship to act
as his father." They were sitting in the garden, watching Winston
point out plants to Suchi while he explained how he'd survived in the
army by learning what was edible and what was not. "He had to
memorize all sorts of information about his fake village and fake family
so it seemed real when the immigration officials interrogated him."

"I didn't know that happened," Howard said.

"Oh, yes, it was very common during that time. Because of the
Chinese Exclusion Act, you couldn't get into the country any other
way. My mother was a 'paper daughter' too—though in reality her
'father' meant to make her his bride. That man died in the first few
months after my mother—just thirteen—arrived."

"And you knew all this?"

Annie shook her head. "Not for many years. I think my parents
were afraid of being found out and deported. It was only in the sixties, after the government changed the immigration laws, that they
told me the truth. I learned my parents' names weren't even their real
names! Can you imagine? I had lived my entire young adult life as
Annie Foo, and suddenly my father was telling me my last name was
actually Kwok." She laughed. "I mean, legally, it didn't matter, since
I was married by then. But my father very much wanted both me and

my brother—my brother especially—to change our Chinese surnames, so we did."

Annie's father must have spent his life believing himself unfilial, Howard thought. It was a feeling he understood too well, only in her father's case it had been worse: not only had he been incapable of caring for his parents in their old age, but he'd been unable to carry on their name. What a relief it must have been for him to finally tell his children the truth! With shame, Howard realized he knew little about the Chinese who had lived in this country before him. Annie was the first Chinese person in his generation he had ever met who was born in America.

"What was it like to grow up in California?" he asked.

"It was wonderful and terrible. I loved my town and my neighbors, the bubble I lived in, but if we stepped one foot outside our block . . ." She trailed off. "Things worsened after the Japanese bombed Pearl Harbor. We were constantly telling people we weren't Japanese. The Caucasian children wanted us to prove it by speaking Chinese. But my Cantonese was terrible, so half the time I made the words up. They didn't know the difference."

"At least your English is perfect," Howard said, remembering how painful it was to catch up with the language the year he'd switched to an English-speaking school in Shanghai. The pains he took to underline words in his textbooks and look them up in his dictionary, a battered pocket-sized volume with a red cover and pages as thin as moths' wings. The many, many times he looked up the word *the* only to realize each time it was a near-meaningless word.

"Your English is good too," Annie said. "Especially considering the age you were when you immigrated to the States." Howard did not correct her assumption.

SUCHI AND HOWARD LEFT CORAL SUNSET TOGETHER IN the late afternoon. Howard noted Winston's lingering hand on Suchi's arm as he helped her off the curb, where a pimply valet was waiting with Howard's silver Ford Taurus.

"Are you sure it's not too inconvenient?" Winston asked Howard as he opened the passenger door for Suchi. "I can call Suchi a taxi."

"It's on my way home," Howard said. "No need to waste money on a taxi." He tipped the young man a few fuzzing bills and waved at Winston and Annie before getting into the car.

"Do you know how to get to your son's house from here?" he asked Suchi once they were buckled in. Suchi nodded, directing him through several turns until he saw the entrance for the 5. Upon entering the freeway, a cascade of red lights greeted them. Cars going nowhere.

"Rush hour." Howard sighed.

Suchi chuckled. "We would have made it out sooner if you hadn't been so enraptured by Annie's stories."

"Me?" Howard said. "What about you? Encouraging Winston to share how he had that salesman begging him to take that new car away for pennies?"

"He forgets he's already told me that story several times," Suchi said. "The price gets more outrageous with every telling."

"I think Winston conveniently uses his age as an excuse to tell the same stories repeatedly."

Suchi laughed.

"He told me he likes you very much," Howard said.

"Ai," Suchi exhaled.

"I take it you're not interested?"

"We're old now," she said. "What's the point? I might die to-morrow."

"Doesn't that make it all the more urgent to seize companionship while you can?" he asked.

Suchi didn't respond. They watched a motorcycle thread its way between the halted cars, disappearing with a roar into the distance.

"Why didn't you tell me you were waitressing at a nightclub?" Haiwen asked.

"What?" He glanced at her. She had tilted her head away.

"Winston told me today you waitressed at a Hong Kong night-club." He hadn't been able to stop thinking about this revelation. As the day had worn on, the lie had felt more and more like a betrayal. "You didn't tell me. When we were in Hong Kong."

She sighed. "It was a shameful job. I knew what people thought girls like me did at those jobs. I knew girls who did those things, and I don't blame them; they had to survive. I just didn't want you think-ing there was the possibility I did."

"You should have told me," he said.

"And what? What could you have done but feel sorry for me or disappointed in me? It was a job, the best-paying job I could get. Sulan was sick, and we needed the money."

"You said you worked at a noodle shop."

"I went through a lot of jobs while in Hong Kong. Working at a noodle shop was one. Besides," she said, "I *did* tell you I was sing-ing at a nightclub. I just didn't tell you I was primarily a waitress there."

Howard furrowed his brow. "I don't remember that."

"Why does it matter, Doudou? It was a long time ago."

He didn't know why it mattered. It just did.

The cars started easing forward. He removed his foot from the pedal and let the car coast slowly ahead. After a brief minute, the cars came to a standstill. He pressed on the brake.

"I just wish you had told me," he said.

"Howard," she said, her use of his English name stinging him, "you couldn't be my hero. Your chance to save me had passed."

Howard didn't respond. If he'd known the reality of her situation . . . He didn't know how to finish the thought. The truth was, he was hurt by the lie. Maybe because, once upon a time, he'd been able to read Suchi's lies. Or maybe because when they were kids, she'd kept nothing consequential from him. But what right did he have to her truths? He'd been the one to break her trust first.

"Let's talk about something else," Suchi said, her voice laced with false cheer. "Why don't you tell me about these friends of yours? Since I know you love gossip so much."

She was teasing him, trying to smooth the tension between them; she must have remembered he hated to gossip. He stared at the unmoving line of cars ahead, at the diminishing marigold glow of the sky.

He took a deep breath. "Sure, why not?" he said, and gave her the lowdown on Jianfeng's scandalous marriage to his new wife (why could he never remember her name?), followed by stories of Tina and George's worst bickering. Suchi laughed, not that demure titter she'd given earlier, but the full-throated shower of abandoned joy he recognized, and Howard felt something bright warm his chest.

After half an hour with hardly any movement in traffic, Howard turned on the radio. A scratchy, quick-lipped report he could just barely grasp mentioned an accident somewhere ahead.

"It sounds like we'll be stuck here for a while longer," he said, switching off the radio. "Do you have a cell phone? Maybe you should call your son."

"I already texted him," Suchi said, waving a clamshell phone.

He was impressed. "Texting is much too complicated for me."

"You know me," she said, smirking, "always trying to keep up with what's in fashion."

He rolled down the windows. Despite the car fumes, whenever it was possible, he liked to let in the California breeze. He was convinced if he inhaled deeply enough, he could smell the sea.

"How do you enjoy living with your son?"

"It's nice," she said. "He mostly gives me my space. His wife, Ronnie, is a white woman, but she's as filial and thoughtful as I could have wished in a daughter-in-law. And I get to spend time with the kids."

He briefly considered warning her this daughter-in-law had been the source of gossip about her. Suanle, it wasn't his business. "How old are your grandchildren?" he asked.

"Nicholas is a year and a half and Abigail is five. They're sweet. Abi likes to sneak into my bed at night and sleep with me." She smiled. "What about you? How did you end up in California?"

So Howard explained to her how, in 1976, the textile company he worked for in Taiwan sent him to Los Angeles to gain a foothold with the garment manufacturers that had sprung up in the city's newly defined Garment District.

"I was the only person in the company with decent English," he said. "Guess all those hours suffering over English phrasebooks came in handy after all."

"Isn't it strange," Suchi mused, "after all of that, now our grand-children rattle off English like it's nothing?"

Howard nodded, about to tell her about the absurd words Jennifer had to spell for her spelling bee, when a car came out of nowhere, zipping past them on the shoulder and kicking a cloud of dust into Suchi's side. Howard frantically rolled up the window as she coughed and sputtered.

"Gangdu!" he cursed in Shanghainese.

She gaped at him, surprised. Then she broke into a cackle.

"It's so unsafe!" he said. "What if someone is pulled over? He could cause an accident."

"You were always such a rule follower," she said. "Such a good boy."

"Not always," he insisted.

"What rules did you ever break?"

His mind flew to the gambling, his unfaithfulness, the lie about his age that had changed his life. The many ways he had hurt the people he loved. He glanced at Suchi. This was, of course, not the moment to bring up any of that.

Suchi started giggling as several seconds passed.

"I yelled at Junjun a few times, when she was annoying me while I was practicing."

Suchi raised an eyebrow. "That's the best you can do? Sulan and I used to rip each other's hair out and claw each other's arms."

He scratched his chin. "Kissing you?" he said. "That was surely against the rules. Your father would have killed me."

"That doesn't count! I kissed you first!" She swatted him, her cheeks pink. "Try again."

He tried to come up with a memory from their childhood, but his brain was blank.

She chuckled. "See? Good Doudou—"

Howard jerked the steering wheel to the right. The car swung onto the shoulder and he pressed down on the gas, the vehicles to his left becoming a blur of shadows, until he spotted an off-ramp. He pulled off and was spit onto a local road that was, if not clear, at least moving.

Suchi said nothing for several minutes. Then she exclaimed, "You're crazy!"

Howard kept his face impassive and stared straight ahead.

She shoved his shoulder. "Ei. What would you have done if the police stopped you?"

"I would have pretended to be a senile old man," he said. He switched to English. "Silver alert," he enunciated slowly.

She started laughing again, louder and harder than before, and it gratified Howard to know that, at least for him, her laugh remained the same.

OFF THE HIGHWAY, THEY COASTED THROUGH THE RITZY Laguna Beach neighborhood, gaping at the opulent oceanside mansions neither of them could ever afford, and slowly passed the famed beach. The sun was setting and the sky took on a smear of lavender and pink and gold, bright and lovely over the glinting sea. They rolled down the windows, letting the wet breeze dew on their skin. They'd stopped talking by then, taking in the beauty side by side in silence.

"I've always wanted to live by the ocean," Suchi said after several minutes.

Howard wondered if the ocean reminded her, as it did him, of home.

"Have you been back at all?" he asked.

She shook her head, staring out the window.

"I went back once," he said. "It was . . . different. Nothing was the same. I felt like the old man in that He Zhizhang poem,[2] a stranger in my own hometown."

She didn't respond, and he didn't continue.

Eventually he drove through enough back roads to believe it was safe to reenter the highway from a different on-ramp. The highway had cleared up some by then. It took another hour before they pulled up to Samson's house in Monterey Park. Suchi had been quiet for most of the drive and Howard hadn't wanted to disturb her thoughts. Instead, a familiar symphony hummed gently through his head. While the blanket of haze hadn't entirely lifted, he felt, for the first time since Linyee's death, a sense of contentment.

"Let me walk you to your door," he said, unbuckling his seat belt.

"No need." She smirked. "We're not lovers on a date." She slung her purse over her shoulder. "Thank you for the ride."

Irrational panic gathered in Howard, the way it had at that Hong Kong tea shop all those years ago. He was certain she would walk out of his car, into the house, and he would never see her again.

"Wait," he said. "Can I have your phone number?" He picked up his cell phone from the cupholder and waved it around. "It's so easy these days."

Suchi looked at him askance. "Do you even know how to input

a new number?" His face must have fallen, because she laughed. "I may be the same age as you, but I'm glad to know I'm not nearly as helpless. Hold on." She took her phone out of her purse and flipped it open. "Tell me your number."

He looked at her sheepishly.

"You don't know your own number?"

"*I* never call it," he said in defense. "I have it written on a piece of paper in my kitchen so when I need it . . ." He trailed off.

"Aiya," she said. "Do you have some paper?" He rummaged through the center console and produced a small spiral notebook. She riffled through it. "So many notes," she mused. She peered at his most recent entry, sounding out the vocabulary he'd had to have his granddaughter help him spell. "'Ex-no-puh . . . ex-ee-no-fo . . .'" She paused and switched back to Shanghainese. "What is this word! At this age, still trying to learn! You always were the more studious one."

"That's because you were effortlessly smarter than me. I had to study to keep up."

"Ha!" She flipped to a clean page and scribbled her number down. "Here," she said. "Just don't call me after ten o'clock. I'll be sleeping."

"Do you think I'd be awake then?" he said.

"I don't know," Suchi said. "You used to be a night cat, always tired at school."

"You forget how old I am now."

Suchi smiled. "I do." She placed a hand on his arm. "Do you know how to get home from here? Go back the way we came, turn left at the end of the street, then right after two intersections, and if you follow that road, it will get you to the freeway."

Howard nodded. He watched her careful steps up the path and to the front door. He would leave once she was safely inside.

IT TOOK HOWARD ANOTHER HOUR TO GET HOME— despite Suchi's directions, he'd still gotten turned around for the better part of half an hour—and by the time he stepped through his door, the serenity he'd garnered from the day had vanished. He was agitated and lonely; he missed Linyee more than ever. She would have known how to find the route on the map and helped him navigate; she would have known how to charm a passerby for directions.

Yijun, his younger daughter, picked up the phone on the sixth ring. "What's wrong, Ba?" she answered in Mandarin. She was slightly breathless.

"Nothing," he said. "Did you eat yet?"

"Yes, we just finished dinner." Of course. It was past nine o'clock in Chicago.

"How are the kids?"

"They're good," she said. "Tim's getting ready for bed, but I think Kevin is still up doing his homework. Do you want to talk to him?"

"No need," he said. "Homework is important. I don't want to disturb him. What about Robert? How is Robert?"

"He's fine, he's in class right now. We're both busy with teaching these days. And Robert is working on a new book."

"Oh, a book. What is it about?"

"The evolution of huaigu poetry," she said. "You know, the kind Li Bai made really popular."

"That's great," Howard said, proud of his son-in-law. He and

Linyee had been adamantly against Robert when Yijun had first started dating him in graduate school. Yijun had told them he was African American, and the only things they knew about African Americans were from the movies and the news, a montage of gangsters with guns and criminal mugshots. Yijun told them, first patiently, and then not so patiently, that what they saw on TV wasn't representative of Black people and certainly wasn't representative of Robert. He spoke fluent Mandarin! He studied classical Chinese literature! He was a music aficionado too! If they just gave him a chance, she knew they would love him. But they were worried for their daughter and refused to meet him. After many months of fighting, Yijun, who, unlike her stubborn older sister, had usually been keen to please her parents, not only refused to break things off with him but threatened to elope. After this, they relented.

Wouldn't it be hypocritical of us, Linyee had pointed out to Howard, *considering what we went through with my father?*

Now, after hundreds of beers shared over conversation on music and history, Howard loved Robert like his own son; in fact—and he would never reveal this to his older daughter—he favored him over Yiping's husband, Adam, despite Adam's Chinese heritage. Adam was a workaholic who (from what Howard could gather) barely had time to spend with his own wife and kids, much less his in-laws when they were in town. Whenever Howard and Linyee visited Yiping in Maryland, he couldn't shake the feeling that Adam viewed them only as a nuisance to be dealt with. In contrast, Robert always welcomed them to Chicago with a warm hug, already excited to play Howard the new record he had purchased or proud to share some accomplishment of Yijun's she had been too modest to tell them herself. It shamed Howard to remember his own closed-mindedness.

"And how about you, Ba?" Yijun now asked. "How is everything?"

He thought about telling her about Suchi. Yijun had been the more curious of the two girls when they'd been young, wanting to know his story, about how he had ended up in Taiwan, about how he had met Linyee. She once told him he was the reason she'd decided to go into China studies, and he'd been touched. But he'd never mentioned Suchi. As far as either of his daughters knew, he had only ever been in love once, with their mother. He wondered if they would feel betrayed if they knew the truth. He had a feeling Linyee herself had suspected there had once been someone else, but she'd never asked, although whether it was out of respect or denial, he didn't know.

"I went to Wei's eightieth birthday party last week," he said. "I saw many of me and Ma's old friends."

"Oh, that's great! Maybe we should start planning your eightieth too."

"Please, no," he said, dismayed. He hated the idea of a big formal event. So many people staring at him, expecting to speak to him, so many people he would not be able to hide from.

"I'm teasing, Ba," Yijun said. "I know you hate things like that. Ma, on the other hand . . . If she'd lived until eighty, she would have loved it." She sighed. "It's too bad we couldn't even give her a seventieth."

Linyee had been in rough shape by her seventieth birthday. She'd been five years his junior, and yet it was as if she'd been the older one, confined to a wheelchair, her limbs jerky and stiff, her appetite gone, dementia settling in. A party had been impossible—it would have made her anxious and confused. She'd died three months later.

"Ba, is there something else?" his daughter asked. "Really, is anything the matter?"

"I was thinking of your mother," he said, the crushing feeling escaping with his words. He guiltily realized that while he'd been with Suchi today, he had not thought much of Linyee. For a few hours, he'd forgotten that yawning emptiness. But now that he was alone again in the house they'd shared for the last two decades, he wished she were here. He wanted to tell her about his visit with Winston and the ridiculously extravagant Coral Sunset, about Annie's remarkable upbringing, and yes, even about Suchi. Linyee had been his best friend, the person with whom he'd shared the details of his days, the person who had listened and helped him untangle his frustrations, the person who had exclaimed over all of his minor victories as if they were her own. Without her, he had no one to help him sift through the confusion of nostalgia and affection that arose in Suchi's presence.

Yijun sighed. "I know, I miss her too." He thought he heard a tremble in her voice. Even as a child, she had been the more sensitive one. While Yiping had been headstrong and independent, Yijun had lingered behind, preferring to stay close to Linyee, wanting to help her mother mend clothes or do dishes or listen to her read. "Ba, why don't you consider moving in with Jiejie like she keeps asking you to?"

"Your mother is buried here."

"I know," she said. "But we worry about you, cooped up all alone in that house."

"I get out," he said. "I told you I went to Wei's birthday party. And I saw Winston and some friends today."

"Okay," she said. "I just don't want you to be lonely."

84

"Winston tried to introduce me to a woman," he blurted.

Yijun paused. "Oh?"

"A friend of his, at the retirement community he lives in."

"And? What was she like?"

"She was nice," he said. Why was he was telling her this? He wasn't even interested in Annie. "She's about your mother's age. But she speaks perfect English. She was born in San Francisco to Chinese parents who came over in the early twentieth century."

"Wow," she said. "I haven't met many of those." She coughed. He could hear a faucet being turned on in the background. "So what did you think? Were you interested in her?"

"It's only been a year since your mother has gone," he said. "I was married to your mother for nearly fifty years. How can a woman I just met take her place?"

"Ba, I don't think anyone expects you'll replace Ma. But maybe you should keep an open mind. It might be nice to have a companion."

"No one can replace your mother," he repeated stubbornly.

"Ba," Yijun said. The sound of the faucet stopped and her voice sounded hesitant. "You know me and Jiejie will be happy as long as you're happy, right?"

"She's not my type. She's too garish."

"Okay, okay," she said. "You were the one who brought it up."

"I just wanted you to know I have friends. I'm not lonely. You don't need to worry."

"I know, Ba." He heard the faucet turn back on. "Listen, I have to go. I have to finish the dishes and then I have papers to grade. But I'm happy you called. Call anytime, okay?"

He replaced the wireless receiver into the cradle on the kitchen wall. Taped next to it was the pink Post-it where Yijun had written his cell phone number. He rummaged through the plastic caddy on the counter until he found the nearly finished roll of Scotch tape. From his notebook, he tore the page Suchi had written on, and with two long pieces of tape, he affixed her number underneath his.

His head was still stuffy, agitated. He tried to conjure up the symphonic movement that had buzzed while he'd driven Suchi home, but the ghost melody wasn't enough to soothe him.

He went into the living room and scanned the shelf until he found what he was looking for. Brahms's Symphony No. 1 in C Minor. Gingerly, he placed the record on the turntable and watched for a moment as the vinyl gained momentum, spinning around in a dark blur. He raised the arm and positioned it before the second track. He sat down on the couch and closed his eyes, listening to the Vienna Philharmonic fill the space of his empty house.

HE HAD IMAGINED THIS VERY PIECE—BRAHMS'S LOVELY second movement—through two years of marching with his unit through the desolate countryside of northern China, hiking through dusty mountains and wading through icy rivers he could no longer name. His lifelong habit of muting the world so he could focus on the melodies in his head had been handy through nights of cold, hunger, boredom, fear. From that first battle, at the moment when his commanders had shouted *Sha!*—the word almost lost amid the chaos of machine gun fire already rhythmically punching the air—he had instinctively shut everything out. Moving forward with his rifle, he tried to listen only to the single lonely violin that closed out the end of the movement. He would not stop to think about his friends falling around him, would not see the humanity oozing from them, soft and raw. He would not hear the percussion of explosions happening somewhere near or far nor heed the popping bullets landing with a metallic ping or airy thud or gooey thwack. He would go forth in this horde of men, kill if he must kill, but if he were to die, it would be with Brahms's strings reverberating in his mind.

In later months, it was Bach, his Double Violin Concerto in D Minor. Or Mendelssohn, his Violin Concerto in E Minor. Sometimes Mozart. Or Sibelius, Bruch. Music he no longer was certain he remembered how to perform in its entirety but could hear in his mind as clear as the recordings his old violin teacher, Mr. Portnoy, used to play on a prized Victrola. Mr. Portnoy once told him music was a composer's conversation with God, that in playing or singing, anyone—priest or pauper, Christian or Jewish, old man or young woman—would have an audience with the heavens. Aside from the occasional temple visits his parents had forced upon him as a boy, Howard had never been religious, but he felt an element of truth to this, for he did experience something otherworldly vibrate in him when he played particularly well.

So when, in 1949, he found himself finally back in Shanghai—or rather, on its banks—hurriedly boarding a crowded military ship to flee the encroaching Communists, he turned once again to music. As a bomb sent a spray of water not two dozen feet from where he and his fellow soldiers ducked, he retreated into the meditative opening chords of the third movement of one of Beethoven's string quartets. He tried to catch a glimpse of his childhood home through the chaos, regretful there had been no opportunity to stop by the shikumen and find his family and ensure their safety, no chance to hold Suchi, but the music carried his prayers—that he would live to see them again, that they would remain well until that day came.

The music didn't stop after he stepped off the boat and into Keelung Harbor in Taiwan. It wouldn't stop until nearly a year and a half later. In that time the military moved him around—from northern Taiwan to the sweltering Penghu Islands to Zhoushan Island, off the coast of Ningbo and so close to home he considered stealing a boat or swimming across the strait. By mid-1950, when he found himself back in Taiwan, building military housing he didn't qualify for during the day and squatting in an elementary school at night, the music had begun leaking away, like a sieve had opened up in his brain. Notes, colors, and textures he had once known perfectly disappeared—he awoke in panic at night trying to recall if a phrase rose to an F or an F sharp, if it had been a cello or a viola that had entered a measure. And then one day, he tried to conjure up Brahms and found the symphony had vanished. Not a single note of it remained in his memory. All he had left was the echo of the feelings it had once evoked—of hope and regret and faith that life held meaning.

Years later, once he was able to afford a record player, he walked into a music store and found a recording of the Brahms symphony. That night, after they had finished dinner and Linyee was cleaning up, he set the needle on the record. The opening swells ripped through him. The pain, the terror, the homesickness—they all flooded through his system. He remembered: his friends who had fallen right next to him; the surprised faces of the men he had shot; the ache in his fingers after his unit had been commanded to retreat, his hands unable to loosen their grip on his gun.

Yijun, five at the time, had sidled up to him with an anxious expression on her face. "What is it, Baba?" she had asked, her voice a whisper. "Why are you crying?"

Over the next week, he returned to that record store every day to purchase all the pieces he had forgotten, playing them nightly with the same terror and captivity. Linyee said nothing, until on the sixth night, in bed, she turned to him and said, "You're scaring the girls, you know. They don't understand why their father sits for hours, listening to the same music repeatedly, weeping." He began to explain, but she hushed him. "I don't need to know what it is those pieces dredge up. I assume it's something you're working through. I just wanted you to know the girls are watching."

The next night he started to remove the new record from its sleeve—Mozart's violin concertos—but he stared at the partially torn plastic wrapper and put the record down. He went to the closet and found the battered brown case he had hidden behind his clothes. He plucked at the A string, the one he'd had to replace with an erhu string. It sounded slightly off in timbre but workable. He called the girls over.

"I want to play you one of the earliest songs I ever learned, a folk song you both will recognize," he said, cradling the violin to his neck. Their faces were curious, expectant, shining. He lifted the bow and closed his eyes. His fingers, miraculously, remembered the first familiar notes of "Jasmine."

APRIL–AUGUST 1945

Shanghai

T HE LAST GASPS of the Japanese Army's hold over China were taking place, but they did not know that yet. Apa frantically followed news of the war through the radio, local gossip, various newspapers, and other sources he did not name, relaying the information through his terse responses, the way his eyebrows knit together, his daily shifting mood. The day he received word the Japanese had lost Iwo Jima to the Americans, Apa closed the bookstore early, went out, and came home with a rare treat—a bottle of Coca-Cola. He poured it among the five of them and raised his glass to China's formidable allies. Suchi was delighted by the sweet syrupy drink, the loveliest thing she had consumed in months, maybe years, savoring how it fizzed her nose and prickled her tongue, how it left her teeth squeaky and metallic. Now, according to Apa's sources, Germany had surrendered, and Apa remarked, "It's only a matter of time before the Japanese do too."

There were air raids every few days now, low US fighter jets that vibrated the buildings long before the sirens went off. They often heard the distant staccato of Japanese antiaircraft artillery returning fire, sporadic and hollow like New Year firecrackers. Apa tried to explain to them about the politics surrounding the war—their own current government, a puppet government installed by the Japanese; the machinations of Stalin and Hitler and Chiang Kai-shek and Roosevelt (now dead) and Mao Zedong. Suchi was fourteen now, he said, Sulan seventeen; it was time they understood the world from a bird's-eye view, not just the way the war affected their everyday lives.

But Suchi didn't know how else to make sense of what was happening. She didn't understand tactical battle strategies or the struggle for political power. What she understood was scarcity and hunger, the pang in her belly never quite sated by the porridge they ate most days of the week, more grit than rice. She understood destitution, the desperation ragged on the faces of the swelling numbers of refugees squatting in the dusty corners of her city. She understood danger, the current of it running beneath the surface of everyday living, made live one morning when, not fifty meters in front of her on a busy street, a man was shot in the leg and dragged shouting into a dark car. And she, of course, understood death, had herself passed corpses fatting flies on the sidewalk, her face averted, though she'd overheard boys in her class say a good look would tell you if the victim was one of starvation or of the Kempeitai.

Most of all, she understood fear. In particular, fear of the Japanese. She had been afraid of them nearly her whole life, having heard people murmur what they did to girls and women was worse than death, and though she hadn't been able to fathom what that unspeakable horror could be, it had loomed over her like a shape-shifting monster. When the Japanese had finally seized control of the International Settlement two years ago, her fear had reached a fever pitch:

her nightmares of being chased and bayonetted by faceless soldiers coincided with her new daily lessons in Japanese language and customs at school. The nightmares eventually slowed, not because the threat had gone away, but because she'd grown accustomed to its presence, a low habitual hum in the background that only spiked when a Japanese sentry asked for her identification card or a group of swaggering soldiers patrolling the streets stared at her for a beat too long.

Apa wanted her to care, and it wasn't that she didn't. But how could she care about the war *apart* from what was happening in front of her? And how could she *live* if she only focused on the death and fear and hunger? It was exhausting to constantly remember she and her family could die in any number of terrible ways at any given moment. When once Suchi told Apa she was sick of hearing about politics, his voice had grown low with disappointment. "I've shielded you from too much," he said. "You haven't known real suffering. Most people don't have the luxury of turning their face from this."

Suchi knew Apa was right. She knew she should try harder to educate herself, to listen more closely to the latest headlines shouted by the newspaper boys, to ask Apa to explain how the actions of a few powerful men affected the lives of millions. But it was spring, and the cherry blossoms were blooming, white-pink explosions that showered down like sweet snow when one pulled on their branches, and Suchi was in love.

She wasn't sure when it had happened. Doudou had never struck her as anyone worthy of romantic affection—in fact, the suggestion of it only a couple of years earlier by a neighbor had been mildly revolting to both of them and they had pretended to gag and run away. He had been her best friend for years; they had walked to school together every day until he had switched to a foreign-run missionary middle school. Now that they were in separate schools, they anticipated the times they met even more, with Suchi bursting at the seams to tell him about her day and Haiwen eager to show her the newest piece he was working on. She'd always paid attention to him—deciphering his expressions, reminding him to eat, teasing him for his quirky habits. It was true that over time she had begun to collect this information more carefully, more intentionally. And sure, there were the occasional stray thoughts about whether he might like the purple ribbon she put in her hair, if he'd notice the scatter of pink pimples dusting her forehead, possibilities that fluttered in her gut like a trapped moth.

But *love?* It had never crossed her mind until one day, after Suchi had snapped at Sulan for misplacing one of her gossip magazines, Sulan had responded, "Don't take your lovesickness out on me!"

"What on earth are you talking about?" Suchi demanded.

"Haiwen has been so busy practicing for his upcoming recital, he's hardly paid attention to you."

"So?" Suchi said. "It's important. His teacher always invites his friends to these recitals, and this year, some faculty members from the music conservatory will be in attendance, and if he makes a good impression *now*, they might invite him to join the Youth Orchestra, usually only reserved for conservatory students, or maybe it will help him when he auditions—"

"Sure, but you've been in a foul temper about it all month."

"I have not."

"You have."

"Why would I be? That's his business. It has nothing to do with me."

"Zhang Suchi, are you an idiot? You're in love with him."

For days afterward, the word *love* tumbled in her mind. Sulan was completely off-base, she thought. Haiwen was a brother to her, someone she had grown up with. She was fond of him, but it wasn't *love*, not that kind, anyway. For one, she found it completely irritating how he spaced out, following whatever thread of music had hooked itself into his brain, even if she was in the middle of telling him a story. She found his hair, the way it stuck up in all directions, and his teeth, crooked and one slightly blackened from a cavity, unattractive. He'd sprouted many inches in the last year and now towered over her, awkward, a mess of gangly limbs, and his head, which once had seemed so big for his torso, was now a mere pin atop his shoulders. Ugh, Suchi thought, she could never, ever be in love with him.

A few days later, on a drizzly afternoon, she came out of her school gates to find Haiwen waiting for her under an umbrella. He straightened up quickly when he caught sight of her, and she saw his school shirt had come untucked from the back of his slacks, a wrinkled mass flapping behind him. She waved as he drew near and smiled to herself. He was always so disheveled. "I've been so busy I forgot to tell you the details of the recital," he said. "It's quite a bit away, on July twenty-fifth. But I hope you'll come."

"Of course," she said. "But why couldn't you tell me at home?"

"Oh," he said, as if he was confused by the question. "I thought you might need an umbrella."

Love crashed upon her in a pastel splash. Sulan was right, Suchi thought as they trudged home through the rain together. She loved his stupid hair. She loved his tedious aloofness. She loved the mystery of the music she couldn't hear behind his eyes, even more than the music that came from his fingers. She loved him, and she felt dumb that Sulan had known before her.

Suchi sat with this knowledge for a week, an eternity. Now that she'd admitted it to herself, she was certain the obviousness of her love emanated from her in a cloud, each molecule announcing her feelings as it brushed Haiwen's shoulder.

Suchi agonized over what to do about this turn of events. She worried about ruining their friendship, that to confess these feelings would be to irrevocably change the comfort that hummed between them. But Suchi was not one to hold things in. That she had withheld such an important revelation was nearly intolerable to her. She was losing sleep, unable to focus on the chores her mother gave her, filing books wrong at the bookstore. She decided, finally, to tell him.

SUCHI WATCHED HAIWEN LIFT THE NEEDLE OFF THE record, recrank the Victrola, switch the motor back on, and gently place the needle on the record again. He lay down on the ground, curled alongside the gramophone, his right ear pressed into the courtyard's slate tile. For a few seconds there was nothing but the scratch of the needle, and then out of the static, a single lonesome violin, like a child emerging from the dark woods.

He had already played the record through once—Suchi had caught him at the end, and not wanting to interrupt him, she had waited at the doorway. But her palms were damp, and she was worried she would lose her nerve if she waited any longer.

"Doudou!" she called as she leapt in front of him, twirling. The skirt Sulan had helped her sew bloomed like a petal.

"Susu," he said, sitting up. He fiddled with the machine so the music played more quietly and turned to her with an expectant smile. Her heart contracted.

"I was watching you," she told him. "You listened to this record the whole way through once already."

"Twice today," Haiwen said. "This is the third time."

She laughed. "So dedicated," she said. "I noticed you were listening on your side again." He had told her it was a habit from when he'd lived in the big European-style house with wooden floorboards. He'd liked to listen to the gramophone and radio with his ear pressed to the ground so he could feel the vibrations of the music through his body. Although it didn't work in the same way with stone tiles, it was a habit that gave him comfort. Suchi had thought it odd at the time, but now she found it endearing, a quirk of his that made her chest swell. "What are you listening to?" she asked.

Haiwen's face brightened. "Sibelius! Mr. Portnoy just played this copy of his violin concerto during lesson and I loved it so much he lent it to me. This violinist is Jascha Heifetz; Mr. Portnoy said he came to Shanghai back in the late twenties and he'd met him. Isn't he amazing? Mr. Portnoy says he was even more amazing in person."

Suchi couldn't stop smiling. This was the only time Haiwen was ever forthcoming with his words—when he was excited about something musical.

Haiwen was still going on. "This concerto though! Listen to the cadenza in this first movement, but wait, it's a few minutes in . . ." He turned up the volume.

The music was dark and unnerving. It reminded her of the feeling she got when she passed Japanese soldiers on the street, who, in the last year, had begun eyeing her as she walked to school. An urgent desire to cross the road, slip into some back alley where they couldn't watch her.

"It's like," she said, hesitating, "the violin is the heroine of the story."

Haiwen nodded. "That's exactly it."

Suchi imagined herself as the violin, its notes dodging Japanese soldiers, kidnappers, gang members, spies. But then a lovely turn, the discovery of sanctuary. The tenderness caught her breath.

"I like this better than some of the other music you've played for me. Like that . . . What was his name? Ba . . . Bu . . ."

"Bach," Haiwen said. "He's a genius."

"That was so messy sounding, so much going on," she said. "I didn't know what to listen to."

"That's how Bach is. It's amazing how he can get so many threads going on at the same time and yet together it sounds perfect."

Suchi wrinkled her nose. "You know I don't understand the music you listen to, anyway." As soon as she said the words, she regretted it. She was suddenly conscious of how uneducated she was on this thing Haiwen loved so much, how stupid her earlier comments had probably sounded. "Speaking of music though," she said, "I heard a new Bai Guang song on the wireless receiver the other night." Although the Japanese had ordered radios to be confiscated, many families, like theirs, still held on to them in secret and played them with the volume turned low. "I keep turning on the radio hoping it'll play again, and it's starting to get on M'ma's nerves. She doesn't like how I hover over what she considers *her* radio, even though Apa said the only reason he hasn't already sold it on the black market is so he can stay informed."

She plugged two fingers in her ears to block out the violin croon-ing on the gramophone, and squeezed her eyes shut, trying to recall the evocative tune, something that made her think of intriguing dark rooms and mysterious women.

"*Yanbo liu, ban dai xiu . . . huayang de yaoyan, liu yang de rou . . .*"[3] She trailed off and blushed. "I can't remember the rest, but it's so sexy and jazzy, you have to hear it. It's perfect for her low voice! I wish I sounded like her. Maybe if I listen to it enough times, I can figure out how to sing it the way she does, kind of the way you listen to those records over and over." She added, excitedly, "And there's a violin part in it too! So you can play it for me while I sing. Wouldn't that be fun?"

"I'll see if I can catch it being broadcast," he said, giving her a sweet smile, and again she felt that warm rush of gratitude. Haiwen patiently tried to reproduce accompaniment to the pop songs she loved, ignoring how frustrated she became when he couldn't get it based on her hums alone. Suchi knew he didn't enjoy this type of music himself, the shidaiqu, or as Apa referred to it, "yellow music," as if it were degrading or pornographic somehow. They didn't un-derstand, she thought. This music moved from her ears through her ribs down to her fingertips and toes, igniting each piece of her. It transported her to a different place, a different body, a different world. And the women who sang the songs! Glamorous, elegant, beautiful. She was sure even Haiwen's mother appreciated their star quality. Wang ayi nearly looked the part herself in the way she dressed, the way she held herself. Suchi had wondered if she went out to dance halls and nightclubs, but she'd never asked Haiwen; it seemed impolite.

"By the way, is your school participating in the city-wide school choir competition?" she asked.

Haiwen shook his head.

"Oh, because our school was assigned 'East Asian Nations March.' I don't actually like it that much, but guess who sings the radio recording? Bai Guang!" She clapped her hands together. "Do you think," she asked dreamily, "it's possible for me to become as talented and beloved as Bai Guang someday?"

"Of course," Haiwen said. "You already practice all the time. I bet Bai Guang started off as a girl who just liked to sing songs she heard on the radio too." He paused, then cracked a smile. "And anyway, Bai Guang probably doesn't know how to sew her own skirts for performances. You have that advantage."

Suchi's cheeks warmed. Haiwen had noticed her new skirt. To hide her embarrassment—and the skirt's uneven hem—she gathered the fabric in her lap and mumbled, "It doesn't matter, Apa will never let me be a singer, anyway."

"Why not?" Haiwen asked. "Doesn't he always say that girls can do anything?"

But Haiwen misunderstood Apa. Apa was progressive about many things when it came to women—he insisted to M'ma, when she lamented not having produced him any heirs, that girls were as good as boys, and encouraged the girls' curiosity by bringing them piles of books from the shop—but one thing he couldn't stand was his daughters' infatuations with Shanghai's starlets. He considered singers and actresses barely a step above prostitutes. "They exploit themselves for everyone's gaze," he said. Suchi and Sulan still purchased entertainment magazines without their father's knowledge and pasted pictures of Bai Guang, Zhou Xuan, Yao Lee, and others in scrapbooks they kept hidden beneath their schoolbooks.

"Apa says that all the time, but that doesn't mean he wants me to be a singer. Anyway, he doesn't know what he's talking about," Suchi grumbled. "Have you noticed that most of the women in the neighborhood are wives or mothers? The ones who work are almost all factory workers or waitresses at eateries or assistants to their husbands for whatever business they've opened. I want something more. Travel, adventure, glamour!" She sighed.

For several months now, a growing awareness of the futility of everything Apa had pushed her to be had begun gnawing at her. It had started with the arrival of her new teacher, Hu laoshi, a power-hungry, petty man who enjoyed picking on students for the smallest infractions—if they answered too slowly or their shirts weren't well ironed or they didn't understand his terribly explained lessons or they wore too bright of a ribbon in their hair. He berated them for being stupid and useless, reminding them that their unimpressive family backgrounds meant they were only good for being vases to be placed on their future husbands' shelves, and that was if they were lucky enough to be pretty. The rest of them, he said, were destined to become factory drones, so trying to teach them was like playing a lute to a cow.

At first Suchi had only cared about not invoking Hu laoshi's wrath: she'd studied diligently for all of her subjects, had been prepared any time he had called on her, had worked hard on all the assignments he had given her. She'd thought once he realized she was a quick learner, he wouldn't be able to find fault in her, that she would show him she was meant for more than what he believed. She was wrong. At first, he had seemed mildly amused by her aptitude, but that had quickly turned to annoyance, then anger, boiling over on the day she tried to point out an error she noticed in one of the characters he had written on the board. He had whipped around and hurled a piece of chalk at her, narrowly missing her face. "Arrogant fox!" he had bellowed. "Don't you know entire dynasties have been brought down because a woman believed she was smarter than everyone?" Wu Zetian, Yang Guifei, even the recent, most reviled Empress Dowager Cixi—he spat the names of these infamous women as proof Suchi was headed down a dangerous path.

So she had stopped trying, had folded herself into obscurity, answering questions just often enough to avoid being accused of laziness but not so much as to invoke Hu laoshi's wrath again. Mediocrity was a safe place to be, even if it did not bring her the same joy as excellence. But once there, once she stepped out of the inertia of achievement she'd been caught in for her whole young life, she realized that in a way, Hu laoshi was right. School *was* pointless. What was it all leading up to? She saw the way M'ma worried about money for groceries; they wouldn't be able to afford university. And while she had once delighted in being *good* at school, what were these lessons actually teaching her? Math was rote memorization, which she could do easily enough, but most bookkeeping positions were given to men. Classical Chinese was dated and impractical. Even geography seemed laughable to her, what with the way occupations kept shifting as the war ravaged on. Sure, Japanese language could certainly be useful, but it felt like a skill of survival, not something that excited her, and in fact, when combined with Japanese culture lessons, made her feel sick. And then there were the "womanly arts": sewing, embroidery, painting, sketching. Those classes might have been fun if they'd been allowed to be creative, but instead they were graded upon their ability to replicate uninspiring premade samples. She spent more time in Apa's bookstore, reading travel memoirs and translated foreign novels, and dreaming of a different life. The singing competition was the first exciting thing that had happened at school in ages.

"Maybe you can convince him," Haiwen said. "Doesn't he realize being a singer takes guts? Didn't you say he respects those who are courageous?"

He looked at her with such seriousness that it took everything in Suchi not to reach out and touch him. He was the one person in the world who believed in her wholeheartedly. She felt an urge to confess then, to take his hand and tell him, but at that moment, he whipped his head back toward the gramophone. "Here!" he exclaimed. He cranked the volume a little higher.

The solitary violin slid up and down as if running stairs, before turning an odd corner. It was jarring, frantic at parts and lonely in others. But oddly enough, whenever Suchi thought she couldn't bear it anymore, it became tender, like a woman stroking her hair.

"It's so different from everything else I've listened to," Haiwen said. "All the scale figures, the double stops, the trills and leaps . . . It's messy but beautiful, don't you think? It feels like how an actual human is inside."

They listened to the rest of the record without talking. Suchi, aware of the warmth of his body beside her, snuck glances at Haiwen's intent face. How he stared off at nothing, lips slightly parted. How his head moved to the music in gentle circles. How his fingers waved lightly on his forearm, touching invisible strings. She found herself committing these things to memory. Little gems.

The movement ended, and Haiwen stopped the Victrola. He sighed—a contented sound.

"Is that what you're playing for the recital?" Suchi asked.

He shook his head. "Mr. Portnoy says most of his friends prefer the classics—Brahms, Mozart. This would probably be too modern for their taste."

"So what will you be playing?"

"Beethoven's Spring Sonata," he said. "It's pretty, and of course I'm working hard on it, but . . . it's nothing like the Sibelius concerto." He looked dejected. "Mr. Portnoy thinks it's too advanced for me, anyway. He says we can revisit it for my music conservatory audition in a few years."

It was strange, Suchi thought, how things she had known about Haiwen for years presented themselves as new. Now she found herself charmed by how passionate this Sibelius piece made him, so different from his usual neutral self.

"You'll impress those teachers no matter what you play," she told him. "And when you apply to the music conservatory, they'll remember you."

Haiwen lifted the record from the machine. "What if—" he started, and stopped. He kept his eyes focused on what he was doing.

"What if what?" Suchi prodded.

Carefully, he slid the record back into its sleeve. "What if they don't like me?" he finally said in a quiet voice.

"Of course they'll like you!" Suchi exclaimed. "How can they not?"

Haiwen gave a short, sharp shake of his head, though whether he was shaking off her comments or his fears, she couldn't tell. He turned to look at her, a smile just a pinch too bright on his face. "Why did you stop by today? Any reason in particular?"

A damp trail sprung along Suchi's spine. She looked at Haiwen's expectant face, at the tension that hadn't quite eased from his brow. She shook her head vigorously. "Can't I drop by and see my best friend when I want to?"

A WEEK LATER, M'MA PUT SULAN AND SUCHI TO THE task of mending some old clothes she piled on the table in front of them. There were navy and brown qipao with tears in the seams and a few of Apa's shirts and pants requiring patches. Some clothing was in such poor condition it would have to be repurposed for scarves or small jackets, even dishrags. Sulan suggested she might be able to patch some of the more salvageable cloth together and make new dresses. M'ma agreed, grumbling. "Nyau lausy was right. The fortune teller warned me the little money we had would disappear as if our pockets have holes! I told your father, but he doesn't listen; he insists on spending money on his . . . politics . . . instead of using what's left over on useful items. He acts as if we aren't in the middle of a war, as if we can guarantee there will be food on the table tomorrow. If he has leftover money, shouldn't he be thinking about your futures? Laelae, soon we'll have to find you an appropriate marriage match—how can a young woman show her face wearing shabby old clothes like this? Your father never thinks about these things!"

Sulan frowned. "M'ma, I'm too busy these days for suitors—"

Suchi cut her off. "Nyau lausy tends to be pretty accurate, right?"

M'ma peered at the patch she was mending. "He said you would get a lot of colds, didn't he? I warned you to stay away from cooling foods, to eat more ginger, especially during your monthlies, but you didn't listen and how many times have you been sick so far? You've——"

"Where does this fortune teller live, anyway?" Suchi asked, interrupting her mother's familiar refrain. "How come you never take me with you?"

"Out in Hongkou, in the ghetto where all those poor European Jewish refugees live," her mother answered. "Nowhere a young lady should go, especially now, with all the air raids and increased patrols. I wouldn't go now myself." She sighed. "It's too bad, I don't think he can afford to move anywhere else."

TWO DAYS LATER, SUCHI WAITED AT HAIWEN'S SHIKU-men for him to come back from his lesson. She played with Junjun, who wanted to show her the present she had received for her ninth birthday, a wooden jewelry box that opened to reveal a twirling ballerina and a tinkle of a foreign melody. Suchi, whose birthday had passed several weeks earlier, felt a streak of envy. She had never received anything so pretty. Every year, Apa gave them books, and though Suchi loved reading, she wished just once to receive something shiny and precious.

When Haiwen returned a little before dinnertime, he seemed tired. Junjun ran to him and threw her arms around his waist. "Susu jie is here," she said. "I was showing her my music box."

Haiwen patted his sister on the head and looked at Suchi. "Were you waiting long?" he asked in Shanghainese.

Suchi hesitated. Was this a stupid idea?

"I was thinking—" She stopped and restarted. "So my mother has a fortune teller she sees once a year, right after the Spring Festival, Nyau lausy. The fortune teller tells my mother what to watch out for, what ailments we might have, as well as advice and predictions about how hard things will be." She paused and twisted a strand of hair around her finger. "Maybe if you know the recital won't go too bad, you won't be as stressed. Or maybe the fortune teller can tell you how better to prepare."

Haiwen looked at her dubiously. "My mother says fortune tellers are part of the old backward ways," he said. "And what if he tells me it will go terribly? Then I'll just be worried."

"Or," Suchi said, "you'll practice harder. The fortunes aren't a sealed *fate*."

Haiwen sighed but listened to Suchi because he always did.

THEY MET THAT WEEKEND, EARLY IN THE MORNING BE-fore Haiwen's afternoon lesson. Suchi rode sidesaddle as Haiwen pedaled his bike through the International Settlement toward Hongkou. The breeze cooled the summer stickiness on their skin, but Suchi felt wet with nerves. They traveled the most straightforward route they could—Apa had warned them time and time again never to venture too far out, that the destitute on the fringes of the city grew more desperate each day, that danger lurked beyond the borders of what they knew.

Several meters from one of the checkpoints, Haiwen slowed. Beneath a sign reading STATELESS REFUGEES ARE PROHIBITED TO PASS HERE WITHOUT PERMISSION stood a bored-looking Japanese soldier. Suchi shuddered.

"Are you sure you want to do this?" Haiwen asked.

She steeled herself. "Yes."

The Japanese guard held up a palm as they parked the bike and drew close. "Identification," he barked in heavily accented Mandarin.

Haiwen handed over his identification card, but Suchi froze, realizing she had left hers in a different purse.

"Well?" the guard said impatiently. He looked the two up and down and frowned.

Suchi could feel the exact moment Haiwen realized the reason for her hesitation. A failure to bring identification could be life-threatening, depending on the soldier. She could be dragged in for questioning by the Kempeitai, she could be disappeared the way suspected spies were disappeared, she could suffer whatever it was they did to women.

For a moment, Suchi did not react, the cold sweat beading along her neck. Her nightmares prickled her skin, the false memory of a bayonet in her stomach. Then, as if someone were drawing strings upon her face, she felt her features rearrange into something soft, innocent, and girlish. Smiling sweetly, she responded in Japanese, her voice a pitch higher than normal. "Sorry for the trouble, sir." She bowed. "It's our elderly uncle, who lives here. My brother and I received word he has suddenly gotten very sick. I'm afraid I was so worried, I ran out without my identification. Please forgive me; it won't happen again."

Suchi stood, the smile taut on her face. She noticed a sprinkle of acne on the soldier's cheek; she realized he couldn't have been much older than herself. After an agonizing few seconds, he jerked his chin. "Well, I guess there's nothing that says Chinese can't move freely in and out. Don't forget your identification next time."

Once they were out of earshot of the soldier, Haiwen looked at her with an expression of both admiration and concern. "Someone's been paying attention during their Japanese classes," he half-joked. She could hear the nerves jagged in his voice.

She shook her head. "I just figured if I ever came face-to-face with a soldier who wished me harm, he might be kinder if I could speak his language."

"Looks like you were right," he said. "The way you were talking and acting . . . I've never seen you like that before."

She shrugged, trying to slip the grip of fear from her shoulders. Whatever she had just done, she had not done it consciously and probably couldn't replicate it if she tried. She hoped she wouldn't need to.

The street they'd been let onto was grimy, littered with old cans and broken glass, mangy dogs rooting around in the gutter for food. The stench of recently emptied chamber pots wafted in the air. Several young foreign children in patched-up clothing ran by Suchi and Haiwen, singing in a language neither could understand. Despite the run-down appearance of the ghetto, there were businesses thriving on the streets. A bakery advertised sweets in both Chinese and a foreign language; next door was a milliner whose hats appeared well constructed despite the cheap material; beside that was a music store, selling secondhand instruments: a rusty flute, a beat-up violin, a few scattered harmonicas, an accordion stretched out like teeth. In front of these stores were mobile Chinese vendors with more familiar offerings: bamboo baskets, thread and cloth, boiled water from tiger stoves, haircuts, ear cleanings.

"It's not *too* different from our neighborhood," Suchi whispered. "Except for the foreign signage." The truth was the condition of the streets and buildings and the appearance of the people themselves all pointed to a certain destitution that made her want to flee. Suchi had learned from her father that when the Japanese had seized Shanghai, they had forced all the recent Jewish immigrants—the ones who had come from Germany and Austria and Poland, not the Russian Jews who had been around for a while, like Mr. Portnoy—into this cramped settlement, which had already been bursting at the seams with people, both Chinese and foreign. *It's better than what their kind are rumored to be enduring back in Europe*, her father had said. But he never elaborated further what that meant.

They went into a Chinese-owned tobacconist and asked the surly man if he knew of a Nyau lausy who was a fortune teller. The man picked his teeth before answering them. "En," he grunted. "One block over, down the alley in the row house between the Hungarian café and the stocking store. You can't miss it. He leaves food out for the stray cats and dogs. As if there weren't people starving in this neighborhood!"

In front of a dirty gray door, they found plates of rubbery chicken feet and glistening raw fish tails littered on the stoop. They knocked. A few seconds passed; they heard the bustle of someone shouting in Shanghainese, "Coming!"

An old man wearing wire spectacles and a changshan opened the door, a calligraphy brush dripping with ink in one hand. "Who are you?" He blinked with disinterest.

"Excuse me, Nyau lausy—" Suchi began, but the man turned his head before she finished her sentence.

"Nyau lausy! Young folks here to see you!" the man called up the staircase. He turned to the two, letting them into a grimy, dim foyer. "Go on up."

They climbed up the rotting wooden stairs. Suchi tingled with apprehension. She had no idea what to expect. Would he read her palm? Touch her head? Would he go into a trance? Or would he be able to tell everything just by looking at her face?

At the top of the stairs was a short hallway with a door. They knocked and it opened immediately.

A woman slightly older than Suchi's mother stood in the doorway. Her gray hair was swept cleanly from her thin face. She had on a navy changshan, similar to the one the man downstairs wore. Suchi had never seen a woman in a changshan before.

Suchi smiled uncertainly. "Ayi," she said in Shanghainese, "we're looking for Nyau lausy—"

"Yes." The woman was curt in her response. Suchi was confused.

"You're Nyau lausy?"

"Yes." The woman looked impatient. Her eyes flicked to Haiwen, then behind their shoulders, as if expecting someone else to show up.

"Ayi—" Suchi started.

"Lausy." Haiwen was correcting Suchi's choice of honorific. "Nyau lausy."

Suchi was still trying to understand. She'd assumed all fortune tellers were old men;[4] she hadn't expected a middle-aged woman.

Haiwen elbowed her gently in the rib cage.

Suchi shot him an annoyed side glance but said, "Nyau lausy. We're so sorry to bother you like this. I'm Tsan Suji and this is Waong Haeven. We were wondering if we could trouble you to do a reading for him?"

"Tsan Suji? The name sounds familiar," the woman said.

"My mother is Sen Sieu'in," Suchi said. "She's a client of yours and she speaks highly of you."

"Ah." The woman paused. "You have an older sister. And a father who sells books."

Suchi nodded, surprised by her memory.

"Hmm," she said, looking between the two. "I don't normally do readings for children without their parents."

"We're fourteen," Suchi protested. "Our nominal age is fifteen." She hated being looked down upon because she wasn't an adult yet. Haiwen nudged her side, but she ignored him. "In many villages, people at our age marry and fortune tellers tell them what days are auspicious. Why shouldn't we get a reading done?"

Nyau lausy's face cracked into amusement. "That's right. You're spirited." She gestured at them to follow her. "Come in. I'll bring you some tea."

A stone of annoyance formed in Suchi's throat, and she bit it back. She didn't like that this woman already seemed to believe she was familiar with Suchi, just because she'd known Suchi's mother. She didn't know anything about her.

The apartment was old and sparse but clean. Nyau lausy gestured at two chairs in front of a long wooden table and sat across from them. She poured water from a kettle she had left heating on a portable stove into a smaller pot containing tea leaves and let it soak. Waiting in silence, Suchi felt anxious. She glanced at Haiwen, who sat with a placid expression and didn't look her way. After several minutes, the fortune teller poured the tea into two ceramic cups and placed one in front of each of them. She poured herself a cup and sipped at it before speaking. "So, you want a reading."

Suchi leaned forward. "He has a recital coming up and—"

Nyau lausy narrowed her eyes at Suchi. Suchi stopped talking, although her annoyance ground more insistently. Nyau lausy focused her attention on Haiwen, who was palming his cup.

"I have a violin recital coming up," he said. "Some important people will be there from the music conservatory, and I'm just wondering . . . I guess I want to know if it will go okay."

"I'm afraid I can't be that specific, but let me take a look." She pushed over a brittle sheet of old newspaper and a pen. The newspaper bore years-old news about Nationalists agreeing on a truce with the Communists at the very start of the war against the Japanese. "Please write your full name and birthday." Haiwen wrote his information down in a gray, smudgy margin.

Nyau lausy took the paper back and read it. She ticked her thumb across her remaining four fingers, silently counting something invisible.

"You're like a well," she told Haiwen. "Clear and still, but if a man dropped a stone in, he would find it to be quite deep. You display little of your emotions, but you feel things keenly. You are sentimental. You transfer all that you don't know how to share into another world you live in. One of your imaginings. And yet, in life, you try to be practical, to be obedient, to do what is expected of you. You aren't a rule breaker."

While Suchi was mildly impressed by the woman's accuracy, she mostly felt impatient. Why was the fortune teller telling them what they already knew?

As if she could sense what Suchi was feeling, Nyau lausy ticked her fingers before speaking.

"You have fairly good ming. You will find success far from home," she said to Haiwen. "You'll have many mentors and friends who will help you, but not here. The further you journey from the place of your birth, the better your fortune."

Taken aback, Suchi glanced at Haiwen, who appeared stricken.

"What do you mean?" she asked. "Does that mean he won't get into music school?"

The fortune teller shook her head. "I can't tell you something that specific. I can tell you this year is the beginning of some fluctuating luck—good things will be tempered by bad things and vice versa. It will be like that for two years. Then there will be a hard period for several years, where your luck will be closed to you, where you will find everything is a struggle."

"Just when I'll be auditioning," Haiwen murmured.

Suchi could feel Haiwen deflating beside her, his dreams draining away. This was her fault; she shouldn't have brought him here.

"Well, isn't there anything you can do to change it?" she demanded.

Nyau lausy ignored Suchi. She looked with kind eyes at Haiwen. "Nothing is set in stone. That's something you have to understand. The I Ching tells me what it tells me, but it doesn't mean anything is definitive." She paused. "You know the word *mingyun*, right? Your personal destiny in this life?"

Haiwen nodded, but Suchi refused to react.

"Think about the two characters that make up the word. Ming is the inherent nature of your life as given to you by the gods. It's a destiny that can't be changed, the way the innate characteristics you are born with can't be changed. But what is yun? Yun is where flexibility comes in. Yun is fortune that changes with the seasons of the universe but can also turn depending on the actions you take, the choices you make. Together ming and yun make up a river, one that wants to carry you to a particular destination but moves fluidly, possibly diverging if a tree falls along its path or a large rainfall swells its banks. You, too, can change the path of the river; you can even swim upstream if you want to. Just expect it will be tiring, not as easy as moving with the current."

Haiwen nodded again, and Suchi was seized with irritation at how earnestly he was taking in everything Nyau lausy was saying.

The woman continued. "You might have a harder time in two years than you would right now; you might have a harder time being successful in Shanghai than you would in Chengdu. But if what you want is to stay, you can stay. You'll just have to work harder than you otherwise would have. It doesn't mean you can't be successful or attain your dreams. But I tell you what I know so you can be better prepared, whatever choice you make."

"I understand," Haiwen said. "Thank you, lausy."

"Don't look so sad, child," Nyau lausy added. "It's wartime. This period is hard for everyone."

Suchi couldn't tell if Nyau lausy was saying this because it was something she interpreted from the reading or because she felt the need to be an ayi with kindly advice, but it didn't matter. Both possibilities incensed Suchi with their totally useless outcomes. "Can't you give him a charmed amulet of some sort, something to change things?"

Nyau lausy focused her gaze on her. Suchi noticed her eyes were almost gray in color, clear and intense. "Tsan Suji," she said, sliding another strip of newsprint toward Suchi. "Remind me of your birthday."

For some reason, with Nyau lausy's eyes on her, Suchi felt chastised, as if she were a little girl. She obediently jotted down her birthday.

The fortune teller started calculating on her fingers again. She stopped and looked at Suchi. "You're very stubborn."

Haiwen burst into laughter. "Well, you can't say she's not accurate," he murmured. Suchi scowled.

Nyau lausy smiled and continued. "You're passionate, smart. You have a natural curiosity, a natural ability to learn new skills, to expand your knowledge, to adapt, but it's one of the things that makes you lonely. You feel lonely often, and the more you learn, the more it sets you apart and the lonelier you become, though you try to hide it. It's why you are fiercely loyal to the people important to you. For the people you love, you can turn into a dog with a bite."

Suchi loathed this woman. She seemed so smug, so certain of herself! Sure, she wasn't exactly *inaccurate*, but what a lack of humility, to assume she *understood* Suchi! Her mother had probably revealed Suchi's temperament in her previous visits. It meant nothing that she could recite it back to Suchi.

"You wear your emotions everywhere—on your face, in your words, in the way you move. But it's not because you can't hide it. You just don't want to. If you wanted to, you would be adept at hiding your emotions. You are like an octopus; you can change your skin to match the sand or sea."

Aha! Suchi broke into a grin. The fortune teller was finally wrong. Suchi was a terrible liar; Haiwen and Sulan could always guess how she was feeling (although, a voice nagged at her, if this was the case, why hadn't Haiwen already guessed how she felt about him?).

Nyau lausy checked her fingers again. "Unlike Haeven's, your luck is better if you stay close to home, not as good if you leave. These next two years will be very good for you; your luck is open. Things will come to you easily. You just have to allow it."

"That means I don't have to study as hard at school then, I guess," Suchi joked. Haiwen shook his head.

Nyau lausy frowned. "A boat doesn't get to its destination by current alone; it still requires steering. You have good opportunity luck right now, but not if you squander it."

"I've been telling her she needs to work harder for months," Haiwen said, nodding.

Suchi was stung by his betrayal. He was supposed to be on her side. He was supposed to understand. She swallowed her hurt. "It's not like I'm failing," she muttered.

"Yeah, but ever since that teacher got into your head, you've given up."

Suchi felt a spike of anger toward Haiwen. Didn't he know how pointless doing well in school was when you couldn't afford to go to university? *He* had the whole world open to him. Someday, after this war was over, he might tour the globe, meet singers and celebrities. He'd have the cosmopolitan life she dreamed of, but she'd still be trapped in their longtang, probably mending clothes and minding children like her mother.

"You know my school isn't fancy like yours, where the graduates go on to attend pricey universities and run around with the upper echelons of society. We don't even learn English, which might actually be useful if I ever want to travel abroad or work in a foreign-run company. That's why I'm going to be a singer. I *know* for a fact that your background doesn't matter, just your voice. And I can keep practicing."

Haiwen looked stricken. "Well, of course you're going to be a singer. I just thought—I mean, you were always so happy to be at the top of your class. It just seems so unlike you to suddenly not care."

Suchi didn't answer. She glanced at Nyau lausy, who was looking serenely between the two of them. This was her fault. *Look at her,* she thought. *Dressed like a man.* As if that were all it took for the world's doors to open to a woman. She was a fraud, Suchi decided. She'd been wrong about Suchi's temperament; she could be wrong about everything else.

"Suchi, I'm sorry," Haiwen said.

The fortune teller looked at them with a small smile on her face. She counted on her fingers again. Then she stared up at them.

"Are the two of you . . . a pair?" she asked, holding her two index fingers out and sliding them together.

"No," Suchi exclaimed, her face flushing pink. She didn't dare look at Haiwen. "We're good friends. That's all."

Nyau lausy hesitated. "I see," she said. She smiled slyly. "That's too bad. You make an excellent match. You have strong yoefen."

"What does *that* mean?" Suchi asked, flustered, her voice coming across as more defensive than she'd intended it. She knew, of course, what the word *meant.* She'd heard it tossed around by girls in school who had crushes, what they called "yuanfen" in Mandarin. But what did it *mean* for Haiwen and Suchi?

"You'll find yourselves pulled toward each other again and again," the fortune teller said. "Like you're tethered to each other with string." She folded her hands. "It's a predestination more than anything. But like I told you earlier, this is meaningless in the scheme of your own actions. You have destiny with many people in this world.

Perhaps your friendship is the fulfillment of that destiny. I'm just telling you what I see."

Suchi opened her mouth again—though she wasn't sure if it was to ask another question or argue with her—but Haiwen cut her off before she had the chance. "Thank you, lausy," he said. "We appreciate your time. We're sorry again for barging in on you."

Nyau lausy smiled indulgently at Haiwen.

On the table, Haiwen placed the two silver dollars they had brought between them, nearly worthless in this wartime economy, yet all the two could part with. Nyau lausy pushed one coin back at them. "I don't do this to make money. But the dollar will balance out the slight tilt in the universe I've caused by telling you your fortunes."

She pocketed the coin, nodded curtly, and stood up. The session was over.

Outside, Haiwen and Suchi said nothing. They walked side by side until they passed the checkpoint—the Japanese guard gave them a brief nod and Suchi thought she even saw a tiny flash of a smile—and hopped back on the bicycle. After ten minutes, Suchi couldn't contain herself any longer. "I'm mad at you," she said in a pouting voice, poking at Haiwen's ribs.

Haiwen jerked his neck around, the bicycle swinging. "I know. I'm sorry. I didn't mean to—" He stopped abruptly and was quiet for a moment. "I just think you shouldn't squander your opportunity luck. Look, if things can come easily to you, why wouldn't you take advantage of that to do even better than you might normally? Maybe if you do well enough you can get one of those scholarships I hear some of the universities give out. Or if you want to get a good position at a big company, I think you could! You're already so smart, smarter than me."

"That's not true," Suchi protested. "And I'm not talented like you. I'd much rather have a gift like yours."

"Too bad I don't have luck on my side," Haiwen said. Guilt streaked through Suchi; Haiwen might second-guess himself because of what that woman had told him. Her silence must have betrayed her feelings because Haiwen added, quickly, "It's okay. I mean, if what she says is true, I'll just have to work extra hard. I'll practice twice—no, three times—as much as I do now. But that's good. It's an incentive."

"I don't even know if I believe in these things," Suchi said. "My father says traditions are important, but some old-world rituals are just superstitions, things to keep the masses in check."

"She was accurate about our personalities," Haiwen said.

"Yours, maybe. I don't know about mine. What was that about being an octopus? I can't lie to save my life!"

"You seem octopus-like to me," Haiwen said, smirking. "You always have so many arms to poke me with. Maybe I should start calling you Zhang Suyu," he added, making a pun with her name.[5]

"Hey!" Suchi said, crossing her arms heavily. The bicycle teetered with the sudden shift in weight.

"I'm kidding," Haiwen said, glancing back at her. "Don't be upset, Susu. I only half believe this stuff, anyway."

"I'm not upset."

"You looked ready to throw tea in her face," he said.

Suchi cracked a smile. "See? I'm terrible at hiding my emotions. She's wrong."

"Yeah," Haiwen agreed. "In that case, she couldn't be more wrong."

Neither talked about the other thing the fortune teller had said, about their yuanfen. But of course, Suchi couldn't stop thinking about it.

SUCHI STOOD BY THE BOOKSTORE'S BACK SHELF, SECRETLY thumbing through a copy of Su Qing's *Ten Years of Married Life*. She was marveling (and feeling slightly breathless) at the fact that a woman writer could so boldly write about her marriage and bed-chamber antics, when her father's voice cut through the air. "Tsan Suji!" Suchi quickly shelved the book. Her father had used her full name. With trepidation, she went into the adjoining room, where Apa was sitting. When he looked up at her, she knew she was in trouble.

"I bumped into your teacher this afternoon," Apa said, his words clipped and tight. "He mentioned you are doing poorly in class, that your essays are sloppily done and that you seem ill prepared for lessons. He asked if having you skip a grade of middle school might have been a mistake." He stared at Suchi intently. "Was it a mistake?"

Suchi was furious. After all that grumbling Hu laoshi had done about the waste of time it was to teach them, he had the gall to complain to her father about her poor marks?

Sullenly, she muttered, "What does it matter if I get good grades or not? I'm not going to university anyway, and I don't need good grades to be a singer."

Apa's voice rose in fury. "What have I told you about singers? They're no better than—"

"What about Bai Guang?" Suchi asked defiantly.

"What *about* that woman?"

"You think she's just a lowly prostitute, but she's so respected, our school choir is singing one of her songs for the city-wide competition!"

Apa gave her a hard look. "What song?"

"'East Asian Nations March,'" she said. "It's all over the radio and it's state sanctioned and that goes to show you can be important and still be a singer!"

For a moment Apa said nothing, and Suchi thought he was digesting the information, reevaluating his opinion on the singer. But all at once he was a mass of action and sound—his newspaper cracked against the table, his chair nearly toppled over from the sudden force of being shoved backward as he leapt up. Suchi jumped in surprise.

"*State sanctioned?*" he roared. "Have you forgotten *whose* state we're under? Have you not been paying attention to *anything* I've been telling you? Heavens, I thought that teacher of yours was a fool, but now I see that you, precious daughter, are the fool! Think, daughter, think! Why would this government want all of you youngsters to learn this song that glorifies this idea of a Japanese-controlled Asian state? Why do you think this song is all over the radio, presented by popular celebrities? That precious Bai Guang of yours is nothing more than a Japanese-loving traitor, using that pretty voice of hers for Chen Gongbo's propaganda so she can become rich and famous! And you have the audacity to use her as an example of *why* you should be a singer!"

Suchi's breath quickened. She had been so excited about the singing competition she hadn't stopped to think about *who* had sanctioned that song or what those lyrics meant.[6] But surely what Apa

121

was saying about Bai Guang was an exaggeration. Surely she had been coerced and had no choice. Did women have a choice when it came to the Japanese? Did anyone?

"I should have sold that radio on the black market! You want to be a song girl, but what does a song girl do? She sells her voice, her body, her face. My daughters will be better than that. Even if I'm not a wealthy man, that doesn't mean my daughters shouldn't be just as educated, just as smart. In fact, my daughters will be *better* than the frivolous offspring of rich Japanese collaborators. My daughters will have a purpose, a conscience, a role in remaking this world. Do you understand?"

Suchi nodded quickly. Her face burned with shame.

"Think long and hard about the person you want to be in this life," Apa said. His voice had evened, but the words came out through his teeth. His hands had found his newspaper again, and it crinkled under his fingers. "I didn't raise you to be a fool, but if that's who you want to be, make that choice now so I don't have to waste any more time on you."

Desperation spiked in Suchi. Apa's pride in her was draining away, as surely as if it were blood from her veins. She wanted to please Apa, but she didn't know how to be the person he wanted her to be. What was the pathway to this ideal woman he expected her to become? She wanted to explain the situation, to tell him how Hu laoshi hated her for being *too* studious, how he wasn't the only one, how all her teachers seemed irritated whenever they learned she was *good* at school. She wanted to tell Apa that even if *he* believed she was meant for great things, that women could do whatever men could do, the rest of the world didn't agree, that she'd heard all the good positions at the best companies went to St. John's graduates, that everyone still expected women like her to become nothing more than wives and mothers. What he wanted seemed impossible.

"Apa—" Suchi started to say.

"Go," he said. He sat back down in his seat and snapped his paper open. She knew the conversation was over.

When, a few weeks later, her school did not win the competition, Suchi was relieved. She had mouthed the song along with everyone but could not stomach truly singing it. That night she went home and tore out the pictures of Bai Guang she had pasted into her albums over the years. While she still loved popular music, she never listened to that hanjian singer again.

EIGHT DAYS BEFORE HAIWEN'S RECITAL, THE UNITED States bombed Hongkou, the worst air raid yet. Thousands of residents dead, many of them Chinese, the reports said. A stench of sulfur, rubber, and something Suchi tried hard not to identify wafted in with the summer breeze.

"I thought the United States was our friend," Sulan said to Apa.

"But this is Japanese-controlled territory now," Apa said. "So as far as America is concerned, we're all the enemy."

Suchi thought of the children and the vendors she had seen that day. The people walking the streets. Nyau lausy. What had happened to all of them? Suchi felt guilty she had been so rude to Nyau lausy. Who knew if that woman was still alive?

Everyone stayed indoors for several days, unsure when the next air raid might be, if the next time, their heads might be the ones the bombs rained down upon.

Six days later, as people carefully resumed daily life, Haiwen came to Suchi. "The recital's been postponed indefinitely," he said. "Because of the bombings." He paused, and she could tell he was trying hard to mask his disappointment. "Is it selfish to have such thoughts when so many people have died? I mean, it's terrible, and I keep thinking about the people we saw that day, and I know I shouldn't even *think*—"

"I understand," Suchi said. She wanted to reach out and stroke his arm. Instead, she hugged herself.

"It seems Nyau lausy was right. Things aren't going my way . . . or anyone's way, really." He attempted a half-hearted smile. "At least she said the bad will be tempered by good, right?"

Suchi thought about confessing her feelings then. But she wasn't sure—would he see her confession as good or bad?

"Let's go for a bike ride," she said.

"Now? But what if—"

"Just a short distance," she said. "Take me to the music conservatory. I've never seen it before. I want to see the place where you're going to end up in a few years."

Haiwen smiled, a wide grin. "All right," he said.

Amid M'ma's concerned shouts—"Where are you going? It's not safe right now!"—Suchi gathered a purse, checked she had her ID card, and went back out, where Haiwen was waiting with his bike.

They rode toward the French Concession, braking and tilting their heads at the sky every time the low roar of a plane passed somewhere overhead. Haiwen rode through longtang communities and smaller roads as much as possible, ignoring the occasional shouts, suspicious looks, and hollow, hungry faces they encountered. Eventually, they passed the manicured, serene greenery of French Park, seemingly untouched by the war, and turned onto rue Lafayette.

The school was not as romantic as Suchi had imagined. She had expected an airy greenhouse, with music filling its halls and lawns, but it was quiet because of the raids. A simple black gate with hastily painted lettering announced the school. The building façade was gray with soot, and weeds peeked out between cracks in the bricks. The windows were dirty, and Suchi couldn't see much through their smeared surfaces. It seemed a depressing place to be.

"When we win the war and overthrow the Japanese, the conservatory will be even better than it is now," Haiwen said. "All the students and faculty that fled to Chongqing will come back. And I'll be in the thick of it then."

Suchi glanced at Haiwen. His head was tilted up at the buildings. She gazed at his face, at his eyes shining like pearls, and realized that when he looked at the school, he saw none of what she saw. In his expression, Suchi could still glimpse the child she'd first watched in the courtyard, playing that too-big violin. In so many ways, Haiwen had never changed from that boy. Sweet and solemn and earnest. Pulled along by a singular dream.

Suchi didn't understand what that was like. She had been saying for years she wanted to be a singer because singing gave her immediate joy in a way nothing else could. But she had also fantasized about becoming a singer because she'd begun suspecting that without a university degree, or at least a prestigious McTyeire high school degree, becoming a star was the only way for her to experience the excitement she craved. Now, after Apa's outburst, she felt naïve and frivolous at best, unconscionable at worst.

She had been thinking, over the last few weeks, about what Apa had said. About the person she wanted to be in this life. The only answer she'd arrived at was that she wanted to be a *good* person. Beyond that, what shape that life took, she didn't know. There were so many things she wanted from her future. She didn't want to be like M'ma, cooped up in her own world, judgmental and afraid of change. When the war was over, she wanted to *do* things, to *live* more than survive. Travel to places like Hong Kong or England or France, get there on a sturdy ship that cut through the gray seas. Learn brush painting and calligraphy. Speak English well enough to converse with a European without blushing. Start a little garden where she could tend her own kumquat and lemon trees. Dance until sunrise in a room of beautiful strangers. Read every book ever written. Life was dynamic and vast, and she wondered if she'd ever be able to experience enough of it to feel satisfied, if she could die happy knowing she'd only gotten to rub up against the small corner of the world she lived in.

Apa wanted her to be *more*. He wanted her to be the smartest she could be, the most courageous she could be, not for the mere sake of it, but because he wanted her to do something that would make a difference in their changing world. His definition of *good* was someone who helped the people around them, even when they themselves felt powerless. But what if Suchi couldn't?

She was still staring at Haiwen and he was still staring at the music conservatory. It was different for him. He was driven by his love for music and that alone. It was something she both envied and respected—the purity, conviction, and single-mindedness of his devotion.

Maybe it wouldn't be so bad becoming nothing more than a wife, she thought, *if I'm his wife.* Maybe she couldn't change the world, but she could change one person's world. She could spend her life supporting Haiwen, making sure he reached his dreams. The good luck the fortune teller said she had would temper the bad luck he was destined for. She could be a partner to him, she could use what multifaceted talents she had to build him a home, a space in which he could succeed. They could travel the world together, have adventures together. His achievements would be hers, too.

Maybe that could be enough.

"I can't wait to visit you here," she said.

Haiwen turned, his eyes still in a distant fantasy, and slowly focused back on her.

"After I'm done with high school," she continued, "I'll be so bored with my life, I'll sneak out all the time to see what you're up to."

"Oh, Suchi, I almost forgot." He took out a folded-up piece of newspaper. "Look."

It was a job ad for the Central Air Transport Corporation, several years old it seemed from the yellowing of the paper. The airline had been looking for stewardesses for their commercial flights.

"Where'd you get this?" Suchi asked.

Haiwen turned it over. On the back, she saw, in her own hand, her birthday. "I noticed this on the back of where Nyau lausy had you write your information, so I took it."

"Why are you showing this to me?"

"I know it's not as glamorous as being a singer, but it would involve travel, meeting people from different places and . . ." He stammered and trailed off, looking down at the paper fluttering between his fingers. "I mean, all commercial flights have stopped since the war intensified, but I'm sure once it's over they'll be looking again. So maybe this is something you could do, you know, while waiting for the singing stuff to work out."

She thought of herself flying high in the air, visiting far-off destinations, and felt a small bubble of possibility. It took everything in Suchi not to throw her arms around Haiwen. Instead, she took the ad and carefully tucked it into her purse.

On the bike ride home, Haiwen was silent. His white shirt had once again come untucked, and it flapped in the breeze, revealing a small triangle of pale flesh. Suchi inched her hand close to it, trying to feel its warmth. As they wheeled near the longtang's entrance, he said quietly, his voice almost swallowed by the wind, "Thank you for today."

"Thank *you*," she answered. She touched him gently on the small of his back, avoiding the exposed skin.

"TURN ON THE RADIO! THE JAPANESE ARE SURRENDER-ing! Those dogs have surrendered!" Apa burst into the room where Suchi was eating lunch with M'ma, Siau Zi at his heels. M'ma put her bowl and chopsticks down in a hurry, turning toward the radio, but Apa was already crouching in front of it, fiddling with the dial. After a few minutes of whiny static, the receiver caught and a crackling, distant voice filled the air. The familiar Japanese sounds and syllables gave Suchi chicken skin, and she suppressed a shudder.

"That's their bastard emperor, Hirohito," Apa said.

Although nobody understood the classical Japanese the emperor was using, for four and a half minutes, they all listened intently, absorbing each word as if it were from a disgraced god. Distantly, Suchi could hear the lone laughter of a child; she watched the light of the late-morning sun flicker through the panel cracks onto the floor. The voice was staccato and lilting, bloodless and thin. Suchi wondered if Haiwen would hear music in it, if there was something to unravel in the rhythm of Hirohito's voice, the voice of the nation that had held her people captive her entire life. The words were meaningless, but their drone made it hard for Suchi to breathe. She didn't know what to feel; she felt nothing. There was a before—her whole life was a before—but following these words, there would be an after.

The speech ended abruptly, with no fanfare, no further comment. The airwaves simply fell silent. They said nothing for a while, just continued to stare at the radio, as if to move would be to wake from a dream. But slowly, Suchi became aware of a hum that was growing outside their windows. People were cheering, whistling; celebratory shouts threaded throughout the alleyways like a dragon on the breeze until words were no longer intelligible and the longtang was a cacophony of feverish joy and relief.

Apa was already drinking with Siau Zi; M'ma was weeping. Suchi thought of Haiwen, practicing at Mr. Portnoy's for a recital he still hoped would happen. Had he heard? Did he know? She gathered a purse and a light scarf, closing the door on M'ma's fretful calls for her to stay home, Apa's merry encouragement for her to celebrate with friends, and emerged out onto a raucous, joyful Fourth Road. She saw people tearing papers—posters? Money? Newspapers?—and throwing them like confetti. Some chanted anti-Japanese slogans, others sang patriotic songs. Several were waving flags, the yellow triangles from Wang Jingwei flags ripped off so only the bright red and blue of the original Republican flags remained.

She ran as fast as she could, not bothering with trolleys that would never make it through the crowds. After forty minutes, she reached Mr. Portnoy's building, a tenement in the French Concession that Haiwen said his teacher shared with four other musicians, Russian Jews like him.

Suchi rapped on the door urgently. When no one responded, she tried again. She was holding her fist up for a third time when the door flew open and Mr. Portnoy, a rotund bearded man in his fifties, regarded her grumpily.

"What?" he said in accented Shanghainese. "Who are you?"

"Sorry to bother you, lausy," she said, giving a bow of her head. "I'm Tsan Suji, Waong Haeven's friend. Is he here?"

Mr. Portnoy frowned, drawing his bushy eyebrows together. "He's upstairs, practicing. You can talk to him when the lesson is over."

But Haiwen had already appeared at the top of the stairs, his violin in hand. His face creased with worry. "Suchi? Suchi, is something wrong?"

As he came to the door, the emotion Suchi hadn't felt back at home swelled and burst. "Oh, Doudou! It's over! The Japanese have surrendered!"

"What?" Mr. Portnoy said.

"On the radio—the emperor—"

Mr. Portnoy disappeared upstairs and a few seconds later, they heard the squeal of the radio and then the foreign-language station, the announcer speaking rapidly in English Suchi couldn't keep up with.

"I can't believe it," Haiwen said. He looked around, listening to the excited shouts. "We didn't know—the room is covered in rugs and drapes for soundproofing." He looked Suchi up and down. "You're dripping with sweat. Did you run here?"

"I knew you wouldn't have heard," Suchi said, feeling foolish. She put a hand self-consciously to her hair. She must have looked a mess. "I wanted to tell you."

Haiwen threw his arms around her. The sudden action startled Suchi. He smelled like the peppermint oil he massaged into the rose-colored callus on his neck. His hold was solid yet yielding, and her skin tingled with warmth against the light cotton of his shirt. She didn't know whether to hug him back; her arms hovered awkwardly at her sides. Before she could decide what to do, he pulled away. She wondered if he had felt her pulse twitching in her neck, if her face burned as red as it felt.

"Let me get my things and we'll go home," Haiwen said.

Sitting on the back of his bicycle, she pictured wrapping her arm around his waist. Instead, she gripped the seat frame with one hand, the other one cradling his violin case tightly.

The streets were teeming with even more people than before, rowdier too. They approached a crowd of thirty or forty people blocking their route. As they pedaled closer, Suchi realized something odd: the shouts coming out of the people's mouths were jeers, not cheers; their faces were distorted into hatred, not elation. The people closest to them were craning their necks to catch a glimpse of the center of the crowd. "Hanjian!" one person shouted, his arm gesturing wildly. "While you were collaborating with those pigs and living a comfortable life, our countrymen suffered!" Through a brief parting of bodies, Suchi glimpsed jerky limbs on the ground, a strange dance. A sharp, strangled cry startled her, and reflexively she grabbed a fistful of Haiwen's shirt.

"They're beating someone," Suchi whispered.

Haiwen said nothing. He braked and turned the bike around and veered off in a loop, toward a smaller, quieter street. A few minutes passed.

"Who were they beating?" Suchi asked. "A Japanese soldier?"

Haiwen didn't respond.

"But I heard them calling the person a hanjian," she added. "So the person was . . . Chinese?"

Haiwen kept cycling. The road had European-style houses typical of the French Concession's wealthier parts and was mostly unscathed by the war. Breezy trees lined the block.

"I suppose—" Suchi said aloud. "I suppose he deserved it. For being a traitor to his country."

There was a pop. The bike jerked and the pedals spun in a creaky whir, useless.

They jumped off the bike and Haiwen got to his knees, examining the chain. He spent a few minutes trying to pull it back over the gear, but it would not take. The chain was twisted somehow, a link unyielding.

"Maybe if we both pull on it . . ." She reached toward the chain, but Haiwen waved her hand away with black-greased fingers.

A few more minutes passed. The shouts were distant now but still audible. Haiwen glanced up toward the sound and then back at the chain, frowning. Suchi could tell he was getting increasingly frustrated.

"Let's just walk," Suchi said. When he didn't react, she switched tactics. She crouched near him. "I'm getting hot," she said.

He pulled on the chain harder, yanking on the stuck link. His tongue slipped out, a little clam foot.

"Don't ignore me," she said lightly.

He wiped the sweat dripping down his nose and left a streak of grease.

She started laughing. "Your nose!" she said.

He glanced up at her, and in his flinty eyes, she saw he wasn't just frustrated—he was angry. Haiwen—who rarely displayed anything close to a temper—was absolutely livid.

And all because of a bicycle chain.

"It's okay," she said. "I don't mind walking."

Haiwen shook his head. "I have to get you home," he said, his voice strained. "Those crowds—if anything were to happen—" He gave the pedal an angry spin.

She understood then.

"Doudou," she said, her heart tender.

Haiwen turned, his eyes narrow and stormy. That was when she kissed him.

FEBRUARY 2008
Los Angeles

HOWARD HAD BEEN cataloging the things about Suchi that hadn't changed. Her laugh, of course, was the first. But also: The way she played with her hair when she was in deep thought. Her quiet intake of breath and wide eyes when something delicious was placed in front of her. The way she pursed and swizzled her lips from side to side when she was trying to make a decision. The freckle underneath the corner of her right eye. Her affectionate teasing. The way she prodded for his thoughts when he was too silent or took too long to answer a question. Her love of fruits, any kind of fruit, and the voracious, unladylike way she bit into them.

These were the anchors he held on to when so much else about her had become unfamiliar. It wasn't just her age or her appearance—he thought she had aged beautifully—it was her whole being. She was more subdued now, more even-keeled. She still liked to tell him all the details of her day, but her speech didn't have the same electricity behind it. Of course he couldn't have reasonably expected she would remain girlish and energetic forever, but what perturbed him more was that now there was something about her hidden from view. Where once she had worn her heart on her sleeve, he found he could no longer easily guess what she really thought or felt about anything. Where once she had been curious and probing, she now seemed content with focusing on the present.

"We never talk about the past," Howard said to Suchi one day as they ate lunch at a trendy Taiwanese eatery. They had been sharing meals like this every other day for the last couple of weeks, after an initial awkward suggestion by Howard the day after he dropped her off.

"What do you mean?" Suchi reached for the sautéed greens. "That's all we talk about."

It was true—most of their conversations, if not about the mundanity of their day or updates on their children and grandchildren, revolved around their childhood. Comparing memories of old friends and neighbors, jokes they had shared, incidents that made them laugh. But while they rubbed up against the painful things, they never confronted them. They remembered each other's parents fondly without ever discussing what might have happened to them. They talked about dates they had been on without explicitly acknowledging they once had been in love. And they never spoke of anything beyond Shanghai.

"I mean," Howard struggled to explain, "we don't talk about anything that matters."

Suchi plucked at the oyster omelet with her chopsticks. The sticky tapioca starch, doused in pink sauce, stretched and snapped, a glistening gray oyster tugged along. She picked up the slice and put it in her bowl.

"What's the point in talking about unhappy things?" Suchi said. "We only have a few days left on this earth. I'd prefer to pass them with things that make me happy. Like this." She took a bite of the omelet and smiled. As in their childhood, Howard found her equal parts endearing and frustrating.

"Have I changed?" he asked.

Suchi chewed thoughtfully. "In some ways," she answered. "But haven't we all?"

"How?" Howard pressed.

"For one," she said, swallowing, "you didn't used to ask me so many questions." She laughed. "You were always serious. In your own head. You haven't changed in that regard. You're just . . . surer of yourself, perhaps. Maybe a little sadder. But we all are. It's just what happens."

"Do you want to know how you've changed?"

Suchi shrugged. "We all change."

"Little Susu would have begged me to tell her."

Suchi laughed. "Little Susu was a very impatient, nosy girl. I hope I've changed in that sense." She placed some tofu into Howard's bowl. "Hurry up and eat."

The eatery was playing a Mandarin pop ballad Howard had heard dozens of times, its lyrics mostly unintelligible aside from a repetitive phrase—something something *cute girl*. His grandson Charlie had played the song repeatedly in the car when Howard had gone to visit last fall. Freshly back from a summer in Taiwan with Love Boat, a summer program for Taiwanese American teens, Charlie told Howard the singer, Jay Chou, was one of the most popular musical artists in Taiwan; he'd even given Howard one of his CDs for Christmas, saying the last song was about war and he thought Howard might relate. Howard had taken one listen to the first track and couldn't tolerate it. It was some sort of lyrical rap that hurt his head, and worst of all, he couldn't understand the singer's Mandarin—it all came out in one thin stream of mumbled vowels. He'd tried skipping to the end, to the song Charlie had mentioned, but the opening bars featured a percussion of bullets set over soaring violins that made Howard wince, and he'd shut it off.

Ever since Charlie had returned from that trip, he'd taken to proclaiming to his family that he wasn't Chinese, he was *Taiwanese*, and corrected his mother whenever she called herself Chinese. This upset Howard greatly. "If I'm Chinese, then you're Chinese too," he admonished his grandson, and anyway, Charlie's other grandparents were from Hong Kong, which had rightfully been returned to China a decade ago. But Charlie insisted Taiwan was its own country and Hong Kong could *barely* be considered a part of China, which made him Taiwanese and Hong Kongese, at the most.

Yiping, his older daughter, told Howard to ignore him. "It's a phase, you know teenagers, they have no sense of nuance," she said, but it was hard for Howard not to take it personally, hard for him not to feel like his grandson was wielding a knife to his heart and slicing it to shreds. The only comfort he had was knowing that if Linyee were alive, she'd secretly be pleased, even if she might pretend to be on Howard's side.

"You hate this song, don't you?" Suchi asked. She was looking at him, a smile playing on her lips. "You have that look—the look you'd get when I forced you to listen to the popular ballads I loved on the radio. Your brow would furrow just a little bit, your eyes would pinch for a second. That's how I knew you hated them even though you'd never admit it."

"I didn't hate them," he protested. "I played them back for you."

"Only because you loved me," she teased. Her words caught in Howard's lungs. Suchi's face froze for a millisecond before smoothing out. "In any case, you were not as mysterious as you thought you were. Perhaps inscrutable to others, but you had certain tells. For instance, I always knew when you were focused on that other place in your head, the one constantly listening."

Howard thought about the years his head had fallen silent, when he'd found music in nothing, had been left only with the yawning emptiness of his tangled consciousness. How lonely those years had been. In the months since Linyee's death, he had noticed that blankness reoccurring occasionally; it terrified him.

"What are you doing for Chuxi?" Suchi asked. "Spring Festival is almost here."

"Oh," Howard said. "Winston invited me to join him at Coral Sunset."

He didn't tell Suchi that Yiping had offered to fly him out to Maryland so he could stay with them for two weeks, the way he had last year, his first Spring Festival without Linyee. But he couldn't stomach the idea of gritting his teeth through the "nutritious protein shakes" Yiping made him each morning, or the gentle yet insistent suggestions he make his stay a permanent one. He knew he was lucky his daughters loved him this much—he'd heard stories of children who threw their parents in nursing homes and never visited them (and in fact, he was surprised Adam had agreed to the possibility of his moving in with them at all)—but when he was around them, particularly Yiping, he found himself advancing into an age he didn't quite *feel* yet.

"I was wondering . . ." Suchi started, suddenly shy. Her fingers twisted in her chin-length hair. "Well, would you like to have dinner with my family?" As if suddenly aware of her fidgeting, she abruptly clasped her hands in front of her. Hurriedly, she added, "It won't be anything fancy—I'll be doing most of the cooking, though Ronnie has been eager to help. I don't know what kind of Chinese fare they'll serve at Coral Sunset—it might be quite luxurious! But in case you want something homier, you're welcome to come."

She shifted her eyes down, and Howard cataloged one more thing that hadn't changed: Suchi's surprising shyness.

"I would be honored," Howard said. He resisted the urge to reach over and cover her palms with his.

SUCHI'S SON, SAMSON, OPENED THE DOOR WHEN HOWARD rang the doorbell. "Welcome, Suksuk!" he said, shaking Howard's hand vigorously in the foyer. Samson looked nothing like Suchi, except in the eyes; his eyes were the same shade of almond as Suchi's—expressive, warm. A little girl in a cranberry-colored velvet dress came weaving between his legs. Two pink barrettes clipped wavy chestnut pigtails on either side of her head.

"Who're you?" she asked, stopping short in front of Howard. She stuck a finger in her mouth, and he could see she was missing a front tooth.

"Abi, we talked about this, remember? This is Aniang's friend, Uncle Howard. He's joining us for Chinese New Year."

"Are you Aniang's boyfriend?" Abigail asked, her finger migrating to her left nostril.

"*Abi*," Samson said, swatting at her hand. "Don't pick your nose."

"I didn't know Aniang had friends," Abi continued, oblivious to Samson's admonishment. "I thought old people can't have friends."

"Abi!" Samson scolded. "Stop asking so many questions of our guest! He hasn't even finished walking through the door." He turned to Howard. "Please come in. I'll take your coat and there are slippers for you over here."

The house was spacious and bright. The décor was warm and inviting without being flashy. There were photographs everywhere on the walls, mostly of the kids—swaddled on beds, sitting on Santa's lap, blowing out birthday candles—though there were a few of Samson and Ronnie as well. Howard followed Samson into the living area, which opened up into the kitchen. The floor was strewn with toys and the television blared cartoons. Beside the couch was a playpen in which a chubby starfish of a toddler slept. Suchi was stirring a pot on the stove while a tall, pretty brunette stood at the island and pleated dumplings.

"Hi, I'm Ronnie!" she said, waving. "I'd shake your hand, but mine's covered in flour and raw pork, I'm afraid. But it's so nice to meet you."

Howard nodded and smiled. Despite living in America for over thirty years, he still felt a twinge of embarrassment when confronted with white people. He was acutely aware of his accent, his fumbling English.

Suchi looked up and broke into a smile, her lips painted a soft red, bolder than the coral pink he'd grown accustomed to. Her fuzzy sweater was the color of dates; her hair was combed back to reveal gold earrings in the shape of sunflowers. Could he have guessed this was what she'd age into, that she would still be so striking?

"Doudou, I hope you are hungry, we've cooked so many things!" she said in English.

"Who's Doudou?" asked Abi, who had followed them into the kitchen.

He crouched down and looked at Abi's round, serious face. "I'm Doudou."

"You're Uncle Howard."

"Do you know what 'doudou' is?" he asked. Abi shook her head. "It's a bean. Like a . . . a hongdou, a, a, what do you call it . . ."

"Red bean!" Samson called from the living room. "You love the red bean soup Aniang makes."

"Right, those sweet beans in your soup," Howard said. "So when I was a baby, I was very, very small. Like a little red bean. So my mother called me Doudou for a nickname."

"Then when he was a teenager, he grew to be very tall, so instead of a little hongdou, he was a sijidou, a string bean!" Suchi said, laughing.

"Can I call you Doudou too?" Abi asked.

"Abi, be respectful . . ." Samson warned.

Abi glanced at her father. "Can I call you Uncle Doudou?" she revised with grave earnestness. The adults erupted into laughter. Abi's brow furrowed and her lips protruded into a tiny pout. So like Suchi.

"You can call me Uncle Doudou," Howard said, patting Abi on the head. She brightened up immediately and ran back to the living room, plopping herself in front of the TV.

Ronnie caught Howard's glance and rolled her eyes. "Thank you. She's a handful."

Just like her grandmother when she was young, Howard thought. As if she knew what he was thinking, Suchi made an exaggerated sniffing sound and bent over her pot.

~

"MOM, YOU'VE REALLY OUTDONE YOURSELF," RONNIE said once they were all seated at the dining room table. In the center of the round table were so many dishes there was hardly room for their bowls and small plates. Crisp golden spring rolls, bean sprouts and tofu skin in vegetable broth, sautéed garlic bok choy, fried longevity noodles, rice cakes with salted cabbage and pork, and a whole carp, steamed with scallions and ginger.

"Wah, rice cakes *and* noodles," Samson said, rubbing his belly. "Good thing I quit that Atkins diet! Please," he urged Howard. "Help yourself. You're the guest."

Howard began heaping food onto his plate but then paused. He gazed at the glistening noodles, at the vegetables and soup.

"What is it, Doudou?" Suchi, seated next to him, asked in Shanghainese. "You don't like it? I tried to make the Shanghai favorites, though I did add less salt since we're both supposed to be watching our sodium—"

"No," he said. "It's just that this is the first time you've ever cooked for me."

Her face blanked for a moment and the disconnect Howard had experienced over the last several weeks set in—in these moments, Suchi was a stranger to him, obscured. But in the next moment, she laughed. "Well, eat more! I can't promise you'll ever receive this honor again!"

"Everything is delicious, Mom," Ronnie said in English as they dug in. "What a feast."

Suchi beamed. "Nali nali, I couldn't have done any of this without your help."

"I only sous-cheffed. And wrapped those ugly dumplings."

"I want dumplings!" Abi shouted. A flake of spring roll hung off the corner of her lip. "Where are the dumplings?"

"We'll have them at midnight," Suchi said. "To bring fortune in the new year."

"Breakfast for you," Ronnie said.

"But I want them nooow!" Abi collapsed into a tearful meltdown. Her screams woke up her baby brother, who started fussing in the playpen.

"Oh god," Ronnie said, her face collapsing into her palm. She stood up after a moment and went to pick up the baby. "I'm so sorry about this," she said to Howard, touching his shoulder as she passed.

Howard looked at Suchi, who smiled and shrugged. "Isn't this what the Spring Festival is about?" she said to Howard in Shanghainese.

Scenes from past Spring Festivals flickered through his mind. Last year, his first without Linyee. His grandchildren bickering, the ache to have his wife by his side. That empty space transforming, filling with Linyee's presence. Linyee before she grew sick and confused. Linyee smiling radiantly while the grandchildren bowed, chubby hands outstretched for red envelopes stuffed with twenty-dollar bills. The children's faces changing, the clothes becoming shabbier, the red envelopes thinner, until it was his daughters' faces, his daughters' palms. Their bright smiles of excitement, their hands over their ears as fireworks crackled. His and Linyee's fortune.

His mind drifted to an even earlier Spring Festival. His first with Linyee. Her pregnant belly protruding as if she'd eaten one too many good meals—Yiping. Him, Linyee, Zenpo, Lau Fu, Lau Fu's wife, Lau Fu's new baby and mother-in-law. All crammed into the two-room low-level juancun housing Lau Fu had been assigned.

There'd been a bounty of fish, vegetables, and liquor, but what he remembered was gazing past all of that, across the table, at Linyee's face glowing as Lau Fu's wife handed her the infant to hold. Her radiant smile, one he hadn't seen in many months because her father still refused to speak to her over half a year after they'd eloped. He'd hoped reminders of the family they were building together would help her forget, momentarily. It was something he, too, tried to focus on.

Parts of that get-together were blurry to him now—there had been sorghum liquor and old stories, maroon faces shiny with drink. Li Tsin—had they talked of him? Or had they avoided inauspicious topics? He couldn't remember anymore. What he remembered was the surge of affection he felt through his drunken haze. He was lucky to be sitting at this round table, surrounded by such warmth and tenderness. So many others had nothing. His compatriots, dead on the battlefields or at the bottom of the ocean. Families back in China— he wouldn't allow himself to think *his* family—starving.

But sometime after—maybe it was when the women were clearing the table or when Zenpo and Lau Fu started affectionately calling each other names over a round of xiangqi—he'd slipped out into the lanes of the juancun. The low residences that made up the military dependents' village had recently been renovated with concrete and surrounding brick walls, the government's attempt to reinforce hastily erected bamboo, straw, and mud shacks meant to be temporary. Haiwen remembered how hard they had labored to put up the structures they believed were only needed for the couple of years they would be stationed out here. Over time, they'd cracked and sagged, worn down by typhoons, earthquakes, and thunderstorms. The new walls made the narrow corridors between houses darker and more imposing, and he felt suffocated. A few stragglers were still setting off firecrackers, the lonely pops less festive in the dead of night, each burst a flash of a wartime scene he didn't want to remember.

He exited the village and walked until he was far from any residences, threading through the district's empty streets until he found himself on the grassy bank of the river, not far from where he had hauled the rocks that formed the foundations of the house he and Linyee lived in. The new moon was a fingernail snagged on a veil of clouds, making the night stars easily visible. He looked for the brightest star, what he hoped was the North Star, and oriented himself in its direction. He crouched on the ground, staring at the bright pin of light. Softly, he called for his mother, his father, Junjun, Haiming, Suchi. "Happy New Year," he whispered.

FOR DESSERT, THERE WAS A BEAUTIFUL PLATTER OF eight-treasure rice pudding. Suchi listed out the ingredients layered in concentric circles between sticky rice—red bean paste, lotus seeds, pineapple cubes, red dates, dried longans, goji berries— finished with an osmanthus sugar-water glaze and shaved tangerine peel. Abi, who had calmed down considerably after Suchi boiled her several dumplings to have for dinner, stared at the dessert in rapt delight as a slice was handed to her. "I want to eat this every day," she announced after she bit into her piece.

When everyone had finished their dessert, Suchi announced, "Who wants a hongbao?"

"Me!" Abi said, jumping out of her chair and rushing toward Suchi.

"Nuh-uh," Samson said. "That is not how we do things. Remember what you have to do."

Abi stepped away from Suchi and bowed her head, holding out both her hands. "Um."

"Gunghei," Samson prompted in Cantonese.

"Gunghei," Abi repeated.

"Faatchoy."

"Faatchoy."

"Say it all together now."

"Gunghei faat—faatchoy."

Suchi smiled. "Xinnian kuaile, siau noe," she said, handing the red envelope to Abi, who took it with both hands happily.

"What do you say?" Ronnie prodded.

"Thank you, Aniang."

"Mommy and Daddy have one for you too," Samson said.

Abi stood in front of her parents and repeated the ritual. Waving the two envelopes around, she exclaimed, "I'm rich! I'm going to buy the most biggest LEGO set ever!"

"Don't forget to put the yasui qian under your pillow," Suchi said. "It's luckier if you sleep on it."

"And lucky for the college tuition fairy who picks up the money in the middle of the night to put in investment funds," Ronnie tossed out. Samson laughed at Abi's confused look.

Howard smiled. Although he'd come in with judgments about Ronnie, he'd found she was warm and funny and seemed genuinely to care about Suchi and her family. She was hard not to like. Perhaps, he thought, if he got to know her better, he would warn her about saying too much about family matters to friends. Perhaps she didn't realize how easily gossip spread within the Chinese American community.

"Wait," he said, waving Abi over with a palm. "I have one for you too."

Abi tucked her chin into her chest, shrugging, a gesture of sudden shyness. She looked up at her parents, who nodded. She made her way in front of Howard and bowed. "Gunghei faatchoy, Uncle Doudou."

Howard suppressed laughter and slid the red envelope into her hands. "Xinnian kuaile, Abi."

She thanked him and ran back into her mother's arms.

"I have one for the baby too," Howard said, giving the other envelope to Samson. He glanced over at Suchi, who was smiling gently. For a second—a moment—he imagined a parallel life. One in which they presided over this New Year's dinner together, where these were their children, their grandchildren. The family they had built together. He blinked, guilt trickling through his body. The mere thought was a betrayal to Linyee. No matter what, that part of his past belonged to her, would always belong to her. And yet, Howard longed for *something*. For *more*.

"All right, little bug, I think it's time to wash up for bed." When Abi started protesting, Ronnie cut in. "Don't you want to sleep on all that money you got? Didn't you hear what Aniang said? It's good luck." This seemed to quiet Abi down.

"Say good night to everyone," Samson said.

"Good night," Abi repeated. She started climbing up the stairs but paused and peered down at Howard from between the balusters. "Will you be here tomorrow?"

"I don't think so."

"Oh," Abi said, pouting, while Ronnie urged her up the stairs. "Okay, goodbye forever!"

Samson rolled his eyes and started clearing the table. Howard stood to help, but Samson waved him off. "Please, sit!"

Howard collected some dishes anyway and brought them to Suchi, who was already rinsing things in the sink.

"You speak Cantonese to the children?" Howard asked in English, curious. He had noticed Samson had instructed Abi to say the New Year's greeting in Cantonese, though Suchi had responded in Mandarin.

Samson shook his head. "I don't really talk to the kids much in Cantonese. Ronnie can't understand it, obviously. They hear me talking to my mother in Cantonese though, and she often responds to me in a mix of Mandarin, Shanghainese, and Cantonese. And Ma often speaks to them in Mandarin. I always hope maybe they'll pick up something that way."

"His father didn't like me speaking Mandarin or Shanghainese when he was growing up," Suchi said in Mandarin.

A dark look passed over Samson's face, but it cleared in the same moment. "She did anyway, when he wasn't around," he said. "So I can understand a little of both, I just can't speak that well." Howard nodded; Shanghainese was an entirely foreign language to his daughters too, which saddened him.

"He has a terrible Cantonese accent to his Mandarin," Suchi joked to Howard in Shanghainese.

"Hey, I understood that!" Samson said.

Suchi gave Howard a sly smile. He had seen that same expression every time she'd played a prank on him when they were kids.

148

"So tell me more about yourself, Suksuk," Samson said while he loaded dishes into the dishwasher. "I'm afraid we didn't get much adult conversation in at dinner. My mother says you two were friends when you were children. What a small world that you ran into each other after all this time!"

He hadn't realized Suchi had told her family they were childhood friends; Howard himself had only told his children he was going to a friend's house for New Year's. How much had she told her son? "Your mother looks the same," he said. He almost said *still beautiful* but caught himself.

"You keep saying that, but it's a lie," Suchi said. "Anyway, back then I was gawky and pimply. Now I'm fat and dowdy. So."

"Don't listen to her," Howard said. "She was always striking, she just didn't know it. All the boys were in love with her."

Suchi laughed. "Now I *know* you are lying! Everyone was in love with Sulan, not me."

"I think all the boys were intimidated, honestly," Howard continued. "Even though she was never particularly tall, the way she lit up like a firecracker when you crossed her made her feel much larger. I think her long legs had something to do with it too. When she was angry, it somehow felt like she was looming over you."

Suchi gave a sigh of exasperation, but Samson laughed. "Oh, I know about *that*," he said.

"But between you and me, I think the boys *liked* teasing her. She had this cute heart-shaped face that flushed in the cheeks and nose whenever she was embarrassed or mad."

"Ma, you sound like you were a heartbreaker," Samson said, delighted.

"Luan shuo," Suchi admonished, and Howard noted with

amusement that her cheeks and nose were red at that very moment. "He's making up tales. None of the neighborhood boys talked to me."

Howard continued, partly to embarrass her and partly because—well, he didn't know why, exactly. Maybe because he could picture young Suchi more clearly than he could remember even his most recent memories.

"Oh, and her eyes. When she was passionate about something, those eyes glinted at you furiously. Her eyes are special, you know." He paused and looked at Samson. "You have her eyes."

"Lighter than most Asian eyes," Samson said. "People always think I'm mixed because of it."

"Your grandfather's eyes," Suchi murmured in Shanghainese.

"Ah," Howard said. From the mist, a memory of Suchi's father struggled to push to the surface. "Yes, perhaps you do resemble Tsan yasoh."

"So you knew my grandfather too?" Samson asked.

Howard nodded. "We grew up in the same longtang—um, neighborhood. I don't know if your mother told you about it."

Samson looked over at Suchi, who was scraping leftovers into plastic takeout containers. "She doesn't talk much about her childhood at all, to be honest."

"I told you," Suchi said.

"Yeah, you only told me bare facts. How you grew up in Shanghai, not rich, not poor. How your father was a bookseller and your mother had bound feet. Everything else I learned from Ayi."

"Sulan?" Howard asked. "What your mother says about Sulan isn't wrong. Sulan was considered the beauty of the longtang."

"I'm not surprised!" Samson's face lit up. "I remember thinking she was beautiful, even as a kid. She was my favorite aunt when I was growing up. My father's sister was severe, but Ayi was warm and funny. She lived with us when I was young. She rested a lot, but she let me climb into bed with her and she'd tell me stories about when she and Ma were little. How they'd fight, how they slept in the same bed, how they chased each other through the alleys of their neighborhood and played pranks on other kids." He paused. "I wonder if any of those stories were about you."

"I didn't know she was telling you all that," Suchi said.

"She told me not to tell you," Samson said. "She said you didn't like being reminded of the past."

Howard stared at Suchi's back, hunched over the sink. She was carefully adding hot water into a pan to soak.

Samson turned the dishwasher on and wiped his hands on a dish towel. "I'm going to see if Ronnie's got the kids handled. Why don't you two catch up? Don't feel in a hurry to leave. Maybe you can tell me more stories about my mother later."

When it was just the two of them, Howard switched into Shanghainese. "Thank you for having me over," he said. "It was such a pleasant night."

"I'm glad you could come," Suchi said, washing her hands. "Would you like some tea?"

Howard nodded. Suchi pinched tea leaves from a metal canister into two ceramic mugs and filled them from the hot water dispenser on the counter. She brought the two mugs over to the kitchen table.

"I'm so happy to have met your family," Howard said, warming his hands around the mug. "Abi . . . she reminds me of you."

"Nosy and tactless?"

"Energetic and curious."

151

Suchi smiled. She was particularly radiant tonight, Howard thought. Her eyes glowed bright and he remembered the time she had snuck a small bottle of baijiu from her father's stores and they each sipped on the terrible stuff, the burn and heat and rancidness of it. How pink her cheeks had become, how tender her expression. She'd been unable to control her laughter, which made him laugh like he had never laughed, and when he kissed her, he wondered how the sharp tang of liquor had disappeared from her lips.

That date had occurred in the early days of their romance, the sweetness of her mouth still electric and new. The first days, weeks, months filled with anticipation and joy. In some ways their routine had remained unchanged. She sat by him while he practiced and sometimes she sang; he waited for her by the gates after school so they could walk home together. She prattled about what had happened each day; he listened and smiled and offered input when asked. She was still her; he was still him. But in all the ways that counted, everything had changed. They held hands, first tentatively, then in a tangled grip, as if they hoped to meld into each other. They snuck kisses when no one was around, sometimes soft and sweet, more often hungry and wet. The air between them was a gap he wanted to close, wanted to spend a lifetime trying to close—he wanted to consume her, to know her wholly. Mr. Portnoy had complained he seemed unfocused; he didn't agree. There were bars of music that made more sense to him, melodies that felt alive and bright in a way he hadn't been able to conjure before.

They'd spent the last warmth of that summer lying out on the grass of French Park, his arm around her, her face buried into his chest, his violin forgotten. They'd listened to birdsong and imagined a future. The Japanese were leaving, Shanghai would be China's again, and this meant they could dream about a war-free life.

The past mingled with the present. He was Howard now, and she was Sue, but here she was, across from him again, still beautiful in every way. "Susu—" he started, then stopped. He wasn't sure what he wanted to say. He wanted to hold on to this moment, or maybe what he wanted was to go back to an old moment, a moment before all the things they didn't talk about existed. Change something, somehow.

"Don't," Suchi said, and the easy smile on her face evaporated. In its place, a mask. While he didn't always understand her anymore, he realized she still saw him, even now.

But Howard felt propelled forward.

"Sometimes I think if only—" he started saying.

"Doudou—" Suchi broke in.

"I think about it all the time," he continued. "What you wrote to me in Hong Kong. About how we can't regret the past. But—"

"We can't," Suchi said. "Everything we've lived through has brought us to here. Me in this house, with Ronnie and Samson and Abi and Nicky. You and your daughters and your memories of Linyee. Changing the past wipes all of that away. I can't do that, can you? We can only move forward."

"You're right," Howard said, though he struggled with this. How he longed to live a synthesis of all the lives he had lived and not lived, a life in which he held on to Linyee and his daughters while still having his parents age beside him, meeting the children he and Suchi would have borne. "I'm greedy," he acknowledged out loud.

"We don't get to be greedy," Suchi said. "We get to be content."

"This is the twilight of our lives," Howard said. "Even if we can't look backward, it doesn't mean . . . It doesn't mean we can't reclaim what we lost or be who we were."

"We can never again be who we were," Suchi said. "It's impossible. We've already missed each other."

He was fumbling. The year after Linyee's death had been passed in a gray, soundless fog, an acceptance that the best part of his life was over and that now he could only muddle through each monotonous day, waiting to die. He was content, he told himself. They'd had a good life. He would not dwell upon regrets. And yet in the month since Suchi had reappeared in his life, he'd discovered he still had things he wanted, wishes unfulfilled. Suchi was the answer to all of those things. He would right history with her. They would restart their lives, cram everything that had been robbed from them into the next five, ten, twenty years.

He didn't know how to explain all this to Suchi. Gone were the days when they understood each other implicitly.

"Yuanfen," he said in Mandarin.

"What?" Suchi asked.

"The fortune teller . . . that fortune teller you dragged me to see when we were kids."

Suchi sighed. "How can you still believe in that stuff after all we've been through?"

"She said we'd find each other again, and we have. Twice now. Don't you think that means something?"

Suchi abruptly stood, her mug in her hand. "It's late," she said, gathering his mug too, although it was still half-full. "You should get on the road. I don't want you to get lost again."

"Suchi," he pleaded. "I know you must blame me for leaving you. Perhaps you have never forgiven me."

"There's nothing to forgive," Suchi said, her voice weary.

"Then why won't you talk about it?"

"About what?"

"Any of it. The past, what happened between us. You won't let me get close to bringing it up."

"What's the point?" She stared down at the two mugs she was holding. "It happened."

"If you want to air your grievances against me, I deserve it. The Suchi I knew would have—"

"The Suchi you knew evaporated decades ago," Suchi interrupted, slamming the mugs down on the table and setting her eyes steely upon him. Her voice vibrated and swelled in a rush. "She was silly and frivolous, and she was killed off in the war, just like everyone else. What took her place is the Suchi sitting before you now, and I survived by not looking backward. So stop trying to revive the dead. You won't find what you're looking for here."

For a moment, Howard felt triumphant, almost exhilarated. This temper of hers, it was familiar. She was, despite what she had just said, still the same person inside. "Suchi," Howard said gently, remembering the many times he'd had to coax her when they were children. "It's my fault. I didn't mean—"

Suchi sagged back down into the chair, like a balloon whose air had been let out. "This was a mistake," she said quietly, covering her face with a palm, red nail polish shining in the dining room light. "I don't know what I was thinking."

"Susu," Howard tried again.

She waved an arm toward the foyer without looking up. "Please go," she said.

"I'm sorry," Howard said. "Can we just—"

She shook her head but said nothing else.

Howard wanted to reach out and touch her hand, to rub her candy-apple nails beneath his fingers. He wanted to melt away whatever fear it was that held her back. But he knew she would not be convinced tonight. He stood up; she didn't move. He got his coat from the closet, put on his shoes. With one hand on the doorknob, he looked back. He would find a way to break through her walls, he told himself. He would fight for her. Then he let himself out of the house, into the crisp winter night.

JANUARY–APRIL 1947
Shanghai

SUCHI SPIED HAIWEN practicing underneath a tent of emptied willow branches, the shadows undulating across his face, bringing him in and out of focus. The sun was a bright yolk in the milky sky, unseasonably warming the day; she'd known he wouldn't pass up the chance to practice at his favorite spot in Huangpu Park after weeks of frigid weather. His arms were aloft with his instrument, his fingers flying across its neck, sheet music he'd carefully hand-copied weighted by a stone on a bench beside him. Suchi loved listening to him practice, to the precise magic that came from his hands. Even after all these years, his talent captivated her as much as it had the first day she'd seen him play.

He hadn't noticed her approach. Close to where he had leaned his violin case, she spied a fuzzy gray ball. She plucked the ball from the ground, pocketed it, then hung a few feet back for several more minutes, watching him absorbed wholly in the fast-soaring notes. When he brought his instrument down, she threw her arms around his waist.

"Susu," Haiwen said, turning with a smile. Hand still holding the bow, he reached out with his index finger and brushed hair away from her forehead. The tender way he touched her made her heart swell. "Why are you here?"

"I just went to pick some things up for M'ma at the black market and had a feeling you'd be here. Is that Paganini again?"

He nodded. "I'm trying to memorize it for my audition." His audition for the music conservatory was in mid-May—although he had just turned sixteen, younger than most students matriculating, several members of the faculty had been impressed by his performances at recitals and with his school's orchestra.

"It sounds awfully hard."

Haiwen bent down to put his violin away. "Mr. Reyes has been showing me a new way to memorize my music."

Mr. Reyes was a forty-something Filipino man who had replaced Mr. Portnoy when he had moved to America the year before. Haiwen had been devastated to lose his longtime mentor, but a friend in his orchestra recommended Mr. Reyes, telling him not to believe the stereotype that Filipino musicians were only good at jazz and popular music. Now Haiwen talked about Mr. Reyes constantly, in awe of the diversity of his musical knowledge and excited by his unconventional methods and musical philosophy.

"He's encouraged me to use my ear *more*, instead of trying to photograph the score in my mind," he told Suchi now. "Trust my ear to tell my fingers where to go next, because my fingers already know. But also to hear the music ahead of where I am. If I stretch the time in my mind, the caprice actually ends up feeling leisurely."

Suchi never really understood what Haiwen was saying when he got technical, but she smiled at how happy he sounded. She took his hand in hers, then yelped. "Your hands are so cold! What happened to the mittens I knit you?"

Haiwen's eyes widened. He patted his body with his palm. His face fell. "I . . . I don't remember. I took them off to practice and . . ." He searched the ground around him.

"Aiya," Suchi said in mock lament. "Do you know how long it took me to learn to knit those? What's the point of giving you anything? You don't cherish my gifts!"

"I do!" Haiwen insisted. "But I can't play the violin with mittens!"

He looked so upset, Suchi couldn't bear to keep teasing him. She pulled the gray ball from her pocket. "Here," she said, waving the mittens at him. "They were on the ground."

"Aiya, Susu, you had me so worried! How can you torture me like that!" He took the mittens from her and put them on. They were misshapen but he held them up proudly.

Suchi laughed and wrapped her arms around him. "You're just so easy to tease," she said, squeezing him.

They walked home hand in hand, taking the long way, looping down the Bund before they cut back west. She looked up at him and he returned her glance, giving her a smile. Her heart contracted. Even after two years, she still felt a giddy thrill when he smiled at her. She leaned into his arm, inhaling the heat of him. They waited for a tram to pass before crossing the street, and when it was safe, he gave her hand two quick squeezes as he always did, his signal that it was safe to go. When they got to the other side, she brought the back of his hand to her lips and kissed it.

She cherished this time together, surrounded by so many strangers that the world became their own. It was different back in the longtang. There was less privacy in Haiwen's shikumen now that Haiming had returned from England with a pretty Eurasian wife, and M'ma still refused to let Suchi bring Haiwen home. Besides, Suchi had grown wary of the gossipy neighbors. Whenever an ayi encountered Suchi alone, she would inevitably ask when she and Haiwen were to be married. M'ma, for her part, muttered that Haiwen better marry Suchi, since no other man would want her after she so publicly flaunted their relationship.

It wasn't that Suchi hadn't wondered about the answer to that question herself. She dreamed of an early summer wedding, during plum rain season, when her favorite sour plums were plentiful—a wedding during rainy season seemed so romantic. But although she and Haiwen had made offhanded comments about their future together—where they might live or the children they might have someday—neither had discussed how far off that future might be. She knew Haiwen was singularly focused on his audition in the spring—perhaps, after he matriculated into the music conservatory and she finished high school or started working as an airline stewardess, they could finally discuss plans for marriage.

"Oh!" Haiwen said. "I almost forgot to tell you the good news. My sister-in-law is pregnant!"

Suchi clapped her hands together. "That's wonderful! Your parents must be so excited!"

Haiwen nodded. "I'm going to be an uncle. Isn't that weird?" He smiled. "Maybe I can teach that little kid to love classical music like me."

Suchi made a face. "You have to at least expose the child to some popular music! Do you want your niece or nephew to be teased mercilessly for having such strange taste?"

Haiwen laughed. "Well, then I guess it's a good thing they'll have the very cool Zhang Suchi as a shenshen!"

Suchi pulled Haiwen's arm closer, her heart warmed by the implication that she would be his wife. "That reminds me, there's a new song by Yao Lee called 'Lovesick Dream' that I absolutely adore. I'd love to practice singing it, so do you think you could—"

She stopped. A familiar roar of voices trembled through the streets, headed their way. More anti-American protests.

In the year and a half since the War of Resistance had been won, tensions between the Nationalists and Communists had risen steadily. Apa had been furious when, after Japan's surrender, Japanese militia continued to patrol the streets with their bayonets; posted notices explained the Japanese would hold off the Communists and "protect the city" until the Nationalists could get to Shanghai. But then the Japanese had been replaced by truckloads of loudmouthed, hooting American troops who treated the city like their own pleasure palace. Apa had grumbled about Generalissimo Chiang's shortsightedness, about the danger of relying upon American aid in this renewed struggle for power. "We owe the Americans too much. What will they want in exchange, do you think?"

And then at the end of December, a Beijing student had been raped by two American marines, and the streets had erupted. They hadn't quieted since. Apa was not the only one wary of the American presence, it seemed.

As the protest drew closer, Suchi made out the words on the signs, the slash and cut of their bold characters. Some banners proclaimed the country had defeated one foreign rapist only to welcome another with open arms; others pleaded for an end to the civil war. COMMUNIST OR NATIONALIST, WE ARE ALL CHINESE! it insisted.

The protestors demanded justice for the student who had been violated and the immediate withdrawal of American troops from Chinese soil, their chants a steady hammer that thrummed Suchi's tendons.

Haiwen pulled Suchi against the buildings, his body shielding her as the crowd streamed past. He shook his head. "Without America, we never would have won the war against Japan. We still need them if we're to win this one."

Suchi said nothing. The protestors' calls had awakened the knotted unease she felt whenever she thought about the Beijing student. She didn't know much about the girl; the privately owned newspapers Apa had given her to read had largely focused on what had happened, and details about the girl were scant. Suchi knew her name—Shen Chong. She knew she wasn't much older than Suchi and was from a prominent family. She knew the girl had been coming home from the movies and had tried to protest but had been too scared to resist much. But Suchi wanted to know what she was *like*. What movie had she come from? Did she and Suchi like the same movie stars? Did she also have a boy whom she dreamed of marrying someday? Had she hoped to travel to America when this war was over? Suchi wondered if they'd have been friends if they'd met. She wondered what her life was now.

"Do you realize," she said as the last protestors trailed away, "that we've never known peace? Our entire lives, this country's been at war."

Haiwen squeezed her hand. "There has to be an end to this, someday."

"But how will it end? Who do you think will win?"

"Whoever is supposed to, I guess."

Haiwen's laissez-faire attitude pricked at her. Tears burned her sinuses. She wrenched her hand away. "You can't just live in your music all the time! Don't you care who wins?"

"Do you?"

"Of course!"

"And who do you hope wins?"

The Communists. The response popped into her head. She'd heard the ideals Mao Zedong espoused from her friends, from Sulan, even from Apa, though he tried not to bias her toward one party or another. The truth was, she didn't understand why Haiwen's family was so staunchly against the Communist Party. Apa said it was because the Nationalists had helped the Wangs take back control of their ten textile mills, but she knew the Wangs were good people who wanted what was fair. And that's what the Communist Party wanted: fairness for all people. It wanted everyone, from farm workers to mothers, to be recognized for their efforts; it wanted to end the widespread famine and poverty that existed in the rural countryside outside of their Shanghai bubble. This all seemed good and right to Suchi. But Apa had cautioned his daughters that ideals and politics were two different things and human flaws always got in the way.

"I just want things to be better for all Chinese people," Suchi answered. "I want the war to end, and for a prosperous peace to finally descend upon us."

"Everyone wants that," Haiwen said, "there's just a difference of opinion on how to achieve it."

"And you think Chiang is the answer?"

"He was tapped by Sun Yat-sen himself." He responded with certainty, as if this alone explained everything.

"We don't live in a dynastic empire anymore," Suchi said, her face hot, "it doesn't matter who the leader before wants. Besides," she added, "Sun Yat-sen tapped Wang Jingwei, not Chiang Kai-shek, and look where that got us."

She walked briskly, her arms folded across her chest. She didn't know why she was getting worked up. Ordinary citizens were like ants to these powerful leaders: invisible, impotent, negligible collateral damage. While the mighty fought, they were trampled into dust to be blown away by the wind.

"Hey," Haiwen said, coming up behind her. He caught her arm. She shrugged him off. "Okay, okay. You're right. Maybe Chiang isn't the answer. Don't listen to me, I don't know anything. I'm just a violinist."

She halted, hugging herself.

"I didn't mean to upset you, I'm sorry." Haiwen reached out and put his hands on her upper arms.

Suchi felt the tension in her jaw loosen. Eventually she relaxed into Haiwen's embrace. He was warm and solid around her, and she felt silly for her outburst. In Haiwen's arms, it was easy for her anxiety about the war to melt away.

"By the way," he said, finally releasing her, "I saw that the CATC's applications for stewardesses are finally open again."

"Ooh, you saw an ad?" She'd had a habit of scanning the papers for any mention that the CATC might reopen flights or be looking for stewardesses. But Apa had so many newspapers scattered around at home, she hadn't always been able to look through all of them.

"A couple of days ago. You still want to apply, right?"

Suchi nodded. While a part of her dreamed of becoming a singer, the practical side of her knew that becoming a stewardess was a more attainable dream. "Did it say anything about an age minimum? Or degree requirement?"

"High school graduates preferred, I think it said. Sorry, if I had known I'd see you today, I would have brought it with me."

"It's okay," she said, feeling buoyant. Since she had skipped a grade, she was only a year from graduating—surely that was close enough. "It didn't say anything about grade requirements, did it?" She gave him a guilty look. She still only made mediocre marks.

Haiwen sighed and swatted her on the head. "No, it didn't say anything about that, Zhang Suchi, you slacker. Lucky for you."

Suchi laughed and grabbed his hand, bringing it down to her cheek. "Imagine if I get this job," she said. "Eventually, once the war is over, we'll be able to travel to faraway places together. I could probably get you a discounted ticket."

"I did see that they're opening routes to Hong Kong," Haiwen said. "My mother is always telling us stories about having tea in the Peninsula and says that the seafood there is the best she's ever had."

"Didn't your mother say Hong Kong has beautiful beaches? Maybe we can sunbathe like they always do in pictures."

Haiwen raised an eyebrow. "I'd like to see you in a bathing suit."

"Don't be crass." Suchi pushed him away playfully, even though his suggestiveness sent a tug in her belly. In their two years together, the most they had ventured were some hungry caresses over each other's clothes in dark alleyways. Suchi knew good girls didn't do more than that, and Haiwen had never pushed her. But she couldn't help but wonder what it would be like to be free to satiate their thirst for each other, once they were married.

Haiwen gave her a crooked smile and scratched the back of his neck, a gesture of mild embarrassment. She leaned into him and plucked his arm so it lay around her shoulder. He brought her in close, kissing her on the forehead.

"Now, what were you saying about a Yao Lee song?"

THE DRAFT NOTICE APPEARED IN THE *SHANGHAI PEACE Daily* a week later, a small square in the corner of the newspaper below loud characters cheering the National Revolutionary Army's new wins against Mao's Communists in the north. Its headline announced the Enforced Military Conscription Act. "Physically fit men between the ages of 18 and 36," the subheader said. Every household with two sons or more would have to enter one son in the draft; those with four sons or more would have to enter two. Students, only sons, and those demonstrating hardship would be exempt.

Suchi's father shook his head and sighed. "Soldiers fight poorly when they've been forced into battle," he said, drinking his tea.

"Thank god we only have daughters," M'ma murmured.

Suchi reread the square. "Waong Haeven's not of age yet," she said. "And he's in school. So will they force his brother to go?"

"I don't know," Apa said. "But the Waongs have enough money and connections. I'm sure they can pay an official to look the other way."

Apa said this with a hint of disapproval in his voice, but Suchi was relieved. Even if Haiwen was safe from the draft, he would have been devastated if Haiming were sent to war.

"The Nationalist army is getting desperate," Apa said. "They're not doing well; the Americans have already started withdrawing their troops. The Communists are gaining support because they're orderly, well-disciplined, and good to the civilians, unlike those rag-tag Nationalist soldiers who will murder farmers for their last crumb of bread. And how can you blame them? Their own officers are fattening their pockets by selling rations meant for them. But you won't see that printed in the state media." He tossed the paper to the side. "Thankfully, there are other journals telling the truth."

"How do you know what the other papers say is true?" Suchi asked her father. "How do you know that's not propaganda too?"

Apa frowned at her. "I don't. That's why I read all kinds of papers, to see what each one says. So I can compare. I consider not just what they're saying but how they're saying it. And I measure what they're saying against what I know of the world, what I've seen and experienced with my own eyes, what I've learned about human nature and history. I don't ingest words like I'm a hollow gourd."

Suchi thought about the whispers among the neighbors about a so-called secret police responsible for the sudden closures of various presses along Fourth Road. "Won't publications like that get in trouble with the government?"

Apa looked annoyed. "Is that a good reason not to tell the truth? Without access to information, ordinary citizens will always be caged in dark rooms, only able to believe whatever people on the outside tell them is true. Why do you think I bothered to keep the damn bookstore open when it was barely pulling in any money?"

Suchi nodded, hunching her head down between her shoulders. Whenever Apa went on one of these rants, she felt like a small girl all over again.

Apa drained the last of his tea and stood up. "Siau Zi and I are attending a meeting this morning," he said. "He's already opened the shop, but, Suchi, I'll trust you to deal with customers while we're gone. We should be back before you have to head to school."

Suchi helped her mother clear away the breakfast dishes, troubled by the feeling that she had let her father down again.

SUCHI STOOD WITH HAIWEN OUTSIDE A PHOTOGRAPHY shop, trying without success to make out her reflection in the glass of the shop's display.

"How do I look?" Suchi asked, smoothing out the collared navy dress she had borrowed from Sulan.

"Perfect," he said, tucking a hair behind her ear.

"I'm serious. This photo is going to go on my application, and I have to look just right. Tsia says the CATC will likely be looking for girls who are pretty, but tastefully so, professional. Someone who looks inviting and friendly."

"You know you always look beautiful to me."

Suchi rolled her eyes, but she grabbed his hand and kissed it. Then she pulled him into the photo studio.

She felt awkward in front of the camera as the photographer directed her to adjust her head and chin, and the flashing lightbulbs made her dizzy. She worried that the difficulty she'd had focusing her eyes would be obvious in all the pictures.

Afterward, she and Haiwen crowded over the two square photos. "Ugh," Suchi said, "is that what I really look like? Why am I holding myself so unnaturally?"

"It's perfect. Look, you can even see the little freckle under your eye." Haiwen thumbed the corner of one photo, as if he were stroking her face. "How many do you need for the application?"

"Just one," Suchi said. "If they like my application, they'll call me in for an interview."

"Could I have the other one then?"

"You want it?" Suchi said, her face warming. She felt both embarrassed and thrilled that Haiwen wanted a picture of her.

"Please?" Haiwen asked softly.

"Everyone will think you have a weird-looking girlfriend," she muttered. She could feel the blush spreading across her face. "But yes, of course you can have it."

Haiwen leaned over and kissed her cheek. Suchi watched how carefully he slid the photo into his wallet, like she had given him something precious. For a moment, she could almost see herself the way he did, and her self-consciousness slipped away.

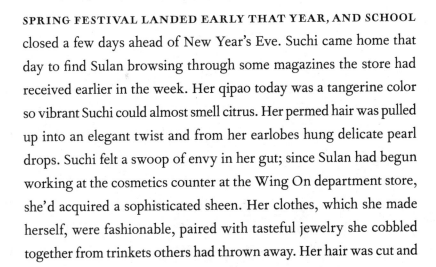

SPRING FESTIVAL LANDED EARLY THAT YEAR, AND SCHOOL closed a few days ahead of New Year's Eve. Suchi came home that day to find Sulan browsing through some magazines the store had received earlier in the week. Her qipao today was a tangerine color so vibrant Suchi could almost smell citrus. Her permed hair was pulled up into an elegant twist and from her earlobes hung delicate pearl drops. Suchi felt a swoop of envy in her gut; since Sulan had begun working at the cosmetics counter at the Wing On department store, she'd acquired a sophisticated sheen. Her clothes, which she made herself, were fashionable, paired with tasteful jewelry she cobbled together from trinkets others had thrown away. Her hair was cut and waved in the latest trend and her eyebrows were perfectly arched. She could have passed for one of the wealthy daughters Suchi sometimes saw in rickshaws or shiny chauffeured cars. After all the years her sister had admired Haiwen's mother, Sulan had succeeded in replicating her elegance.

Suchi wasn't the only one who had noticed Sulan's transformation. Siau Zi, now an awkward bachelor in his midthirties, had begun following her with unblinking eyes whenever they were in the same room. In the eight years he had lived with their family, he had kept to himself and had never, to their knowledge, had a girlfriend, although Apa had offered to set him up with some of his friends' daughters. Skinny and bespectacled, he had always been uncomfortably formal and stiff around the girls, and when they'd been younger, they couldn't resist playing pranks on him: one time they switched out his soy sauce bottle for black vinegar; another time they snuck into his room while he was sleeping and painted his big toe with one of his calligraphy brushes, giggling when it wiggled. He never complained or told Apa, which somehow made him even more pitiful to them.

Now Suchi noticed how he was frozen behind the cashier's counter, his eyes bulging as if he wanted to devour her sister. Sulan was oblivious to his attention. "Oh, Susu," she said when she saw her sister, replacing the fashion magazine she'd been holding. "I was waiting for you!"

She threaded her arm through Suchi's, and they went upstairs into the bedroom they still shared, though these days, more often than not, Sulan was still out with friends by the time Suchi fell asleep. A few times, Suchi even caught her sneaking in at dawn, the smell of smoke and liquor and sweat enveloping her.

Sulan flopped onto the bed and Suchi lay down next to her.

"Did you just come back from seeing Haiwen?" her sister asked.

Suchi shook her head. "He's rehearsing. I came from school."

"I can't believe the two of you haven't gotten engaged yet," Sulan said. "At the very least, he should have his mother discuss it with M'ma."

"M'ma can't stand Wang ayi," Suchi reminded her sister.

Sulan shrugged. "It's not like she isn't expecting it though," she said. "Everyone knows you two will get married someday."

"They're probably waiting to marry you off before me," Suchi teased.

Sulan said nothing. She draped the back of her wrist over her eyes, her pose so feminine and languid, Suchi wondered if her sister had practiced it. "I don't think I want to get married," she said after a moment.

"Why not?"

Sulan put her arm down and sat up, facing Suchi. "Doesn't it seem terrible? Living your life for a man? Look at M'ma."

"M'ma's old-fashioned," Suchi said. "It doesn't have to be like that. Haiwen's mother—"

"Even then," Sulan said. "Her life revolves around her children. I want *more*."

"Like what?" she asked. Although Sulan had always been quietly rebellious, Suchi hadn't considered this might extend to marriage and children. To hear Sulan admit it both shocked and thrilled her.

"I don't know, maybe I'm just selfish," Sulan said. "I sometimes think—" She stopped short and shook her head. "I'm just different from you. You have someone you can be with. I don't."

Something about the way Sulan said this wounded Suchi. As if the fact that she had Haiwen meant she couldn't possibly understand what it was like to want *more*. She thought of the restlessness that occupied her heart. The thoughts she'd had, particularly as she devoured travel memoirs and translated novels, of what it'd be like to see the places they detailed firsthand. Her fumbling, secret attempts to teach herself French and Russian and English from the dusty foreign children's books she'd found in a corner of the store. Just in case. It was true that her desire for adventure was often overshadowed by her desire for Haiwen, but she hated the idea that Sulan saw her only as a lovesick teenager.

Suchi started to argue with Sulan, to tell her that she'd finally sent in her CATC application and that if she was offered the job, she'd be more than a wife, too, but then stopped, watching the way her sister gazed down at her fingers spread across the bedspread, her curled figure small and vulnerable. Her sister hadn't meant to insult her, Suchi decided. She was just worried she'd end up alone.

"You'll find someone," Suchi assured her. "It's never been hard for you to make friends. Why should it be any different with men?" She thought of Siau Zi's lingering gaze on her sister downstairs. "I bet there are men in love with you already and you don't even realize it."

Sulan didn't respond. Instead, she picked up a parcel wrapped in newspaper lying next to her on the bed.

"I brought this for you." She tossed the bundle at Suchi. "Think of it as an early birthday gift." Inside was a qipao the color of plums, embroidered with jade and blush blossoms. Turquoise piping lined the dress and two intricate butterfly knots—the ones M'ma had proudly taught them to make as a way to dress up an otherwise plain qipao—sat at the neck.

Suchi was breathless. Most of the dresses she owned were simple, ill-fitting shift dresses in navy or gray, or the occasional Western dress patterned in checkers or printed with small flowers, patched over many times. Nothing so beautiful and *grown-up* as this qipao.

"How did you afford this?" she asked. Everything was scarce these days—sales were down in the bookstore and the family hadn't had fresh vegetables in weeks. Although Sulan worked multiple shifts to help supplement the family's income, she (to M'ma's disapproval) spent so many of her nights and weekends out with her friends that Suchi couldn't imagine she had much pocket money left over.

"I made it," Sulan said. "Yizhen found the fabric discounted on the black market, so I borrowed some money from Apa. It was irregularly cut and torn in spots, so I hid those parts with embroidery."

"You borrowed money?" Suchi asked. "But—"

"Don't worry. We've been able to sell some of our designs to the other girls at the store and make a bit of money, so I've paid him back already, plus some." She beamed proudly. "Yizhen and I work so well together—Yizhen is good at finding materials and negotiating their prices, and I make the clothes."

"It's beautiful," Suchi said. "I didn't realize you could make something so nice."

"That's what I mean," Sulan said. "If Yizhen and I were men, we could open up our own business. Maybe someday have a beautiful display in the store. But you know those master tailors would never take us for anything more than common seamstresses." She sighed and stretched out onto her belly, propping her head up with one palm. "Well, try it on. I'll make adjustments if I have to."

Siau Zi joined the family for dinner that night, as he tended to do whenever Sulan was home. Suchi felt bad for Siau Zi, but if he believed Sulan would ever consent to being his wife, he was dreaming too big.

"How's work, Sulae?" Siau Zi ventured.

"The same," she responded. "It's long hours, but the girls I work with are great and it's nice to be among pretty things all the time." Apa grunted. He had not approved of Sulan's decision to do what he considered a "frivolous service job" but Sulan had threatened to move into the women's dormitory and keep all the earnings for herself if he didn't let her take the job. It had spawned a terrible fight, but in the end, Apa had relented, grumbling that he had never been able to tame his eldest daughter and he didn't suppose he'd be able to start now.

"Your customers must all be rich, right?" Siau Zi asked. "Do they look down on you?"

"The trick is to flatter them, make them all feel pretty in whatever lipstick shade they ask for, even if it makes them look like toads." Sulan puckered her lips and screwed up her face. Suchi laughed.

"Don't be unkind," Apa said, but Sulan merely shrugged.

"Anyway, *my* job will be nothing compared to what Suji will likely have to deal with on air—" Suchi pinched her sister under the table. Realizing her mistake, Sulan snapped her mouth shut, but it was too late.

Apa looked at Suchi sharply. "What?" When Suchi didn't immediately respond, he turned to Sulan. "Tell me what you were about to say."

Suchi cleared her throat. "I've responded to an ad in the paper for airline stewardesses."

"You've *already* responded? Don't you think you should have consulted me first?"

Suchi looked down at her bowl, trying to steel herself against Apa's rising anger. "I knew you wouldn't want me to do it."

Apa narrowed his eyes and glanced in Sulan's direction. "Was this your idea? As if it weren't enough that you have to do a lowly job servicing the rich, you have to corrupt your little sister too?"

"Tsia had nothing to do with this," Suchi said. "I've been thinking about it for years. It's a good job, Apa, it pays decently and—"

"What kind of customers do you think fly commercial airplanes? Wealthy men, that's who. So being a stewardess is no better than being a waitress at a nightclub, only you'll be trapped in the air." He glanced between Suchi and Sulan. "All the books I've given you. All my reminders that you can be anything you want to be, that you don't have to be factory workers or menial laborers. And this is what the two of you decide to do."

"It's better than a factory job, Apa. I'll be given a nice uniform and everything."

"What about a job as a teacher? Or at a magazine, a press. An office job at a company integral to society."

Suchi bowed her head. "You know my grades are only mediocre. Certainly not impressive enough that anyone would want me teaching their kids or writing articles for others to read."

"Your grades," Apa scoffed. "And whose fault is it that you don't have good grades?"

Suchi let out a hard breath. Although she had improved her grades over the last two years, she had never found the drive to compete for top marks again, and it was a constant source of disappointment for Apa. "Anyway, if I get the job, I'll have to start immediately. So I won't even finish high school."

"What?" Apa exclaimed. "You have one more year!"

Suchi was aware that Sulan and M'ma had grown very quiet at the dinner table. "What's the point of finishing high school if I won't be going on to university?" Suchi muttered.

Apa stiffened. Suchi suspected he felt guilty he couldn't afford to send his daughters to university.

"You're very capable," he said after a moment, "and things are changing. In the new China we'll build once this war is over, we'll need smart women like the two of you. It will be no time for frivolity. You need to be well-read, to be able to articulate your ideas. I may not be able to afford to send you to university, but that doesn't mean you can't cultivate those skills. Finishing high school, being around the right types of people—intellectuals, thinkers—that's how I became who I am and that's how you will too!"

"But what's the point?" Suchi asked. "What am I working toward? Even at the presses and magazines, all I'd be is glorified slave labor to a bunch of men. Is that your dream for me? You keep talking about how I'm supposed to be part of this new China, but what's the endgame of all of this? Who will hire me to do anything serious?"

"I will!" Apa roared. "You will take over my legacy, the way a son would!"

Suchi was stunned into silence. All the times Apa had asked her to help with the bookstore, with bookkeeping and inventory. The many lectures he had given her, his belief that books and periodicals could move the minds of people and incite change—it had never occurred to Suchi he had been grooming her to one day take over.

She glanced at Siau Zi. He was staring into his bowl, the thin bones of his jaw rigid. Surely he had assumed *he* would take over someday?

"How do you expect to run a bookstore—a store of *ideas*—

when you have no idea how to think for yourself, if all you do is fill your head with that yellow music and bow to wealthy people?"

"But," Suchi ventured in a small voice, "why me?"

"Because I know you can!" Apa said. "Because you, unlike your sister, have always loved spending time in the shop and I thought that meant you might actually care about keeping it going. But perhaps I was wrong!"

Suchi glanced at Sulan, who was looking down at her beautifully filed nails.

"You can be so much more than what you allow yourself to be," Apa said, his voice returning to an even volume. "I don't understand why you hold yourself back. I don't know where I've failed. But I want you to be more than another pretty face." He looked at Sulan. "Both of you. Do you understand?"

"Yes, Apa," the girls murmured.

Satisfied, Apa turned to other aspects of the bookstore, asking Siau Zi about a recent shipment of books that was delayed. He responded with a hint of sullenness.

Suchi digested Apa's revelation as she ate. Was this something she wanted? She had never considered it, but now it rotated in her mind like a stone being polished.

SUCHI WAS EAGER TO TELL HAIWEN ABOUT WHAT APA had said at dinner, but for weeks, she didn't have the opportunity. First it was Spring Festival, during which the Wangs packed up and went back to their old family village for nearly a month. Once Haiwen returned, he was immediately immersed in an intense schedule of school, orchestra rehearsals, private lessons, music theory classes, and practice. M'ma remarked in passing that Suchi seemed to be home more often, pursing her lips. "If he can forget you so easily now when you're young and beautiful, what will he be like when you're married?" The moments Suchi and Haiwen were able to steal were brief, and even then, he was distracted. It never seemed the right time to bring up the topic.

"Did you ever listen to that Yao Lee song I told you about?" Suchi asked the next time they were together. She was sitting in his courtyard, watching Haiwen pick through the same two measures of Paganini over and over again, and felt listless. She hadn't heard back from the airline, despite it being over a month since she'd mailed out the application. The unending wait put her in a bad mood.

"Sorry, Susu, I haven't turned on the radio in ages." He frowned and repositioned his fingers. "But I'll get to it, I promise. I've just been busy."

"You're always busy," she muttered.

"It'll be better once I finish the audition," he said. "Promise."

"That's months away," she said.

Haiwen stopped playing. He looked at Suchi and put his violin down and crouched in front of where she was sitting. "Your birthday is coming up in a couple of weeks," he said. "Why don't we do something nice? I'll cancel my lesson that day and we can go to that European café and pretend to be fancy foreigners for a day. I'll even get dressed up."

Suchi lifted her eyes to meet Haiwen's earnest ones.

"It doesn't have to be something that pricey," she said softly.

"Come on, don't you want to try that fruit tart? With the money I got from my New Year's envelopes, I think I can afford a birthday treat."

Suchi broke into a wide grin and threw her arms around him. "Promise?"

"Promise."

~~

SUCHI GRIMACED AT THE SHARP ODOR OF URINE. SHE wanted to wear the qipao Sulan had made her for her birthday date with Haiwen, but the only place to change after school was the toilet. She'd taken extra care to put her hair in rollers the night before so the waves fell in loose curls around her face and, with limited success, had lined her eyes with kohl in a small compact mirror. Now, as she maneuvered her body into the beautiful dress, she was mindful not to let anything dirty splash the hem, or worse, to slip and step into the trough in the floor.

She took one last look in the small mirror and then hurried outside the school gates to wait for Haiwen, nervous with excitement. She felt bad that she'd been so short with him recently. She knew how hard Haiwen had been working toward this audition, not merely over the past few months but his whole life. He hadn't meant to neglect her. Still, she was looking forward to a nice evening with no distractions. No auditions, no applications, no war. No Apa with his disappointed frown or M'ma with her disapproving stare. Just the two of them, pretending they were in a different time and place for just a short while.

Fifteen minutes passed. She craned her neck toward the street, searching for his familiar figure. *He must have gotten distracted again,* she thought, a touch irritated.

Thirty minutes ticked by. Annoyance bloomed into anger, and now her foot tapped in impatience. *Of all the days!* she thought. Was she of such little importance to him that he could easily forget his promise? M'ma's words poked into her thoughts.

By the time forty-five minutes had passed, anger had given way to anxiety. Something terrible had happened to him. He had been hit by a car while biking and was lying injured in a ditch. He had been kidnapped for being the son of a textile manufacturer and was being tortured in an abandoned building while the kidnappers awaited ransom payment. He had been caught in a crossfire shootout between Nationalists and Communists, was dying on the street at that very moment, his bright red blood streaming into the gutter.

When an hour had passed, she could wait no longer. Stomach curdling, she ran back to the longtang. She went directly to Haiwen's shikumen. In the moment before she raised her fist to knock on the door, the possibilities she'd imagined earlier exploded back into her body, choking her.

The door swung open. Suchi was relieved—then livid—to find Haiwen standing behind it. He looked blankly at her. "Suchi?" he asked.

A hundred angry words crowded onto her tongue, but then she noticed his colorless complexion and hollow eyes. The words dissipated; fear began to beat again in her throat.

"What's wrong?" she asked. "What is it?"

"My father," he said. His voice was steady, but Suchi could hear the agitation quivering behind each word.

"What?" Suchi breathed.

Haiwen pinched the bridge of his nose. His words came out clipped and careful. "There's . . . there's a friend of my father's, a prominent editor at the Commercial Press, someone who I guess hobnobbed with a lot of high-level officials. He and my father were friends; my father used to go to his house sometimes. When our factories were controlled by the Japanese, he was the one who lent my father money and helped him out, he was the one who introduced my father to the officers who helped him regain control of the factories. He tried to convince my father to invest in some business or project of some sort, I don't remember what, but Ma and him fought about it and he decided not to do it."

Suchi nodded, wondering where this was going.

"Anyway," Haiwen said, his voice strained, "it turns out this whole time he's been a Communist spy. Now he's disappeared. Some are saying he ran away, but he might also have been captured. I don't know. But because of their connection, they dragged my father from the factory this morning to interrogate him."

"Heavens," Suchi exclaimed, a hand to her mouth. "But he doesn't know anything, right?"

"Of course not! He had no idea! My father, you know him, he loves the Republic!"

"Then . . ." Suchi was afraid to ask.

"They released him. My mother went to the wife of an officer she used to play mahjong with. I have no idea what she did, but they let him go."

"Thank god," Suchi said. "Is he all right?"

"They beat him; my mother cried when she saw his condition. But nothing that won't heal."

"Then everything is okay, right?"

He shook his head. "They told him they'll be watching him. And in exchange for his release, he has to prove his loyalty." Haiwen paused. "First, the factories. Effective immediately, the factories have to cease all normal operations and focus on churning out uniforms. And second——" His voice broke.

Suchi didn't dare move. The back of her mouth was dry.

Haiwen cleared his throat. "The officer apparently said, 'I see you have two able-bodied sons. Do you Wangs feel so superior that you can stand by while other people's sons die for our country?'"

"But *no one* in Shanghai is entering the draft!" Suchi exclaimed. Despite the notice in the paper, few officials in town had been enforcing the draft in Shanghai. The Nationalists were targeting poor peasant boys from rural families, not the urban-dwelling petite bourgeoisie of the city.

"To prove our loyalty," Haiwen whispered, "my brother will have to. They're coming for him on May first. And the only reason they've given us that time is because Ba begged, insisted that Haiming was needed to get the factories running for them."

Suchi put a hand on Haiwen's arm. That was only six weeks away.

"It would have been better if Haiming had stayed in England." He squeezed his hands into fists.

Suchi pressed her palms over his. His fingers were icy. She ran her thumb over the back of his hand, trying to warm him.

"My sister-in-law won't stop crying. She says my brother will widow her and leave her to raise this child alone."

She took him into her arms. He buried his face into her hair and was silent. She wondered if any neighbors were looking out the window and clucking their tongues. After several minutes, Haiwen lifted his head and stepped back.

"You look so pretty today," he said, reaching out to touch a curl.

His eyes widened in realization. "Oh no, your birthday. I was supposed to— With all of this happening, I just— I'm so sorry." He knocked the side of his head with a fist.

"It's not important," Suchi told him. "Another day."

Haiwen drew her into his arms. He held her tightly and spoke into her hair. "I promise." Suchi heard Wang ayi calling Haiwen from inside. Haiwen glanced over his shoulder. "I better go back," he said. "I'll come look for you tomorrow."

Haiwen didn't meet Suchi at school the following day, nor the day after that. She didn't bother him and tried not to fret, but unease curled through her limbs.

GOSSIP SPREAD THROUGH THE LONGTANG ABOUT WANG Chongyi's detainment by the Nationalists. Several people had seen Wang Chongyi's bloody and bruised face upon his return in the afternoon and the shape of the story began to shift as it blew through the alleys. While some speculated he might be guilty of some sort of embezzlement crime, many correctly guessed that he was suspected of being a Communist. This was bringing danger onto their doorsteps, and they could not easily forgive it.

When news of Wang Haiming's imminent enlistment somehow got out, the chatter grew. The few who had defended Wang Chongyi against Communist accusations pointed to this as proof—it didn't make sense for a Communist to send their child off to voluntarily join the Nationalists. New theories began to spring up: some said Wang Chongyi was troubled by how his son had turned out after living abroad and was sending him to the army to teach him a lesson; others said he had gotten mixed up with lingering gang members living in Shanghai; others said Wang Chongyi wanted his son to achieve military glory and had connections that would ensure that success; still others said in actuality, Wang Chongyi was a *Nationalist* spy, a staunch believer in Chiang Kai-shek and all he stood for, and the interrogation was just a façade to confuse the other side. They all agreed that no matter the reason, it was a shame, for the Eurasian wife would be left all alone with her in-laws, with a quickly swelling belly too, and few wanted to befriend her as they felt it was unnerving to look into her eyes—green irises set in Chinese monolids—when they talked to her.

Nobody from the Wang family tried to counter this gossip— they kept to themselves, even more than usual. Suchi didn't see Haiwen at all during this period—she didn't dare bother him and he didn't seek her out. She reasoned to herself that this was to be expected. Haiwen must have wanted to spend as much time with his brother as possible before he left. Still, his absence stung.

She threw herself into helping Apa at the bookstore. Now that she knew Apa's true intentions, her work felt less like a chore and more like a responsibility she could take pride in. The bookkeeping was no longer a dull ledger of numbers but a record of something that might be hers someday; the customers who wandered in asking for specific volumes were no longer nuisances interrupting her own pleasure reading but *her* customers.

After school one afternoon, a little over two weeks after the incident with Haiwen's father, Apa told Suchi he was leaving the bookstore in her hands while he and Siau Zi attended a meeting that would run past dinnertime. As dusk fell, Yu, a young neighbor Suchi didn't know well came in. Suchi tallied comics while he browsed the shelves. After a few minutes, he approached the counter with a wuxia novel and a few coins. When Suchi counted out his change, he smiled warmly at her, his eyes crinkling at the corners.

"Where's the fellow that's usually here? What's his name . . . Zi something or other?" he asked. When Suchi said he was at a meeting, the man laughed, a sound like warm rain. "My lucky day. You're much nicer to look at than that sourface." He leaned close to Suchi, his thumb slowly riffling the corner of the novel he'd purchased. His eyes were locked on Suchi's, and she noticed how smooth and poreless his olive skin was. The pages of the book crackled between them. He asked, "Is your father at that meeting too?" in a low, conspiratorial way, and Suchi blushed.

"Tsan Suji!" M'ma stood at the side door, her lips pursed and eyes glinting. "Isn't it about time you closed up the shop? I need your help in the kitchen!" She glared at the man, who languidly straightened his posture. He tipped his fedora at M'ma with a smile and exited out to the street.

When he was out of sight, M'ma hurried to the front of the shop. She hobbled when she tried to move too fast, and Suchi rushed after her, but M'ma waved her off as she pulled the doors shut. She leaned against the wall, breathing heavily, face pale.

"M'ma—" Suchi started, concerned, but M'ma shook her head.

"Stupid girl!" she said as she headed into the kitchen. Suchi trailed behind her. M'ma scraped at vegetables in the wok, the metal-on-metal loud and grating. "Don't you know when men flirt, it's because they want something from you?"

Suchi pulsed with shame. She had found that man attractive, had liked the attention he had given her. In that fleeting moment, she'd pretended Haiwen didn't exist, and M'ma had seen and known.

Apa and Siau Zi did not return until nearly midnight. Suchi heard

Apa's footsteps fall heavily on the stairs, passing her doorway and going up to the attic bedroom. The door creaked open and slammed, and through the thin walls she could hear low, muffled dialogue. Suddenly M'ma's voice pierced through the air.

"You think I don't know what you're up to? After what happened to Mr. Waong, how can you still be this arrogant?"

What was M'ma talking about? Suchi stepped out into the stairwell and crept up to the landing, pressing her ear against the door.

". . . people are saying he was killed by Chiang's secret police for anti-Nationalist editorials he published in an anonymous left-leaning journal."

"It's just rumor," Apa answered. "No one knows the truth. He might have gone back to his hometown because he grew homesick."

"You must know. You talked about him often when you worked together at the Commercial Press, about how much you admired him."

"I haven't talked to him in years."

"You swear?" M'ma asked. There was a brief pause. "A man came today," M'ma continued. "He was asking about you."

"Who?" Apa's voice had become tense.

"That boy Yu, the one who works as a clerk at the bank, whose father fled to Chongqing last year. He asked Suji about your meeting."

"Did he ask anything else?"

"No, I shooed him away. But Susu . . . You can't leave Susu alone like that. She doesn't think, she's still so young and when a boy shows her any attention—"

"She'll be fine. The bookshop is good for her. She needs an outlet for her intelligence. She wastes so many hours following Waong

Haeven around. She just needs a challenge, and she'll rise to the occasion, you'll see."

"And *this* is the challenge she needs? You can't make her in your image!"

"What's the alternative? Marry her off so she can sit at home cooking and cleaning and raising children? Letting her talents waste away?"

"You never have any issues with it when *I'm* the one laundering your socks and washing your rice!" M'ma's tone was wet with anger. "But you're right, I do think Suji needs a good, stable marriage. I just don't know if we can consider that Waong boy anymore. Sure, the Waongs have the money to keep her fed and safe, but look at the trouble they're in now."

What was M'ma saying? Suchi had to explain to M'ma that it wasn't Mr. Wang's fault, that it was a mistake—

Apa scoffed. "Do you think a family like that even wants their son to marry a girl with no schooling, no cultivation, no money of her own to bring to the marriage?" Suchi flinched. A sour, metallic taste bloomed on the back of her tongue.

"Someone like me, you mean?" M'ma's voice was tight with injury. "I know I've been a disappointment to you. I've never been good enough for you and your big dreams."

"Good god, woman," Apa said. "Will you stop with your martyrdom!"

Silence permeated through the door. After a moment, M'ma said, in a much quieter voice, "Please, I'm begging you, for once, consider your family instead of your ideals. If you care about us at all, you'll give up your projects."

"I care," Apa said. "Everything I do is so my daughters can have a brighter future. Don't you understand that, laubu?" After a pause, Suchi heard Apa sigh. "Forget it. It's tiresome to talk to you about these things, you never understand."

M'ma didn't respond. Suchi waited by the door. She heard the shuffle of feet but no further conversation. After a few more minutes, she crept back downstairs and into bed.

She lay awake long after she was sure the rest of the house had fallen asleep.

⌒⌒

NOW WHEN SUCHI HELPED CUSTOMERS, SHE MADE SURE to be polite but never eager. When there were no customers, she tried to focus on other tasks—her schoolwork, bookkeeping—but she found her mind wandering back to her parents' fight. There were parts of the conversation she hadn't understood—what had Apa done?—but there were many more parts she *wished* she hadn't understood. The part about her flirting with that man. The fact that her mother thought she was stupid. But most of all, that Apa did not think she was good enough for Haiwen.

It had never occurred to her that she and Haiwen might be mismatched doors.[7] No one had ever insinuated such a thing—not M'ma; not Wang ayi, who had always been so kind to her; not any of the neighbors. Of course she *knew* Haiwen's family was different from hers—they had money and had traveled and were highly educated. But Haiwen had never made her feel like any of that made him *better* than her, and it had never crossed her mind. But now she couldn't get Apa's words out of her head. Had everyone been thinking this the whole time? Had she seemed foolish, reaching above her station?

A few days later, Suchi finally received a letter from the airline.

Excitedly, she ripped open the envelope. If she were an airline host-ess, she thought, at the very least she'd be earning good money. It might not be the same as being a university graduate, but if she be-came more worldly, perhaps Haiwen's family might look upon her differently.

She removed the letter. Her heart stammered. The words blurred, focusing in and out:

We regret to inform you that you do not meet our criteria . . .

. . . over three hundred applicants . . .

. . . We carefully considered background, appearance, and education when inviting applicants to interview . . .

. . . McTyeire . . . St. John's . . .

. . . Thank you for your interest and best of luck.

Suchi stared for a beat, a dizzy sick feeling in her stomach. She ripped the letter to shreds. They'd lied, she thought. Why bother saying "high school degree preferred" in the advertisement when in reality you needed a pretentious diploma from one of the top schools in Shanghai? She'd thought it would be different for a ser-vice job.

Forget it, she thought, she had the bookstore. She would work toward taking over. Why not? She had nothing else.

Days passed and still Haiwen hadn't come. Her one indication he was still alive was when Junjun dropped by one afternoon, hold-ing out a small box.

"Erge says he's sorry, but he wanted to give you this, as part of your birthday gift."

Suchi opened the box. Inside was a golden airplane pin, the size of a large button, and alongside that, a scrawled note. *I still want to travel the world alongside you, if you'll have me.*

Suchi wanted to cry. Putting the lid back on the box, she swallowed and pasted a bright smile on her face. She patted Junjun on the head. "Tell your brother thank you."

She wished he'd come himself. But then she thought better of it; she didn't know if she could have faced him.

LATE ONE SUNDAY AFTERNOON, NEARLY FOUR WEEKS after her birthday, Haiwen appeared with his violin case.

His expression was tired and pinched. "Can you get away?" he asked with no preamble.

Suchi, who had been helping to shelve books, looked at her father. He nodded. "I'll get Siau Zi to finish the rest," he said.

Haiwen grabbed her hand and began walking. "I'm sorry I haven't been around," he said. "I've just had some thinking to do, some things to do. I wanted to come but . . ." He trailed off. He looked straight ahead, his face serious and focused. He wouldn't meet her eyes. Something was off.

"Where are we going?" she asked.

"The park," he said, glancing to the side, then darting his eyes away. Cold unease prickled Suchi's skin. Had he heard she'd been rejected by the airline? In their time apart, had he also decided they were not a good match?

When they arrived at his favorite spot, Haiwen told her to sit down on a stone bench. He took out his violin and held it under his chin. He positioned his bow aloft over the strings. For a brief second, he closed his eyes. When he opened them, she knew he was in a different place.

He inhaled sharply and drew out the first note. He slid it upward, controlled and steady, momentum building. At the top, he seesawed back down, his fingers dancing across the strings, then back up again. There was an urgency to this preamble, a wind before a storm.

He took a break. A breath—then launched straight into the storm itself. The bow quivered, flew, a bird battling rain. His hands, quick and precise, as much a dance as it was a spar. His body was upright, slightly swaying, his eyes half-closed, flicking an occasional glance at his fingers as if to check they still existed, as if they were the only thing that embodied his consciousness. The piece went on, one continuous phrase, and Suchi found she was holding her own breath while listening, until he sped straight into the end, a sudden last note he completed with a flourish of his bow.

His arm floated down beside him. He opened his eyes and looked at Suchi, back in her world once more.

"Amazing!" Suchi exclaimed, jumping up and clapping.

"Caprice Number Five," he said, smiling thinly. "I've finally mastered it."

"I knew you could!" she said. "You'll impress them at your audition!"

He bent over and put his violin back in its case.

"Is that piece long enough? How long does the audition have to be?"

He closed the lid. "Let's sit," he said, gesturing to the bench.

Suchi was exhilarated. Haiwen would get into the conservatory, no doubt. She had watched him practice diligently for so many years. He *deserved* to get in. A surge of pride washed through her.

"Your dreams are so close," she said to Haiwen, grabbing his hands. "Despite what that fortune teller said. You worked hard and now you're almost there."

He brought her hands to his lips and kissed them gently. Relief flooded through her at the affection. Her body was hungry for it. Goose bumps raised across her flesh.

"Do you remember what else the fortune teller said?" Haiwen asked her.

"About what?" She laughed, remembering how angry she had been at the fortune teller for telling Haiwen it would be difficult for him. But perhaps it had been a good thing. Perhaps he had worked harder, practiced more, because she had warned him.

"About us."

She smiled, happy he was bringing it up. "She said we have strong yuanfen." She squeezed his hand. "I was already in love with you, so I was secretly thrilled."

"Yes, she said we'd always find our way back to each other, no matter what happens. That there's a thread drawn between us."

He took his violin out again. Standing once more, he shut his eyes. After a moment, he started playing another piece, a simple, slow tune that rang familiar. It took her a moment to place it. And then she realized what it was: Yao Lee's "Lovesick Dream."

He played with his eyes closed, his body swaying as if the piece were one he, too, loved. Beneath his fingers, the jazzy, poppy melody transformed into something elegiac and romantic, more beautiful than the original had been.

He had remembered.

Suchi stared at him, too moved to sing along.

When he finished, he put away his violin and sat down next to her. His eyes were soft and serious. "I wanted to play this for you on your birthday," he said. "I'm sorry I didn't."

He loved her. Truly loved her. He was bad at expressing emotion through words, but his music never lied. How could she have ever, even for a split second, dreamed of being with someone else? She loved Haiwen, would always love only him.

The words tumbled out of her. "Let's get married."

His eyes widened in surprise and his lips twitched. She thought he was going to break into a grin. Because wasn't this what all this was leading to? Wasn't he finally setting their engagement?

Instead, he looked away from her and took a deep, shaky breath.

"Susu." The world tilted. Something was wrong. She pulled her hands away.

"Don't you want to marry me?" she demanded.

"Susu," he repeated. "I can't right now——" Pain stabbed her chest. His gaze, it wasn't serious because he was proposing, it was serious because he was sorry. Sorry for *what*?

"Because of your audition? But that'll be over in a few weeks!"

"There's been so much going on recently, and . . ." Haiwen rubbed his face. "Please, Susu, right now I could really use your understanding."

"My understanding?" Suchi jumped up from the bench. She fought the urge to run away. "I've been so patient! When you've been preoccupied with rehearsals and your brother, I never complained, not once! Do you think any other girl under the sky would have tolerated her boyfriend forgetting her birthday? Would have forgiven him for disappearing for nearly a month? A *month*!"

Haiwen shook his head and buried his face in his palms. "You don't know what it's been like——"

"What about what it's been like for me? My mother thinks I'm no better than a pet to you, to be loved when it's convenient, to be ignored when it's not. Do you know how embarrassing it is to have to defend you?" The sharp pain had spread into a tide of hurt and she was struggling to breathe. When she spoke again, she was quiet. "Is it your family? Am I not good enough for them?"

"No!" Haiwen's voice was sharp. "Suchi, what are you talking about? I'm trying to talk to you about something important here!"

"Why do you get to decide what's important?" She was verging on tears now. "I have important things to tell you, too, but you never have time, never ask." Yu's easy smile flashed through her mind, the way he'd looked at her like she was someone special. "Do you think I'll sit around and wait for you forever?"

All she wanted was for him to take her in his arms, to tell her she meant more to him than anything, more than a stupid audition, more than whatever was going on with his family, more than her lack of breeding or whatever it was that made her not as good as him. It was a selfish, unreasonable need, she knew, but months of repressed hunger had made her desperate for reassurance.

But he shook his head and looked at her sadly. "No," he said, "I don't. Which is why I can't marry you."

His words landed with the force of a bomb. She stared at him, and she thought in his expression she saw something akin to pity. Something in her cracked, loosing a creature ugly and mean.

"Maybe you feel the way your family does," she said, cool and accusatory. "That I'm not good enough for you. Maybe you'd be happier with someone who appreciates the symphony and has a fancy English-speaking education, someone whose father has money."

Suchi pressed on, the words sliding off her tongue, white-hot.

"You know, it's ironic the Nationalists think your father could be a Communist, because it's so clear he's a capitalist. I might not come from a rich family, but at least my father is a man of principles, not someone whose greed is going to get his own son killed."

Haiwen blinked as if he'd been slapped. For a moment, the monstrous thing inside of her was triumphant—she had done it, she'd hurt him the way he'd hurt her! But a split second later, horror poured over her. Her hands flew to her mouth, too late to shove the cruelty back in.

Haiwen picked up his violin. He adjusted his grip on the case handle and began to walk away.

"Wait," she called after him, her voice hoarse. "Wait, Doudou, wait, I'm sorry."

He kept walking, his pace brisk. He did not glance back at her.

"I should never have said that," she said, scrambling to her feet. Her words sounded strangled. Her tongue felt swollen and dry. "I just missed you so much. All I want is to marry you."

Haiwen stopped abruptly. Suchi caught up to him, relief flooding through her as she grabbed his arm. He whipped around, pulling her into a tight, fierce embrace. She returned it, pressing into him, all sweat and rose and menthol. She felt the damp warmth of his breath on her scalp, felt the crush of his arms around her. The soft fuzz of his favorite dress shirt nuzzled her cheek, and beneath it, his heart beat, fast yet steady. Just like his playing.

All was forgiven. All was right. He still loved her. She could wait. Everything else—their differences, their dreams, their future—they'd figure that out. As long as they had each other, they could overcome anything.

After a long time, Haiwen released her. She looked up at him, smiling, expecting him to kiss her. Instead, she found him staring down at her, his gaze pained. "I'm sorry, but I can't," he whispered, and disentangled himself from her arms.

Before she could register what had happened, before she could even call out for him, he was dashing down the street, his violin case bouncing against his leg. And then he was gone.

SHE AWOKE THE NEXT MORNING RESOLVED TO MAKE things right. She would pound on his door until he let her in, she would get down on her knees and apologize for what she had said, she would refuse to go until he took her in his arms. He had to see she had made a terrible mistake; he had to forgive her. She could not live without him.

But when she opened her back door, she found Haiwen's violin case leaning against the wall. Inside, atop his violin, was a note written in his hand: *Forgive me.*

She ran through the alleys, the case hugged to her body. What had he done? She banged on the doors of the Wangs' shikumen. When Wang ayi opened the door with red-rimmed, puffy eyes, Suchi knew something terrible had happened. She began to tremble.

"Where is he?" she whispered.

"Zhang Suchi," his mother said, but Suchi was peering around her, searching for Haiwen.

"Please, Wang ayi, let me see him," Suchi rambled. "I said terrible things yesterday, things I didn't mean, but—"

"He's gone," Wang ayi said, and for one horrifying moment Suchi thought she meant *dead*, the numb shock trying to turn into something comprehensible. But Wang ayi continued, tears falling anew. "He took Mingming's place in the army. He enlisted and didn't tell us until it was already done. He's already reported for duty." Wang ayi stretched out her arms, as if to embrace Suchi, but Suchi stepped back.

"He wouldn't leave without saying goodbye," she said, shaking her head. "He must still be here, somewhere. He hasn't said goodbye."

"I saw him off at the train station this morning," Wang ayi said. "I'm sorry, I assumed, yesterday, when he went to meet you—"

Suchi backed away, turning on her heel.

"Zhang Suchi," Wang ayi called out. "Wait!"

But she was already running through the alleyways, past the ayi who greeted her, past the food vendors, past the children who looked at her curiously. She ran out of the longtang, into the chaotic street she knew so well, and kept going, desperate to get away from the memory of Haiwen, away from herself. Apa was right: she didn't deserve Wang Haiwen—she didn't deserve anyone at all.

APRIL 1993
Shanghai

THE FIRST THING Howard noticed when he stepped off the plane was the way the air smelled, like burnt rubber and yellow dust. He sniffed as he walked across the tarmac, again as he stepped through glass doors toward customs. He thought if he inhaled hard enough, he could unbury the smell he longed for but had forgotten, the lost smell of home.

The customs officer, a bored man with thick eyebrows, took his time flipping through Howard's passport. The passport was brand-new, thin and unbent, bearing the bright gold eagle seal of the United States of America. And yet, Howard had a sudden urge to repudiate the document he had fought so hard to claim, to shout out, "I'm one of you! I'm Shanghainese too!" When the officer stamped his passport, Howard said, "Ziazia," in the clearest, most perfect Shanghainese he could manage, hoping it would be enough.

It was jarring to be in Hongqiao Airport, a place he remembered only as a military base. He had never imagined anyone might freely walk through it. The light of a descending sun gleamed through large panels of glass, and his shadow loomed long as he pulled his suitcase behind him.

On the taxi ride to his hotel in the former French Concession, he stared out the window, stunned by the changes streaming by—the modern vehicles, the widened roads, the new highway, the winking tangle of bicycles, the dazzling neon lights of new buildings. He searched for familiar landmarks but felt disoriented.

Once he checked in, he took a shower, then sat on the narrow bed in his room. His nerves were buzzing and bright, and a sour feeling laced through his gut. He longed to head to the longtang, though he knew it made no sense to go now. But he couldn't stay indoors.

Outside, the streets were unfamiliar to him. The former French Concession had retained its airiness, yet although he could tell many of the buildings—from grimy shikumen to nicer European-style houses—were older, he felt no recognition. Where had Mr. Portnoy once lived? Which street had it been? He tried to recall where the music conservatory had been housed, but it had moved too many times during the war.

A few pedestrians stared at him with unblinking eyes as they walked by. They had marked him as a foreigner, he thought, someone who didn't belong. He wanted to claim he was no different from them, but he wasn't sure that was true.

When he turned onto Dama Lu[8] (which, according to a street sign, had been renamed Nanjing East Road), a strange sensation peeled through him, that of his consciousness being split. He felt as if he were a time traveler caught between two worlds, visions of a future he had only glimpsed superimposing themselves on top of the specter of his past. The Wing On and Sincere Company department stores still stood, their European architecture still gleaming white, their lights brighter than ever, yet they were window-dressed with goods from the wrong era. The road itself was just as expansive as he remembered, perhaps wider, teeming with crowds of pedestrians in modern clothing, but a ghost tram of his memory threaded its way between them, filled with people, many of whom were likely dead now.

He walked to the Bund and stared across the darkened river toward Pudong. What once had been the muted lowlands of a fishing village were now garish skyscrapers that made a jagged slate mess of the sky.

He had known, of course, that his homeland had gone on without him; he had seen evidence of its development and change through the images that trickled out of the country and appeared on the news. But in his dreams, this place was as he had left it, so burned into his brain he believed he could have given turn-by-turn directions had someone asked. Now he found the old knowledge leaking away, uncertain and tenuous.

He returned to his room, where he stared into the contents of his suitcase: boxes of gold-foil-wrapped chocolate, family-sized bottles of shampoo, bags of flour and rice, two Rolexes (one silver, one gold), three silk scarves painted with flowers and butterflies, lavender-scented soap, a Game Boy, two pairs of pearl earrings, a white-gold ring, a large tin of instant coffee, three cashmere scarves and four wool sweaters, a stuffed dog that sang songs when you squeezed it, brightly colored children's books, an album full of photographs of his family. And, squashed into one tiny corner, a change of pants and shirt and underwear for himself. He had wanted to bring two television sets, one for each of his siblings, because that was what Zenpo had said he'd brought when he went back, but they'd been heavy and he'd worried about having to haul so much luggage through multiple legs of flights.

His siblings and their families would arrive the next day. They'd wanted to pick him up from the airport, but neither had been able to take off from work early enough to get to Shanghai in time to meet him. His brother had suggested Howard fly into Tianjin instead and they could take an overnight train down to Shanghai together, but Howard had insisted—Shanghai was the place he had longed for all these years and its soil would be what his feet first planted themselves upon when he returned.

It was strange, the ease with which he could now telephone his siblings after so many decades apart. Howard remembered the fifties and sixties, years he spent in Taiwan worrying about them, through rumors of famine and then the Cultural Revolution, not knowing if they'd survived. He thought back to conversations he'd had with Zenpo, Lau Fu, and other veterans like them, their sentimentality lubricated with cheap liquor. How they'd each admitted to pining for their fathers and mothers, for the pets that had surely died by now, for the wives and children that some had left behind—a past that could never be mentioned in the presence of their new families. They'd reminisced about local delicacies, ponds they had fished in, willow trees they had pulled switches from. These conversations had been hushed, because it was illegal to talk about missing home so openly. Chiang Kai-shek and his regime maintained there was no such thing as "going home" when you already *were* home. There was no going *back* to China when you were already *in* China.

And then, in October 1971, over two decades after Howard and two million other Nationalist and Nationalist-affiliated refugees had fled to the island of Taiwan, the Republic of China lost its

United Nations seat. Despite years of backing Chiang's (anti-Communist) government as the rightful leadership of China, the UN had charged that Chiang and his exiled officials could no longer claim to represent the millions of Chinese citizens back on the mainland. They promptly gave the seat to the People's Republic of China. By the following February, Howard was staring at a front-page photo of Nixon shaking hands with Zhou Enlai, the PRC's premier. The bamboo curtain had lifted.

For several weeks, he allowed himself to mourn. He didn't know exactly what he was mourning for—he had enlisted out of necessity, not patriotism, and he'd always felt ambivalent about fighting his own countrymen, even more so when he learned of some of the things the government had done. Yet for fifteen out of the twenty-eight years he had lived in Taiwan, his identity had been that of a soldier. It was due to his position as a soldier in those years that he had a modest salary, work, any sort of clout. His community was almost entirely made up of people he had met through the military. And, throughout his homesickness, he could convince himself his sacrifice had been for his country, for the true beating heart of China. But the implication that Chiang's government was a rogue government diminished his life to that of a lowly rebel, unwanted and unrecognized by his own home.

It was only seven years later, three years after he had moved to America, when a neighbor originally from Guangzhou mentioned he was searching for the wife he'd left behind during the war, that Howard realized his status had changed. He was no longer in Taiwan, no longer known by his identity as a veteran. He was a resident of the United States, and normalized relations with China meant he had the ability—the right, even—to try to contact his family.

He didn't start immediately—he was still settling into life in America, trying to adjust to the discomfort of being an outsider again. He was working hard to build up Yong Yuan Fabrics' relationships with clients in the garment industry, learning to manage his staff of three, dusting off English he hadn't used for decades to handle inquiries. But it was more than that—everyday living was its own exhausting challenge, from squinting at road signs and bills in order to decipher their meaning to counseling his daughters when they came home in tears because someone had called them a name they did not understand but knew had not been kind.

When, another three years later, he'd felt in a position to begin his search, he realized it would still be a delicate feat. He recalled how, years before Nixon went to China, Zenpo had been overjoyed when he'd finally succeeded in sneaking a letter to his family, only to be disappointed by the response: they had pleaded with him not to write anymore. Having relatives overseas, particularly with the Nationalist government, had already gotten them in trouble, causing them to lose rations and work, and the letter had only made town officials bully them more. Zenpo did not write them again for many years.

Howard hadn't been certain what the situation in China was by then. He'd hoped the United Nations seat and normalized relations with America meant Communists were relaxing their prejudice against overseas Chinese. Still, he'd wanted to be careful. He wrote a letter to his parents that avoided mention of his connection to the army and didn't dare mail it directly to his old address. Instead, he wrote "Sifo Li, Shanghai" on the envelope, along with "Wang Family," hoping that would be enough for a neighbor to know whom the letter was meant for. When that garnered no response, he tried again, this time addressing the envelope to Li Yuping, his mother's name. Instead of signing his name, he enclosed the gold ring his mother had once given him. If it reached her, not only would she know for certain it was him, but she could also sell the ring if she needed money. When he still received no response, he grew bolder and sent several letters directly to the address he remembered on Fourth Road. Finally, he reached out to friends and friends of friends who had family in Shanghai—who said there was nothing to fear anymore—and wrote over and over again descriptions and names of his family, always including his phone number, until in the middle of one night in 1983, a phone call came, rousing him from a dark dream.

The connection was distant and echoey, the uncertain woman's voice reverberating like a ghost from the future. "Is this Wang Hai-wen?" the voice asked in Mandarin, and when he tentatively said yes, it exclaimed, joyously, "Erge, this is your sister, Junjun!"

Howard's throat filled with so much emotion he could not respond. Linyee, awake beside him, looked on with concern, and when he spoke into the receiver, incredulously calling out his sister's name, she burst into tears.

His sister worked in Beijing now, and she explained his letter had reached her by chance. A friend had heard from a colleague that a man in the US originally from Shanghai was searching for his family, and he remembered Junjun was from Shanghai, so perhaps she could help? "When I saw our names, I cried out so loudly that my daughter came running in, worried I had hurt myself," his sister said. Her voice was raspy, matronly. Howard tried to match this voice with the image he had of her, a little girl, and found he couldn't.

When he asked about their parents, she said quickly, "They've already gone," and though Howard had known this was a possibility, he wept aloud. Junjun continued speaking as if she hadn't heard. She told him their father had died during the Cultural Revolution and their mother had died ten months ago from stomach cancer. He sobbed harder. He had missed his mother by months! Mere months. For weeks he existed draped in sorrow and regret, unable to stop thinking about that which could never be reclaimed. If only he had begun searching sooner, perhaps his letter would have reached Junjun years earlier, and he would have been in time. He might have been by his mother's side when she died.

A few weeks later, Haiming called, and the first words out of his mouth after he confirmed Howard's identity were apologies. "I never should have let you go," he said.

"It's in the past, Dage," Howard responded.

"If it's any comfort, my life has been hard."

"That's no comfort at all."

Haiming didn't seem to want to divulge details of what he meant when he said his life had been hard. Instead, he pressed Howard for details about America. "I heard the streets are paved with gold," he said. It was what they'd believed about America as children.

"Sadly, it's not true," Howard told him. He felt awkward saying too much about his life. It was true he and his family lived comfortably—they had a modest house with a tomato garden Linyee tended to and owned little luxuries like a coffee percolator, a color television, and a stereo system that was nice enough that, when he turned on his record player and closed his eyes, he could almost imagine he was in a concert hall. For the first few years before Yiping went to college, the four of them would go to the beach on the weekends. While the girls swam in the frigid waves and Linyee camped out beneath an umbrella, Howard dipped his toes into the surf and imagined the dead cells sloughing off his skin and being carried westward, back onto the banks of Shanghai.

But what he told Haiming was that the weather was nice, work was good, he and Linyee had made many Chinese friends, and he felt lucky.

"You definitely got the better deal then," his brother said. He laughed, a hollow, bitter sound that jarred Howard.

When Howard asked his brother about their mother, Haiming's voice became tight and serious. "I don't know what Haijun told you."

"She said Ma died of cancer, less than a year ago." Howard grew quiet. "She said I missed her by months."

"Bad luck," Haiming said. "She was calling for you on her deathbed."

Sharp, raw grief filled Howard's body. Regret, longing, regret regret regret. It carved a void into his being.

He couldn't continue the conversation.

It had taken him ten more years of waiting—first for his green card, then his US citizenship—before he had been able to book a flight back to Shanghai. In the meantime, he called his siblings once every few months. He longed to bridge the gap between them, but after the initial outpour of emotions, they reverted to a distant civility, the way one might treat a guest in one's home, an outsider to be shielded from overstuffed closets and dirty underwear. Their conversations were always brief—the connection was bad and the rate was exorbitantly expensive, even with a calling card—and they circled the same topics: old childhood memories and updates on what their children and grandchildren were doing. Whenever he asked one of his siblings about what had transpired in the intervening years, they were vague, saying only that they were years of hardship and it did nobody any good to dwell on such sad times.

Now, sitting in his hotel room, he stared at the gifts he had brought and wondered if it was too much, too desperate. As if a handful of things could make up for everything his family had suffered. As if he could close the chasm of years and their divergent paths through money alone.

~

HOWARD WAS AWAKE AT FIVE A.M., DESPITE FALLING asleep only three hours earlier. He went downstairs and ate breakfast from the hotel buffet—a watery rice porridge topped with pickled vegetables, a wedge of salted duck egg, and small, caramelized silver fish—and read the newspaper without really reading it. Junjun and Haiming were coming at nine. As the hour approached, Howard couldn't decide whether to wait in his room or downstairs. In the end, he settled on staying upstairs. He worried that if he sat in the lobby, he might not recognize his siblings when they walked in, and how terrible would that be? This way, they would call up to the room when they arrived, and he would know for sure the people waiting downstairs were for him.

The phone squawked. Howard, startled, jumped up from his bed. His heart was beating painfully fast. The phone rang three more times before he pressed the receiver against his ear. "Okay, thank you," he told the receptionist.

Standing in the elevator, he felt dizzy. The car's beeping descent sounded both distant and incredibly loud. He wiped his hands against his pants.

The doors opened. He saw, standing next to a plump middle-aged woman, his mother. She was staring curiously at him, a half smile on her lips, and Howard froze. He wanted to grab her hands, to thank the heavens for this miracle. He had taken two steps forward when the woman standing next to his mother threw her arms around his neck and began to cry.

"Erge," she kept sobbing into his shoulder. Howard blinked a few times, his hand raised hesitantly in the air. The woman released him and stared into his face. Tears streamed ugly down her round, pink cheeks. In the crinkle of her eyes and the upturn of her nose, he found hints of his baby sister, and he was remembering her at two: how she toddled around the courtyard and clapped while he practiced the violin, the downiness of her hair on his fingers as he patted her head between run-throughs.

"Junjun," he said, a muffled cry of joy, and seized her, this stranger who was not a stranger, crushing her tight against his chest.

When they both had shed enough tears, Junjun let go and gestured to the woman whom Howard had mistaken for his mother, who was discreetly wiping her own wet face.

"This is my daughter, Xuenong." The daughter pressed her palms on her pants, bowed slightly.

"Erjiu," she addressed him.

Howard couldn't stop staring. Now he noticed that she was wearing jeans and a T-shirt, clothing his mother would never have worn, and that she had fringy bangs. But she looked so much like the mother he held in his memory. That beloved face, which Howard had found harder to conjure up over the years, was finally redefined in the lines and contours of his niece's.

"You look just like—"

"I know," Xuenong said. "You're not the first person to say so."

Howard searched for something else to say, but Junjun cut in. "My husband is waiting in the car," she said. "He'll take us to the old neighborhood."

"What about Dage?"

"They're delayed. I checked the train. There are some railway issues, and they might not get in until this evening. But we can leave a message with reception to let him know where we've gone. They're staying here too, right?"

Howard nodded. He had paid for Haiming's family to stay in the same hotel for a week, the longest they could get away from work.

"So we'll see them when we get back."

He was surprised his sister, a mischievous child who had gotten in trouble more than once for trying on their mother's makeup and jewelry without permission, had grown to be so no-nonsense, so brusque, but he supposed it made sense. She worked for the government, relatively high-ranking in the Party according to Haiming.

Junjun led them out of the hotel lobby, into the brisk spring air. She waved at a man sitting in a shiny, if outdated-looking, black sedan. "My husband borrowed this car from a friend of a friend who is a high-ranking official out here," she said, a hint of pride in her voice. She opened the front passenger door. "You sit here. Xuenong and I will sit in the back."

Howard climbed into the passenger seat. Junjun's husband, a man with a moon face and gold-rimmed glasses, flicked a cigarette out the window and held his hand out to Howard. His handshake was firm and vigorous. "Erjiuzi," he said, and it struck Howard that this was the first time anyone had called him by this term for brother-in-law reserved only for his sister's husband to use; that earlier, when Xuenong had called him "Erjiu," that was also the first time he'd been called by that title. There would be, he realized, a series of firsts on this trip, something he was not entirely prepared for.

"Meifu," Howard said, acknowledging him. His first time addressing his little sister's husband.

"Do you know how to get there?" Junjun asked her husband from the backseat.

"Yes."

"Are you sure?"

"*Yes*," her husband responded. He put the car in drive and off they sped.

~

THEY STARED AT THE LONGTANG'S WEST GATE, AT THE worn chiseled characters 思福里[9] still visible above the archway. Howard peered down the guojielou; if he squinted just right, he could almost see Suchi running ahead of him.

They walked in, hesitant, careful, as if they were afraid to disturb the residents. A man in a sleeveless shirt stained with yellow spots crossed their path, a cigarette dangling from the corner of his mouth. He gave them a once-over, then went on. Howard had an urge to tell him, to tell anyone and everybody, that he had grown up here, that this was his home. But there was no one familiar to tell.

Laundry hung from poles overhead, and it billowed gently in the breeze like ghosts waving. The alley was quiet, wooden doors mostly shut. So much had changed: the density of electrical wires, the types of potted plants sitting outside, the colors of the bicycles, the occasional air-conditioning units shoved into too-small windows, the bright plastic awnings erected over some of the doors. On the wall at the far end of the alley hung a red banner, a Maoist quotation about miracles. Parts of the longtang appeared run down, uncared for. It all appeared dirtier, smaller, more crowded than he remembered. And yet, much had remained the same: the doors with their peeling black paint, the rusted knockers, the red brick, the little detail of a flower carved above each art deco doorway. As they passed each shikumen, Howard thought to himself: *This is where Von ayi lived. This is where Zia yasoh lived. This is where En'en lived.*

They slowed at the intersection where the road widened into the main artery. "Remember how the ayi would sit there and crack watermelon seeds or fold wontons while they gossiped?" his sister asked, pointing at the expanse of space visible to their left, now crammed with wooden chairs piled on top of one another, two rusted bicycles, and a sofa whose springs were poking out.

"I remember one of the ayi yelling at you here for yanking on her daughter's hair," Howard teased.

"Oh, Ma," Xuenong responded, "were you a bully?"

"I was not," Junjun retorted. "Tell her I wasn't a bully, Erge."

But Howard wasn't listening anymore. He was peering down the lane, toward the direction of Suchi's shikumen. He thought of the many times he had been down that path, to walk her home or meet her before school or tell her a bit of news. He suddenly recalled the day after their first kiss, how nervous he'd been as he'd walked toward her house, how his heart had thrummed against his lungs. He'd been sure the kiss had been a dream, that he'd imagined the slight chap of her lips, the soft tease of her tongue, that when she opened the door, she'd act as if nothing had happened. But when she stepped through the frame, soft and shy and radiant in a blush-colored skirt

211

he'd never seen before, he knew instantly things between them would never be the same, that he'd never want them to be the same again.

"Erge?" he heard Junjun ask, but it was a distant sound—he was somewhere else, some dimension of the past. His feet moved, three involuntary steps in the direction of her shikumen. He had the overwhelming feeling she was still there, waiting for him, that she had been waiting for him all these years and if he knocked on the door, she would open it, unchanged, still a girl of sixteen.

"Where are you going?" Junjun asked. She jerked her head. "Our shikumen is in that direction."

Howard stopped. The lane was still, bare. She was not down there. With the exception of a single week when he'd been in his thirties, it had been nearly five decades since Suchi had been in his life. Although he wondered—was she happy? Was she okay?—he quickly brushed the thought away. He had Linyee now. That's who was waiting for him at home. *Home*. Was Shanghai still home? Or was home now California, an ocean away?

He turned to follow Junjun.

The road to the shikumen came back to him easily. He knew the maze of this community in his bones, in his muscles. He hadn't been sure he would remember, and it relieved him that he did, that his legs carried him of their own accord. And yet, for all its familiarity, the longtang caused in him a dissonance, a note slightly out of tune. He felt like a lonely spirit pacing the corridors, longing for a friendly face, only to discover no one could see him.

Although the entrance to their old shikumen resembled almost every other door in the longtang, a damp weight descended on him as he approached it.

"Do you want to go in?" Junjun asked.

"I'm sure the people living there now wouldn't want us to bother them."

"I'm the landlord. I could insist."

"You're the landlord?"

His sister looked embarrassed. "The government was— They wanted to accommodate several more families because it was such a large property. But Ma refused to move out. So I managed to . . . acquire the rights to the place. After Ma died, I thought about turning it back over, but Ma would have wanted me to hold on to it. She always worried if she left, you wouldn't know where to find us when you came back. She wanted there to be a home waiting for your return."

Howard thought of his mother, living in the shikumen alone, waiting day after day for him to appear. A fist of regret clenched his chest. How sorry he was to have caused his mother so much grief.

Junjun cleared her throat. "In any case, I rent it out to other people now and have someone manage it for me." She paused. "Don't tell Dage. He doesn't know. He would think I was bragging by telling you this, trying to show off what a filial daughter I've been. Or he'd brush it off as a scheme to line my own pockets."

She said this matter-of-factly, but it raised an alarm in Howard. Over the years, he had picked up on an unsettling current between his siblings through stray comments they'd made.

"It's okay," he said. "It's enough for me that I'm here. Just to see the exterior again is a blessing."

"Nonsense," Junjun said. "You've come all the way from America. You should get to see inside." She knocked on the door, the familiar hollow sound of metal hitting wood rippling through him.

While Junjun explained who they were to the middle-aged woman who answered, he stood immobile. They crossed into the courtyard where he had spent hours practicing. Crowded with racks to dry laundry, it seemed smaller than he remembered, but he sensed ribbons of music dancing across the air, the way they had when he used to lie on the ground with the Victrola spinning, coming to him bright and electric like a live wire.

The woman apologized for the mess as they walked into the first-floor room. Haphazard furniture was crammed into what had once been the sitting room where they'd had dinner and received guests. Ugly white fluorescent light shone from a precarious metal lamp overhead, and a small black-and-white television blared in one corner. It looked nothing like it had when they had lived there—his mother had had a keen eye for design and had made the modest space appear warm and splendid.

The other tenants were out at work, the woman was explaining, her words fast and nervous. She didn't know if the group wished to go upstairs, but she didn't have the keys to the other people's rooms. Junjun started to respond, but Howard shook his head. "It's all right," he said. He didn't want to see any more of how his childhood home had transformed.

As the tenant saw them to the front door, she appraised Howard and asked, "So you're American?"

Pain slivered under his breastbone. "I'm Shanghainese, like you. I grew up in this very shikumen."

She flushed, nodding. "Of course, of course. What I meant was, were you the one who sent the letters?"

His breath caught. "The letters?"

The woman hesitated. "We received some letters with foreign stamps when I first moved in years ago, but we didn't know who they were for; they weren't addressed to anyone and had no signature, just talked about things none of us knew anything about." She looked worried. "We turned them in, reported them. We didn't want to get in trouble."

He felt Junjun stiffen beside him.

The woman glanced at Junjun and quickly added, "We didn't realize it was a relative of yours, comrade, or we—"

"It's all right," he said. "They weren't important. I'm sorry to have caused you trouble." The woman rubbed her hands in her shirt and nodded. The group thanked her and left.

They walked in silence, passing an old woman washing dishes in the sink behind her shikumen. Numbers were spinning through his mind, calculating, comparing. "I sent the first of the letters in February of 1982. A few months before Ma died. I always thought they were simply lost, but now, knowing some had reached the shikumen, perhaps . . . Is it possible . . ."

Junjun shook her head. "I don't know. If she received a letter from you, she never mentioned it to me, to Dage, to anyone. I certainly didn't find anything among her things."

"What about a ring? A gold ring made of two twists braided together?"

His sister frowned. "What do you mean? Any items of value were sold off years ago."

"I sent a ring—"

Junjun snorted. "Through the mail? Erge, you must have known that ring would be stolen long before it could reach Ma!"

He nodded, but he couldn't stop thinking, hoping—perhaps she'd read one of his letters, had gone to her grave knowing he was alive.

Junjun reached out and touched his arm. "If it's any comfort, she often dreamed you were in the room with her. She was constantly talking to you." She removed her hand, and in a falsely bright voice, she said, "Can you imagine what Ma would have said if she could see the state of her beloved guest hall?"

Junjun was trying to cheer him up. He forced himself to swallow his disappointment and faked a chuckle. "We weren't allowed to touch anything in that room aside from the chairs and dining table, if I recall."

"Do you remember when Ma caught me trying to open up the clock to examine its gears?"

At this memory, he broke into a genuine grin. "You were lucky she only docked your snacks for a month instead of telling Ba!"

"He would have seriously whipped me," Junjun said, laughing.

Howard was grateful, suddenly, that his sister was beside him. She shared his past, was proof that what he remembered had existed. They spent another half hour roaming the alleys, reminiscing and joking, and with her, the uncanniness of the longtang felt less bitter-sweet. Even when they passed Suchi's shikumen and he realized the painted bunny near their back door was no longer visible, his flash of sorrow was quickly pushed aside when Junjun sheepishly confessed she had once stolen a comic book from the Zhang bookstore. For the first time since he'd reconnected with his sister, Howard recognized the Junjun he'd grown up with.

Xuenong listened, grinning. "It's nice to have you back, Erjiu," she said. "Otherwise I might never have heard any of these stories of how mischievous my mother was!"

Howard smiled. Inside his bones, a Mozart concerto wove, its notes high and bright.

OVER LUNCH AT A NEARBY RESTAURANT SPECIALIZING in soup dumplings, Junjun and her husband explained the economic reform occurring in Shanghai. Howard mentioned the walk he had taken when he'd arrived, the construction he'd seen across the Bund.

"Oh, yes, Pudong is where it's all happening—" her husband started. Junjun cut him off.

"Shanghai will once again be a financial capital of the world, starting with Pudong. This liberalization will launch China into the next century!"

What surprised Howard wasn't how Junjun touted the Party line—he assumed this was how all Party officials talked—but how zealous she seemed about it. He wondered if the same people who had once insisted landowners were evil were now the same ones erecting tall skyscrapers, hoping the money would pour in.

"How does this fall in line with the idea of Communism?" Howard asked.

Junjun frowned. "We're doing all this for the benefit of the people," she said, a tinge of haughtiness in her voice.

Howard instantly regretted his question. That sense of easiness and intimacy he had reclaimed with Junjun evaporated, and she became a stranger to him once more.

When the bill came, Howard tried to pay, but Junjun's husband grabbed the check out of his hands. "You've returned home after so many years, you must let us treat you!" Howard wondered how much money his sister and her husband made as officials. The friends he'd had who had returned to their families in China had come back with stories of shocking impoverishment; some had returned with only the shirt on their back. He had even been warned by some not to go back at all: *They'll try to wring you of everything you have, telling you it's what you owe them, and it will sour your memory of your family.* Howard had been prepared for his family to be in need—thus all the gifts he'd brought—but Junjun and her husband seemed fine.

HE WAS JOLTED FROM HIS LATE AFTERNOON NAP BY A loud and insistent knock. His head felt stuffed with stones, his breath tasted gray and smoky. He shuffled to open the door, feeling as if he were walking underwater. He was greeted by sound first, then the gruff grab of his shoulder and vigorous patting.

"Doudou, you've finally returned!"

His eyes adjusted to the orange glow of the hallway just as the arm thrust him away. An old man stood before him, his face lined and sagging, the whites of his eyes yellow and filmy. Behind him, a couple in their forties peered anxiously, the man's hands resting on the shoulders of a girl of about ten or eleven who wore her hair in two braids. Howard was confused; his mind was fuzzy. Was this a dream?

"What time is it?" he mumbled, tripping over the words as if he had marbles in his mouth.

"What?" the older man asked. He glanced over his shoulder at the younger man. "See how American your uncle has become! It used to be me tutoring him in English and now look, he's speaking English in his sleep! How our fortunes have switched!"

It took Howard a moment for him to remember where he was. Had he asked for the time in English instead of Mandarin? He stared at the man, who laughed, a distinctive hiccupping sound that rang familiar, and he understood. This was Haiming, his older brother. But what had happened to him? He was only seven years older than Howard but already resembled a man of eighty.

"Dage," he said, rubbing his eyes. He waited for a wave of emotion to hit him, the way it had when he had seen Junjun, when he had seen his mother in Xuenong's face, but instead he felt unease, a seed that was transforming into panic. He had an urge to recoil, to step back into the room, to shut the door.

But Haiming pulled him into a tight embrace. "My little brother," he said. "Ma would be so happy to know you're back. She never gave up hope this would happen someday." His voice was coarse, thick with emotion. Over his shoulder, the young girl was staring up at Howard wide-eyed, her small pink lips slightly parted.

When Haiming let him go, he waved at the man and the little girl. "My son, Jiwen, daughter-in-law, Hong, and granddaughter, Chun'er," he said. The man and woman mumbled hellos.

"Quick," Haiming urged Chun'er, "greet Shugong."

"Shugong," the little girl responded obediently.

Haiming nodded his approval. "We just checked in," Haiming said. "Sorry we missed the morning. The trains were delayed."

"Junjun mentioned." Howard was fixated on his nephew, whom he'd last seen as the slightest bump in his sister-in-law's belly. It dawned on him that his nephew had been named for him, or more precisely, was named with a wish for his return.[10] The emotion he'd been grasping for uncurled. Tears pricked his eyes.

"We're to meet her downstairs in half an hour," Haiming said. "She has reservations somewhere fancy." Howard caught the same dismissive tone he'd heard on the phone before.

"I need to wash my face," Howard said, pressing an index finger to the corner of his eye.

"Go, go," Haiming urged him. "I just didn't want to wait too much longer to see you."

~

AN HOUR LATER, THEY WERE SEATED AT A TEN-PERSON round table in a private dining room. A papered door slid noiselessly open and closed every time a waiter entered to refill tea or bring peanuts.

Howard had noticed that Junjun and Haiming's greeting in the hotel's lobby had been terse and courteous. They treated each other like acquaintances, not family. He wondered if they had become distant after his mother's death and how different things would have been if she were alive now. She'd bring them all together, he thought.

Now, sitting around the table, things were awkward. Junjun and her husband were bickering over the menu. Hong was busying herself with her daughter, who kept grabbing her mother's neck to whisper in her ear, while Haiming, sitting on the other side of Chun'er, kept picking up peanuts with his chopsticks one by one and placing them on his granddaughter's plate. Next to Hong, Jiwen and Xuenong made small talk in Mandarin—it saddened Howard to realize that, like his own daughters, neither his niece nor his nephew spoke Shanghainese—but the two cousins seemed to have nothing in common. Xuenong had an air about her, something effortlessly elegant and unconcerned. She reminded him so much of his mother, who'd had the same quality.

In contrast, Jiwen seemed awkward and shy, as if he wanted to disappear into himself. His movement was heavy and his language simple and brisk, as if he wished only to communicate what was necessary and would be relieved to stop speaking. Haiming had told Howard that Jiwen worked for a construction company in Tianjin, a foreman who managed a small team, but that neither he nor his wife had finished high school. Howard guessed this was due to the Cultural Revolution, though Haiming never elaborated. He wondered how his brother felt about his abrupt change in fortune—after all, he'd been sent to England for his own schooling. Even after their father lost all of his factories to the Japanese, his parents had continued paying for Haiming's tuition, positive that when the war was over, Haiming's education would come in handy for rebuilding. Howard wondered if Haiming could still speak English, or if, like so much else, it had been lost to the intervening decades.

The food began to arrive, each dish exquisitely plated and delicately flavored: jellyfish marinated in vinegar, braised duck web, tofu skin stir-fried with salted pickled greens, "lion's head" meatballs braised with translucent leaves of cabbage, silken tofu and crab meat stew, braised fatty pork cubes in sweet sauce, jade river shrimp sautéed with fresh peas, and raw crab soaked in Shaoxing wine, the last a delicacy Howard had never tried and had only seen his parents eat on rare occasions before the war.

With each dish's arrival, the table oohed and aahed, all except Haiming, who seemed unimpressed. Howard savored each bite. Although the San Gabriel Valley boasted some pretty decent Shanghainese food, it couldn't compare to the complexity of the flavors here.

"The shrimp are so crisp, Gugu," Jiwen commented, and Junjun beamed.

"This is one of Shanghai's best restaurants," she answered. "Deng Xiaoping himself has dined in this very room."

Haiming snorted but took another bite of his pork.

"Ma only wanted the best for Erjiu's homecoming dinner," Xue-nong said. "She was sure you missed the flavors of your hometown." She rotated the lazy Susan until the drunken crab was in front of Howard. "Please, Erjiu, take another piece. I'm sure you can't get this back in America."

Howard brought the cluster of crab to his lips, sucking on the pungent, creamy flesh. He loved how the fishiness was tempered by the sharp sweetness of the wine.

"Deng Xiaoping dined here?" Hong asked. "What a fancy place! We surely aren't worthy!" Howard sensed she meant this genuinely.

"We're hardly worthy enough to be in Comrade Wang's presence at all," Haiming muttered. Howard paused, not certain Junjun had heard. But the flicker of emotion he saw in her eyes told him she had. She blinked and it disappeared.

"Like Xuenong said, there's no question we must have the best on this joyous occasion." She held up a cup of baijiu. A toast, the first of the evening. Howard lifted his cup too, as did all the adults. They threw back the contents of their glasses. The liquor burned a warm trail down Howard's esophagus and into his stomach. This began a series of short toasts around the table: Xuenong commented on how pleased she was to finally meet her long-lost uncle, and Jiwen expressed his happiness at this reunion. Haiming, who had eaten his dinner in apparent ill humor, stood when it was his turn and patted Howard's shoulder. His face was red from the alcohol, his forehead shiny. His expression softened as he looked in Howard's eyes. "It's nice to have you back, Doudou. I hope we can make up for lost time." A shot and subsequent refill punctuated each toast.

By the time it was Howard's turn, he was feeling light-headed from the strong liquor and found it difficult to speak. "Words can't express how fortunate I feel right now," he said. "I only wish our parents were here too."

Nobody said anything, but he saw Junjun nodding. They knocked back their last cup of wine.

"They would be happy the three of us are in the same room," Junjun said.

"Bullshit," Haiming said under his breath.

"Ba," Jiwen said in a low warning tone. He gestured to his wife, an awkward hand signal that seemed to mean *Do something*, but Chun'er was between her and Haiming. Hong shook her head at her husband.

"What?" Haiming said, a little louder, his words slightly slurred. "She's full of shit, and she knows it. Look at all of this. It's a display, to show off how much better she is than we are. But ask her where it comes from! Ask her where she got all of this from!" He directed the last two phrases at Howard, who didn't know how to respond. His brother's eyes were bulging, wild, and a vein glistened in his neck. He glanced around helplessly. A few chairs down from him, Junjun looked stricken. Beside her, her husband's face creased into anger, his hand curling tightly around his glass. Jiwen and Hong seemed anxious, while their daughter tugged on her grandfather's arm, whispering, "Yeye." Only Xuenong appeared impassive, her eyes unreadable as she stared at her uncle, her arms folded on the table in front of her.

"Dajiu," she said, her voice quiet and steady. "I think you might have had too much to drink. Perhaps I should ask the server for more tea?"

"I'm fine," Haiming insisted. "It's just your mother—"

223

"... has gone through quite the trouble to get us this reservation," Xuenong finished for him. "This restaurant is booked for months, but Ma insisted she wanted only the best for her family, that it's what her mother would have wanted. Surely, Dajiu, you would agree Waipo would have wanted a grand welcome for her youngest son?"

"She would have cooked all the dishes herself," Haiming said, but he sounded subdued. "She would have made those turnip pastries Doudou loved the most."

Howard turned to Junjun. "Remember when I got in trouble for eating half a batch she had been cooling to bring to the neighbors? The glaze on their crusts was so shiny and brown, I couldn't resist."

Junjun cracked a relieved smile. "You tried to blame it on me!"

"But Ma knew. My punishment was to help her make the next batch knowing I wouldn't get any. It was cruel."

"You know, up until she died, she was selling those pastries alongside her meat buns?" Junjun glanced at Haiming, whose eyes were now glazed and staring into his glass. "She was well-known for having the best pastries in the area. Her secret was high-quality lard."

Howard struggled to picture his refined, beautiful mother as a roadside hawker. He longed to know more, about the life his mother had lived, how it was she spent her last days toiling away. But he was afraid, now, to set off his brother.

"I miss her," he said, sighing. Junjun nodded. Silently, she reached over and poured more clear liquor into his cup.

HOWARD AWOKE THE NEXT MORNING AT SIX A.M., HIS skull throbbing from all the baijiu he'd consumed the night before.

He made his way down to breakfast, eager for some congee to soak up the liquor sloshing in his belly, and found Haiming was already there, sipping on the thin porridge.

"Good morning," Howard said, setting down the bowl of congee.

"Good morning." Haiming's eyes were bloodshot.

"Where is your son's family?"

"They're still sleeping as far as I know," he said.

Howard nodded and ate his congee. The bland wateriness was exactly what he wanted; his head began clearing almost instantaneously.

"I'm sorry about last night," Haiming said, not looking up from his bowl. "I got a bit drunk and carried away."

Howard stirred his congee. Why did Haiming despise Junjun so much? He didn't know how to ask. Instead, he said, "I didn't know Ma had opened a food stand."

"Yeah," Haiming said. "She started a few years before she died, selling off the last of the jewelry she had squirreled away to buy a modest cart and ingredients. I tried to convince her to move to Tianjin, but she insisted she could eke out a living in Shanghai. She was stubborn. She didn't even let any of us know she was dying. It was only when a friend of Ma's called that we found out she'd been sick for months."

"Why would Ma keep such a thing to herself?"

"You know Ma, she didn't want us to worry. And apparently she didn't want Haijun to get in trouble." Haiming gave a bitter laugh.

Howard didn't know whether to steer the conversation back to safe territory or to push ahead, to make sense of what was going on between his siblings. "In trouble?" he echoed.

"I think Ma was under the impression Haijun would somehow

use her connections to try and move her into one of those high-end government hospitals in Beijing, the ones they only reserve for officials. As if Haijun would ever do anything to threaten her position."

"I'm sure Junjun would have—"

"Forget it," Haiming said. "Tell me about what my nieces have been up to recently."

The abrupt shift in topic frustrated Howard. He was sick of being shut out, as if he were an outsider or a child to be protected. He wanted to know what had happened to his family, why they were like this, why this rift had grown between them.

"Junjun is a filial daughter," he insisted. "Of course she would have taken Ma to the hospital. Ma knew her own daughter." Haiming said nothing, so Howard pressed. "Junjun looked up to Ma, she followed her everywhere, tried on her makeup, her clothes. She—"

Haiming dropped his spoon to the side. It clattered against the porcelain bowl. He stared intently into Howard's face. "Did Haijun ever tell you how Ba died?"

"She said he died during the revolution."

"That's it, eh? Of course that's all she told you."

"What do you mean?"

"Ba was beaten to death by a group of Red Guards." Haiming leaned in, his gaze unwavering. His breath still smelled faintly of alcohol. "Turned in by none other than Wang Haijun herself."

Howard's brain went numb. "That can't be true."

"It's true. She wrote a denouncement, signed it herself. Labeling Ba as a bourgeois, capitalist, foreign-loving dog. We're lucky they dragged only Ba off. She denounced you, too, saying she had severed ties with her traitorous Nationalist brother, though she'll never tell you that."

Howard flinched.

Haiming was crushing the paper wrapper from the chopsticks he had used. "I don't know why they left Ma alone. They just took her things—whatever she hadn't had time to hide—clothes, jewelry, her books. Oh, and all of your records—she cried over those the most."

Images flashed through his mind—of his father shouting, bleeding, of his mother held back as guards ran through their shikumen and dashed records on the floor. And at the center, sweet, cherubic Junjun in her pigtails, her lips twisted, mouthing ugly words, her fingers pointed at the parents who loved her most. But no, his sister had been an adult by then.

"Haijun begged for our forgiveness, years later. She says she had no choice, that comrades had recently dug up her past and discovered her brother was a Nationalist soldier." Howard felt sick; the acid from last night's liquor climbed his gullet and burned the back of his tongue. Haiming, not meeting Howard's eyes, stared at the white wrapper. "She claimed she thought if she could stay on the good side of the Party, it would help us all eventually, cancel out your misdeeds. She said she didn't know they would actually kill Ba, she thought at most he might receive a prison sentence. But I think she was trying to save herself. She was already deep in the Party by that time, but she'd just given birth to Xuenong, who was sickly and fussy, and remarks had already been made that perhaps now that she was a mother, her attention and commitment were no longer with the Party. If they decided she wasn't fit to stay in the Party, it would affect her husband's position too. Ma forgave her, said she understood that everything Haijun had done, she had done for her family. But I never did. I never will."

Haiming paused, the paper now twisted in his fingers, and Howard tried to remember if his voice had always been so harsh. Or had life changed it?

"Despite what Haijun claims, I received no protection. They stripped everything from me and sent me to the farms to shovel shit, to be reeducated. My son, labeled a descendant of capitalist traitors by his own classmates, was sent to the worst countryside in harsh, freezing conditions for reeducation, part of the wave of 'sent-down kids.' He's lucky he survived. Some of his friends didn't. Ellen didn't survive the worry."

The restaurant seemed too empty, too loud. Howard squeezed his eyes shut. He wondered if part of Haiming could also not forgive Howard—for taking Haiming's place and now having the better life, for bringing shame to them even in his absence. The likelihood he had ruined his family's lives burned deep in his ribs. *All of this is my fault*, he thought.

"Dage," he said, opening his eyes, but Haiming shook his head and batted away whatever Howard was about to say.

"I don't want your pity. Despite everything, I can say I lived with integrity. I did the best for my family, even if it wasn't enough to protect them. We don't have the lavish things Haijun and her family do; we don't have high connections. We live a simple life and we barely scrape by most years, but we support each other and that's enough. If it weren't for you, I would be happy to never speak to that woman again. As far as I'm concerned, she's no family of mine."

Howard didn't know what to say. As a child, he had looked up to his brother and had wanted his approval. After his brother had gone away to boarding school, Howard, six years old, had cried himself to sleep for a week. But because of that, he hardly had any memories

228

with him; his brother had always seemed removed, unreachable, someone he didn't really know. Instead, it was Junjun whom he'd watched grow from a baby to a preadolescent, Junjun whom he'd shared inside jokes with and made up stupid games for, Junjun who had been an unconditional fan of his music.

"Perhaps—" he started, but again, Haiming waved him off.

"Don't. You weren't there. You can't understand."

The words stung. But Howard understood the truth behind them. He loved them both, but this rift was not his to repair.

IN THE LATE MORNING, HIS SISTER'S FAMILY ARRIVED with a silver van to pick them up. Haiming barely acknowledged them as he climbed into the back with his family. They traveled an hour outside the city, the bustle and smog receding behind them, to a cemetery.

Narrow plaques crowded together, marking gentle mounds overgrown with grass. "Ma's grave is back there," Junjun said, pointing to a row several hundred meters from where they stood. Howard wanted to know where their father was buried, but he was afraid of the answer. He suspected "capitalist pigs" were not allotted earth in which to rest their bodies. Again, it must have been Junjun who had used her connections to finagle a plot for their mother at all.

Junjun led them to a black plaque bearing their mother's name, a small black-and-white photograph embedded into its surface. Howard stared at the picture of his mother as he had never seen her, at her lined, weathered face, the soft hinge of her jaw, the crinkle in her eye, her white hair pulled into a sensible bun. She was still beautiful, he thought, and he remembered the many times he had woken from a fever or a nightmare as a child to find her cool hands stroking his hair.

"Ma," Junjun said, brushing away the dried leaves that had gathered on the concrete altar in front of the plaque, "I've brought Erge with me. He's finally returned home and has come to pay his respects." She set down two altar candles, a small brass incense urn, and a bowl of oranges.

Howard stood in front of the dark plaque, lit joss sticks pressed between his fingers. A quiet breeze lifted his thinning hair. "Ma, I've returned," he started to say, but his voice broke. How to tell her everything that had happened to him? How to make her understand how he would never stop missing her? He had failed in his duties as a filial son—he had not been around in her old age, to care for her, to provide comfort. He was filled with regret that gaped so wide he felt it was swallowing him from the inside out.

In America, his children had this idea the dead lived in the sky as invisible angels and peered over clouds to observe their family, but Howard believed in no such solace. He didn't know where his mother's soul was, if she'd already been reincarnated into her next life or if she was in some other realm of the dead.

He fell to his knees. Flakes of white ash broke off the joss sticks and snowed upon his knuckles. Tears mingled with snot above his upper lip. He wanted his mother's forgiveness for leaving her, but he would never receive it.

FOR THE REST OF HIS TIME IN SHANGHAI, HOWARD DU-tifully followed Junjun as she took him from neighborhood to neighborhood, showing him how things had been renamed: Fourth Road to Fuzhou Road, French Park to Fuxing Park, Jing'an Temple Road[11] to Nanjing West Road.

She was trying so hard to please him, he could tell. She insisted on treating him to the best restaurants, paying for entry fees to attractions. She was jovial at all times, her chatter upbeat and her laughter loud, but once in a while, when she didn't know he was watching, he caught her face relaxing into its natural state, a downturn of her lips, her eyes sinking into shadows.

On the last morning before his departure, they took an early stroll to watch the sunrise along the Bund. The walkway was quiet, and aside from a few elderly winding their arms and patting their legs as they passed, it was otherwise empty. The siblings stared out at the water in silence, waiting for the faint pink glow on the horizon to turn into the blood orange of the sun.

"Junjun." She turned to him, and in the contours of the early morning light, he could still see the baby sister he had left behind. "I talked to Dage. He says . . . He told me . . . how Ba died."

Her smile faded. Her lips drew into a thin straight line and she folded her arms over her chest. "He's always hated me," she said.

"I want to hear your side of the story," Howard said. "I want to know . . . is it true?"

"You don't know what it was like back then," Junjun said, her voice defensive. "You have no idea."

"I just want to understand," Howard said. When she didn't respond, he pleaded, "Junjun, my favorite sister. Tell me what happened."

Junjun stared back out at the skyline of the unfinished city. "You know, back then, we weren't even as good as the kids. These ten-, twelve-, thirteen-year-olds were running around, willing to turn in their teachers, their friends, their families, all for the sake of a higher ideal. They had pure ideologies we could never compete with. Every day, we were being watched, every day a purity test we could never pass. But we had to try. *I* had to try."

"But Ba, he loved you, he—"

Junjun shook her head. "They knew everything. Records that you had voluntarily enlisted with the enemy. Evidence showing he had voluntarily helped with the war effort with his factories. From their point of view, Ba had colluded with the Nationalists."

"But couldn't you have explained? We had no choice then!"

"It wasn't just that. He had land and factories, he had a foreign education and imported goods. He was a capitalist, someone who had stolen from honest Chinese citizens, who'd profited off their backs. No explanation I could have given would have wiped his slate clean. It would only have made me seem like I was making excuses for this behavior."

"But you could have *tried*!" Howard struggled for a moment, attempting to come out from under the weight of a hundred emotions he didn't know how to name. When he spoke again, his voice was quiet, injured. "How could you personally sign the denouncement? He was your father."

"What was I supposed to do?" Her words came out sharp and ragged and her arms flung out to grip the railing, her knuckles turning white. "They questioned me, asked me if I was like my bourgeois father, my traitorous brother. They pressured me to prove I was different from my blood. I had a sick baby that needed me. Do you see? If they dragged me away, locked me up, executed me, what would happen to her?" She squeezed her eyes together tightly. "Ideologically, he was guilty. You and I both know that's true. But I never thought . . . I thought if I signed the paper, I would have a chance to decide his sentence, that they might go easier on him."

Howard pressed a fist to his mouth. How did she live with it? Had she always had the potential for such ruthlessness inside of her? Would she have done such a thing if it weren't for him, who he was, what *he* had done? If he had never enlisted, if he had been around—

"Erge." Her voice came out in a croak. "I had no choice. You have to believe me."

The sun was halfway into the cloudless sky now, the light dappling brilliantly across the water as if it were littered with diamonds.

The anger he felt, the grief, the helplessness—he didn't know whom he blamed more, Junjun or himself.

~

IN THE EVENING, HOWARD AND HIS WHOLE FAMILY WENT out to a hot pot restaurant. The restaurant was crowded with raucous groups, loud and happy as they drank and ate together. Wisps of steaming broth floated through the air, a jungle of herbs and marrow.

Before dinner, Howard had offloaded the gifts he'd brought, slipping the most valuable items to Haiming and his family first. His brother had been embarrassed. "I'm your older brother, I should be taking care of you," he'd protested, but eventually he had accepted.

The thin slices of lamb and pork were tender and not too gamey, the noodles slippery and perfectly chewy. Howard savored the vinegar of the dipping sauce on his tongue; he savored the sight of his family, broken as they were, sitting around the pot, their chopsticks clattering against one another as they reached into the boil.

No matter what had occurred, no matter the rift, this was his family. His brother and sister, the only ones he had. The war had taken so much. He looked at Haiming, curled over his bowl, his hunched body etched with innumerable tragedies Howard would never understand. He thought of all the ways he owed his brother, could never make it up to him. He looked at Junjun, who quietly picked up slivers of radish. She had been subdued and careful around him all evening, and he felt a small pang of regret that he had ruined their last night together. He glanced at Xuenong and imagined this lovely woman as a helpless, sickly infant. He didn't know if he could forgive Junjun, if it was possible to forgive something that big and terrible, but he knew he would spend the rest of his life trying.

Near the end of the night, as they sipped on sweet walnut soup, Xuenong turned to him and asked him if he'd been able to visit the Shanghai Conservatory of Music. "Ma said you had always dreamed of going there."

He had. The campus was now situated near what had once been Avenue Joffre in the former French Concession. He had walked through the gates apprehensively, expecting to feel a pang of remorse for what could have been, but to his surprise he felt nothing aside from marvel. The campus brimmed with energy: students bustled between European-style villas and modern buildings with instruments in hand; a lone flutist practiced in the spacious courtyard while a study group pored over books nearby; a soprano's aria wafted from an open window. But the idea that this might have been his life seemed foreign to him, a faraway dream irrelevant to his waking reality.

"It's very different now," Howard told his niece. "During the war, the campus kept moving around, even splitting into multiple schools at one point."

"Your uncle was so gifted," Junjun said, the first time she had really spoken all evening. "When I was little, he'd amuse me by making up songs on the violin. Sometimes, if his girlfriend was there, she'd make up lyrics that I could sing along with, then she'd take my hand and twirl me in circles until I got dizzy."

Howard's chest ached. "Suchi loved you," he said.

"Oh!" Junjun exclaimed. "Speaking of Susu jie, I suddenly remembered something I've been meaning to mention. I thought you'd want to know that her mother and Ma were friendly in her last days, funnily enough. She was the one who called Dage when Ma got sick."

"Tsan ayi?" His voice was taut. "Where is she now? Is she still alive?"

"I don't know. After Ma's death I promised her I would try to help her track down her daughters, but I'm afraid I got busy and forgot." She paused. "I'm sorry, I should have thought of this sooner. I might have her phone number stashed somewhere. She could still be alive. She would be in her seventies or eighties now, probably?"

"Do you know if she ever heard from Sulan or Suchi?"

Junjun shook her head.

It was too late; Howard's flight was leaving in the early morning. There was no time to find her, to tell her the little he knew of her daughters.

"Please search for her number if you can," he told Junjun.

For months afterward, Howard asked Junjun for the number, but she never found it.

THE ENGINES' ROAR QUAKED INSIDE OF HOWARD, HIS ribs knocking. He peered out the window, at the skyline of Shanghai, the people, the buildings, its dirt and grass and dust falling away.

Somewhere below were his brother and sister, somewhere below was the ivory of his mother's and father's bones. Was this still his home? Would he see any of it again? He did not know.

Beethoven began to swell, the same bars that had taken him away once before. He remembered being eighteen, catching a final glimpse of Shanghai's shores, not understanding then how long it would be before he returned.

The plane lifted, a split second in weightlessness, then straightened out.

Howard wondered if his daughters' ideas of the dead were correct. Perhaps this was what his mother saw as her soul sped away from earth.

A cloud enveloped them, and Shanghai faded into white.

SEPTEMBER 1948–DECEMBER 1953
Shanghai / Hong Kong

T HE TRAIN STATION was a sea of black heads bobbing. Suchi pressed the violin case tightly to her, excitement electric in her veins as she and M'ma searched for Apa in the crowd. M'ma nearly fell over when someone jostled into her, teetering on her lotus shoes, but Suchi grabbed her just in time. "You should have stayed home," she said, but M'ma shook her head, her expression pinched and anxious. They found Apa and Sulan ahead of them.

"Once you get to Shenzhen, remember you have to switch to a train to Kowloon," Apa reminded them for what felt like the twentieth time. "One of my contacts at the King Publishing Company will meet you there. He'll take care of you while you're in Hong Kong."

He smiled widely, in a way that made Suchi's face hurt.

"Work hard! I expect you two to make some good deals!" He gazed at Suchi. "Especially you, Meimei." *Meimei.* Little sister. He hadn't called her that in years, not since she was a young child. "Don't forget you're as smart as any of the boys. I know you'll make me proud."

"Of course, Apa," she said. Her first business trip, her first time out of Shanghai!

"You have everything?" he asked, as if they could easily turn around and go back for something they had forgotten. "The tickets?"

Sulan nodded, holding them up in her fist. Her face was pale and tight. She was nervous, Suchi realized with surprise. When had her sister gotten so timid?

"And the money?" he added in a low voice.

Sulan nodded again, patting a silk purse of Hong Kong dollars Apa had managed to change. She slipped the purse into a pocket she'd sewn into her black qipao.

"Hong Kong will be unfamiliar," Apa told them. "Whatever you do, stick together and look out for each other. You're family. Don't forget that."

"Do you have the snacks I prepared for you?" M'ma added. "Don't eat them all at once, in case the water and soil there don't agree with you. Do you have your sweaters? It might get cool on the train."

"We'll be fine, we're not babies," Suchi said impatiently.

M'ma began to cry. "You're two young women— I don't—" she sobbed. "Don't talk to strange people, promise me. The two of you trust strangers too easily, you think everyone is your friend, but promise me you won't be stupid."

"We won't, M'ma, we promise," Sulan said, her own eyes glittering with tears.

Suchi swallowed her irritation at everyone's dramatics and tried to comfort her mother. "It's only for a month," she said, her hand on M'ma's back. M'ma shook her head.

"This doesn't feel right," she said. "I shouldn't—we shouldn't—"

"Laubu," Apa chided in a gentle voice they rarely heard him use with their mother. She stopped talking, though she continued to wipe her tears away.

A bell signaled that the train was readying to depart. M'ma grabbed each of their arms tightly, but Apa shook her loose. "They have to go," he said. "They can't miss this train."

Suchi disentangled herself from M'ma's grasp.

"Don't worry, M'ma," she said. "I'll bring back some Hong Kong sweets for you."

Apa was urging them up the stairs to their train car. When they got to the top, he handed them their two suitcases. "Hurry and find your seat before someone steals it."

They squeezed through the train's packed aisle and put their suitcases in the berth above their seats. Still clutching the violin case, Suchi scooted into the hard bench and Sulan pressed next to her. They crowded around the open window and hung their heads and arms out, enduring the smoky exhaust. On the platform, M'ma leaned against Apa, who gripped her forearm, as if propping her up. He appeared so small, his face so tired. Suchi remembered that when she'd been young, his legs had been tree trunks she climbed.

"Apa!" she called, waving. He snapped his head toward her voice. She saw him searching the open windows one by one until they landed on her and Sulan's faces. The train emitted another whistle and crawled to life.

"My daughters," he shouted. "Don't forget to eat!"

"Apa! M'ma! Take care of yourselves!" they shouted back, their arms furiously waving. A pang of homesickness seized Suchi. This would be the first night of her seventeen years she would spend away from them.

Their hair whipped in the gaining breeze as they tracked their parents' figures until they were tiny specks in the receding distance. Then even those specks vanished.

Sulan slumped into the bench next to Suchi. She glanced at the violin case hugged in her sister's arms.

"I can't believe you brought that thing," she said, her voice thick.

"I don't trust M'ma not to throw it away while I'm gone," Suchi retorted. Her sister shook her head and looked away, pressing her fingers to her eyes. Suchi tilted her head toward the window, not wanting to miss a thing.

THE NEXT DAY, GROGGY AND STIFF, THEY DISEMBARKED at Lo Wu, the last town before crossing the border into Hong Kong. After waiting two hours in a snaking line of hundreds, Suchi and Sulan purchased their seats to Kowloon. The trip was around three hours, brief compared to the overnight ride they had just taken. Suchi watched the rolling hills and open expanse of land stream past. She remembered all those years ago, trying to imagine what this place was like when Haiwen had first mentioned his parents had lived here. Now she was disappointed by how plain it appeared—she had expected a city that rivaled Shanghai in its glamour. But so far, it seemed to be simply another countryside.

Kowloon Station was much livelier. The sisters emerged from the stately building into a stifling afternoon. The sun was high and unforgiving, and the stink of salt and oil and decaying fish hung heavy in the humid air. The harbor was populated with junks and sampans on a placid sea, and in the distance, on the other side of the water, was the dense skyline of what they assumed was Hong Kong Island. On the road, a throng of pedicabs, automobiles, and buses competed for space behind swarms of people. The girls scanned the crowd for a man who appeared like he might be searching for them. They realized they didn't know Apa's contact's name.

Ten minutes, then twenty went by as they gripped their suitcases with sweaty hands and peered hopefully into the thinning crowd. Pedicab drivers came up to them, speaking Cantonese, pointing at their vehicles. The girls waved them off. Suchi was sticky and uncomfortable in the cotton qipao she was wearing, and her armpits were beginning to stink with dampness. After forty minutes, the girls looked at each other.

"Maybe he didn't realize we were coming today," Sulan said.

They waved down a pedicab driver. "Can you take us to King Publishing Company?" Suchi asked him in Mandarin, but he shook his head, uncomprehending. He looked at her scornfully, responding in Cantonese. Even without understanding his words, the girls caught the exasperation behind them.

After trying another pedicab driver, they appealed to a British officer, but he only frowned impatiently at their flustered, halting English.

"What should we do?" Suchi fretted.

"Hey, you two," someone called in clear, accented Mandarin. The girls turned toward a middle-aged woman who was approaching them. She was wearing a simple navy qipao and her graying hair was pulled into a bun. Suchi breathed a sigh of relief.

"Ayi, you can speak Mandarin?"

"I've been watching you. You don't know where you're going?"

"Someone was supposed to pick us up," Sulan said. "But they must have confused the dates of our arrival."

The woman nodded. "You're from Shanghai?"

"How did you guess?" Suchi asked.

"Your accents. Your clothes. There have been a lot of Shanghainese refugees coming in these days, running from the Communists, and they all have an air about them, the same air you two have."

Suchi couldn't tell if this "air" the woman spoke of was a good or bad thing. She thought she detected a slight distaste in the woman's voice, but she could have been imagining it.

"We're not refugees," she told the woman. "We're here on business."

"Do you know how to get to King Publishing Company?" Sulan asked. "Our father's friend, he works there. If we can get there, we should be able to find him."

"Do you have the address?" the woman asked. They shook their heads. She sighed. "Listen, I have a boardinghouse not far from here. I suggest you stay for a night, rest, and search for this friend of your father's tomorrow. I can take you there now. I'll only charge you two dollars a night."

The suggestion of a bed tantalized Suchi. In addition to the clammy film she was now covered in from the humidity, she became aware of how much her back ached from sitting on the train's hard benches for a day, how swollen her feet were inside her traveling boots. She longed for a bath, a bed to lie flat in. She glanced at Sulan, hopeful her sister felt the same way, but Sulan was already responding to the woman in a firm voice.

"No thank you. We have to find our father's friend. He's expecting us."

"I can help you," the woman insisted. "Don't worry."

Her sister shook her head. "We'll figure it out ourselves," she said. She pulled on Suchi's sleeves, leading her down a crowded street.

"Why did you do that?" Suchi complained when they were several meters away. "It wouldn't have been so bad to rest a bit before searching for the company."

Sulan held on to Suchi's elbow. "You're so dim," she said. "Have you already forgotten what M'ma said? What if that woman was a brothel owner, looking to kidnap us? Or maybe she would have robbed us of our money while we were sleeping! I've read about these things happening, you know."

"She seemed nice," Suchi said, still thinking longingly of a bed.

"When will you grow up?" Sulan said. "You can't be this naïve forever."

They wound through the narrow streets and alleyways, searching for anyone who spoke Mandarin. They found a few people, but no one knew of King Publishing Company.

After several hours of walking, Suchi's feet were sore. She was hungry. She began to regret her stubborn insistence on bringing Haiwen's violin, as it meant she could only lug her suitcase with one arm. They stopped into a small restaurant and ordered by pointing at the handwritten menu hanging on the wall. Sulan extracted several precious Hong Kong dollars to pay for their meal.

"We can't walk around aimlessly forever," Suchi said. "Maybe we should go back to that woman."

Sulan shook her head. "Not her," she said. "We'll find somewhere else to stay."

After some asking around, Sulan found a small boardinghouse she felt comfortable with, run by a young widow and her two daughters, sweet-cheeked girls of seven and nine. They openly ogled Su-lan, who, despite a long day of travel and Hong Kong's unforgiving heat, still looked enchanting in her black qipao, navy felt hat, and coiffed hair. Watching the girls reminded Suchi of how she and Su-lan had once been starstruck by Haiwen's mother. Had this been what Wang ayi had seen on their faces, this poorly concealed awe and longing?

The thought of Haiwen jolted her grief back into the forefront of her mind. She wondered where he was, if he was injured, if he was alive. Regret for the things she had said to him crept into her belly, but she pressed it down deep where it could not hurt her.

FOR A WEEK, THEY RETURNED TO THE TRAIN STATION, hoping Apa's contact might appear on a different day, that he had misremembered the date they were arriving. But nobody ever seemed to be looking for two young women.

"We should give up," Sulan said as they walked back to the boardinghouse after the seventh day.

"We can't!" Suchi said. "How are we supposed to do any of the work Apa asked of us if we don't find the publisher?"

Sulan stopped walking. She stared at her sister. "Tsan Suji."

"I promised Apa." Apa had asked her to make him proud. A vicious hunger crawled into her breast. She wouldn't let him down.

"Come on, Susu," Sulan said, her voice light and even. "You can't tell me you don't know what's happening."

"What are you talking about?"

Sulan gave a snort of laughter. "And Apa thinks *you're* the smart one and *I'm* the frivolous one?"

Suchi felt her temper rising. Her sister was patronizing her, and worst of all, she didn't know why.

"Come on, dummy, think about it, will you? Inflation is through the roof. Apa's business is barely holding on—"

"That's why he needs us to make some lucrative deals with the Hong Kongers!"

"Then why wouldn't he come himself? Why would he have us come instead? Especially me? Why would he ask me, when I've never shown any interest in his business?"

Suchi had assumed it was because he felt Suchi was too young to go alone.

"You're so stupid," Sulan snapped. "Apa was sending us away to keep us safe."

"Safe?"

"From the war. From the Nationalists, the Communists, from whatever might happen if Shanghai falls again. In case you haven't noticed, the war isn't exactly going well."

Truth ripped through her. With clarity, she saw all she had ignored: the way Apa's smile had been too wide to be real, the multiple reminders Apa had given about sticking together and staying safe, M'ma's unending tears and fretfulness.

"You knew?" she asked. "Apa told you?"

"No," Sulan said, "but it was obvious. He had me sew jewelry into the seams of all of my clothing, saying you never knew what kinds of bandits might be in Hong Kong, and it was better to have some capital stashed away. And one afternoon I returned early without telling them, and I heard him and M'ma fighting. He wanted M'ma to go too, but she wouldn't—she didn't even want us to go. She thought we should all stay together."

Tears pricked at Suchi's eyes. "Why didn't you tell me?" she asked. With regret, she thought of how she had snapped at M'ma before they left.

"How was I supposed to know you didn't know? I thought you were feigning all that excitement for Apa and M'ma's benefit. I didn't believe you could truly be that self-absorbed!"

Sulan's words stung. Suchi felt as stupid and silly as her sister implied, and she was ashamed. "So was the contact fake too? Have you let me wander around aimlessly for days for no reason?"

Sulan shook her head. "As far as I know, that contact was real. I think Apa hoped he would house us and take care of us. I don't know what happened to him."

"How long will we be here?" Suchi asked.

"I don't know," Sulan said. "Probably until Apa thinks it's safe for us to go back."

THE GIRLS ADJUSTED SLOWLY TO THEIR NEW LIFE. Their first priority was to find work, since the cash Apa had given them could not last them forever, and they wanted to pawn the jewelry only as a last resort. But despite Sulan's high school degree, she had a hard time landing a job. She was still, even here, competing with other Shanghainese girls, daughters of rich businessmen who had gone to St. Mary's Hall or the famed St. John's University, who spoke perfect English and knew how to type. Eventually, she found a job assisting a tailor who was also originally from Shanghai, putting her many years of sewing her own clothes to use.

Suchi fared even worse—unlike Sulan, she had no specialized skills. With her poor Cantonese, no one would hire her to work in their shops or restaurants. She could get a job at one of the nearby factories—that's what most refugees were doing—but Sulan had heard of women who had been locked in the factories and made to work until their fingers bled and forbade Suchi from signing up.

In the end, Mrs. Chan, their landlady, offered the girls discounted room and board if Suchi would help her and the girls with the daily chores needed to keep the boardinghouse running. Suchi liked Mrs. Chan, who could not have been much older than thirty and had a kind smile, and she liked the girls too, who insisted on being called by their English names, Shirley and Betty. While Mrs. Chan patiently communicated with Suchi through a combination of hand gestures, miming, and sentences scribbled in Chinese on slips of paper, Shirley and Betty delighted in teaching Suchi words in Cantonese, giggling at her awkward pronunciations.

Once they were settled, Sulan and Suchi wrote Apa a letter, telling him the contact had never appeared—did he have a name or address? Could he check what had happened?—and that they were safe. They described Hong Kong, the fishy tang of the harbor, the beautiful view of the city and beyond from the top of Victoria Peak, the pale British buildings that reminded them of home, the surprising frequency with which Shanghainese pierced through the singsong of Cantonese on the street.

They didn't admit they only knew of the Peak's view through postcards; how hearing their childhood language made them ache; how usually the speakers were rich Shanghainese merchants and their families who, despite their common hometown, would never have accepted the sisters into their fold. Nor did they tell him about the less fortunate mainland prostitutes who lingered down by the harbor where the British navy men anchored, or describe the shantytown that had cropped up on a hill not five blocks from where they lived, overcrowded with mainlander refugees who spent most of their day waiting in long lines for a ladle of rice from charity organizations.

Apa's first letter arrived within a few months, stating he had tried to get in touch with the contact, to no avail. "He's a thief, forget about him," Apa wrote, but did not elaborate. "Hold on and take care of each other in the meantime," he added. "It's no longer safe to return. Your mother and I will follow as soon as we can." Suchi and Sulan counted their expenses, putting aside what they'd need, and everything else they sent to Apa. Another letter came around Spring Festival. "We are still trying to get money," Apa said. "Inflation is rising so fast, we can't keep up. There are stories of people wheeling cartloads of cash in order to buy a single cup of rice. But soon." The girls sent more money, a hundred Hong Kong dollars, which was all they could spare, and hoped it would be enough. In mid-May, a letter dated early April came from Apa saying they had given up on getting the necessary funds for tickets and were searching for an alternative way to get to Hong Kong. The letter was cryptic as to what that alternative might be.

Two days after Apa's letter arrived, they woke to the news emblazoned on every newspaper.

Shanghai had been "liberated" by the Communists.

Apa was too late.

MOONLIGHT SPLASHED ONTO THE FLOOR. IT WAS THE evening's quietest hour, and everyone else in the boardinghouse was asleep. Suchi sat up in bed and peered out the window down into the street. Directly in her view was an old banyan tree whose twisted roots had broken through the pavement, cracking and raising a hill in the cement. It was ghostly and beautiful at night, silver where the moon hit its branches.

Four years had passed since they had first arrived in Hong Kong—in that time, Suchi's hands had become cracked and calloused, and Sulan had begun complaining of backaches from being bent over the sewing table for too many hours. Suchi's Cantonese was now at a conversational level, while Sulan, who spent her days conversing with the mainlander patrons at the tailor's shop, many of whom were from Shanghai, had not progressed past basic formalities like *please* and *thank you*. Sulan had befriended some Shanghainese women her age who lived in the shantytown and sometimes went out with them to eat, but Suchi spent most of her time at the boardinghouse, growing closer to Mrs. Chan, who insisted she and Sulan call her "daaize," Cantonese for "big sister." In turn, Suchi treated Shirley and Betty as if the girls were *her* little sisters (and in fact the younger girls called Sulan and Suchi "daaize" too). She learned Mrs. Chan's husband had died of pneumonia the first winter of Japan's occupation of Hong Kong, leaving Mrs. Chan to figure out how to make ends meet.

"Failure wasn't an option," she said when Suchi asked how she'd been able to bear it. "I had two little ones to think of. I had no time to feel sorry for myself. I could only move forward."

Each month for the last few years, Sulan and Suchi had prepared packages of oil and rice and whatever money they could spare and gave it to a courier who promised to get the commodities to their parents. Apa had written a few times since the Communist takeover, but although he'd mentioned how scarce things were, his letters were falsely upbeat and gave no hint of any plans to leave Shanghai. Suchi knew people still arrived from the mainland—the streets were filled with recent transplants and the shantytown was growing more crowded every day. Word was it was much harder to enter Hong Kong than it used to be, because the British did not want China's problems on its soil and policed its borders tightly. And yet people continued to find ways. Suchi knew Sulan, like herself, held on to hope Apa and M'ma would find a way to cross the border and join them.

But several months ago they had realized it had been too long since they'd heard from Apa. Now, nine months had passed with no word, but they still sent the packages. "Maybe it's the censors," they reasoned, and continued to wait, neither of them willing to voice out loud the unthinkable possibility it could be anything else.

The gnarled branches of the banyan tree filled Suchi with unbearable sadness. Her eyes traced the lines of each root and vine, searching for their connections, following where one tucked in and disappeared into the shadows, and where it reappeared and branched into another limb. She loved the tree's complication, its chaotic beauty, and yet she couldn't decide if she felt its unruliness was one of creation or destruction.

Her memories bubbled more easily to the surface at this hour, things she didn't want to remember but couldn't bear to forget: Her family around the dinner table, bickering, Apa lecturing them. The fragrance of the rosewater M'ma bathed her feet in at night. Lying out on the terraced rooftop with Sulan, the night chatter of Sifo Li in the background. Haiwen playing the same pieces repeatedly; Haiwen gliding a thumb across her cheekbone. She even allowed herself to fantasize about what her other self, the self who lived in a Shanghai without war, would be doing now. She'd be sleeping next to Haiwen in their shared bed. Perhaps there would be a child between them, nursing. The moon that shone would be casting a light on their two faces, the loves of her lives, and she'd feel a contentedness she'd never experienced before.

It was like pressing down on a pimple, painful but irresistible. But by doing so, Suchi found no relief, only regret.

Earlier in the day, as she was collecting dishes from the boarders' morning meal, the sharp, mournful notes of a violin had wafted in from somewhere down the street, and for one disorienting moment, she had thought it was Haiwen. She was halfway out the door, her arms still laden with plates, before Sulan called out and asked her where she was going. Suchi turned to her, confused, then turned back toward the street, listening for the music. Whatever piece it had been had evaporated, replaced by a popular radio program.

In recent weeks, Mrs. Chan had begun coyly suggesting she introduce some men to Suchi or nudging her when younger, eligible boarders came to stay, but Suchi couldn't even think of it. To open herself up to other men meant accepting, on some level, that Haiwen was gone. That he was dead, or at least as good as dead.

In the year between when Haiwen had joined the army and Suchi had left for Hong Kong, no one had heard from him. She had no idea if he was alive, if he'd been killed in action or if he'd been captured by Communists once they'd won the war. The awful things she'd said to him burst through her skull whenever she imagined these terrible possibilities, loud echoes that haunted her despite her best attempts to block them from her memory. She thought back to the airplane pin, the last gift he'd ever given to her, and, not for the first time, felt a pang of regret she had not brought it with her.

Suchi climbed out of bed and retrieved Haiwen's violin from the bureau, opening the case. The strings appeared nearly translucent in the moonlight. She held the instrument in her lap as if it were a homing beacon that would lead him back to her.

She wished her body would let her forget. She wished, like Mrs. Chan, she knew how to move forward.

~

"SOUKEI MUI," MR. WONG CALLED OUT. SUCHI TURNED. She had reluctantly gotten used to the Cantonese pronunciation of her name over the last five years, though it sounded rough to her ears. Mrs. Chan and the boarders, all single men, appended *mui*—"little sister"—to it, even though she was twenty-two and old enough that she knew some of the men hoped she might entertain ideas of something more.

"Mr. Wong," she said to the jovial older man, lifting up the pitcher she was holding. "Do you need more water?"

"The congee is excellent today," he said. "Tastier than usual. Did you make it?"

"I did, in fact," she said. "Betty hasn't been feeling well since last night, so I said I'd take over the kitchen so Mrs. Chan could focus on her. But you're overpraising me. It's just water and rice, a little ginger."

"And something else," Mr. Wong prodded. "Plain congee doesn't taste nearly as good."

"Mushroom stock," Suchi said, leaning over with a mock whisper. "I used the water left over from dried mushrooms we were soaking for lunch."

"So smart!" Mr. Wong laughed appreciatively, banging the table with his palm. "Most boardinghouses serve cheap watery gruel!"

"Growing up during wartime makes you resourceful," Suchi

responded. "My mother taught me all sorts of tricks to transform the meager ingredients we had into tasty meals."

"Amazing," Mr. Wong said. He rubbed his stomach. "Would you ever consider marrying an old bachelor like me? I could use the care of a woman who can cook." Mr. Leung, the only other current boarder, was reading the newspaper next to Mr. Wong. He smirked without lifting his eyes from his reading.

Suchi laughed. She was used to the fake proposals she got from the many men who came through the boardinghouse—and played off the ones she suspected were a bit more sincere. Sulan was the one who had suggested a little friendly banter—nothing that could be mistaken for overt flirtatiousness—would put these lonely men in better spirits, which made them more likely to be courteous boarders who cleaned up after themselves and treated everyone kindly.

"Oh, Mr. Wong, I'm afraid you'd get sick of my temper rather quickly! Just ask my sister!"

Sulan was hovering at another table, wiping it down.

"Is it true?" Mr. Wong asked her in Mandarin. "Does your sister have a bad temper we have yet to see evidence of?"

Sulan gave Suchi a coy glance. "Oh, any man who can put up with my sister's temper must be a saint," she deadpanned, making the men chuckle.

After Mr. Wong and Mr. Leung left for the day, the sisters stacked the dishes and brought them to the kitchen.

"You know," Sulan said, "I know those men were joking, but . . . maybe it *is* time you considered looking for marriage prospects."

"Not you too," Suchi said, rolling her eyes.

"You're not young anymore," Sulan said. "There's a man I met, the brother of one of the Shanghainese women who visits our shop.

He was studying to be a doctor before they fled here. They live in a crowded shack in the shantytown, but if he can finish his studies here and start a practice, he'll be in good shape. And if you marry him—"

"Are you kidding me?" Suchi said. "Are you trying to marry me off to some student who lives in worse conditions than us?"

"He's Shanghainese, he'll understand you better than any of the Cantonese locals."

"If he's so great, why don't *you* marry him?"

Sulan narrowed her eyes. "I told you before, I'm never getting married."

"If you don't want to get married, why should I?"

"You're different," Sulan said. "You need—"

"I need what?" Suchi asked, her voice rising. "You think I can't be independent like you, work a decent job like you? You think I need someone to take care of me?"

"Actually, yes," Sulan said. "You've always had someone to coddle you. First Apa, then Haiwen."

"I'm not the one who has to charm everyone I meet, even dirty refugees living in sheds!"

"The only thing that separates us from those people in the shantytown is luck. It's luck we found this boardinghouse, it's luck I found a job. It's luck the money and jewelry we had weren't stolen or discovered. It's luck we left Shanghai before the Communists won the war. It's all luck! All of it!"

Suchi gritted her teeth. "Is it luck too that Apa and M'ma aren't with us? Is it luck we've lost all contact with them? I didn't know he was sending us off for good. But you did. You should have threatened not to go unless they came. Now we have no idea what's happened to them, and that's your fault."

Sulan said nothing. After a moment, she said, "I promised Apa I would look after you. But I can't look after you a whole lifetime. I know you want to be loyal to Haiwen, but—"

"Don't . . ." Suchi warned.

Sulan sighed. "If you marry someone, I'll feel better. Apa would feel better."

"Don't use me as a way to assuage your guilt," Suchi snapped.

Sulan looked stricken. For a long moment, she didn't respond. Then she said, "I'm going to work."

Suchi gathered the remaining dishes and sat out back, scouring them vigorously. Why was everyone in such a hurry to marry her off? Why couldn't people mind their own business?

When the dishes were done, Suchi washed the dirty linens and clothes the men had set aside. As she picked through the pile of shirts, pants, socks, and underwear, she mused about how far she had come from her first weeks here, when she'd been embarrassed to touch the men's intimate clothing. Now she hardly glanced at them as she scrubbed.

Her anger ebbed. Her sister was just trying to help. Suchi knew this. *You're selfish, self-absorbed.* She had caused Haiwen pain before he left and now he might be dead. She had been too excited about traveling to notice her parents' anguish and had snapped at her mother. And now she had turned her guilt onto her sister.

As she was getting ready to prepare lunch, Mrs. Chan came downstairs. Dark shadows ringed her eyes.

"Both the girls have fevers now," Mrs. Chan said. "And rashes."

Suchi clucked. "Should we call a doctor?"

Mrs. Chan shook her head. "House calls are too expensive."

"There's leftover congee," Suchi said. "Maybe eating will help?"

She ladled a bowl for Mrs. Chan to bring up to the girls. Mrs. Chan headed halfway up the stairs but turned back.

"Oh, I almost forgot," she said. "A letter from Shanghai arrived yesterday. I put it in my apron to give to the two of you, but with Betty so sick I forgot. It should still be in there."

Suchi's heart leapt.

She rummaged through Mrs. Chan's apron and pulled out the thin envelope. She was about to tear it open when she noticed the handwriting on the front. It was not Apa's. Suchi looked at the sender. *Xu Haowei.* Who was that? She looked more carefully and realized the letter was addressed only to Sulan. Could it be an old classmate of Sulan's? A boyfriend she didn't know about?

It hit her. Siau Zi, Apa's old employee, the one who'd had a crush on Sulan. She had read the characters 徐豪瑋 to herself internally in Mandarin, because it was the language she had learned to read in, but if she read them in Shanghainese, it was pronounced Zi Ghau-wei . . . Siau Zi's full name.

How had he gotten their address? Why was he writing? Something must have happened to Apa. He was sick, or injured, or—

Suchi put the envelope down. She stared out the kitchen window, into the dusty alleyway.

The naked pain on her sister's face after she had accused Sulan of causing whatever had befallen their parents lingered in Suchi's mind. She had spoken her sister's secret fear out loud. Suchi regretted her words, sorry she understood her sister so well she instinctively knew how to hurt her the most.

Suchi pulled the letter out. Another slip of paper fell and fluttered to the floor, but she scanned the letter first.

Miss Tsan Sulae,

*You might not remember me, Siau Zi, the boarder who
lived with your family for many years. It took me some time
to track down your whereabouts, but I'm happy to be back in
touch. Unfortunately, I bring bad news.*

*It seems your father has been accused of betraying his
country. It has been discovered he is the author of several
articles written during the war, criticizing the Party for its
War of Liberation and betraying its ideals. On top of that,
evidence has surfaced that his store has been a front for
an undercover publishing house for years, avoiding
regulation and taxation. Our nation's great leader is
working hard to eradicate the toxic capitalist elements that
poison the country, so this accusation is very serious. Both
your father and mother are likely to face consequences for
this deception.*

*However, as I have recently risen within the ranks of
Communist leadership, I may be able to help him. That is,
of course, if I have an official reason for doing so. Miss Tsan,
if you come back to Shanghai and marry me, I will vouch for
him as my father-in-law, and make sure he and your mother
are protected from being labeled "bad elements."*

*I have enclosed a one-way ticket back to Shanghai and
the necessary entry visas. I await your return.*

Sincerely,
Comrade Zi Ghauwei

Suchi stared at the paper in shock, then growing fury. Behind the letter was a visa document. She picked up the paper that had fallen to the floor—a single train ticket. How dare Siau Zi? After all her father had done for him—taken him in as an apprentice, given him a place to live. How could he use Apa's life as a bargaining chip to fulfill his own lovesickness?

Her fury was slowly replaced by the horror that at that very moment, her poor proud Apa might have been suffering. She glanced at the date of the letter, over two months old. Where was Apa now? Had he been thrown in prison? Was he in a labor camp? She had heard stories about rich people being shamed, beaten, their heads shaved and oil poured on them. But her father wasn't rich. He was a regular man who loved his country. Surely those who interrogated him would see that? Her father had always insisted country was before party, that what mattered were everyday Chinese people. Wasn't that what the Communists also believed? If they talked to him, they would know he wasn't against them, he was with them, and had always been.

Suchi shoved the envelope and its contents into her apron. She couldn't tell Sulan, not yet. She had to consider how to present the information to her. Or perhaps Suchi could write Siau Zi herself and beg him to help. She could lie and say Sulan was too sick to make the trip back, but entreat with him on the basis of the years they had lived together under one roof. She was sorry now that she had played so many practical jokes on him, that she hadn't been kinder.

Suchi passed the rest of the day in a haze, relieved that Mrs. Chan was preoccupied with the girls.

In the evening, while Suchi was serving a simple dinner for Mr. Leung and Mr. Wong, Sulan came home, looking tired and sullen. Suchi wanted to apologize, but somehow, the words stuck to her mouth. She fingered the envelope in her apron. As Suchi pondered how to tell her sister about the letter, Mrs. Chan came running down the stairs.

"I think something's wrong," she said, her expression frantic. "Betty is making funny sounds. Her breathing is strange." Suchi ran upstairs, with the men behind her. She hesitated for only a moment before crossing the threshold into Mrs. Chan's room. The girls were lying side by side on the pallet, their limbs tangled in damp sheets. Betty was making a gurgling, wheezing sound. Suchi reached out and touched her forehead and pulled back immediately, startled by the heat. She looked over at Shirley, who was moaning quietly.

"We have to get them to a doctor," Suchi said. Mrs. Chan's face was ashen.

"Tell her I know someone," Sulan said. "The man I was telling you about earlier. He's been acting as the doctor in the shantytown. His rates will be reasonable. I can take them there." Suchi translated this for Mrs. Chan, who seemed overwhelmed. Mrs. Chan nodded. Mr. Wong and Mr. Leung offered to carry the girls.

Suchi felt helpless as she watched them disappear down the street. The shantytown was sprawling; she didn't know how long it would take to get there on foot or if it was well lit at night.

The girls had to be all right. She thought about their giggles, high and clear like bells. How Shirley, the younger, quieter one, followed Betty around the way Suchi had once followed Sulan. They had only recently sprouted into the beginnings of young womanhood, limbs elongating, baby fat dissolving, but they were still silly and bright and loved playing games with her. Suchi wasn't a religious person, but in that moment she said a quick prayer to the heavens.

Suchi kept herself busy for the next hour, wiping the tables and sweeping the floors. She collected the sweat-soaked bedsheets from Mrs. Chan's room and washed them. As she was stirring a new batch of congee, Sulan, Mr. Wong, and Mr. Leung returned.

"The doctor thinks it's measles," Sulan said, "and a serious case at that. He was able to spare a tablet of aspirin for the two girls to split between them. The fevers came down a bit right before we left. The doctor wants to watch them overnight. He's worried Betty has contracted pneumonia."

"What can we do?" Suchi asked, and then remembered the money.

At first, despite Apa's silence, they had continued sending packages, on the off chance he was receiving them. But word got out that the particular courier they'd been using had been reselling package contents on the black market and keeping the cash for himself. So the girls began putting aside the money to one day buy passage for Apa and M'ma once they got back in touch. But now.

"Can we go to a pharmacy and get medication? Could that help?"

Sulan hesitated for only a moment, understanding what Suchi meant to do, before she nodded in agreement.

The nearest pharmacy was twenty blocks away. It was closed when Suchi and Mr. Wong got there, but Mr. Wong rang the doorbell over and over until someone answered the side door. After explaining that they needed medication for measles and pneumonia, the pharmacist gave them two glass bottles, aspirin and penicillin. Suchi paid for the pills, peeling off months of Sulan's salary. She thought of the girls' smiles, the way their eyes turned into half-moons when they laughed, and she felt nothing had ever been more worth it.

Mr. Wong took her into the shantytown. Trash littered the pathway and there was a smell—of rot and damp and too many sweating bodies. People squatted outside cooking dinner over small charcoal stoves. Oil lanterns flickered in the darkness, some strung between poles overhead. The residents with their drawn faces, the messily constructed abodes—all of it made her want to avert her eyes. She wondered how many of these people were like her, folks who had previously lived a middle-class existence, who could never have fathomed living in conditions like this.

The shack the doctor and his sister lived in was crowded on every side by precarious lean-tos and piles of refuse. Mrs. Chan jumped up quickly when she saw Suchi and Mr. Wong. When she heard they'd brought medicine, she started crying.

"It's nothing," Suchi said, struggling to contain her own tears. She sat by the girls, brushing the hair from their sticky foreheads. They weren't as hot as before but seemed so pale and fragile, all the brightness gone from them. Worry pinched her throat. "Will they be okay?" she asked the doctor.

"The medications you brought will help greatly," he responded, surprising her by using Shanghainese. "We just have to get through this night. But I promise I'm doing everything I can." He had a nice face, she thought, open and kind. Perhaps, when this was all over, Suchi would get to know him after all.

"Do you want me to stay with you?" she asked Mrs. Chan, who shook her head.

"Go home and rest," she said. She smiled weakly. "You've already done enough."

"I'll be back tomorrow," Suchi promised.

SUCHI SNAPPED AWAKE IN THE DARK, DISORIENTED. Something pulsed heavy and strange in the atmosphere. What time was it? She fumbled, trying to understand what had woken her.

The moment she stepped outside, she was hit with the wrongness of the air. It was alive with a high chatter that seemed windborne, like thousands of leaves falling. And the smell—

She lifted her eyes and saw the orange glow on the horizon.

Sulan was next to her, asking, "What's going on?" but Suchi was already running. Her heart was pounding with her pace, with the shrieks of alarms careening in the distance. *Please*, she thought.

She saw the catastrophe before she reached the edge of the hill. The shantytown was on fire, blazing in breathtaking destruction. She gaped. People were screaming, running, clutching things as they fled. Roofs caved in, sparks tumbling with them.

"Mrs. Chan," she breathed.

"Oh my god," Sulan said. "Oh my god." By then, Mr. Wong and Mr. Leung were also beside them.

She took one step forward, then another, then another. The fire roared, its heat licking at her skin even from this distance. She had to get to the girls, to Mrs. Chan, she had to—

A hand wrenched her back. "You can't," Mr. Wong said.

She wrested free. "We have to get the girls, Mrs. Chan can't carry them both!"

She glanced at Sulan for backup, but Sulan was staring dazedly at the blazing fire, her face pale and slack.

"The firefighters and police are already here," Mr. Wong said. "Let them do their jobs."

"If you go in there, the firefighters have to save you too," Mr. Leung added.

"I'm going," she said, turning away. "I can't do nothing."

"Susu!" Sulan's call was strangled, anguished. Suchi turned. Her sister's eyes were staring at her, pleading, glossy, full of fear. Suchi saw, suddenly, what it must have cost her all these years to act the big sister, to be the rock for Suchi. If something were to happen to her, Sulan would be all alone.

A cacophony of collapsing metal and wood shattered her thoughts. "Get back, get back!" bystanders shouted. A wave of acrid smoke hit their noses and they buried their faces into their sleeves, coughing.

"There's nothing we can do," Mr. Wong said gently, pulling on Suchi's elbow. "The best thing is to go back and wait."

The fire was put out nearly six hours later, close to dawn, by which time everything had burned to the ground. A plume of gray smoke floated over the whole smoldering area. The trees were dusted white with ash, as if Hong Kong had experienced its first snowfall in history. By afternoon, residents had begun migrating back, picking through the ruins for any possessions that might have survived. But Mrs. Chan and the girls did not come home.

Mrs. Chan's landlord gave the sisters one week to move out. They wept as they packed their things. "This is all my fault," Sulan murmured. Suchi hid Siau Zi's letter inside a small tear in the lining of Haiwen's violin case. She promised herself she would tell her sister about it eventually, once they were in a better place.

DECEMBER 1981
New York City

T HE SNOWFLAKES WERE powdery nickels planting themselves on the taxi window. In the front seat, the cabbie honked his horn and cursed. "Come on! What, a little snow and suddenly nobody in this city knows how to drive no more?"

Howard was going to be late to his meeting with the designers. Their offices were down at a studio on the Lower East Side, and he was still on Thirty-Fifth Street, crawling through traffic lights.

He'd forgotten what a marvel snow was. It never snowed in Southern California, his home for the last five years. He had not seen snow since the war, when the army had been marching in northern China. It had piled up without end then, white and loveless, a cruel punishment. His toes, his fingers, his ears, his nose—they became so suffused with chill they felt on fire. One night after a particularly bloody battle, after he'd written Suchi yet another remorseful letter that he wasn't sure she would receive, he had been staring at her picture, heartsick and homesick, and had foolishly fallen asleep without properly insulating his bedroll. He'd awoken half a day later in the infirmary, and after frantically searching, was immediately engulfed by regret that he had lost the photograph somewhere in the snow. But he was lucky to be alive, they said, lucky the photo was all he had lost.

He didn't want to dwell on that now. He was inside, warm, safe. From the haven of the taxi, he could appreciate the beauty of the snowflake, its miniature geometry. Like much in this world, what was beauty and what was torment depended upon the context.

Thirty minutes later, he emerged from the cab. The wind was biting, its teeth cutting into the exposed skin of his cheeks and neck. He hurried inside the run-down building and into an elevator.

Howard stepped out on the fifth floor into a spacious, open loft lit only by tall windows on facing sides of the room. It was a mess— bins overflowing with spools of thread and fabric were stacked next to long worktables where sewing machines sat. Metal racks bursting with colorful clothes—some finished, some not—pressed against the room's wooden beams. An army of headless, armless dress forms lined one window, half of them naked. Yet Howard saw no signs of any actual, living humans.

"Excuse me?" he called out in English. "Hello?"

Somewhere, from behind a pile of purple fabric, a petite Asian woman popped into view. Her hair was permed and piled high on her head, and her eyes were framed by bright blue eye shadow. From her ears dangled lime earrings in the shape of seashells. She wore a fuzzy, oversized eggplant-colored sweater, its left side slipping off and revealing a bare shoulder. At first, he thought she was very young, in her late twenties or early thirties perhaps, but as she approached him, he realized from the crows' feet in her smile she was older, around her midforties.

"Hello! We weren't sure you were still coming, what with the storm and all." The woman gestured at the windows, where the snow was swirling in view. She had no discernible accent.

"I'm sorry I'm so late," he said. "I'm from Yong Yuan Fabrics. My name is Howard Wang."

"I'm Momo Yamamoto," the woman said, inclining her head. "Welcome to Peach and Orchid. My partner should be here soon— she went to run an errand." She glanced around. "I'm sorry it's such a mess. We only moved here a few months ago and we haven't fully unpacked."

"No problem," he said. *No problem* was one of his favorite English phrases. It disarmed sticky situations, offered a measure of vagueness when he did not want to lie but knew better than to tell the truth. It was a phrase that meant many things and yet also nothing.

"Did you bring the samples?"

Howard held up his briefcase.

"Great," Momo said. She led them to a table by the window. He pulled a folder from his bag. Inside, stapled on poster board, were squares of different dyed denim, from indigo so dark it was nearly black to the palest powder blue.

"I know you are mainly interested in our denim," he said. "These are all factory-made with our high-quality yarn. One hundred percent cotton. Most is made with synthetic dyes, but this and this"—he pointed to two vibrant panels—"is dyed to order with local Taiwanese plants."

Momo fingered each panel, lifting them to inspect their much lighter back sides. "Yes, we're specifically interested in the denim dyed using traditional natural methods," she said. "Our whole spring collection will center on elements of Asian cultures." She studied the two Howard had highlighted and pointed at the one on the right. It had a special weave where the weft, a bright light blue, was thicker than the warp, which included two shades of blue, a dark indigo and a more royal blue, resulting in a slight checkerlike pattern that gave off a complex texture from afar. "I like this one. But with the non-synthetic dyes, will you be able to provide us with bulk quantities in a short turnaround?"

"It's doable," Howard said, and began laying out the possibilities.

A dull clang rang through the warehouse, followed by the sound of the elevator door opening. "The snow falls so much!" a woman's thickly accented voice said, slightly breathless.

"We're back here," Momo called out.

The woman came into view, limping as she leaned a brown wooden cane against a table. She paused to unknot a chunky gray knit scarf from around her head. It was dotted with melting flakes, as was her silvery hair. When her face emerged from the mound of yarn, he saw her nose and cheeks were red from the cold.

"Hello," he said, rising and holding out his hand as she came toward him. Her steps were slow and deliberate, her feet dragging slightly now that she no longer had the aid of a cane. "Howard Wang, Yong Yuan Fabrics."

"So sorry to be late," the woman said. Her fingers were icy and slight in his palm, but she smiled at him warmly. "Sulan Chang."

A shock ran through him. He knew many Chinese had their last names romanized in strange ways when they immigrated to the United States. Zhu became Chu, Jian became Chien, Guan became Kwan, and Zhang became Chang. Could this be the Sulan he had known? He hadn't seen her since she was nineteen, and at the time she had been a slim beauty with milky skin. The woman in front of him was carefully made up and the jewelry she wore accentuated her simple black tunic sweater, but lines creased her angular face and silver streaked her hair.

The woman looked at him uncertainly and gently tugged on her hand. He realized he had been holding on to it for a beat too long and hurriedly released it, mumbling apologies.

"Su-chan," Momo said, waving her over, "come look at this denim. It would work wonderfully with some of your designs, especially that jacket you sketched the other day."

Sulan sat down in a chair close to Momo. She and Momo discussed which denim might work for their plans and requested samples of several other fabrics the company manufactured. They asked some questions, which Howard did his best to answer, but he had difficulty focusing. He was studying Sulan Chang, trying to make up his mind about whether she was the Sulan he had grown up with. At certain angles, she definitely resembled Suchi's sister, but her fragility made him doubt himself. He couldn't imagine this to be the Sulan he'd known.

"I think we're leaning toward 312F," Momo said. "But we'll discuss and call your office if we want to put in an order. Does that work?"

Howard nodded, a bit guilty he had not done a thorough job at making his sales pitch today but grateful they seemed to be interested anyway. He rose from the chair, and so did the two women, though Howard noticed Sulan rose with much more difficulty. He put away the sample portfolios and shook Momo's hand, then Sulan's. He was about to turn around but decided, *What the hell.*

"By any chance, are you from Shanghai?"

Sulan frowned, but Momo clapped a palm over her mouth. "How did you guess?" she asked, delighted. "Are you Shanghainese too?"

"I am," he said, watching Sulan. He switched to Shanghainese. "Did you live in Sifo Li?"

An emotion tugged at Sulan's lips. Was she about to smile or grimace?

"I grew up there." He paused, waiting for her to respond. When she didn't, he added, "Waong Haeven."

"My god." She dropped back into the chair. Momo looked from Sulan to Howard and then rushed over to Sulan, placing her hands on the back of Sulan's neck.

"Su-chan," she said in a hushed, intimate tone. "Daijobu? Do you need something?"

Sulan shook her head. She closed her eyes and pressed a hand to her forehead. A moment later, she opened her eyes. "Wang Haiwen," she said, switching to Mandarin, and while it was strong and clear, so different from her halting English, it was less intimate than Shanghainese. "I can't believe it's you. You're alive?" He parted his lips to speak—he had so many questions!—but Sulan continued, a tinge of hostility creeping into her voice. "How can you be alive?"

Howard closed his mouth.

"After all this time . . . I can't believe . . ." Sulan sputtered. "Do you know how much my sister has suffered? Did it ever occur to you?"

Regret, contrition, guilt—they rose to the surface from the deep place they'd lived all these decades. He thought back to the last time he saw Suchi, in Hong Kong, all the things left unsaid between them. He thought even further back, to the way he had left her in Shanghai. He felt a pang of longing. "Sulan, I—"

"I don't want to hear it," she said, cutting him off.

Howard fell silent. After a moment, he asked, "At least, can you tell me how she is?"

"She's married. Has a son. A wonderful boy. Smart, sweet, good-looking."

Although he'd expected she was married—was, of course, *glad* to hear this—he felt a twinge in his chest. "That's great," he responded, hoping he sounded neutral. "Is she—" He hesitated. "Is she in New York as well?"

She shook her head. "She's in Hong Kong."

He nodded. So she was still there. "And you're in New York, running your own label."

Sulan pursed her lips. "Susu wanted at least one of us to pursue our dreams," she said. "She helped make this happen."

"So Suchi's singing—"

"What singing?" laughed Sulan. An ugly sound. "She has a husband to please. A son to raise. Not like me. I'm a spinster no man will love." She said the last sentence in English and glanced over at Momo, who kept a worried hand on Sulan's shoulder. At hearing a phrase she understood, she smiled at Sulan.

The animosity that rose off Sulan pained him. He yearned to learn more about how Suchi was doing, about the lives they'd led in

Hong Kong, but he realized their childhood familiarity gained him no mileage.

"I wish—"

"It doesn't matter what you wish," she said. "None of it matters anymore."

He couldn't blame her.

She exhaled heavily. "I wish you didn't tell me who you are." She'd switched back to English. "I like your company's product. But. I don't think I feel good working with you. Too many bad memories. Maybe you ask them to send someone else."

"Okay," he said quietly, his stomach clenching. "No problem."

"Please go," she added in Mandarin.

He nodded dumbly, hefting the briefcase containing all the samples. "I'm sorry," he said, turning toward the elevator.

"Goodbye!" Momo called out, false cheer in her voice. "Thank you!"

～～

HOWARD FINISHED A SECOND GLASS OF WHISKEY AT THE Irish pub across from the middling Manhattan hotel he was staying at. He glanced at his watch. Linyee would be getting ready to play mahjong with her friends for the evening, and he could still catch her for a quick phone call before she left the house. He wondered if he should tell her about running into a childhood friend from Shanghai. He could imagine her delight. *What a wonderful coincidence!* she would say.

When he entered the hotel's automatic doors, he stopped in his tracks. Sulan was seated in the cramped lobby with her cane across her lap. She rose stiffly when she saw him.

"I hope you don't mind. I—I called your assistant and said you had forgotten something. She told me where you were staying," she said. "Do you have a moment to talk?"

He took a seat across from her.

"I'm sorry about how I reacted earlier," she said, though she did not sound contrite. "You took me by surprise."

"No problem," he said in English, then switched to Mandarin. "I understand."

"No," she said, "you don't. I was very angry at you, for a long time, for breaking her heart, but our situation wasn't your fault, I know that. That's just the way things were back then. We had no control over anything."

Howard nodded, less out of agreement and more to show her he was listening.

"But Suchi . . . She's been unlucky. Part of that is because of me." Sulan rubbed at her leg, as if trying to rub out an invisible spot, and he wondered what kind of injury she had that she needed a cane already.

She stopped rubbing and looked up at him. "She's never forgotten you. I know she hasn't. She never says anything, she never talks about the past, but I know you live somewhere in her secret heart."

He thought about that night, about the note she'd left him. "But she's married."

"It's an unhappy marriage," she replied.

He said nothing.

"Tell me, honestly, do you ever think about her?" She studied him, her eyes flickering from one side of his face to the other. "You must," she added before he could respond. She began to rub her leg again. "You know, Suchi has done so much for me over the years. I'm the older sister, and yet she has had to take care of me. Now it's my turn to protect her, but I don't know how, I don't know if I can. But you appearing like this. Perhaps this is the heavens' way of giving me an opportunity to help her for a change."

"I don't understand," Howard said.

"When we were young, I used to envy the two of you," Sulan said, as if she hadn't heard him. "You were so in love, and everything seemed predestined. You would be a violinist and my sister would run Apa's store or be a singer or a stewardess or whatever it was she wanted to do. You would travel the world together. You would have children and be happy. I was jealous of how easy it appeared for you two, how perfect. And in another time, maybe that's how it would have turned out."

Sulan drew an envelope from her pocket. "I was going to leave this for you at the front desk, but I thought it would be better if I gave it to you myself."

She held it out to Howard. Its contents were light and thin, almost as if nothing were inside.

"It's Suchi's phone number in Hong Kong," she said. "Her husband is often gone during the weekdays—nights too, but that's more unpredictable—so your evening is best."

What was Sulan talking about? "I really don't understand," he repeated.

"My brother-in-law is . . . unkind," she said. "He's unfaithful, impatient, and has a pride you only disrespect if you want to see his terrible temper." She paused. "Like I said, my sister has suffered."

Her words landed heavy and bright as a knife.

"I've told her to leave him. She has excuses—her son, her responsibilities, her lack of financial resources—but I think she's afraid." Her eyes were glittering but hard.

"Maybe she still loves him," he said, struggling to make sense of what Sulan was saying. He thought of the troubles his own marriage had once suffered. If Linyee had had a sister who had counseled her to leave back then, would she have listened? He had once heard no one fully understood a marriage but the two people in it. Perhaps there was something Sulan could not see.

She shook her head. "If you called her, if she knew you were waiting on the other side . . ."

"But I'm already—" he started to say, but stopped. The word *suffered* echoed tinny in his ear.

"You once loved my sister more than anyone. If you still love her, even a little bit, please call her. She needs you." Sulan paused. "It's not too late, you know. The two of you—you still have a chance."

Howard smoothed the envelope in his grip. He cleared his throat. "Thank you," he said.

Sulan nodded. With some difficulty, she stood, bundling her jacket around her slight frame. "Please," she said, before slipping back out into the snowy night.

~

HOWARD UNLOCKED THE DOOR AND WENT INTO HIS room, taking off his wet coat and shoes. He put the envelope on the narrow writing desk. He imagined opening it, dialing the number on the paper inside, imagined the surprise and relief palpable in Suchi's voice. He imagined her anxious expression at airport arrivals as she scanned for him in the crowd, the beauty of her smile when she found him. He fantasized about her thigh, warm against his in the taxi. And later: The tremble of her breath. The softness of her skin. The curve of her body nestled against his.

He would make her a promise—he would protect her, let no one ever hurt her again. They would start a life together. In New York, if she wanted. Or California.

The thought of California stopped his fantasy. Linyee.

His wife picked up on the third ring. "I'm almost out the door!" she said, her voice bright. "You nearly missed me!"

"I'm sorry," he said. "I got caught up."

"How did the meeting go? Does it seem they'll sign on?"

He hesitated. "Some of the specialty denim excited them," he responded. "But I'm not sure what will happen."

"Mm," she said. He heard the faucet being turned on and off and pictured her hands shaking away droplets, could hear the faint clink of her jade bracelet knocking against her watch. "I saw on the news it's snowing in New York. Did you bring warm enough clothes?"

"It's a bit chilly," he admitted, "but nothing to worry about. I'm mostly in taxis, anyway."

"Don't catch a cold! You're getting older you know, not young and spry like me."

He smiled. She loved to tease him about their six-year age gap as if it were decades.

"By the way," she said, "I finally took your violin in for repairs. It should be ready by the time you come home." She laughed. "Before you say I shouldn't have troubled myself, that you'd have done it yourself, let me just remind you you've been saying that for months. I miss hearing you play."

Howard was surprised, then moved. He hadn't realized Linyee had been listening to his idle playing with any attention. He had worried it irritated her, because she never said anything, never reacted.

"Thank you," he said.

"Oh! I almost forgot to tell you!" Her voice had grown quick with excitement. "So, I also asked them if it was possible to patch up the lining in your case because it was all torn, and the man was feeling around the edges and discovered a gold ring lodged in a crack in the paneling."

The breath knocked out of his lungs. Had it been there this whole time?

Linyee continued, her words amber with marvel. "Isn't that remarkable? I wonder who it belonged to."

When he'd returned from Hong Kong with the violin all those years ago, Linyee had assumed he'd purchased it from an antique shop or flea market, and he hadn't corrected her. Now he worried she'd want the ring, to keep it for herself, and Howard found—to his dismay—he couldn't let her have it.

"It's mine," he said, squeezing his eyes shut. "It must have fallen in."

"I've never seen you wear a gold ring before," his wife said. "It's small, a woman's size."

"Does it have a twist in it?"

"Yes!"

"It belonged to my mother. She gave it to me before I left. I thought I'd lost it. I don't know how it got there, of all places."

"What a precious object!" Linyee's voice was tender. "Good thing it's been found. Don't worry, I'll put it in your drawer."

"Thank you," he said. He was filled with both gratitude toward his wife and an acute awareness of the debt he owed her.

"I better go, or I'll be late!" she said. "Stay warm! I hope you're eating!"

He hung up the phone and squeezed his fingers against his temples, trying to calm his breathing. He could still recall the surprise of that ring against his skin when his mother had pressed it into his palm, intended for Suchi. The weight of what she'd told him. *More than ever, we need to keep our loved ones close.*

Howard walked over to the desk and picked the envelope up. The words Sulan had used rang in his ears. *Temper. Unkind. Suffered. Please.* He rubbed his thumb over the paper's surface, feeling the slight raise of the sheet inside. He tried to picture Suchi's face, her sad eyes, but all that came to mind was Linyee, the brightness she carried with her, a brightness that had brought him out of a loneliness he'd thought would consume the rest of his life, that had pulled them through the worst times, a light he had once threatened to dim. Could he really do it? Break her?

Once, during some of their more troubled years, Linyee had accused him of living too much in the past. "You don't know how to see what's in front of you," she said, "you don't know how to let go."

Suchi had been a memory that sometimes felt realer than reality, a path not taken, a regret he couldn't reconcile. Now she was *actually* real. He could breathe her back into his world with one phone call. Briefly, he indulged again in the fantasy—her voice, the airport, the warmth of her body. The life beyond. This he could not get past.

Because he knew the life beyond could not conform to a fantasy. It would be messy, it would be hurtful. He could not right Suchi's life without leaving Linyee's in shambles. He owed a debt no matter which way he turned.

Howard ripped the envelope into fourths, then into progressively smaller pieces. When the shreds were too numerous for him to continue, he cupped them and carried them to the toilet. He watched them swirl away. He would appreciate what was in front of him. His children. His wife.

FEBRUARY–AUGUST 1965
Hong Kong

THE EXTERIOR OF the club was shabby, its windows blacked out and its awning streaked where polluted rainwater had continuously dripped from the barred windows above. An electric sign, unlit in daytime, dimly indicated the nightclub's name, first in Chinese—百樂門[12]—and then below, in English, Gate of a Hundred Delights.

Suchi hesitated. She could still turn back, she thought. Instead, she stiffened her shoulders and pulled open the door.

The interior was nicer than she'd expected. Mirrors lined the back wall, giving the room the appearance of being more spacious than it was. Small round tables crowded the center, with several booths around the perimeter. Up front were a modest stage, two microphones, and behind them, a set piece that looked like a giant fan. The space was bright, all of its lights exuding a bluish hue, but Suchi imagined at nighttime, these lights were dimmed in favor of the sconces dotted around the wood-paneled walls and the single presiding crystal chandelier. The club smacked of a lost time period, or at least was trying hard to approximate one.

She called out hesitantly in Cantonese. "Hello? Anyone here? I'm looking for Mr. Fong."

A brawny man with a shaved head and wearing a blue dress shirt appeared from some back room. A toothpick hung from the right corner of his thin lips. He looked her up and down. "You're here for a job," he said.

Suchi nodded. "My name is Cheung Soukei. Lo Fai told me you're hiring more waitresses."

"Fai's a good girl," Mr. Fong said, grunting in approval. He gave Suchi a once-over again. "How do you know her?"

"She's my roommate," Suchi said. Fai was one of four other girls Sulan and Suchi had moved in with three years prior. She was loud and nosy, and when she'd overheard Suchi whispering to Sulan about how she was worried about making enough money this month to pay the rent, she'd poked her head around the sheet they'd hung to divide their bunks from the others and told them Baak Lok Mun, the club she worked for, was hiring. "It's better than the brothels and opium dens around here," she said, gesturing. She meant the seedy locales of Kowloon's Walled City, places everyone knew were owned by the triads, the organized gangs of Hong Kong. "It's on the Hong Kong side, owned by a legitimate businessman."

Suchi had resisted at first. She had been washing laundry for Mrs. Kwok for the last year, with Sulan joining her when she'd had to stop tailoring due to her worsening eyesight. While it hadn't been much money, it had covered the essentials. But ever since the reports about the famine and classicides in China had begun rolling in, Sulan had begged off work more and more, saying she felt dizzy and unwell. She stopped eating as much and spent most of her time rolled up in her covers in bed, claiming a headache that never fully went away. To make up for her sister's illness, Suchi took on her share of washing, and often by the end of the night, her fingers were blistered and bleeding, her tender skin sloughed off by water and bleach and detergent. Even then, Suchi could not do the work of two, and Mrs. Kwok, who paid them by the kilo, pursed her lips while doling out thinner wads of bills.

The amount Fai said the bar girls made in a single night was what Suchi made in a week. "Especially if one of the men likes you," Fai said. "They'll throw cash at you to show their affection."

Suchi didn't ask if the women were expected to sleep with these men who tossed bills so carelessly. But Fai told her anyway. "Some women do *those* kinds of favors for the guests—I never have, of course—but I hear you can make a lot of money this way. Who knows, some rich man might take you for a 'little wife,' put you in a nice apartment up in the Peak."

At first, Suchi had been too prideful. She imagined her father's disappointment if he knew she was even considering such an indecent job. But two weeks later she'd nearly drowned after falling asleep and tipping into the tub. She asked Fai for the club's address.

Now she fought the urge to screw up her face in disgust as Mr. Fong drew nearer to her.

"Have you ever waitressed?" he asked.

"I worked briefly at a banquet restaurant several years ago," she said. It had been a happy time; she'd made good money at the restaurant, a relatively high-class establishment. Sulan, meanwhile, had worked as an assistant to a well-regarded tailor and garnered a loyal following from several customers who liked her handiwork. At one point, the sisters had saved enough money that they'd begun to dream of opening their own shop—Suchi would run the business end of things and Sulan, of course, would design and make the clothes. But then they'd had a rough winter: they took turns lying in bed with flu, stomach virus, and bronchitis in succession and by the time Suchi recovered, their savings had been spent through and Suchi's boss had replaced her. Despite her experience, she couldn't find another position that paid quite as well. Sulan, never fully recovering from the illnesses, was unable to return to work at her previous capacity, and the two found themselves suddenly unable to afford the small room they shared. That was when they had moved in with Fai and the other girls, and, after two years working at three different noodle stands, Suchi began working for the laundress.

"Your Cantonese is not bad for a mainlander," Mr. Fong said. "Let me guess. Chongqing? Hangzhou?"

"Shanghai," she said, and he nodded.

"You're prettier than those country girls." He pantomimed running a hand along the curves of her body. "All city style."

Suchi said nothing as he circled around her, sucking on the toothpick.

"You're a little old though," he said. "How old are you?"

"Twenty-nine," she lied. She was coming up on thirty-four, but people had often remarked she looked young for her age.

Mr. Fong frowned.

"Look," he finally said, "this job is nothing like working at a restaurant. Our guests are lonely men who are willing to part with their money in order to not feel lonely. The job is about being intuitive to their needs. Lighting their imagination. Keeping them happy. Get it?" Suchi nodded. "Whatever you do, own it. It's okay if you drop a drink, just make sure to fawn over them as you clean up your mess. If you feel offended by something they say, feel free to reprimand them, but do it while batting those pretty eyelashes of yours. Understand?"

"Yes," she said. A dull feeling spread through her as a small voice urged her to leave. There were other jobs, other ways to make money besides spending her days stroking the egos of little men.

"Sometimes a customer might want you to dance with them, which you should, for one song, no more, unless he offers to pay for the time you should be working tables. Otherwise, tell him we have taxi dancers for that pleasure." He waited for Suchi's reaction. She nodded. "Now, we don't force any of our girls to, uh, have relations with the guests. But if some handsome young man catches your eye"—Mr. Fong winked at her, making her stomach churn—"we can arrange for it to happen in a safe place." He smiled then, and she saw his teeth, though yellow, were perfectly straight. She imagined that in his younger days, he might have been a good-looking boy. "We want to make sure you're protected, of course, and that you get paid what you're worth."

Suchi knew his real motivation: he wanted to ensure he got a cut of any money that changed hands. A wave of nausea passed through her, and for a second she thought she might throw up this morning's congee on the man's shiny shoes. But she took a deep breath and the moment passed.

"You'll receive fifty-five dollars a week," Mr. Fong continued, "not counting tips." He smiled at her again. "Unlike other clubs, we're generous here. We let you keep your own tips. It encourages you girls to work hard."

She did a quick calculation. Between her and Sulan, they had barely been able to scrape together a hundred dollars a month. She hated it, but the fact of the matter was, this job would make it easier for both of them. It would only be temporary. Just enough so she could take her sister to the doctor, get her the medications she needed, and nurse her back to health. Once Sulan could work again, they wouldn't need this anymore.

Mr. Fong was scrutinizing her, brow furrowed. "Well?" he demanded. "If you don't want the job, there are plenty of other girls who do, believe me."

For a moment, Suchi hesitated—but then her body was moving, transforming, somehow knowing exactly what to do. From a remove, she observed her face rearrange itself into an inviting smile, her shoulders drape and tilt toward Mr. Fong, her arms languidly reach out and nearly tap him. *How quickly a body learns to adapt*, she thought, before she heard laughter, high and girlish and so unlike her, coming from her own mouth.

"Please excuse me," she heard herself say. "I was so stunned by your generosity, I forgot to respond! Of course I want the job. I'm so grateful for the opportunity."

Mr. Fong grunted. He went to the back and came out with a silver qipao—what they called a cheongsam in Hong Kong—draped over his arm. He threw it at her. It was made of cheap shiny fabric and had moth-bitten holes in the shoulders.

"You start tonight," he said. "Be back at nine."

THE WORK WAS EXHAUSTING. SHE SPENT HER FIRST evening masking her unease around the patrons, local men who were well-off enough to spend money frivolously but not wealthy or socially acceptable enough to gain entrance into the truly high-class clubs. The nights after were spent perfecting the smile and laugh she used for them, sweet enough to be attractive but not alluring enough to be memorable. Over the next few weeks, she learned to read the guests' moods and temperaments and, accordingly, shaped the sound of her voice and transformed how she held herself, whether she pouted or flirted. There were a few drunk men who solicited her, but she'd been able to disarm most of them with a laugh, teasingly slapping their hands away and distracting them with another drink. If they persisted, she led them into the arms of one of the five taxi dancers. Once in a while, Mr. Fong had to get involved, but it put him in a foul temper, and he'd withhold Suchi's tips for the evening as punishment.

But while the men sometimes leered at her as she served their drinks or pinched her ass as she walked away from their tables, they were mostly interested in the singers onstage, Angela and Lily, two young women who rotated every other night, the prized blossoms in Mr. Fong's bouquet. They wore vibrant cheongsams made of jades and scarlets and golds, with matching hairpieces. They covered Hong Kong English pop songs, old Cantonese standards, shidaiqu imported from Shanghai (including Bai Guang, whose songs still made Suchi's stomach twist), and American and British pop songs, backed by a dance band comprising four tired-looking musicians.

The first time Lily broke into the familiar melody of "Lovesick Dream," Suchi had been so startled she nearly dropped the tray she was carrying. The man she was serving looked at her oddly, but she quickly recovered. "Her voice is just so lovely, I forgot where I was!" she said, laughing that unfamiliar laugh that had now become hers.

The man smiled indulgently, patted her on the hand. "It's good you can appreciate talent," he said. Suchi had hurried to the bathroom, where she stood for five minutes, wiping away her tears.

After a month, the job became rote, numbing evenings of pretending to be someone she was not. Even the music she had once loved became background noise, though sometimes Suchi found herself humming along. She remembered, briefly, her old dream of being a singer, but when she watched how the men crowded these women after they finished onstage, she realized her father had been right: that life was just another form of prostitution.

During the day she tried to prod Sulan out of bed. She was getting worse. She rarely bathed, murmuring that it exhausted her to stand for so long under the water; other girls complained she was stinking up the room with her sour odor. She ate little, though Suchi regularly brought home treats from the club's kitchen—fried dumplings, barbecue pork, even the occasional seasoned squid.

"Zhang Sulan," she said one day, exhausted and impatient, "if you don't get up, you're going to die!"

"Well, maybe you should let me," her sister responded from beneath the covers.

"How can you say such a thing!" Suchi hissed. "What would M'ma and Apa say! After they sacrificed so much to send us here, to make sure we survived—"

"M'ma and Apa are dead," Sulan said. "It doesn't matter what they think."

Suchi pulled the covers off in one violent jerk. Sulan lay curled up on her side, motionless. Suchi thought of the letter, the one she had never shown Sulan, at first because she was too distraught and guilt-ridden after the fires, and then, as her sister became increasingly morose and withdrawn, because she didn't have the heart to put that impossible burden on her. Instead she'd responded to Siau Zi herself, saying Sulan was too sick to return to Shanghai but begging him to help Apa anyway. She could send money, she offered. She could send jewelry. She had received no response to that letter, nor any of the others she had sent in the intervening years, and the guilt of what she'd probably let happen to Apa was something she pushed deep into her belly. Now, staring at Sulan's slack, useless figure, the ugly thought came to her that she didn't know if it had been worth it, trading Apa's life for Sulan's.

THE FIRST TIME LAM SAIKEUNG WALKED IN, SUCHI TOOK no notice of him. Only when she scurried to the booth where he was sitting with two colleagues did she get the sense that he was unlike the others.

He wasn't handsome. His hairline was receding, his lips were colorless and thin, and he was pale, too pale, almost sickly. But there was a quiet confidence in the way he carried himself that morphed his features into something interesting. Suchi noticed he sat in a posture both languid and erect, his arm draped around the back of the booth with a feline gracefulness. His face was a smooth sheet of unconcern; he hardly glanced at Suchi when she took his order for a scotch and soda. He lit a cigarette and turned his attention back to his friends, who were arguing animatedly. As she turned to fill the order, he caught her eye and smirked, his eyes sliding toward his companions and back again, as if to say, *Can you believe these two?*

Suchi smiled back indulgently, the way she had practiced in the mirror, because she wasn't sure what the correct response was to his gesture.

Later, when she returned with the drinks, the man said, without glancing at her, "So you're familiar with this song."

Suchi's plastered smile faltered. She hadn't realized she'd been mouthing the lyrics to Lily's cover of Yao Lee's "Rose, Rose, I Love You" aloud.

Quickly, she regained her composure. She giggled. "Oh, I've been caught!"

"This Mandarin version isn't performed as often as the American version these days," the man said, not returning her flirtation. His attention was on Lily. "I'm surprised you know the words."

"It was popular when I was a child in Shanghai," she said without thinking. Then, realizing she had revealed too much, she added, "But of course we all know the words to the songs by now. We hear them every night."

"You're from Shanghai then," the man said, finally turning to her with interest. "Did you escape during the war or the famine?"

"The war," she answered. She was nervous at the serious turn the conversation was taking. "But who needs to talk about such depressing stuff right now? We're all here to have a good time, aren't we, gentlemen?" She appealed to the man's companions, who laughed boisterously and held up their glasses in salute as she hurried away.

For several hours, the man didn't try talking to her again. But as the night wound down, Lily already sitting offstage with a group of the club's VIPs, the man found Suchi at the bar.

"I'd like to hear more about your childhood in Shanghai," he said without preamble.

She looked up from the glass she was rinsing, confused. "What?"

"You said you grew up in Shanghai. I've never been, but I've seen pictures, movies. Isn't that what this"—he gestured at their surroundings—"is all about? Fong's obsessed with replicating 1930s Shanghai. But I'm more interested in learning about the real thing."

Was this a proposition? Suchi checked his tone for a hint of euphemism, but both his voice and face were stoic.

"I have three other tables," she said. A clumsy excuse, since most tables were empty, and the ones that weren't had drunk men draped over them. This man, however, appeared entirely sober, despite the many drinks she had brought to him during the night.

"I'll pay for your time," he said. Suchi was certain now the man was propositioning her.

She smiled brightly. "Oh, you wouldn't want to waste your money on me. I hear Angela's from Shanghai too. She performs on Tuesdays, Thursdays, and Fridays. Maybe you should see if her schedule is free."

Before he could respond, Suchi floated away from him toward the other tables, hoping the rage she felt was hidden behind her smile.

～

THE MAN CAME BACK SEVERAL MORE TIMES OVER THE next month. Each time he asked if she had time to talk; each time she deflected him. His interest in Suchi did not go unnoticed by Fai. "His name's Lam Saikeung," she told Suchi one day. It was nearly dawn; they were getting ready for bed after a long night at the club. "It's said he's recently made a lot of money through his shipping business. If he continues to rise like this, he'll become one of the wealthiest men in Hong Kong in no time."

"That's nice for him," Suchi responded, combing her hair.

Fai brushed her teeth and spat out the cloudy water. "I'm just saying, if you won't sleep with him, I might."

"I thought you didn't sleep with guests," Suchi said.

"I'm waiting for the right man."

"Right," Suchi said. She tucked her toiletry box under her arm and headed back to their bedroom.

SULAN BEGAN MOANING IN PAIN AT NIGHT. AT FIRST SU-chi thought her sister was having nightmares, but Sulan insisted the pain was real. Her back felt like there were hot pokers inside; her arms spasmed, then fell dead beside her. The other girls complained about Sulan's nightly interruptions. After about a week of this, Sulan consented to seeing a doctor.

The first doctor, an old man who laid two fingers on Sulan's wrist to take her pulse, told them she had several important meridians blocked. He slid eight slender needles into different areas on her scalp, rotating the needles vigorously as Sulan gritted her teeth.

"The block has gone away," he told them afterward. "But it's only a temporary fix for your internal imbalance. You'll have to come back twice a week for at least three months if you want to permanently rid yourself of the pain." He gave them a prescription they filled at the traditional pharmacy down the block, expensive parcels of mixed roots and herbs they brewed into a daily tea for Sulan to drink.

For the first few days, Sulan claimed she felt better. And she did appear better. She washed up every day, seemed in a better mood, had an appetite, and cleaned the room while the girls were all at work. She even began talking again about searching for their parents. But on the fourth day, Sulan was back in bed, not wanting to drink the medication the doctor had prescribed, claiming it made her nauseous. Within two days the pain came back. Suchi urged her to go back to the acupuncturist, but Sulan said she had no desire to be prodded like meat being tested for doneness. "Besides," she said, "we don't have the money for it." Suchi couldn't argue with her on that last point.

A few weeks later, Suchi convinced Sulan to see a Western-educated doctor suggested by one of the other waitresses. He was expensive, but Sulan had begun sleeping so little due to the pain that purple bruises had formed under her eyes.

The doctor, a severe-looking white man, pressed his fingers around various parts of her legs and arms, asking her where the pain was in heavily accented Mandarin. "It doesn't hurt right now," she responded like a sullen child.

He took an X-ray to make sure there were no broken bones.

In the end, he told her there was nothing wrong with her. "It's a phantom pain," he said, "probably brought about by stress. There's nothing that can be done. I suggest you rest in bed more."

Suchi felt angry, both at the doctor and at Sulan. *All she does is lie in bed!* she wanted to shout.

The bill for that visit was more expensive than the visit to the Chinese medicine doctor and the herbal medications combined. Suchi couldn't believe she had spent so much money just to have the doctor declare the pain was in her sister's imagination.

Suchi couldn't force Sulan to revisit the traditional doctor, but she began going to the pharmacy weekly, filling the doctor's prescription and handing over a sizable portion of her tips. Every night, before heading to work, she forced Sulan to sit up in bed and drink the stinking brew. Sulan did so without complaint but, immediately after, slipped back beneath the sheets.

Sometimes, after another humiliating night of men swiping at her ass, Suchi came home and stared at her sister's sleeping figure. She thought about what the British doctor had said—that the pain was phantom—and she felt the urge to drag Sulan out of bed and force her to stand up, to do something, anything. *I miss them too!* she wanted to yell. *But if I gave in to my sadness, we would both die on the streets.*

ONE NIGHT LAM SAIKEUNG CAME INTO THE CLUB ALONE. He'd been coming several times a month, sitting where he knew Suchi served. Suchi watched as he was led by the hostess to his usual booth. Before the hostess left, he leaned over and said something to her. Suchi took a deep breath, readying herself to reject Lam Saikeung's advances again. But then Mr. Fong appeared and sat down next to Mr. Lam. The two spoke briefly, and she saw Mr. Fong glance up at her. In the next moment, they were shaking hands and Mr. Fong was coming up to her. "Make sure to take special care of booth number three," he said, his grin extra toothy.

Clammy, cold rage flooded beneath Suchi's skin. Lam Saikeung had gone directly to Mr. Fong like he was her pimp. And now she was simply expected to serve him and do his bidding. The nerve! No job was worth this. She stomped over to the booth, not bothering to put on her friendly act, imagining snatching his cigarette from his fingers and throwing it into his face. By the time she was in front of

him, she was shaking so hard, she couldn't speak. She tried to for-
mulate her anger into words, but before she could, Mr. Lam, without
turning to look at her, gestured next to him. "Cheung Soukei, you're
here. Please sit."

"What?" she hissed. Or tried to hiss. The phrase came out more
a whisper.

"I've bought your time for the rest of the night. You don't have
to wait any tables. Just sit and talk to me."

Mutely, Suchi obeyed, berating herself for being so spineless.

"I hope you're not angry," he said. "But you're always too busy
to have a conversation, so this was the only way." He looked at her
and for the first time cracked a smile. When he smiled, his features
somehow softened and warmed. His eyes were dark and charismatic,
and she understood how he had become successful in business; his
was a face that, when turned toward you, made you feel you were the
most important person in the world.

She hardened herself against him, even as she rearranged her
face into something sweet, innocent, naïve.

"That's so thoughtful of you, Mr. Lam," she said. "I'm flattered.
But you see, it's unfair of me to leave the other girls to pick up my
slack. If I'm not working, each of them will have to carry my tables,
and yet they'll still be paid the same—" She stopped herself, for she
didn't want to badmouth her boss.

"Yes, Mr. Fong mentioned that." Mr. Lam frowned, and briefly,
the warm façade slid away. In another blink, it was back. "He's quite
the businessman, but I suppose everyone is in this era. In any case,
I've compensated the other girls' wages as well. And emphasized I
expected the money to be treated as gratuity."

Suchi tried not to let her irritation show. To be wealthy was one thing, but to throw money around so things bent to your will was another.

"You should be flattered," Mr. Lam continued, "I'm doing all this to get to know you."

"Why me?" Suchi said, and then flinched. She hadn't meant to sound demanding.

Lam Saikeung gave no appearance of noticing. "I told you. I want to hear about your childhood in Shanghai. One day we'll be able to trade freely with China again, and I'd like to know a little bit about the place from someone who lived in its crown jewel."

"Why not Angela?" she asked, more gently this time.

Lam Saikeung glanced at the stage, where the girl was currently singing "The Ding Dong Song," an English version of "The Second Spring" that was an insult to the original. Suchi thought she saw a flicker of disdain pass across his face. He took a drag from his cigarette. "I dislike fighting dogs for leftovers."

Suchi, who had hardly exchanged two words with Angela, felt defensive on her behalf. Although it was probably true Angela had slept with patrons, she had always been sweet to the rest of the girls.

"In any case," Mr. Lam said, "I want more mature company, not to babysit little girls." He tapped his cigarette against the glass ashtray and smiled, and Suchi understood that he had guessed she was older than she'd let on. "Satisfied? Do you have other questions?"

"No," she said, realizing she had already implicitly given her consent to this conversation. She had sat down, she had engaged, and now it was too late to back out. Well, she thought, it was just a conversation.

"Good," he said. "So why don't you tell me about where you grew up?"

It had been a long time since Suchi had allowed herself to reminisce; she had not wanted to become like Sulan, debilitated by painful memories. Her mind came up blank and for one panicked moment she feared that because she had squirreled the past behind a wall, the memories were inaccessible to her forever.

But no. A spark of M'ma's voice rang in her ear, and the images flooded back, flickering so rapidly, she barely had time to grab one and examine what it was. The first thing that came to her was the painted bunny by the back door of her shikumen, so she began there, providing a detailed picture of each room to Mr. Lam. From there she remembered the rest of the longtang, taking him down alleyways, introducing him to neighbors she hadn't thought of in a long time. The memories came in a steady stream now, and she moved through them, trying not to let herself dwell long enough on any one for her to grow emotional. She shared how she and Sulan used to creep up to the rooftop during the Battle of Shanghai to watch the smoke drifting from the city, how her mother sat in the alleyway on nice days to embroider tiny silk shoes. She described Apa's bookstore. She did not mention Haiwen.

Now that Lam Saikeung knew he could buy her time, he came frequently, once a week, sometimes twice. Fai, who couldn't resist passing along gossip, gleefully told Suchi the other girls resented the arrangement. "They're taking bets on how long it will be before you sleep with him, before he takes you as his 'little wife.'"

Suchi retorted she would rather slit her wrists than be anybody's mistress. Fai looked at her skeptically. "A man *never* just wants conversation, you know." Suchi secretly worried about the same. But over the weeks, she cautiously let some of her anxiety go. Mr. Lam was always respectful; he never touched her and never made her feel as if she were there for any reason other than to talk to him. She began, if not to enjoy the nights talking to Lam Saikeung, to at least not dread them. It was a night when she got to be off her feet, when other men could not grab at her.

When at last Lam Saikeung tired of her stories, he began to tell her his.

His grandfather had been a merchant from Guangdong who moved his entire family to Hong Kong amid the turmoil in the late 1800s. Lam Saikeung, who was ten years older than Suchi, had grown up in a young Hong Kong, one the British were still figuring out how to govern. He was an adult by the time the Japanese came, and he remembered the terror of the battle fought on the tiny island, the subsequent chaos, brutality, and suffering.

"There wasn't enough food, not enough work," he said, "so they deported people without jobs to China. Can you imagine? Growing up your whole life here and suddenly you are thrown on a boat to a new land?" A dark look spread across his face. "They violated women, killed men. The people of Hong Kong were reduced to dogs, fighting over grains of rice, over menial work shoveling shit. It was a terrible time."

By the time the Japanese were defeated and kicked out, Lam Saikeung was twenty-five and had been keeping himself, his mother, and his sister alive by trading through the black market. He was good at making friends, at convincing people to do favors for him, at charming rice and oil from greedy merchants and gold and jewelry from desperate taaitaai. "I always prefer to do things the nice way," he said offhandedly, and Suchi heard the implication. While others went hungry, Lam Saikeung's family always had full bellies. Once the British reasserted their control of the island, and with the new war brewing in the north, Lam Saikeung began to export commodities to Guangdong and beyond, until, a few years after the Communists had won, he decided the risk was no longer worth taking. Instead, he bought a ship and decided to go straight. In the last fifteen years, he had steadily become one of the largest importers of goods from Europe and was now poised to capitalize on Hong Kong's growing textile industry.

"A lot of these textile men originally came from Shanghai, like you," he said, and Suchi finally understood. He was a man whose success was built upon his ability to create the illusion of intimacy.

His dream, he told her one night, was to have a fleet of over a hundred ships, to have his name emblazoned across the seas.

She told him she was sure it would happen for him.

"What about you?" he asked.

The question startled her.

"Surely this isn't your dream," Mr. Lam added, a rare teasing tone in his voice.

Haiwen flared across her memory like a sudden off-key note. She thought of the things she once longed for, fantasies that had come true: She had traveled, she had seen something other than her longtang, she was in Hong Kong hobnobbing among singers and well-to-do men. But the reality was nothing at all like what she had imagined. Now what she wanted most was impossible—her family, Haiwen, the comfort of home. All her dreams lay in the past.

"I used to want to be a singer," she offered. "When I was younger, I would stand on a rock in my friend's courtyard and practice songs I heard on the radio."

"Ah, well, you're in the right place for that," Mr. Lam said.

Suchi shook her head. "I'm happy to serve drinks." She had no desire to be Angela or Lily, no desire to be ogled by men any more than she already was.

But Lam Saikeung excused himself, leaving Suchi to sit awkwardly as the other girls walked past her and threw her dirty looks. Several minutes later, Mr. Lam was back. "Mr. Fong has agreed to let you sing on the nights that I come, provided it's early enough in the evening that Angela and Lily haven't come on yet."

Suchi felt panic rising, but Mr. Lam saw fear as weakness. She schooled herself.

"Thank you," she said demurely, casting her eyes down. "I'm grateful for the opportunity."

Mr. Lam laughed. He put a hand on her knee, the first time he had ever touched her, and it took everything in her not to jerk her leg away. He patted her gently. "After all you've given me, isn't it time I gave you something back?"

～

TWO NIGHTS LATER, SUCHI TOOK THE STAGE. SHE LOOKED out into the dim room, at the smattering of guests, including, of course, Lam Saikeung, and felt she might throw up. The girls were watching and probably hoping she'd fail.

Lily had lent her a pink cheongsam embroidered with peonies, insisting she needed something flashier for the stage. She and Angela had shown her how to crimp and style her hair, had helped her to

apply makeup appropriate for the evening—skills she was embarrassed she didn't have at thirty-four.

"Don't be nervous," Angela said. "Pretend your long-lost lover
is out there in the audience sitting somewhere you can't see. Sing
to him."

But onstage, it was difficult to ignore the sound of coughing, of
men laughing loudly, of Ah Lui the bartender yelling out orders. She
shut her eyes. She tried to mute the room, to telegraph her spirit past
the boisterous men; past Lam Saikeung, who sat in his usual languid
manner in his booth; past Mr. Fong, who stood in the back with his
arms crossed. She searched beyond the nightclub, beyond the seedy
streets, beyond Hong Kong itself, and across the harbor. She searched
for a shadow of Haiwen. She knew he was out there, somewhere in
the hazy distance, on a horizon she could not make out. She pictured
him, his violin cradled between his chin and shoulder, his arm raised,
bow hovering above the strings, and was struck with a certainty: all
she had to do was sing the right notes and he would know, he would
feel she was alive, he would launch his bow upon the strings and play
with her.

She heard the band give the cue to go. A blare of horns introduced the beginning of "Lovesick Dream." Her eyes snapped open
and she began.

APRIL 1975
Taipei

HAIWEN WAS DOZING in his wicker chair after lunch, half-conscious of his girls arguing in their room. The radio was on in the background, playing some golden oldies, and he was dreaming of his mother humming the tunes under her breath as she applied makeup. He was crouched in a corner, watching her reflection in the vanity, the way she blotted her red lips on a square of rice paper, the way she primped her hair. She caught his eye in the mirror and smiled at him. *Doudou, you little mouse! What are you doing there? Are you listening to Mama singing? Are you listening? Are you listening?*

He was being shaken. "Are you listening to this? Are you?" He opened his eyes to find Linyee standing over him, her hands on his forearms. When she saw he was finally awake, she let go and gestured at the radio, shaking her head. "I can't believe it."

"What is it?" he asked, but she didn't respond. She was staring at the radio, one hand over her mouth.

He craned his neck forward, trying to make sense of the crackling announcement.

". . . with his wife and Premier Chiang Ching-kuo by his side. We mourn the loss of our fearless leader, the president of our great nation . . ."

"What is this about?" he demanded. Disbelief was pulsing at his brain, blocking him from understanding the words.

"President Chiang is dead," Linyee breathed. "He had a heart attack last night."

"Lord Chiang[13] is . . . dead?" Haiwen echoed, but Linyee was captivated by the radio broadcast, which had now launched into a statement Chiang Kai-shek had prepared a few days earlier.

". . . you should not forget our sorrow and our hope because of my death. My spirit will be always with my colleagues and my countrymen to fulfill the three people's principles, to recover the mainland and to restore our national culture . . ."

Haiwen rose abruptly. "I don't believe it."

His wife turned and stared at him. "What?"

He paced the room. "It's propaganda. It has to be. Probably to deceive the Communists. If they think Lord Chiang is dead, they'll let down their guard. It must be a trick, a new strategy."

She scrutinized him. "These last few months, there's been several reports of President Chiang being ill . . . He was almost ninety, hardly expected to be young and healthy."

Haiwen shook his head. "He can't be dead."

"But he is!" She turned the radio dial to another station, which was reporting the same statement, the same news. "See? Every station is saying the same thing."

"But the media is completely state controlled!" he said. "Of course they're all saying that. They have to make the Communists believe it!"

His wife followed him as he went into the kitchen and poured himself a glass of hot water. "Perhaps if you called some of your friends who are still in the military. Lau Fu, for instance. He'll know."

Haiwen guzzled the entire glass. The water scalded his throat as it went down. "I'm going out," he said.

He rode his scooter aimlessly for a while, passing flat rice paddies on roads he knew his comrades had helped to construct, past electrical poles he knew they had put up. Birds dotted the wires, but otherwise he saw nobody and nothing. It was only as he traveled into the heart of town that he began to see people crowding in twos and fours outside buildings, looking somber. He heard someone shout, "Chiang Kai-shek has passed away!" The news was being whispered around him, traveling through the streets like a fast-blowing wind. Without knowing where he was going, he rode on, until he found himself in front of what used to be his favorite pachinko parlor.

He stared at its shaded windows, at the barely perceptible flash of lights within. His fingers twitched. It had been quite some time since he'd come. A decade ago, shortly after his second daughter's birth, he'd been a frequent visitor, the gambling a distraction from an inexplicable emptiness that Yijun's birth had triggered. After Hong Kong, after the week he'd run into Suchi, he'd quit playing, quit any form of gambling altogether, and his marriage had been saved because of it.

He sat outside the parlor for a long time, but he did not go in.

IT WAS NEARLY DARK BY THE TIME HE PULLED UP TO Treasure Hill, a community where houses built with rocks lugged up from the riverside by the residents' own hands were dotted haphazardly across the foothills. He climbed a zigzag of uneven stone steps and alleys to Zenpo's house and saw Lau Fu loitering outside. The man had tears in his eyes. Haiwen knew that beneath his shirt he still had a Republican sun tattooed on his torso, fuzzy characters encircling its rays. *Recover the Lost Country. Exterminate Commies.* Phrases that had been etched upon all of them, visibly or not.

Haiwen put a heavy hand on his friend's shoulder. Together they rapped on their friend's door.

"Brothers!" Zenpo cried when he saw the two men standing there. Zenpo was already drunk. He teetered dangerously as he let them in. His cramped house was cluttered with empty bottles and old newspapers and had a musty, moldy smell. He led them to the round dining table. "Seems our inimitable leader has finally departed," Zenpo said, raising a glass filled with pale yellow liquor. "And with him, the hope of taking back our nation."

"Don't say that," Lau Fu said.

"Ah, Lau Fu, still the charming loyalist." Zenpo poured them each a glass. "Drink, drink."

They had come together while building officer housing in Keelung in 1955. They'd discovered they were each from the Zhejiang/Jiangsu region, and therefore each spoke some variation of Wu. In a place where so little remained of home, having this shared language, even with their regional variations, was a relief to them. For years, they'd been each other's family, despite the differences in their personalities. Once upon a time, there had been four of them: Lau Fu, the oldest, the leader. Zenpo, the crass jokester. Haiwen, the confidant. And Li Tsin. Young, tenderhearted Li Tsin. Even now, Haiwen couldn't think of the boy without sorrow washing over him.

The three men drank several more glasses in silence before Lau Fu raised his glass and said, "To President Lord Chiang Kai-shek, may you rest in peace. Rest assured we will continue your fight to win back the mainland." He wiped his eyes.

Zenpo snorted. "You don't actually think that will happen, do you? You can't believe that after all this time, it could still happen. If we couldn't win the mainland back with Chiang, what makes you think we can win without him?"

"Lord Chiang is counting on us," Lau Fu said. "Our job is to—"

"Bullshit," Zenpo said. "What military action have we taken against the mainland in recent years? Threatening flyers thrown out of a window over Fujian? Broadcasts about the great republic on some radio wave we hope their people will pick up? Covert espionage so fucking covert not a single person knows about it?"

"There are plenty of things the higher-ups know that we don't," Lau Fu said. "We have to trust they're working on a strategy."

Zenpo poured himself another and glanced at Lau Fu. "It worked out well for you, didn't it? High rank, subsidized housing, wife, kids, pension." The bitterness in Zenpo's voice surprised Haiwen. "No wonder that while the rest of us have lost hope over the years, you've grown more loyal than a dog."

"You—" Lau Fu started to rise in his chair, but Haiwen cut in.

"Come on, brother, how can you say such a thing? You know Lau Fu barely sleeps with how much work he takes on." Despite Lau

Fu's steady income from the military, he and his wife washed laundry every night to earn extra money to afford their children's tuition. During the day, his wife sold soy milk and youtiao out of a cart.

Zenpo looked at Haiwen. "That's not a problem you have though, right? Your ming is better than mine, what with your fancy Shanghai schooling. Not all of us are so fortunate as to be offered a management job in the private sector."

Haiwen was hurt and surprised by the bitterness in Zenpo's voice. He had been congratulatory when Haiwen had retired from the military in 1964 after running into a former colleague of his father's. Mr. Hsieh, who owned a textile business, remembered that Haiwen spoke some English and hired him on the spot. It had been a lucky turn of events—Linyee had just gotten pregnant with their second child, and they'd been worried about feeding four mouths on a meager military salary. Even now, when he thought of it, he felt a mix of gratitude and regret—even in his absence, his father had saved him, and yet, he was unable to be a filial son, was too far to do anything to care for him in return.

Haiwen looked into his glass. "I've asked you if you wanted me to pull some strings, I can still ask Mr. Hsieh—"

"Yeah? And what do you think your boss would say when he learns of my background?" Zenpo swallowed another shot of liquor, loudly sucking his teeth afterward. "Some of us are stupid farm kids fit only for hard labor."

Haiwen didn't know what to say. Zenpo had it the most difficult of the three of them. The fact that he had been forcibly drafted meant he'd had no chance of promotion because the military would always doubt his loyalties. Unlike Haiwen and Lau Fu, Zenpo never married, because in order to do so, he'd have to declare the pregnant wife he'd left back home dead, and he refused. With little more than a primary school education, Zenpo wasn't qualified for jobs in the private sector, so he continued to work for the army's veteran association, farming land in remote areas, building highways and tunnels. Though the pay was decent, it was often dangerous—Zenpo had seen colleagues blown to bits by dynamite while paving roads through the rocky canyons surrounding Taroko Gorge; he himself had lost the use of one of his fingers when a rock rolled down the cliff face he'd been chiseling and crushed his hand. Yet, through it all, although Zenpo constantly cursed the work and his luck and other officers, he'd never shown resentment that his lot had turned out so different from that of his friends. Until now.

Haiwen shook his head. "Brother—"

Zenpo swallowed what remained in his glass. "You know, I can't tell anymore if I'm luckier than that jerk Li Tsin, or if he had it right."

At this, Lau Fu slammed down his glass. "How can you say that! Li Tsin's death was a tragedy!"

"Tragedy, eh?" Zenpo said. His words were loud and slurred. "Isn't the official party stance that those who commit suicide are traitors?" He waved with his arm as if batting the comment away. "Forget it. I can't expect you to understand. Why would either of you want to go back when you've made such good lives for yourselves out here?"

"Of course we want to go back!" Lau Fu exploded. "Which one of us doesn't long for home? Which one of us wants to die on this foreign soil?"

"It's not foreign though, is it?" Zenpo said sarcastically. "Isn't that what you and your ilk keep reminding us? It's China. All of it is fucking China. It's just not Mao's fucking China! It's that idiot

Chiang's fucking China, and what kind of China is this? The Forbidden City is probably bigger than this whole shit-filled island!"

"Brother, I think you've drunk too much." Haiwen tried to pull away Zenpo's glass, but his friend's palm was firmly clutched around it.

"I envy Li Tsin, I really do," Zenpo said. Haiwen realized he was crying. "He was the smartest one of us all. I'm a sniveling coward compared to him." Zenpo wiped his face with his forearm, his head bobbing.

Worry settled into Haiwen's heart. He glanced at Lau Fu, hoping his friend might help him get Zenpo into bed, but Lau Fu was staring at the ground, his jaw tight. A moment later, he poured himself the remainder of the bottle, threw it back, and stood up, his chair scratching along the dirt floor.

"No, you're a treasonous coward," he said to Zenpo. "I should report you, but that would be a waste of our country's resources. You put those who gave their lives for this country to shame. You put the president to shame." He stalked out the door.

"Shame is losing a war and not being willing to admit it!" Zenpo shouted after him. "Shame is lying to your people even after your death!"

Haiwen glanced from the door to Zenpo, whose head had collapsed onto the table.

"Let me get you some water, brother," he said. "Then perhaps we can put you to bed."

Zenpo waved him off, his other hand clutching the empty glass.

"It's a hard day," Haiwen said. "It's a hard day for all of us."

"Every day is hard," Zenpo murmured. "It's just that on some days you're able to forget."

A FEW DAYS LATER, HAIWEN AND LINYEE WATCHED THE
news anchor on their black-and-white television announce that
Chiang Kai-shek's body would be moved to Sun Yat-sen Memorial
Hall, where, for one week, citizens could pay their respects before he
was escorted to Tzuhu, his favored lake retreat.

"We should go," he said. "All of us."

"What?" Linyee said. "But the lines will be incredibly long and
we both have to work."

"We have to pay our respects."

Linyee was silent for a moment. She glanced at the hallway toward the girls' room. When she spoke, her voice was low. "But what
did he ever do for you?" Though she said this calmly, Haiwen could
sense her fury. "He tore you from your family, left you stranded in
a foreign land. He's the reason you have nightmares, the reason you
cry out at night."

Haiwen shook his head. "He was my general," he said. "It's my
duty to pray for his safe passage into the next life."

Linyee looked at him askance. "I don't understand you," she
said. "All these years, even if you never said so, I know you've felt
no particular loyalty to the Nationalist cause. And why should you?
They coerced you into joining a losing war. They treated you like
nothing. Low salary, no identity card, no housing, no pension. We're
lucky they'd changed the rules about marriage when we met, or you
wouldn't even have been able to start your own family! If it wasn't
for Mr. Hsieh, you'd still be toiling away at some pitiful low-salary
job for the government and we'd still be living in that moldy dump
you built yourself in Keelung."

Haiwen balled his fists tightly. "That's beside the point."

"If you want to go, you can go," she said. "But I won't go with you."

"Why not?" All he wanted was his wife's support. Was this too much to ask?

She didn't immediately respond. Finally she said, almost in a whisper. "He's not *my* general."

Haiwen turned to stare at her, offended. "He was the last hope for millions of Chinese——"

She took a breath. "Sometimes I think you forget who I am. You married a Taiwanese woman. I'm *Taiwanese*. I didn't grow up in China, I wasn't born there. I'd never even met a person from China until you all came over. My whole life, everyone in authority, they forced us to be more like them. First the Japanese, then you lot. Demanding we change our language, our customs, our clothes, telling us this would make us more civilized, more cultured. When I was younger, I believed it too, I was so desperate to seem more educated, more cultivated. I wanted to be deserving of the storied Chinese empire my mainlander teacher kept talking about; I wanted to shed my Taiwaneseness."

"'You lot'? So what am I now, just some outsider to you?" It stung, that the suspicion and ostracization he'd experienced from locals all these years was something that his wife might share.

"Are you even listening to me?" Linyee's voice was tight.

"I heard you comparing me to the Japanese." He spat the word *Japanese*.

After a moment, Linyee said, "You know, if you ask my father, he would say that life under the Japanese wasn't that bad. They improved the public health and education systems, they built roads and spread the use of electricity. For oyster farmers like my family, these were welcome changes."

Haiwen stiffened. Whom had he married? How could she love him and say these things? "Don't you know what they have done?" he demanded. He felt sick. Forget the crimes they had committed in the mainland; in Taiwan alone, a catalog of atrocities: local women raped and kidnapped, aboriginals slaughtered, dissenters murdered.

"And don't you know what the Nationalists did? What Chiang did?" Her voice was calm, but the words pricked Haiwen nonetheless.

"Why are you with me then? Why marry me if I represent everything you and your family hate so much?" Although his relationship with his father-in-law was now civil, if not warm, Haiwen had never forgotten the early history between them: the months of tears his wife had shed after her father had disowned her, the verbal attacks he had mutely endured when they went to beg for his acceptance after Yiping was born.

"Aiya, old man, can you stop getting so defensive? You are my husband. I chose you because you are thoughtful and kind, generous and open-minded. I would choose you again; I have no regrets. I'm just saying . . . I saw the Nationalists and their entire history and the war they brought with them through rose-colored lenses because that's what I was taught to believe."

"And now?"

"Now I know better," she said. "Don't you?"

Although Linyee's voice was light and steady, her words felt like an accusation. He thought of the stories he had heard of the early years—whispered behind closed doors, trickled out after rounds of drinks—things that even now, nearly three decades later, no one dared speak openly about. The protests that ended in blood-washed streets. The intellectuals rounded up and strung together in the middle of the night, never to be seen again. The radio host who was shot and died in his ten-year-old son's arms. The young college students executed for having the wrong kinds of books. The spies, the informers, the interrogations, the baseless accusations, the forced confessions.

"You know I wasn't even in Taiwan during the *incident*," he sputtered. "I had nothing to do with—"

Linyee put her palm over his, stilling him. "I know you had no hand in those terrible things. But they were committed by the government you worked for, headed by the man you mourn for now. So while I can appreciate that for you, he was the leader of the country you still believe exists in your heart, to many of my people, he was nothing more than a dictator."

Haiwen let her words sink in. The heat ebbed from his face. He said, quietly, "He wasn't always like that, you know. When I was very young, when we were at war with the Japanese, he stood up to them, he protected us. He was our hero. He was carrying on Sun Yat-sen's dreams for China, for a republic free from the tyranny of dynastic rulers."

"Heroes are men," Linyee said. "They're corruptible. And President Chiang had been corrupt for a long time. Haven't you ever wondered how, with all the foreign support and money they had, the Nationalists were able to lose the war?"

Haiwen said nothing. What could he say?

Linyee sat with him, watching the footage of mourners on the television a while longer. Then she patted Haiwen's leg, stood up, and left the room.

HAIWEN DID NOT GO TO SUN YAT-SEN MEMORIAL HALL
to pay his respects. Instead, he watched the news report after work
every night, transfixed by the scenes of long lines, of the Generalissimo's stately portrait adorned with flowers alongside his casket, of
the older men and women weeping with such distress they had to be
lifted by their armpits and carried out. He was surprised one night
when, among the line of old soldiers, he saw Zenpo's face, grief-
stricken.

Ten days after the Generalissimo's death, Linyee announced
that, with the day off, she would go to Keelung to visit her father,
who had not been feeling well. Yiping, his older daughter, said she
planned to go into the streets and watch Lord Chiang's funeral pro-
cession with her classmates. "Don't you want to come and send him
off?" she asked when Haiwen made no move from his chair. "Aren't
you supposed to, as a former soldier?"

"You go," he told her. "I think I might be catching a cold."

"I'll stay with Ba," Yijun told her sister, and Haiwen was moved
by how mature she seemed at ten. "We'll catch the broadcast later
when they replay it on television."

Yijun ladled him a bowl of turnip and pork rib soup Linyee had
left, but he wasn't hungry. He kept staring at the television. When,
several hours later, the television leapt to life, he straightened in
his seat.

The broadcast began in the memorial hall, where a line of choir-
boys sang a mournful, angelic hymn. After the casket containing
Lord Chiang's body was closed and covered with the Republican
flag, twelve pallbearers in pale suits and black armbands lifted it onto

their square shoulders and took slow steps down the aisle. The Chiang family trailed behind, their expressions difficult to make out on the small screen. In the plaza, a brass band played Chopin's funeral march, and Haiwen thought to himself how truly hopeless the piece sounded. The casket was loaded into a funeral hearse, a truck outfitted with hundreds of white blossoms.

In another few minutes, the hearse was speeding down the very roads President Chiang's army had built, followed by a motorcade of black cars, scooters, and small vehicles bearing his portrait. Haiwen was astounded by the snaking crowd waiting to pay their last respects alongside the vehicle's route. Some people wore black armbands of mourning, others wore white paper hats or white headbands. Many held signs of memorial and tribute. Government officials, lined up in dark suits at the front, knelt and touched their heads to the ground as the hearse passed, while citizens behind them bowed deeply in respect. For the sixty kilometers of its journey, from Jenai Road in Taipei all the way up to the mountains leading up to Tzuhu, mourners accompanied the hearse.

When the hearse arrived at Tzuhu, the casket was brought out again on the pallbearers' shoulders. As the brass band restarted the somber funeral march, Haiwen was overcome by a grief so powerful, he could not contain himself. A sob bubbled up in his gut and burst through his throat. He was choking on himself, unable to stop.

Yijun, who had been sitting cross-legged on the floor beside him, looked up at him in alarm.

"Ba," she said, her eyes wide with concern. "Oh, Ba." She stood up and awkwardly patted his arm.

Haiwen didn't want his daughter to see him like this. He wiped his eyes with the back of his hand. But instead the tears rolled down faster, fat droplets mingling with snot. He was aware he was making a small, howling animal sound.

"Oh, oh, Ba, please." Yijun's eyes welled up.

She was such a good girl, his younger daughter. So sensitive, so caring. But what she could never understand, what her sister and Linyee could never understand, was this complicated grief. He didn't give a shit about Chiang Kai-shek. It was true, everything Linyee had said. It was because of President Chiang he had been forced to join the army, because of President Chiang he had seen his friends' brains blown out, because of President Chiang he'd shot and killed his fellow countrymen. It was because of President Chiang they had lost a winning war and retreated to this jungle. It was because of President Chiang he was separated from his family, from Suchi, forbidden to reach out to them. And yes, it was because of President Chiang so many locals hated him, because of President Chiang so many innocents had suffered and died for simply trying to live a just and fair existence.

But it remained that President Chiang had been his last hope—the last hope for all of them, Zenpo, Lau Fu, every last military man who had left for Taiwan not knowing they would be here for this long. Without President Chiang, there would be no reclaiming the homeland, there would be no returning to China. Without President Chiang, there would be no way to take back what was lost. Everything that had still seemed possible was now extinguished forever. Returning to Shanghai once more, sleeping in the shikumen he had grown up in, being reunited with his family. How could he explain this kind of despair? How could his family ever know what it was like to have one man, however flawed or despicable, be the only option for hope? As long as President Chiang had lived, there'd remained a frayed thread to hold on to, and now even that thread was gone.

Haiwen cried. For everything he had lost, for everything he missed. His nephew growing up. His sister getting married. Caring for his father and mother as they aged. The chance to marry Suchi and share a life with her—though this was, of course, a sorrow complicated by his love for Linyee and the girls. His children would never learn Shanghainese, never bite into his mother's flaky turnip pastry and watch a wisp of hot steam curl out of it. The old regret of never getting to study at the music conservatory or become a professional violinist—a regret that had once caused pain to twist in his chest if he even *heard* a violin—split open again, a fresh wound.

Yijun crouched by him, stroking his arm. "Ba," she said, tears running down her face. "Ba, please."

He was scaring his daughter, but he didn't know how to stop. A coil inside him had sprung and he couldn't shove the grief back inside. He felt Yijun stand up and walk away, and he was relieved. He didn't want her to keep watching him.

But a moment later, she was back. "Ba," she said, nudging him. "Ba, maybe this will help." He opened his eyes. Blurry through his tears, Yijun cradled his violin case. She held it out to him.

"Play something," Yijun said. "Please?"

He shook his head and pushed the case away.

"Ba," Yijun insisted. "It always calms you. Just try."

She put the case in his lap. He stared at it. It was battered, worn on the edges, leather peeling in some parts to reveal soft felt underneath. This case had survived so much.

He lifted out his violin. He placed it under his chin, slotting the strings into the hard ridges carved into his fingers. Immediately, a sense of comfort washed over him. For so many years, this instrument had been an extension of himself, an extra limb, a true voice. He grasped for the bow and pulled it along the strings. It sang, slightly out of tune, but in a way that was intimate, familiar. He twisted the pegs, closing his eyes while he searched for the pitches that would slide perfectly into the notes in his mind. When each string had clicked into tune, he stopped.

"What's wrong?" Yijun asked.

When he was young, he had a piece for every occasion and experience, every joy or misery or frustration, a perpetual soundtrack to accompany his days. But back then, his concerns had been shallow, immature, juvenile.

Notes from the mourning songs for Lord Chiang, the patriotic ditties they'd sung in the army about returning to the mainland, the national anthem—these all drifted into his head but did not stay. They were all manufactured tunes meant to tell a simple story. There was no piece to encapsulate the enormity of this.

"I don't know what to play," he said, opening his eyes, the bow falling down with his hand to rest in his lap. Yijun was staring at him, her body still, as if she were afraid to breathe.

"Anything," she said. "What about 'Jasmine'? That was the first song you ever played for us."

Haiwen closed his eyes again, thinking about that day, the girls' delighted expressions. He'd been pleased this modest song had so transformed him in their eyes. Their faces dissolved into Suchi's and Sulan's. In another blink they were replaced by his mother. Mama. Her head bobbing as he practiced the folk song, a proud, dreamy smile on her lips.

He brought his bow back up and pulled out one hesitant note, pushed out a second. The instrument vibrated, pulsing with life. A third note appeared. Then a fourth. A fifth, sixth, onward and onward, the notes from his violin chasing the notes in his head, each one a confirmation of its own existence. It began to feel as if the instrument were breathing—as if *he* was breathing.

From "Jasmine," he seamlessly transitioned to Massenet's "Meditation," his mother's favorite, the last piece he ever played for her. He felt the breeze on his neck, the tears glinting in her eyes, the glow of a lowering sun. He didn't let the quiet of the final note last too long before he moved on to the next piece—Paganini, which dredged up similar pain, similar bitterness—then the next, Sibelius, cycling through pieces he had learned and loved, a quilt of Bach, of Brahms, of Mozart, sections pulled to the surface by muscle memory. When he had exhausted his classical repertoire, he switched to the popular songs Suchi had loved, starting with "Lovesick Dream" and followed by other jazzy melodies whose names he no longer remembered. Out spun the nursery rhymes Junjun had loved and the English songs his mother used to hum. He did, eventually, play the anthem, but it was slower, more mournful, and he found himself changing it, transposing it so it ended in a minor key, not entirely bereft of hope, but not completely triumphant.

He kept playing even when Yiping and Linyee came home. He heard Yijun whispering about him after she pulled her mother and sister into the kitchen, felt when they returned to the living room. He finished playing the series of children's songs his daughters had chanted when they were little and switched to a popular Taiwanese ballad Linyee used to sing to the girls as she bathed them. When he finished, he held the bow over the violin, his eyes still closed. He heard the keen of a mosquito by his ear, the quiet breathing of his family.

"Laogong," Linyee finally said, "I brought home some braised pork over rice. Are you hungry?"

Haiwen brought the bow down and opened his eyes. His family was watching him, their expressions carbon copies of one another's, concerned, careful, full of love.

"Yes," he said. His neck was drenched in sweat. His fingers ached. "Let's eat."

JANUARY–MARCH 1966
Hong Kong

S UCHI HAD BEEN singing at the club for five months. Now she sang in the early hours on most nights, for a small but devoted following, which, of course, often included Lam Saikeung. The people who liked her said they were drawn to the purity of her voice, the vulnerability of it.

Every night she stood onstage and conjured up her loved ones' ghosts and willed them to hear her. Every song was a prayer that somewhere Haiwen, Apa, M'ma were alive, that they could be kept alive by the sheer force of her memory. It wrenched her.

It had been nine months since Lam Saikeung had first stepped into the club. Suchi had learned from Fai's gossipy sources that Mr. Lam had recently bought out a competitor, making him the second-largest import/exporter in Hong Kong. "He should be going to the swanky clubs in the Peninsula," she said, "but he keeps coming back to our dinky little joint because of you."

In addition to waitressing and singing, Suchi now also spent hours before work poring over English primers. Lam Saikeung had hired a private English tutor for Suchi. "If you're going to sing English songs, you should understand what you're singing," he said. "One day you may have British audience members."

Suchi practiced her English with the new Filipino band Mr. Fong had been able to poach from another club thanks to Lam Saikeung's patronage—their English was better than their Cantonese. She particularly got along with the pianist, Oscar, and the saxophonist, Prince, who had played in Shanghai during its heyday. Suchi loved hearing about what the dance halls had been like, how they'd mingled with Black American jazz musicians who came through. It was the opulent fairy-tale life Suchi had dreamed of when she was young, and rather than making her homesick, the stories filled Suchi with a sense of joy. She could nearly imagine that world still existed, untouched by time or reality, a bubble of dance and music.

Some of the girls grumbled that it was unseemly for Suchi to flirt with the Filipino men, but Suchi ignored them. The men treated her like a sister, laughing, teasing, and sharing stories with an easy sincerity that asked for nothing in return. It was a relief to be herself after an evening of acting the part of the smiling, pliant hostess.

In all this time, Mr. Lam never attempted to sleep with her. Suchi relaxed into their unusual relationship, even allowing herself to develop a guarded affection for him. Perhaps he really was a gentleman, someone who had taken an interest in her career and wanted to help her, and nothing more.

OF COURSE, THIS WAS NOT THE CASE.

Two weeks into their tenth month of knowing each other, Lam Saikeung arrived before opening. Ah Lui was polishing glasses, the band was warming up, and the girls were trickling in, changing into their silver cheongsams. Mr. Lam knocked on the door of the dressing room, where Suchi was applying makeup. The other girls in the room looked confused and hurriedly zipped themselves up before opening the door.

"I'd like to speak to Soukei alone," Mr. Lam said. The girls glanced at Suchi, who sat in front of the mirror in the loose black dress she wore for her commute, and exited the room. Mr. Lam closed the door behind him.

"You're here early," Suchi said, retouching the line of kohl she'd drawn around her eyes. She turned to Mr. Lam and smiled. "I'm a bit of a mess, I'm afraid."

"I like you in your natural state," he said, taking a seat on a chair near her. It was an odd thing for him to say, uncharacteristically sweet, and it put Suchi immediately on guard.

"Is something the matter?" she asked, searching his expression. But his face was warm and neutral. It was the face he often maintained for her, the one that drew her into his charm, that made her forget who he was to her: a man who had paid his way into her life.

"Everything's great." He grinned. "Business is better than ever. My company, my fleet—it's all grown a hundred fifty percent in the last year. I just purchased my mother a large house on the south side, near the ocean. I married my sister off to a competitor who is now going to be a partner as he expands his trade to Singapore. Everything is stable, finally. The future is certain."

Suchi was nodding, smiling, unsure of where this was going. "That's wonderful."

"All of this means I can settle down and start the next phase of my life. I'm getting old." He ran his fingers through his thinning hair, as if suddenly self-conscious. "Forty-six is too old to be a bachelor. My mother is worrying about grandsons."

Suchi continued to smile and nod, though the smile felt frozen on her face. Acid seeped into her stomach. "Oh, but you've been a busy man. Plenty of men—"

"I would like you to marry me," Lam Saikeung interrupted. For a moment he looked like a little boy, his eyes wide and earnest and expectant.

"Me?" Suchi asked dumbly.

"Yes." He continued to stare at her. She wanted to tear away from his gaze.

"But," she stuttered, "but I'm just a bar girl."

"You're a singer," he interrupted.

"Not really," she said, "I'm not very good."

"You're wonderful." A statement. His smile had disappeared.

"But I'm not of the social status to—"

"Being a self-made man means I get to marry whomever I want!"

Suchi froze, her next words evaporating from her tongue. Lam Saikeung's pale face had turned splotchy. After several tense seconds, he sighed and the color seeped from his skin. He continued in a measured voice. "I just—I just don't want you to worry about that. You're a smart, talented woman. Hardworking. I like that about you. I don't want to marry a frivolous young woman who's been pampered by her parents her whole life. I want a woman who's had to scrape her way through life. A woman who's seen loss. That's you."

"I have—I have my sister to think about."

Mr. Lam's voice grew impatient. "I'll take care of your sister once we're married."

"She's not well," Suchi said, thinking fast. "I'm worried the excitement of an engagement would strain her further."

"Or give her something to look forward to. What woman doesn't love planning a wedding?"

Panic was roiling through her gut. He had been nothing but kind to her and she wanted to repay him, but not like this, not with a lifetime tied to his.

"Please," she said, "it's so sudden. Give me some time to think about it."

The warmth on Mr. Lam's face dissolved. "All right," he said, standing up.

When she went onstage an hour later, the booth he normally sat in was conspicuously empty.

FOR SEVERAL WEEKS, LAM SAIKEUNG DID NOT COME TO the club, but news of his proposal spread quickly. Suchi had made the mistake of telling Sulan within earshot of Fai, who caught on to enough Shanghainese to understand the gist of things. By the next evening, Suchi could tell everyone was looking at her differently. "She thinks she's too good for that man?" she overheard someone say.

What the other girls thought didn't bother her. She was more worried about how to say no to Mr. Lam. She agonized over how to couch her rejection to save his ego, how best to show him she wasn't worthy of him, that he deserved a woman whose social status rivaled his, a woman whose past wouldn't become a source of gossip in tabloids.

A month after Lam Saikeung's proposal, she stepped onto the

stage and saw him sitting in the booth, his eyes intense and unsmiling. His sudden appearance jarred her, and she missed the entry into her song. She recovered by the third bar, but she was shaky and off-key and kept forgetting the words.

Offstage, in the dressing room, she struggled to unclasp the buttons on her cheongsam, her hands trembling. She could hear Lily's clear, powerful voice onstage, trying to erase Suchi's disastrous performance from everyone's minds. She tried to remind herself that she had nothing to be afraid of, that Lam Saikeung cared for her, that he might be hurt when she rejected him, but in the end, he would see it was for the best.

The door opened. She looked up.

Lam Saikeung's silhouette darkened the frame. He walked in and closed the door quietly behind him.

"Soukei. I've given you a month," he said. "A month distraction-free, a month to remind you what life without me might be like." He stepped closer. "Did you miss me? I missed you."

"I'm so grateful to you, Mr. Lam—"

"Saikeung. Call me Saikeung."

"—I don't want you to think I don't appreciate everything you've done, your friendship and charity—"

"I want to hear you call me Saikeung," he said, stepping closer. Suchi had never noticed until now how *tall* he was. She usually saw him seated, and his short torso had made him appear not much taller than Suchi. But now she could see he had long legs, legs that covered the distance between them swiftly.

She shifted backward.

"Saikeung," she said. She was babbling now. "I'm a bar girl, and an old one at that. I'm nearly thirty-five. Who's to say I can even bear those grandsons your mother is so anxious about? What will you tell your mother about me?"

"This is the twentieth century," he said. He was very close to her now. She could smell the heat on his skin. "We aren't living in the old country anymore."

She took another small step backward. Her heel jammed into the bottom of the bureau behind her. "You deserve someone young and beautiful, someone pure and untainted—"

He stopped short, his face unreadable. "Are you saying you're not . . . *pure?*"

Why had she chosen those words? Suchi thought quickly. If she lied to him, told him she had already lost her virginity, would that make her unappealing to him? Would he lose his interest in marrying her? She stared at the vein in his neck. It throbbed blue.

"I'm pure, of course I'm pure," she said. "I just meant, someone who hasn't worked in a place like *this.*"

But the seed of doubt seemed to burrow into his brow. He stepped up to Suchi and grabbed her wrists. She gasped, more out of surprise than pain. "How can I be certain?" he asked. "I assumed you were, given how you had given me such a hard time. But I don't know what you were doing when I wasn't around. Whose affections you entertained, whom Fong might have thrust you onto. The other girls whispered to me about your . . . strange affection for those Manila men, but I thought there was no way you could entertain them in *that* way. I trusted you."

Terror ran cold through her veins. "I didn't . . . I never . . ."

"I want to believe you," he said.

"Of course I've been faithful to you," she said. The words popped out of her mouth before she could stop them. Why did she say that? Who was to say she was his? But they worked, and his face softened.

"You know I love you," he said. He was stroking her wrists now, even as he gripped them. She felt the rough calluses of his thumbs flicking across her skin. "As soon as I saw you walking across the room, I knew I wanted you for my own. I knew you were special. And you are! Just look at you! Look how you've blossomed under my care!"

"Mr. . . . . Saikeung," she stammered. She tried to calm her voice, make it smooth like honey, the voice she used on the most irritable guests. "Maybe we can go outside and talk. I know Ah Lui just got in a bottle of that scotch you like. I can go get some for you—"

"There's only one thing I'd like to taste," he said, and dipped his head to kiss her.

She went limp. He released her hands to push her head into his and she felt the slippery wetness of his tongue inside of her. He must have eaten something with cilantro, she thought. She hated cilantro and now the taste was invading the insides of her mouth. Her mind fled to another kiss, a different kiss, from long ago. Haiwen and his tenderness. Haiwen and the fire that had warmed between their lips. How was it that what she had experienced with Haiwen and *this* could be described by the same word, she wondered.

His hands moved downward, roving over her small breasts through the fabric, over her bottom, around and up toward her thighs. He shoved at the fabric of the green cheongsam impatiently, and she heard it tear. *I'm sorry, Lily*, she thought. She would repair it later.

She was pressed up against the bureau inside which the singers' dresses hung. The square knobs dug into her back. She felt him hot against her thigh, a fleshy rodent burrowing, searching. The pain was sharp and filled her so completely, she gasped. He mistook this for enthusiasm. "Yes," he murmured, "yes, yes." The knobs dug deeper with each thrust. She wondered if she would have angular bruises on her back in the morning. In the distance, she could hear Lily crooning a cover of Judi Jim's "Colours of the Rainbow," a Hong Kong English pop song she'd heard a hundred times before and whose saccharine melody she had never particularly liked.

With a loud groan, Lam Saikeung finished. A trickle of wetness, like she had peed herself, dripped down her thigh as he pulled away.

He took out a handkerchief from his pocket and wiped himself with it, inspecting it after he did so. He broke out into a smile, the warm smile she had seen many times, the smile that had led her to believe she was safe. "You were being truthful," he said, his voice so sweet that for a moment she could imagine he was saying it in response to something else, a gift she had given him willingly. He tucked his shirt in his pants, slicked his hair back with his palm. He kissed her on the cheek. "A May wedding maybe," he said, walking toward the door. "When the flowers are in bloom."

SAIKEUNG BEGAN COMING TO THE CLUB EVERY EVENING. He reverted to chastely keeping his physical distance from her, doing no more than occasionally brushing her knee. Even that action made Suchi want to jerk away, but she restrained herself.

She fantasized about ways to kill him. Picking up the lowball glass in front of him, shattering it on the floor, and using the sharpest slice to cut open his throat. Grabbing one of the chef's knives from the kitchen and stabbing him in the groin in one swift downward motion. Dropping rat poison into the scotch she poured for him, smiling sweetly as she watched him choke and die a slow, painful death.

She did none of those things. She sat with a smile pasted on her face, nodding as he told her and his companions about his latest business deal, how big his fleet was, the wonders of his travels.

She told no one what had happened. She wanted it erased from her memory, for it to recede far into a place where the details would no longer torment her, where she wouldn't have to relive every hot breath and rough thrust he had stamped upon her. Where she wouldn't have to chastise herself for being so foolish, for believing he was a different kind of man than she had first assumed.

He told her the night after it happened that they had gotten carried away, but that he wanted their second time to be proper, as man and wife. He'd said this as he'd slipped a diamond ring on her finger, one she made sure to wear when he was around but hid in the bottom of her purse as soon as she was away from him.

Every day, as she lay down to sleep, Suchi dreamed about another life, the one she'd almost had, the one in which she was married to Haiwen, safe in a bed they shared. In that parallel life, that alternate version of her knew nothing about this seedy club, had never heard the name Lam Saikeung. Suchi envied her bitterly.

SULAN'S SYMPTOMS GREW WORSE. SHE COMPLAINED that her vision was almost always blurry, that she was seeing double. Her fingers were numb and stiff. Some days, her headache was so bad, she threw up. The pain in her back and legs kept her up most nights, and Suchi often returned from work to find Sulan awake, moaning. The acupuncture and medication were no longer having an effect.

Suchi tried to be a good nurse: she made hot towels for Sulan's head, ginger tea to calm her stomach. But as she did it, she resented her sister; in her secret heart she blamed Sulan for everything that had happened.

On a rainy Monday, Suchi's only day off, Suchi woke to the sound of Sulan keening as she tossed in bed below her, a high-pitched wail that reminded Suchi of a goat being slaughtered.

With difficulty, Suchi helped Sulan dress, and together they hobbled down the four flights of stairs. Sulan kneeled on the dirty, wet sidewalk, hunched in pain, while Suchi tried to hail a taxi. After fifteen minutes, one squealed to a halt, and Suchi directed it to the British medical center, the exclusive one the rich foreigners went to, where Saikeung took his own mother.

The blond receptionist looked at the rain-soaked women skeptically. Her cheeks were drawn and sharp, her expression a portrait of disapproval.

"Please," Suchi pleaded in English. Sulan was gasping in pain. In a flash of desperation, Suchi added, not knowing if it might help, "I am Lam Saikeung wife, Cheung Soukei. He come here many time."

The woman pursed her lips and sighed. She called someone and spoke to them in low English, too fast for Suchi to understand. After a moment, she nodded and hung up. "Second floor," she said loudly. "Dr. Jones."

To Suchi's relief, Dr. Jones spoke Cantonese. She explained to him the symptoms her sister had been experiencing for the last year.

"We saw another Western medicine doctor, when she first started getting sick," she said. "He said it was psychological. That it was a result of stress."

"Has there been stress?" Dr. Jones asked.

Suchi wanted to laugh. Every day since they had left Shanghai had been stressful. Instead, she said, "Well, there's the news coming from the mainland." She glanced at Sulan, who lay on the examination table with her eyes closed, her breathing shallow. "My parents—we don't know where they are, we left them in China during the war and we haven't heard from them in over a decade. Now with the famine..."

Dr. Jones nodded, his face solemn. "That might be a factor, but let's run some tests."

They poked and prodded Sulan with needles, causing her to cry out. He asked her to estimate how often she had been in pain, how long she had been in pain, when the pain was the worst. He had her walk for him, he tested her reflexes, he listened to her heart, her lungs, he checked her eyesight. He asked her if she had gotten the flu around when her symptoms started. He asked her about her low moods and when they had started. When he was finished, he sent Sulan home with powerful painkillers, large tablets he promised would help her sleep.

A few days later, they returned to Dr. Jones's office.

"Well, I don't think it's phantom pain," he said. He explained to the two sisters that he suspected Sulan had a disease called multiple sclerosis, a nerve disease. "I haven't seen it much in Hong Kong," he said, "so I doubt the doctor you went to before was looking for it. But your blood work has ruled out the more common stuff. And so many of your symptoms are similar to those of a British woman I met who was just diagnosed with this."

Relief overtook Suchi. Finally! A diagnosis! "What's the cure for this?" she asked.

Dr. Jones hesitated before replying. "There's no cure, unfortunately. There's research being done, and some new treatments being tested, but to be honest, we don't understand the disease. The symptoms manifest differently person to person, which makes it difficult. They come and go for some, or they get progressively worse for others. All we can do is try to figure out how to keep Sulan's symptoms under control."

"This disease . . . is it fatal?" Suchi's chest felt tight.

Dr. Jones paused. "Not exactly. We've seen some people live for decades. It's usually degenerative, and the symptoms can make it harder over time for patients to walk or talk. I won't lie: some do die rather young. But for other people, with management of the relapses, they can live long, full lives."

Suchi started crying. Through her tears, she translated what Dr. Jones had said to Sulan, trying to soften the news. She felt terrible— terrible she had not believed her sister, terrible she had blamed her for all the misfortune in her life, terrible she had not supported her and cared for her with a generous heart. Sulan was the last of her family, the only person left in this world who truly loved her.

For a moment Sulan said nothing. Suchi wiped her tears from her face. But slowly, Sulan began to smile, the corners of her lips stretching until she was grinning widely. It was the first smile Suchi had seen from her in a long, long time.

"I knew it," Sulan whispered, "I knew I wasn't crazy. I knew I wasn't making it up. The monster. It finally has a name."

Dr. Jones prescribed medication and more painkillers immediately. He advised Sulan to do her best to get some exercise every day.

He told her she would have to start coming every week, so he could stimulate her blood circulation and monitor her symptoms.

Through the stunned haze of their new reality, Suchi also came to the dim realization that all of this—the medications, the weekly doctor's visits—would cost a small fortune, more than she could ever make, even with her singing income.

But when they went to inquire about the bill, they were told there was no balance to pay. "Your husband has settled it," the blond woman said. Nausea tightened Suchi's gut.

"What happened?" Sulan asked as they walked away.

"Lam Saikeung," Suchi responded, trying to keep her voice neutral. "They must have called him and told him we were here. He paid the bill."

"Have you decided to marry him?" Sulan asked.

"I don't know," Suchi said, although she knew now she had no choice.

THE WEDDING WAS SET FOR EARLY MAY, A MERE TWO months away. Saikeung told Suchi not to be concerned about the details. It would all be planned, he said. One day, she walked into the dressing room and found an expensive wedding gown, shipped in from Paris, draped over her chair. It was cream colored, overlaid with delicate lace and tiny silver beads. She stared at it but did not try it on. Every day, little by little, Suchi felt her freedom slipping away.

A month and a half had passed since that horrible night. Despite overwhelming fatigue, Suchi felt she had barely rested in all that time. Now that Sulan slept soundly through both evening and daytime, Suchi was alone with her thoughts. Nightly, she revisited all the decisions that had led her here. If only she had locked the door that night. If only she hadn't told him of her dream to be a singer. If only she hadn't sung along with that stupid song. If only she had never started working at that godforsaken club. If only she had kept washing laundry, until her fingers bled, until her palms cracked, until the skin sloughed right off her body.

If only she had never come to Hong Kong.

When she did fall asleep, she had dreams of dying. She was drowning or suffocating or bleeding out; she never died but was always in the process of it. It was painful, torturous, and she longed for the end both in dreams and upon waking. Even after she was fully awake, the violence churned in her stomach, sending her to the bathroom to vomit.

She spent more and more time in the shower, weeping.

She moved through the days robotically, mentally crossing them off, not knowing what she was looking toward anymore.

"YOU'RE LOOKING PEAKY," DR. JONES REMARKED TO SU-chi one day as Sulan lay back on the examination table, receiving medication from a drip. "Are you getting enough sleep?"

"Yes," Suchi lied.

"I hear you're getting married," the doctor said, smiling warmly. "I hope the stress isn't wearing you out. I'm not certain what Chinese weddings are like, but I remember when my wife and I were planning our wedding, it was quite the involved affair."

Suchi blinked. Of course Dr. Jones knew about the wedding. He was Saikeung's mother's doctor after all. No place was safe. Even her sister's doctor was in Saikeung's pocket. The doctor's office suddenly felt unbearably hot; the acrid scent of medical disinfectant stung her nose. A wave of nausea engulfed her, and before she could stop herself, she had thrown up all over the floor.

Sulan looked startled. The doctor stared at the vomit and then up at Suchi.

Suchi wiped her mouth with the back of her hand, her eyes watering, her throat aching acid.

"Have you been feeling sick today?" Dr. Jones asked. He walked over to a cabinet and brought out a clean towel, which he laid over the puddle of vomit gently, as if he were hiding what was unpleasant. He handed her another one for her to wipe her face. "Did you eat something bad this morning?"

Suchi shook her head. "I'm fine," she said. "I just sometimes get . . . stress sickness."

"Stress sickness?"

"Just recently. In the last few weeks. What with the wedding . . ." She smiled weakly, aware of the stench emanating from her breath.

"In the last few weeks?" The doctor frowned. "What about food? Can you eat normally?"

"Nothing greasy," Sulan piped up. "Greasy things make her sick. She can't even stand the smell." Suchi tried to contain her irritation that Sulan had chosen this moment to demonstrate the limited Cantonese she knew.

Dr. Jones's face lit up. He asked Suchi if he could speak to her privately in his office. When she was seated across from him, his mahogany desk between them, he smiled warmly before asking, "When was the date of your last menses?"

SUCHI LAY IN BED, SLEEPLESS. SHE LISTENED TO THE girls with day jobs rise, their quiet whispers as they navigated the shared closets, as they shuffled into the bathroom, as they put on makeup and left for work. She heard Fai rustle and snore in her sleep. The gray light filtering through their small window shifted in tone, brightening to a steely white. After a time, Suchi climbed out of the bunk.

She went to the bathroom and brushed her teeth. She stared at herself in the small mirror nailed above the sink. She looked thin and gaunt. Under the harsh fluorescent light, she could see blue veins beneath the translucence of her skin. She had never considered herself particularly beautiful, but she now hated the face that stared back at her. She applied makeup, trying to blot it out, but when she was done, the kohl rimmed under her eyes and her mouth pouting red, she thought she looked like a whore. *Isn't that what I am?* she thought. She didn't remove the makeup.

She went back to the room and searched through the bureau she and Sulan shared. The drab clothes she wore on her commute to work mingled with the many bright cheongsam Saikeung had begun gifting her. She hated it all, she wanted to shred them to pieces. Then her eye caught on a dress pushed all the way to the side. It was the plum qipao Sulan had made for her years ago, the one she wore on the day Haiwen forgot her birthday.

Suchi slipped the qipao over her head. It was snug, made more for a young girl's body than the curves of a woman, but Suchi had lost weight recently. She brushed her hair and pinned it up into a bun. After a moment's thought, she took a canary-colored scarf Sulan had given her and wrapped it around her hair.

On her bed, she left a bundle containing nearly all the cash and jewelry she had, the stack of letters Apa had sent almost fifteen years ago, and the diamond ring Saikeung had given her. She wrote a simple note saying she was sorry. She tried to think of something else to say, but the words wouldn't come. So she added, "I have gone to look for Apa and M'ma," and left it at that.

She pulled Haiwen's violin case out from under their bunk, careful not to disturb Sulan, and reached into the torn corner of the case's lining, feeling for an edge. Instead, her hand touched something cool and cylindrical lodged in the corner. She tugged it out. An unfamiliar gold ring winked up at her. She had never noticed it in the lining before and she wondered how long it had been in there. Was it Sulan's? Had her sister discovered her hiding place? Suchi turned the ring over in her palm, examining its elegant twist. Briefly, she slipped it on her ring finger. It fit perfectly.

Suchi reached into the lining a second time and found what she'd been looking for. Siau Zi's letter. Its thin envelope was wrinkled and fragile from the many times she had read it. If Sulan had discovered this hiding spot, it would mean she knew of all Suchi had kept from her. How long had she known? Was it this letter that had triggered Sulan's sadness, her illness? After a moment, Suchi removed the ring. None of that mattered. It was too late to change anything. She dropped it back into the hole in the lining. The letter, she folded and put in her purse.

It was noon by the time Suchi exited the building. She could smell a fragrant mixture of seafood and garlic and onions in the air. She browsed the outdoor market, taking in the reds and purples and greens of the fresh vegetables spilling out of baskets. She bought an orange and peeled it right there on the street corner, savoring the sweet burst on her tongue as she bit into it. She watched the people walking through the winding alleys of the Walled City—middle-aged men, young women, little boys—and wondered how many were toiling, starving, trapped in a cage of a room with two other families, unable to get ahead.

She made her way to Tsim Sha Tsui and paid for a ticket on the Star Ferry. As the boat backed out from Kowloon toward Hong Kong Island, she stood by the railing and scanned the horizon, thinking about that day eighteen years ago when she and Sulan had set their eyes on Hong Kong's harbor for the first time. The skyline had changed, but the apartment buildings still seemed like shoeboxes crammed together to her, ready to be undone by the next typhoon or a single match.

She was going to jump. The thought had come to her in the middle of the night, and as the hours had passed, it had crystallized into certainty, an imperative. She knew it would be unfair to Sulan, and briefly, she worried about how her sister would take care of herself without Suchi to force her to go to the doctor, to take her medication.

But Suchi couldn't bear what her life would become if she kept living it. She couldn't bear spending another day in this body, this body that had betrayed her, this body that refused to let her forget the terrible night she desperately longed to erase from her mind. She wanted to take a knife and carve her womb out of her stomach, but she didn't have the fortitude. So instead, she would jump.

The ferry crossed the harbor slowly, the putrid stench of rotting fish and human waste wafting around her. Junks bobbed in the distance. Would this ocean take her back to Shanghai, back home? She wondered what was left of her city, of the little longtang she had grown up in. She longed to see all of it again.

"We're here!" a voice beside her shouted, and Suchi blinked. They had arrived at the other side. Suchi had not jumped. As people around her gathered their things and crowded at the exits, she sat, unsure of what to do. A worker came up to her and said, "Miss, we've arrived at Hong Kong Island."

"I forgot something, I have to go back," she said. He frowned, but she smiled at him in the way she knew how to do, and he shrugged and went away.

She would jump this time, she thought as the ferry began to move again. Right when they hit the middle of the crossing, where she guessed the water was deepest. She leaned over the railing so she could gauge how far they were from Kowloon. The scarf whipped around her head in the breeze. The boat moved steadily forward, churning the waves. Suchi lifted her right foot and placed it on the railing, catching her kitten heel. She stood on the tips of her left toes, testing her balance. Right at that moment, she caught the eye of a boy, maybe three years old, standing further down the deck from her, holding his father's hand. The father faced the approaching skyline of Kowloon, but the little boy was looking at Suchi curiously. He had two fingers in his mouth, a string of drool linking his lips to his knuckles. His eyes were wide and round.

For several long seconds, Suchi stared back. She willed him to turn away, but he kept sucking his fingers calmly, occasionally blinking from the wind stirring in his face.

She could not do it.

Again, the ferry docked. Again, she had to explain to the worker she was, most definitely, on her way back to the Hong Kong side.

He felt a hesitant hand cover his. It was cold, slight. Suchi was next to him. Tears streaked down her pale face, leaving dark tracks of mascara, like the transgressions of a calligraphy brush someone had forgotten to put away.

HAIWEN HAD COME TO HONG KONG ON A TWO-WEEK business trip. His boss had brought him along, trusting his eye as they visited factories and potential trade partners. "Everyone thinks you're quiet because you're shy, but I've figured you out by now," Mr. Hsieh had said. "You're just busy observing."

Haiwen and Linyee had been having problems: Haiwen had been spending an increasing number of nights at the underground pachinko establishments, which often turned into a hand or two of cards. Though gambling was illegal in Taiwan, the dens were an open secret, and Haiwen didn't see the harm in trying to make a quick extra buck at a silly game. But the more he played, the harder he found it to stop. When he lost, he became reckless, wanting to cover his losses before Linyee discovered he'd lost his week's salary. But a man can never keep a secret from his wife for long. Over the last few months, there had been less and less money left over for Linyee to purchase clothes for the girls' rapidly growing limbs or for extra bones to make soup. One day, she had finally confronted him. "Think about your daughters!" she had hissed. "What will their lives be if their father is arrested for gambling?" She had been glad when he'd announced he'd be going to Hong Kong. "Get your head on straight before you come back to us."

So now he was in this bustling city, where his parents had once lived. When he'd first arrived, he'd felt a pang of homesickness, the trams and crowds reminding him of Shanghai.

Today was the first afternoon Haiwen had no meetings, so in the late afternoon, he had boarded the Star Ferry to Kowloon. As the boat crossed Victoria Harbor, a pit the size of a walnut rose to his throat. This view of the sea reminded him of the panicked ship ride to Taiwan. At the time, his commanders had promised them all it would only be for a few months, that soon they would defeat the Communists and return home. It had been seventeen years. He was now nearly twice the age he'd been when he'd left.

The ferry had docked in Kowloon and he'd examined the map the man at the hotel had hastily drawn for him. He followed its directions through a winding alleyway, between buildings so close together, the racks of drying shirts and underwear hanging from one balcony almost touched those of the apartment across the street. Finally, he found it, a nondescript door with a broken lock. The inside of the building smelled wet and moldy, like clothes that hadn't been properly aired out. He climbed the stairs up to the third floor and knocked on the second door. A man opened the door a crack. "Dim aa?" the man asked, looking Haiwen up and down.

In Mandarin, Haiwen told the man a friend had referred him. "He said you can get letters to the mainland." He held up a thick sealed envelope.

The man looked at the envelope and stepped out into the hallway. As the door briefly swung open, Haiwen glimpsed a young boy sitting on the ground with his legs crossed, writing in a workbook.

"A hundred sterling," the man said in Mandarin.

"I was told it was fifty."

The man shook his head. "That was before. It's a hundred now."

"But it was fifty not even a few months ago." Haiwen was trying to keep his rising frustration from his voice. His colleague had said this man had reasonable prices compared to other middlemen, but even then, the only way Haiwen had been able to put aside the original fifty was by gambling for several nights in a row before coming to Hong Kong.

The man folded his arms and loomed over Haiwen. "Do you know what is happening in China right now? First, there is a famine. People are eating sticks and weeds, they're eating their dogs. Second, there are rumblings that now that Mao has taken over the Propaganda Department from Lu, he has something big planned. This is making it very difficult for me to convince anyone to go into the mainland. People are barely escaping with their lives—how much do you think I have to pay someone to go in the other direction?"

"I only brought fifty with me," Haiwen said. "Please, I haven't seen my family in almost twenty years. I just want them to know I'm okay."

"Given the news I'm hearing, they're probably not okay," the man said. Haiwen's face must have looked stricken because the man quickly dropped his arms. His demeanor softened. "Listen, brother, I understand. Yours isn't the first sob story I've heard. And I want to help you, I really do. But this is the reality. The risks of going through the mainland are too great right now. Even with a hundred, I honestly can't guarantee your letter will get there." He tapped the letter clutched in Haiwen's hand. "I'm an honest man. I have no desire to use a man's deepest sorrows to swindle him. I can try my best to get the letter to your family, but I will need one hundred sterling."

Haiwen returned to the harbor, waiting for the next ferry to arrive, the envelope still clutched in his palm. He had stayed up all night writing the letters, the first ones he'd tried writing since the days he'd spent marching across China's countryside during the war—one for his parents, one each for his brother and sister, and one for Suchi. He had drafted and redrafted them. His first letter to his parents had detailed everything—the battles he'd been in, the deaths he had seen, the escape to Taiwan, the first months and years of loneliness and withering hope, his marriage, his daughters' births, his current job, the nightmares he had, the gambling. He had thrown those pages out and rewritten them, this time only including the good things, the happy things, stories about his daughters and how he was making good money, how it never grew terribly cold in Taiwan. This didn't feel right either. In the end, he had chosen a mixture of the two—he mentioned the war but glossed over its horrors. He mentioned money was tight but that he was lucky to have a great job and a boss who believed in him. He told them he missed everyone but was confident one day the country would be reunited, and so would they. He enclosed a picture he had taken with his family last fall, Yijun, only two months old, swaddled in Linyee's arms and Yiping, three, sitting in his lap. It was the first picture they had taken together as a family, and both he and Linyee looked somber and tired.

His letter to Suchi had been similarly complicated. With her, too, he had the impulse to write down everything. After half a lifetime of spending almost every day together, missing nineteen years of each other's lives seemed inexcusable, and Haiwen had felt an imperative to fill in all the gaps. In his mind, she was the same girl, his first love, his most intimate friend, the one person to whom he could confide anything. But then, as he was writing, he came to the part about Linyee, and he realized he could not go on. Things *had* changed.

It occurred to him that Suchi, too, had likely already moved on. The idea produced a sharp pain in his rib cage, one that surprised him.

He decided, instead, to write something simple but true: He was sorry he had left without saying goodbye. He was sorry he had not married her. He would have if he could have. For a while he had thought of her every day, but now he was married with two daughters, and he hoped she, too, had found happiness.

He wanted to tell her he still loved her, but he didn't know if that was fair, or true.

He'd gotten on the crowded ferry back to Hong Kong Island, found a place to sit near the railing, and stared out at the turbulent gray waters. He wondered if he should just toss the packet overboard. It seemed the sea had better odds of carrying his letters successfully to Shanghai. As he thumbed the corner of the envelope, he began to slide its edge between the bars.

That was when he heard his name.

WHEN THE FERRY DOCKED, SHE LED HIM WORDLESSLY to a tea shop a few blocks from the port. She brewed fragrant jasmine leaves and poured the tea for him, reaching across the table toward a celadon cup. He found himself captivated by the small cleft on the inside of her wrist where two ligaments met.

He was the first to break the silence. "How have you been?"

"I'm doing well," she answered. "And you?"

"I'm doing well too." The silence returned, taut and thick. A traditional-sounding Cantonese love song twisted in the background.

"I'm learning English now," she offered. In English she said, haltingly, "Hello, my name is Suchi. Would you like some tea?" She cracked a smile at him.

"I've been reviewing my English too," he told her. "I work in the textile industry, and my boss thinks there are opportunities to work with American companies. Guess that private high school education was worth something after all."

"That's great," Suchi said, nodding. Another awkward silence drifted between them. She had become thin, Haiwen noticed. Her shoulders sloped slight and white from her qipao, like delicate porcelain sculptures.

"Why aren't you in Shanghai?" he finally asked, because it was the question he most needed the answer to. All this time, he had imagined she was still there, and with every story that sifted through to him—about the Communists and their Great Leap Forward, about how they had punished those with land and money, about the famines and the suffering—he had worried.

She brushed a strand of loose hair behind her right ear. "My father. He was being cautious. He liked what the Communists stood for, but you know how he was—he distrusted political factions. When the war showed signs of only getting worse and stories of violence in the countryside kept trickling through, he came up with some excuse about sending us to Hong Kong for business. I was silly and young enough to believe him, but Sulan knew it was a ruse—who had the money to take business trips? Our train tickets must have cost my father everything he had."

Haiwen pictured Suchi's father, a wiry man with a thick head of hair he oiled back. He was not a cheerful fellow and had been stern with Suchi and her sister, but with Haiwen, he'd been kind, if gruff, in contrast to Suchi's mother, who had not been able to hide her dislike.

"They were going to join us once they scraped together enough money, but with the rise of inflation . . . Then it was too late." She cleared her throat. "For a while Apa sent us letters, even after the Communists took over, but the letters stopped fifteen years ago."

Suchi sipped at her tea. Her face was placid, expressionless, and it unnerved him. She had never been one to mask her emotions well, and yet, now she spoke about her parents as if she were talking about a rainy day. Haiwen wondered what she was omitting. Although he envied her—for she'd had at least a couple years' contact with her family in a way he had not—he wondered if it was somehow worse, to have that contact abruptly cut off, with no knowledge of why.

"Perhaps they found somewhere else to go," he said. "Your father would make sure to keep your mother safe."

Suchi gazed at her teacup. "Sulan keeps hoping we'll find some kernel of information about them, but I try not to think about it. I'll drive myself crazy if I do." Her eyes shifted upward at him. "You must know what I mean."

An ache wrung Haiwen's chest. The truth was, Haiwen thought of his family nearly every day, turning his favorite memories over in his mind like a hard candy to be savored, terrified if he didn't, he would one day forget them. Once in a while he'd get caught up in his life, focused on work or his children, and then when he realized a few days had gone by since the faces of his parents and his siblings had flashed through his mind, the guilt spread through him as heavy and full as if he had killed them with his own hands.

The one person he had tried not to think about was Suchi. He was a poor husband in so many ways, but this, at least, was something he could do for his wife.

"I tried to send a letter to my family," Haiwen said. "I actually—just now—I went to a man someone told me could get a letter to them."

Suchi shook her head. "Before, two or three years ago even, when people were coming in and out of the mainland more easily, there was a chance. But now? Impossible. Those men who say they can will just take your money and gifts. Don't waste your money or your hope."

Suchi touched the back of his hand gently. The roughness of her slender fingers startled him, and he resisted the urge to grab her hand, to inspect it. "I don't know if it means anything—I know I've been gone for nearly as long, but—" She withdrew her hand, cupping it under her chin. "At least in that last year, they were doing fine. They were worried about you, of course, but they were getting by. Your brother and father were working a lot. The government still insisted on using the factories to produce fabric for uniforms, which I don't think your father was happy about, but it meant for a while they got a stable subsidy each month, which was better than nothing."

Haiwen was relieved. Maybe it had worked, then. Maybe his enlistment had proved their family's loyalty, enough that they could be trusted, given subsidies. Maybe it had made their lives easier, for a time. If that was the case, then it had been worth it.

"Oh!" Suchi continued. "Your sister-in-law gave birth to a boy. They hadn't yet decided on a name when I left, so they all called him Siau Noe—which seemed apt because he drank so much milk! He was a sweet, plump baby who screamed if anyone besides his mother tried to hold him."

Haiwen shook his head in wonder. A nephew. He had never known this nephew. He wondered if he ever would.

"What about my sister?" he asked.

"Junjun was fine," she said. Her face lit up, remembering. "The last time I saw her, she confided she had a crush on a boy in her class and asked me for advice."

A boy! He was hit with a wave of fresh sorrow and regret. Junjun had only been eleven when he'd left, completely uninterested in boys. How could she have grown up so much in the year between when he had left and when Suchi had last seen her? By now she was surely married, possibly with children. He had missed everything.

"It's your turn," Suchi said. "Have you been in Hong Kong long? Have I somehow missed you this whole time?"

"No," he said. "I live in Taiwan. The military sent us there when things started looking bad."

"Oh." The furrow above her nose creased. She looked down into her teacup, rotating it a little between her fingers. When she spoke again, her voice was quiet, airy. "I worried you were dead. When you didn't write. I imagined, all the time, that your body was rotting somewhere on a field, that you were a ghost, nameless and lost, who couldn't find your way to your next life, all because nobody had properly buried you."

"I did write," he said, needing her to know. "I wrote whenever I could. They probably threw out the letters we wrote and told us they'd sent them to boost our morale."

Suchi continued in that slightly hoarse voice, her words growing more rapid. "I told myself not to voice such thoughts. I had to believe you were alive, that any moment the war would be over and you'd come home."

"I would have come back, if I could have," he said. "At the time, they told us—they assured us—it would only be a few months."

"I refused to believe you were dead," she said. "Because . . . because if you were dead—if you were really dead, I'd never forgive myself for what I'd said to you that last day. I'd feel like I'd cursed you."

The guilt that had hummed in the background of his days roared to life. "Susu—"

She looked at him. Her eyes were heavy, bright. "Do you know what my first thought was when I realized we would be in Hong Kong for the indeterminate future? I thought, *What if Doudou comes back and I'm not there anymore? How will he know where to find me? Will he wait for me?* I couldn't stand the idea that you would believe I had abandoned you, as if I were trying to get back at you."

At those last words, her voice broke. She was still the emotion-filled Suchi he'd known, not the stony-faced woman she seemed. She started to weep, her nose turning red, wet drops streaking down the mascara paths marked by her previous tears.

"Why didn't you tell me?" she asked. "Why didn't you tell me you were leaving?"

"Susu," he said, his voice trembling. He squeezed his eyes shut. He could still see the stricken expression on young Suchi's face. "I was foolish, I was a coward. I regret every day the way I left. I don't have a good reason except that I was young and I couldn't face breaking your heart."

"I thought you were punishing me. For saying those awful things." Suchi's face collapsed into her palms. He watched her shoulders slumped and heaving, heard the occasional strangled sob muffled by her hands.

"Susu, please don't cry," he said, feeling helpless. "I'm so sorry.

Everything is my fault. I never should have left you. I don't deserve to be forgiven."

After a few minutes, she wiped her eyes with the back of her hand. "Doudou, you idiot." She sniffled and smiled, though the tears continued to fall. "I'm not upset. I'm just relieved. I'm so relieved you're alive."

He had to go; his dinner appointment with his boss and a potential partner was in two hours and he still had to return to the hotel and review his notes for the meeting. But he wanted to see Suchi again.

"Tomorrow," he said. "For dinner?"

She hesitated. "I can't in the evenings. I work at a noodle shop and dinner is the busiest time."

"After dinner then," he said.

She bit the bottom right side of her lip. "I have to go home to Sulan."

"Then I'll come to you."

"No," she said. "What about breakfast? I can meet you in the morning, before your first appointment. Perhaps at seven?"

They made plans to meet at a congee shop around the corner from his hotel. They walked to the intersection, where she indicated she was going in the opposite direction.

On impulse, he pulled her in by the shoulders and embraced her.

She felt the same in his arms. Her head still met him right at the armpit, her ribs still felt thin enough he was afraid they might break if he held her too tightly. Even the light touch of her fingers on his spine felt the same. The only thing different was the floral perfume she now wore, and even then, he was certain if he buried his head deeply enough, he would still find her sweet, salty, powdery scent.

After a moment, he released her. She gazed up at him. He took a step back and raised a hand in a stationary wave. "Tomorrow," he said.

HAIWEN WAS AT THE SHOP HALF AN HOUR BEFORE HE was scheduled to meet Suchi. He hadn't slept well. He couldn't turn off his thoughts. Memories of their years together flashed in a haphazard fashion through his mind—one moment he was recalling their first kiss; the next he was remembering Suchi at twelve, yelling at some boys who'd taunted them. The memories, which he had kept at bay for so many years, barraged him, and he found himself wishing he'd kept a journal of all their days together, because the fact that he could not remember exact details—had she been wearing a red ribbon in her hair or an orange one when they kissed? Was the first time he had seen her at school or in the streets of their longtang?—it tormented him.

He drank two bowls of warm soy milk and tried to concentrate on the files for his meetings later that day. The words were meaningless pictures, and he observed their shapes and lines, half-marveling at the absurdity of such simple human strokes attempting to represent and encompass the entire experience of living.

Suchi was late by ten minutes, during which Haiwen fretted she might not show at all. But at twelve after seven, she rushed in. Her hair was windblown, and her makeup was smudgy around her eyes. She looked tired. "I'm sorry to be late," she said, breathless.

Haiwen didn't want her to guess he had worried. "I used to be the one who was always late, if I recall."

Suchi's face relaxed as she lowered onto the stool. "You were! I hated it so."

He chuckled. "Then I suppose I have no right to be upset at you today."

In fluent Cantonese, Suchi ordered two bowls of pork and preserved-egg congee, with a side of sliced youtiao. For a moment, they stared at each other awkwardly. The two decades that had gone by weren't immediately obvious—she was more mature, certainly, and of course her manner of dress and makeup made it clear she was no longer the teenager he had left, but she still looked like *her*. Zhang Suchi.

"Tell me about Taiwan," Suchi said. "What is it like? I know nothing about it. Someone told me they'd heard it was an island of primitive natives and poor laborers."

Haiwen told her when he had first arrived, Taiwan had seemed like a jungle. Rice paddies, mountains, summer air as thick and hot as the congee they served in this shop, and residents who didn't trust people like him. "We were warned they'd been so thoroughly brainwashed by the Japanese, they no longer considered themselves Chinese."

Suchi shook her head. "How difficult. They're lucky that the Nationalists came to liberate them then."

He thought of Linyee and inwardly flinched. She would despise Suchi, not for being his first sweetheart, but for what she had just said.

For his wife's sake, Haiwen thought he should correct Suchi, tell her that things were more complicated than she made them sound. But it was too hard to try to explain the tension between the waishengren and the locals. He himself didn't fully grasp the island's dynamics, particularly beyond his bubble. There were prejudices and histories he was still struggling to learn, even after all these years of making Taiwan his home. The disdain his wife felt for a particular Hakka neighbor of theirs, whom she called "cheap," and in turn, the times he'd heard that neighbor's husband rant about the "lazy, drunk" aboriginal men he worked with at a construction site. Being on the outside of it, he didn't understand the assumptions that had embedded in the people who had grown up with them.

"It's actually not too bad," he told Suchi. "The people are hard-working and cordial. And the government has transformed Taipei, the capital, into a real city. They paved large roads for cars, built tall buildings, created infrastructure, made everything more . . . civilized. By 'the government,' I mean people like me, former soldiers who no longer have anything better to do."

"I can't imagine it," she said. "An island full of displaced soldiers."

The shop owner's teenage son placed the bowls of white congee in front of them, and Haiwen began to eat. He didn't feel like talking about Taiwan anymore. It was a home not of his choosing, one that never felt like his. He missed the sharp smell of Shanghai's winters, the buttery flake of his mother's turnip pastries, the warm bustle of his neighbors in the longtang going about their day, the salty sting of the sea. Taiwan was fine, but it could never settle into his heart.

"Tell me, do you still sing?" he asked Suchi, reaching for a piece of youtiao.

An expression he could not read crossed her face. "Yes," she said. "I've been given a few opportunities in Hong Kong."

His chest expanded. He was so relieved, so happy, to know that despite everything, she'd been able to keep singing. "That's wonderful," he said. "Imagine that. You thought you'd never fulfill that dream in Shanghai, and now here you are."

"Yes," she said. "Yes, I'm very lucky." Again Haiwen felt a sense of disorientation, something unfamiliar and unnerving in her that he couldn't quite place his finger on. Suchi swallowed a mouthful of congee. "What about you? Do you still play violin?"

Haiwen decided to tell her the truth. "Not much, no."

"Oh!" she said, her face blinking in disappointment. "How could that be? Who is Doudou if not a violinist?"

"I don't own a violin. They aren't exactly plentiful in Taipei and anyway, I don't have the money to spare."

"Oh," she said. "So if you had a violin—" She paused and gazed at him. "It's something else."

He stared at his hands. After all this time, Suchi could still read him. "It would be hard to play. I don't have scores, so the only music I could play would be what my hands remember." He paused. "Once upon a time, I could have sounded pieces out from memory, but . . ." He exhaled, a sudden burst of breath. "The music is gone. I can't hear it anymore."

Suchi put a hand to her cheek. "What do you mean?"

"I mean," he said, "remember how you used to complain I was never truly present? Because I was always listening to something buzzing in the back of my head? All of that noise—it's gone. I can't hear anything, not Brahms, not Bach, not Sibelius. Nothing. And my mind is unbearably empty without it."

"How? Why?"

"I don't know," he said. "It trickled away little by little during the war, or maybe sometime after it, I don't know. But I woke up one day and realized it was all gone." Without warning, Haiwen found his eyes threatened with tears. He couldn't speak. He swirled his spoon, watched flecks of green scallion and translucent brown century egg appear and disappear in the white porridge.

Suchi began talking. "I remember I could tell when you were angry at me; you could never come right out and tell me, 'Susu, I'm upset.' You would always mumble things were okay and go home. But if I visited your house later, wanting to apologize or make it up to you, I would hear the sharp notes of that Russian folk song."

"It wasn't a Russian folk song," he said quietly. "It was Prokofiev."

She sucked her teeth and laughed. "I never could remember those foreign composers. My point is, you were terrible at expressing your emotions directly, except when you played the violin. It's how you made sense of the world."

"Maybe that's why I can't hear it," he said. "The world stopped making sense when I left Shanghai."

"Or maybe things stopped making sense when you stopped playing," she said.

He looked away. He wanted to confide in Suchi about the gambling. He wanted to explain how the possibility of winning helped fill his echoing head, how the occasional times he did win gave him a high that felt a bit like when he ran through a piece perfectly for the first time. But it was impossible to discuss without mentioning Linyee.

"I spend all my time trying to make my life make sense," he told Suchi. "I keep reflecting on the past, trying to figure out how I got from there to here. What choices I could have made differently."

Suchi nodded. "I understand that feeling," she said softly. "But maybe . . . maybe there's no point in doing that. Maybe it's this obsession over things we can't change that is killing us. Maybe we have to stop thinking about it and move forward with our lives."

"But aren't you afraid of forgetting?"

"No," she said, shaking her head. "I'm afraid of a lifetime of remembering the things I want to forget."

Haiwen figured out what had been bothering him. The Suchi he remembered had been fearless in a way that belied her vulnerability. She'd been a ferocious puppy, growling and pouncing at any threat that came near her or the people she loved despite any underlying insecurities or fears she might have had.

But Suchi now, as beautiful and alluring as she was, seemed guarded and weary. On the surface she seemed to be a more mature, contained version of herself, but he was struck with the certainty that Suchi's assured demeanor masked fear. Haiwen wondered what it was she had endured, but he didn't know how to ask, if he had a right to ask.

A fist squeezed inside him. He stared at her pale hands, folded elegantly on top of each other on the sticky linoleum table. A mosquito landed on her wrist, but she didn't seem to notice. It drifted away, leaving a pink pin drop on her skin.

"What do you sing?" he asked.

Suchi paused. "Shidaiqu has gotten very popular here. And some English pop songs I've learned, although my English is still pretty terrible."

"And they pay you?"

"It's not every day they get a real Shanghainese woman to sing the old Shanghai standards, after all." She flashed him a brief smile, one that was teasing and flirtatious; Haiwen had never seen her smile like that before.

"Can I come and watch you?"

"Oh no," she said quickly. "It's at a private club. For rich British and Hong Kong businessmen. Very expensive."

"I'm here on business," he said. "I could take one of my clients. They may even know you already."

Suchi shook her head, giving him another coy smile. "Come on, stop it. I would be too nervous if you were there! Do you want me to embarrass myself in front of all those powerful men?"

"I've heard you sing thousands of times," he said. "Since when have you been shy?"

"We were kids!" Suchi said. "Now stop or I'll regret having met you for breakfast."

She said this in a light teasing tone, accompanied by another smile, and Haiwen began to suspect it was an unconscious tick, this new expression of hers, what she did when she was being stubborn without trying to appear stubborn. Because that was something he *knew* about Suchi, something he was sure could not have changed: once she had decided she didn't want to do something, she would not change her mind.

"I have to go," Suchi said, putting several coins on the table and standing up. She suddenly seemed exhausted. "Don't you have work too?"

Haiwen rose also, gathering her coins to give back to her so he could pay for breakfast, but she waved him off. Outside, he asked her if they could meet again the next morning. She hesitated.

"I might be busy," she said.

"With what?" When she didn't immediately answer, he pressed.

"Please. You don't know how many years I've spent pretending you were around to talk to."

"Tonight," she said in a rush, as if she were giving in. "It's my night off. There's a noodle shop down the block from here. I'll meet you there at eight."

HAIWEN HAD A SPEECH PREPARED. HE WOULD TELL SU-chi about Linyee as soon as she sat down but emphasize that the fact he was married didn't mean he hadn't truly loved her. He believed part of him would always love her, and his marriage couldn't change that fact. He would tell her that for the first few years in Taiwan, he hadn't even considered being with another woman (he would not tell her, of course, of the prostitute to whom he had lost his virginity), because he had been certain the day would come when he'd return to her and they would be married.

But little by little, things began to change. Whispers that the war would never end. That the Generalissimo had no concrete plan for victory, and they might never return. Somewhere along the line, Haiwen too began to lose faith. He had found no way to get a letter home, though he'd heard rumors it could be done if you knew the right people. He had no idea if Suchi had received his earlier letters, sent from the field, or if she even knew he was alive. Reports trickled in that the families of intellectuals and landowners were being stripped of their assets and sent to languish in farms no better than prison camps. He feared that Suchi, with her education-minded father, was lost to him, perhaps dead (he could not allow himself to speculate on what fate had befallen his own family, with their factories). So when he sat down at a small food stall ten years after landing in Taiwan and met the friendly, pretty daughter of the owner, he allowed himself the interest. She reminded him of Suchi in her openness, her vivacity, but she was gentler than Suchi had been, less stubborn and willful. After six months, he married her.

He knew this explanation wouldn't be enough. It couldn't be enough. But it was all he had.

When Suchi came in, this time right at eight, he started to say, "I need to—" but she cut him off.

"I have something for you."

She placed it on the table in front of him. His violin case.

The words evaporated from his tongue.

The brown leather was scuffed and scratched, showing tender fuzz at the edges where it had been chafed too many times.

"I kept it for you," she said.

He opened the case. Inside was a bundle wrapped in navy cloth dotted with white flowers. He unwound the cloth. His *violin*. A gift from his parents the year he had been accepted into the Youth Orchestra, to replace his shoddy student instrument. He still recalled how stunned he'd been when he'd lifted it out for the first time. The pride on his father's face, the joy on his mother's. *His* violin. He spread his hand across the lacquered wood and brought the instrument to his face. That familiar scent of sawdust and forest and burgundy heat.

He looked up at Suchi, who was watching him wordlessly.

"I didn't think you would still have this."

"Sulan said I was foolish for bringing this with me. We had to be selective with what we packed, and she warned me this would take up too much room, but I had to make sure it was okay."

As Haiwen lifted the instrument under his chin, a sense of completeness overcame him; he had not realized how his body had ached for this phantom limb. He slid his left hand into place along the neck, savoring the dig of the strings into his finger pads. Those specific calluses were still there, useless hard bars permanently embedded into his flesh. He plucked at the strings with his right hand. They had warped and loosened over time and were badly out of tune; the A string had completely snapped. Haiwen heard, faintly, the ghost of a melody trying to break itself into his consciousness. He held his breath, feeling the notes search for footholds along the walls of his mind. But they slipped, receded, and were gone. Haiwen put the violin back in the case.

"I don't know what to say," he said.

"'Thank you' would be nice," she teased, smiling a real smile, and he saw hints of the Suchi he remembered.

"Of course. Thank you."

The shop owner came to take their order—Suchi ordered a wonton noodle soup for herself, and he followed in bad Cantonese, ordering a bowl of fish ball soup.

"Yesterday you said the music was gone," Suchi said. "But maybe it's because you've been lacking your own instrument."

"I don't even know if I remember how to play anymore, to be honest," he said.

She cut him off with a sharp shake of her head. "You might be out of practice, but the violin is in your bones. *You remember.*" She shook the case lightly, insistently. Suchi had always had an absolute belief in him.

"You haven't changed," he said.

"What?" She sat back.

"Yesterday . . . Earlier . . . I worried you must have suffered a great deal these past few years, enough to defeat you. You seemed a bit . . . guarded, fragile. I thought, *Zhang Suchi has really changed.* But now I see you haven't. And I'm relieved."

Suchi twisted her chopsticks between her index and middle finger. "But I have changed. So have you. We've all changed."

Their soups arrived. He stared into the steaming bowl, at the rings of scallion floating on the thin gray soup. He pondered the ways in which he had changed, but it was more accurate to catalog the ways in which he had failed. As a father, a husband. He wanted to be a good man; he wanted to give his family more, to buy his wife a new dress or his daughters presents that would make them laugh. But every time he found himself with extra money in his pocket, he just forgot. He forgot about Linyee. He forgot about his daughters. He forgot about everything except the possibility that his luck might change that night. And afterward, he was always sorry. His daily failure was apparent in the fatigue painted on Linyee's face. He didn't deserve her.

"But you're still you," he said. Unlike him, who had lost himself, he wanted to say. "You're still the vibrant, ferocious Suchi I've always admired. I'm grateful for that."

Suchi said nothing. After a moment, she pushed his bowl toward him and pulled hers closer, dipping her spoon into the soup.

The distance between them that had momentarily collapsed when he'd received his violin now lay wide again. Haiwen scooped out a white fish ball.

"What did you want to tell me earlier?" Suchi asked.

Dropping the half-bitten sphere back into the soup, Haiwen thought of the speech he'd prepared, all he'd planned to say about Linyee and the girls.

"I wanted to ask you if you remember the color of the hair ribbon you were wearing the first time we kissed."

She looked surprised. Then she laughed, that real, clear laugh of unabashed delight he had loved. "It was purple," she said. "What in the world made you think of that?"

"Huh. Purple. I thought for sure it was red or orange."

She shook her head. "It was purple. I remember because it was the first item I owned in purple, and I thought it was the most beautiful color I had ever seen. I wore it every day around that time because I wanted to impress you."

"Was that in March or in April?"

"Are you testing me, or do you simply have a terrible memory?" she teased. "Don't tell me you've forgotten this! It was August fifteenth! The day Japan surrendered. How could you forget?" She pulled her face into a pout, and for a second he saw the young girl he had grown up with.

He tried to tug her words into place, and finally a small sliver of her purple hair tie emerged. A moment later, it brought with it other details, a long-forgotten image snapping into his consciousness.

"Oh, that's right," he said. "We were riding home on my bicycle and the chain slipped off. I was getting frustrated because I couldn't get it back on." He paused. "I was worried because some of the celebrations over the Japanese surrender had become violent. If something had happened to you, it would have been my fault for not protecting you."

"I know. That's why your frustration was so endearing," she said. "You were so serious, so annoyed, but I was just happy to celebrate that victory with you. I had wanted to tell you my feelings for so long." She smiled. "It was the most impulsive thing I'd ever done. And you—you grew so still."

The kiss came back to him, the sensation, the surprise. Music had always followed him wherever he went, but the moment she'd pressed her lips on his, the world had gone silent.

He remembered how his body had vibrated in that hush.

"Your lips were so much firmer than I expected them to be," Haiwen told Suchi.

"I didn't know what I was doing! I was trying to be confident."

"I just mean I had always imagined your lips to be soft, like a cloud." He smiled. "Your hair was in one braid that day. I remember wanting to run my fingers through your hair but being worried I would mess it up."

"Oh, I wouldn't have minded," she said, laughing.

The memory warmed him, even as it caused a dull ache to radiate through his chest. That day he had gone home feeling he was the luckiest person in the world. While everyone he knew had been debating about the Japanese surrender, he'd paid no attention. His life would be bright, whatever happened, because he knew the girl he loved felt the same way.

Suchi folded her hands on the table and leaned in. "What else? This is fun."

He went through a list of questions that had nagged at him the night before, which led to their arguing over details they couldn't agree on ("That fight was *definitely* because you were upset I had been talking to Boyang," she said, while he insisted it was because he had said hello to En'en before saying hello to her) and laughing over memories they each hadn't thought about in decades ("Remember the time you and Sulan stole my bow to use as a fishing rod?"

"I'm so sorry. I was eight. I had no idea how expensive those things were").

The shop owners were mopping the floors and throwing them dirty looks when Suchi suggested they should leave. Outside in the balmy air, Haiwen wasn't ready for the night to end. He asked Suchi if she wanted to go to a little bar near the hotel. She hesitated but agreed.

The place was just a cramped corridor, with a dark wooden bar long enough to seat six stools and a jukebox in the corner playing a sultry pop ballad heavy with strings. Only one other person sat in the corner, a balding man drunkenly pontificating at the bartender. Haiwen and Suchi sat down at the other end of the bar. Haiwen ordered a whiskey, and Suchi ordered a glass of red wine.

"One more," Haiwen said after they'd exhausted most of his questions. "I forgot. Do you remember the first time we met? I can't seem to."

"You don't remember when we first met?" Suchi exclaimed, sipping her wine. "I'm actually offended."

Haiwen could barely remember a time when Suchi wasn't in his life. All of his earliest memories were fuzzy, on a jumbled timeline that included her.

"You had forgotten your lunch that day. I saw you sitting quietly at your desk, with no food. You just sat there, staring straight ahead. Later, once I understood you better, I came to realize you were probably hearing music in your head. But at the time I remember thinking you looked so kelian, and so I came up to you and gave you a meatball."

"I *was* probably hearing music," he said. "I probably didn't even care that I forgot my lunch."

"Do you remember or not?"

He searched again and came up empty. "No," he said, disappointed in himself. "I have so many memories of you, but in all of them we're already friends."

"Aiya," she said with an exaggerated sigh. "I see how little I have meant to you."

He watched her laugh, noted how she still talked with her hands and played with her hair. He noticed all the ways in which she was the same girl he remembered, the ways in which she had never changed, and he felt an urge to seize her, to squeeze her so tightly she might melt into his bones and become a part of him, an organ that could never be cleaved away again.

The jukebox, which had been playing ballad after ballad, went silent. The drunk old man cursed loudly and, with dangerous effort, slid out of the bar stool and teetered over to the wall where the machine stood, his fingers jabbing at the buttons with difficulty. A saccharine melody started winding through the bar.

"Do you ever think about our last weeks together?" Haiwen asked. He was feeling warm from the liquor. "The way they could have gone. The way they went."

Suchi stared down at her glass, which the bartender had kept continuously filled. "I used to, all the time."

"I wish . . ." He paused. Years of guilt pulsed through his body. "I wish I had been less self-involved during those weeks. I wish I had known how to let you in."

Suchi bit her lip. "And I wish I hadn't said the things I did, that we hadn't parted in that awful way."

"At the very least, I wish I had let you know how much you meant to me." He gazed at her, adding softly, "You deserved more."

She sighed. "We were both young. Maybe it's time to forgive ourselves."

Haiwen watched her swirling her wine. "Do you ever wonder what our lives would have been like, if only?"

"Yes," she said, taking another sip of her wine but not lifting her eyes. "I do."

Haiwen watched her lips part gently after she lowered her glass. He longed to put a finger on those lips, to see if they were as soft as he remembered. He reached out and her eyes darted upward. His hand stilled in front of her. An inch from her skin.

"Susu," he said. He did not close his palm. He felt the light condensation of her breath.

Her voice was velvet and heavy when she spoke next. "Take me away from here."

HER HANDS WERE CLAMMY IN HIS AS THEY STOOD IN the hotel elevator. He could feel the knocking of his heart in his throat, and his eyes swam slightly from the liquor. He led her down the dim, carpeted hallway until they were in front of his room. Part of him did not want to release her, worried she might disappear, but he let go to dig the key out of his pocket. As he unlocked the door, he began to feel anxious. Alcohol pulsed loudly through his veins.

He turned on the lights and regretted it at once. In the harsh yellow of the room, he suddenly felt sober, uncertain. The energy that had buzzed between them on the way home faltered. Suchi removed her shoes and coat and walked in, taking in the faux-rococo opulence of the furnishings, the small television set.

"Fancy," she said. "I wasn't aware I was in the company of roy-alty." She bowed in mock deference. "Your Highness."

"Stop," he said, heat traveling to his throat.

"I always knew you were a little bourgeois," Suchi continued to tease. "Even back then. You loved your European music with all those names I couldn't pronounce. Tsai-something-or-other."

"Tchaikovsky," Haiwen said, "and Russia is in Asia."

Suchi snorted. "You're still the same," she said, sitting gingerly on the edge of the bed. She began combing her hair with her fingers. He realized she was nervous.

He switched off the light.

"Hey," Suchi protested. "I liked seeing the palace furnishings."

Haiwen removed his jacket and hung it on the back of a chair. Nerves prickled through his body. "Excuse me for a moment," he said.

Inside the bathroom, Haiwen unzipped his pants and tried to urinate. But his penis was partially erect, and all he could think about was how Suchi was outside the door. He felt his belly tighten and his penis harden. Reflexively, he began to stroke himself, several firm jerks, before guilt crept in. No. He couldn't do this.

He reentered the room. Suchi looked up expectantly at him, shy and lovely, a small rosebud of a smile forming on her lips, and he felt a knot of desire tugging him toward her. He knew he should tell her to leave, but he couldn't bring himself to. He sat down awkwardly next to her on the bed, his hands resting on his knees. She reached out and placed a tentative hand over his. Her hands were soft, warm.

Abruptly, he stood up to turn on the television and it blared to life. On-screen, a long-haired woman in white emerged from a burial mound. It was one of those ghost movies with bad special effects that

Linyee hated. One time they went to the movies, not knowing the film was scary, and by the time they realized, it was too late. Haiwen had to check behind curtains and closet doors for a month. He had grumbled about it at the time, but now it seemed endearing.

"I have to tell you something," Haiwen said in a rush. The words sounded loud in the room. Suchi turned to look at him, her face bathed in the light of the television. "I'm married."

She blinked twice, as if a flash had popped in front of her eyes. He waited for her to say something, and when she didn't, he continued, a cascade of words falling from his mouth.

"We—Linyee and I—have two little girls, Yiping and Yijun. I'm sorry I didn't tell you earlier. I should have, I meant to."

"Oh," she said. She stood up and looked at her hands as if she didn't know whose they were.

"Wait," he said. "Please don't go."

"Oh," she repeated.

He knew the best thing would be for Suchi to leave, but he couldn't bear it. He was certain he would never see her again if she walked out the door.

"I'm sorry," he said.

She sat back down and placed her hands in her lap, staring silently at the television. Her profile was flickering pale blue, her ear receding into the shadows. He wondered what her life had been these last two decades, if she had counted more joy than sorrow. If she would consider this one more sorrow on top of whatever she had already endured.

"Susu," he breathed.

She turned and looked at him, her eyes a question.

Words escaped him. What he wanted more than anything at that moment was to live inside her skin, to know all the things she had experienced, to absorb them into himself and let them mingle with all the things he had been through so the space between them could be erased.

Suchi, somehow sensing this, or perhaps feeling the change in the air, began to shake her head. Her eyes filled with tears. "Don't," she said, shielding them with the back of one hand.

Two steps and he was kneeling in front of her. He had a palm on her face, a thumb pressed against the mole by her eye, brushing away the fat tears rolling down her cheeks. She put up a hand and covered his, bringing his fingers to her lips.

A deep ache spread through his body. He savored the featheriness of her lips upon his fingers and leaned in to kiss her. Her lips were the same as he remembered them. Tender, gentle, uncertain. He felt her hands go up, felt several fingers pressing gently into the nape of his neck, pulling him up toward her. He kissed her harder, and she responded, her gentleness turning into a hunger he now remembered from their last days together, when he'd been too self-absorbed to cherish it, each kiss a promise she would stand by his side. He had taken that fervent love for granted.

Suchi broke away from his mouth to kiss his ears, his neck, the base of his throat, then craned her neck toward his lips again, her hands fierce on his shoulders, on his back, traveling down to his trousers. Dimly, he thought he should stop, that he should pull away, but she was undoing his belt buckle, sliding off his pants. She lay back and pulled him toward her. "Touch me," she whispered urgently, placing his hands over her dress on her breasts.

Soon he was pushing the dress upward, his hands finding her breasts beneath the fabric, their nipples swollen but tender beneath his flicking fingers. She pulled the dress over her head, urging her body toward his. He, too, pulled his shirt off, and now they were both only in their underwear. He stopped for a moment to take her in. He had spent so many adolescent years imagining her naked body. He had pictured her small but delicate breasts, her flat and perfect stomach, the smoothness of her skin. He hadn't imagined that when he finally saw her naked, they'd both be fully grown adults, scarred and lumpy and imperfect in many places. He noticed the slight sag of her breasts, the doughy paunch of her belly, the stretch marks that shone on her thighs. He wondered, briefly, if it was possible Suchi was still a virgin.

"Don't stop," she said, pulling his face toward her again and erasing his thoughts.

He sucked on one breast, then the other. He moved his face up to kiss her again. She reached underneath the elastic of his briefs and pulled his erection free and stroked him. His kisses were ragged pants. He let his fingers trail down past her stomach, hooking inside her underwear and finding it warm and wet. He pressed a finger into her, and when she gasped, he slid in another. He broke away from her to peel away her underwear, and when he took off his, they were both finally naked.

He started to position his body over her, but she shook her head. Kissing him, she maneuvered until they had switched places, her breasts suspended above him.

When she eased down on him, something shattered through his veins. He gazed up at her, but she had thrown her head back, her eyes closed and lips parted. He angled up to kiss her, and she opened her eyes and locked them on his. He couldn't read what was behind her expression. A moment later, she leaned forward and wrapped her

371

arms tightly behind his neck, as if she would never let go. Her mouth pressed beneath his jaw, making soft sounds of pleasure, mounting in their volume, until she dug her fingers into his skin and squeezed her knees around his hips so forcefully that for a second Haiwen thought he might break. With a groan, he came, a climax so fierce his body erupted into goose bumps and his toes flashed cold.

For several seconds after it was over, she didn't release him, her arms still tightly around him. Finally, she loosened her grip and rolled over next to him. Breathing heavily, he reached over to stroke her face but froze. She was crying.

His heart stopped.

"What's wrong?" he asked. "Did I hurt you?"

Suchi shook her head. Instead, she curled up into his body, leaned her face into his shoulder, and sobbed. He put his arms around her, stroking her shoulder. He held her until her cries subsided and evened out into deep breaths. He, too, fell asleep.

HE AWOKE WITH A START. AN ORANGE SUN WAS JUST beginning to warm through the curtains. The television was still on, now the morning news. Haiwen glanced beside him, but Suchi was gone.

He found, folded on top of his violin case, a note.

I'm getting married, so don't worry about me.

I'm glad we met again. My heart is at ease now because I know you're alive and well.

We can't regret the past, so please don't spend too much time dwelling on it.

Don't give up on playing.

FOR FOUR OUT OF THE FIVE REMAINING MORNINGS HE
had in Hong Kong, Haiwen sat in the congee shop until he had to go
to work. He knew she probably wouldn't appear, but he couldn't let
go of the hope he might be wrong. In the evenings, he persuaded his
boss to take their potential buyers to several private clubs, but he
never saw Suchi at any of them.

On the fifth morning, he woke up, packed, then opened his violin case. The only evidence she had not been a dream. As he gazed
at the instrument, he realized the date. Suchi's birthday. A small ache
twinged in his heart. He reached for the tear in the lining—wider
now than the small hole it had been when he'd last had the instrument in his possession—and swept two fingers inside. When he felt
nothing, he pressed around the outside. He wondered if Suchi had
found the ring, if she'd known it was for her. It was too late to ask.

In the afternoon, he strolled the streets, absorbing the people
pushing their carts or driving their taxis or sweeping the sidewalks,
and imagined Suchi's life threaded among theirs. He purchased rock
candy melted into animal shapes from a street vendor for Yiping. He
went into a jeweler and purchased a jade ox charm for Linyee. Then
he walked to the ferry terminal and gazed at the outline of the mountains across the harbor, noticing how the haze made them seem like
they were slowly being erased.

OCTOBER 1972
Hong Kong

S OUKEI WATCHED, HALF aching, half bemused, as a single, fat tear eased out the corner of her son's right eye and rolled down his plump cheek.

"Samson," she said gently, crouched in front of him. She held his two little hands in hers.

He stared past her as if she weren't there, at the legs of adults as they strode by, at the children who stared curiously at him. Perhaps they were wondering how any kid could be unhappy at the Lai Chi Kok Amusement Park, arguably the dream destination for any Hong Kong child.

She might have known better what to do with a tantrum, but her son had never been like other five-year-olds, who would throw themselves on the ground or stamp their feet when upset. Even as a toddler, he'd burrow into blankets when he wanted to cry, embarrassed by his emotions. She wondered where he'd gotten that from. She'd been so different at his age, hadn't she?

"Siau noe," she cooed. "Talk to Maami."

His lower lip pursed into a pout.

She sighed. They had been only a few meters from the zoo, where the park's star attraction, an elephant named Tino, resided, when Samson had suddenly stopped and pulled his hand out of hers. Now for the last several minutes, he'd refused to walk or speak and she didn't know why.

Soukei had thought this part of motherhood would get easier with time. After all, he was no longer a newborn who could only shriek his discomfort; he had words now. But she'd found that her son required coaxing and patience to feel safe enough to reveal his feelings, and while she did her best to maintain a mask of boundless empathy, inside she (guiltily) was often brimming with exasperation. *Just use your words!* she wanted to say. *Just tell me what's wrong so I can help you.*

She tried to follow Samson's line of vision to see if she might glean a clue about what had upset him. Instead, she caught the eye of a woman staring at them in contempt. Perfectly made up, she clutched a designer purse in one hand and a beautifully dressed little girl's palm in the other. A shock of rage went to Soukei's head. *What are you looking at? I bet your daughter throws tantrums anytime she doesn't get what she wants. Isn't that what rich kids do?* But she'd forgotten— her child was a rich kid too. Six years, and she still often forgot whom she was married to. Anyone who didn't know her well—most people—would hear her husband was Lam Saikeung and assume she was one of the taaitaais of Hong Kong, the wives of rich Hong Kongers who whiled away their hours lunching at a different high-end restaurant each day, hair perfectly coiffed, decked out in designer threads from head to toe. Still others who knew of her origin might assume, the way her own mother-in-law did, that she had trapped Lam Saikeung into this marriage by purposely getting pregnant. If only they knew.

The woman was long gone, but Soukei was stewing in a fizz of sorrow and rage. She nearly missed the quiet mumble of Samson's voice.

"What's that?" she said. She swallowed the bitterness in her mouth and stroked her son's cheek tenderly. "Can you say that again?"

"They said Tino is sick," he repeated softly.

"Who said?"

"The workers," Samson said. "They walked by and I heard them say it. They said Tino is sick and hasn't been eating."

It always surprised her how little escaped her son's attention, how much he absorbed from the world around him. She hadn't noticed any workers, hadn't heard their conversation. But then again, she found it easy to block out Cantonese when it suited her—if she wasn't paying attention, the language turned into a blur of ambient noise.

"I'm sure he's okay," she said, rubbing Samson's shoulder. "Everyone gets sick sometimes. It's probably just a cold. Nothing to be upset about."

"But what if—" He stopped and took a small shuddering breath. "What if Tino dies like Bunbun?"

Oh. Now it all made sense. They were here because of Bunbun, after all. Her son's pet rabbit had died the night before after a three-day hunger strike. She'd tried to explain death gently, murmured something about how the rabbit had gone for a long sleep and they wouldn't see her again, but Saikeung had intervened. "Death is a fact of life," he'd said. "Animals die. People do too. This is the first hardship your young life has ever had to face. Get used to it." Samson had nodded sagely, and Soukei had wondered if he'd understood what death was at all. But that evening, she passed by his room and heard him sniffling into his pillow. When she woke him in the morning, his eyes were still swollen and red. She'd thought a trip to the amusement park to see his favorite elephant would cheer him up. Obviously, the gods had other plans.

"Oh, baobei, I'm sure Tino will be fine. Everyone gets sick sometimes, but that doesn't mean they'll die. You were sick just last month, and look at you now, you're all better, right?" The furrow of his brow indicated he remained unconvinced.

"But why did Bunbun die then?"

"Sometimes animals—and people—get so sick, they can't get better. But that's not most of the time. Most of the time everything is okay."

She was sure she was messing this up somehow. While she didn't agree with Saikeung's harsh methods, it was true that death was a fact of life. But she didn't know how to break this reality to her son while still offering comfort, how to help him accept it without making up lies about animal heaven, how to prevent him from being terrified every living creature he cared for might one day, randomly, drop dead in front of him.

"Even though Bunbun is gone, we still love her very much, don't we? We can think about all the good memories we had with her, and she stays in our hearts that way. So it's almost like she's not gone. Like how you always fed her the celery you didn't want and she would gobble it up so quickly. Or how she always cleaned her bowl and pushed it into the corner of her cage after every meal, like a very good rabbit. Aren't these nice memories?"

She was aware of how stupid and empty she sounded, and she wasn't even sure she believed this advice, so she stopped, certain Samson would see through the inanity of her words. But after a moment he gave the tiniest nod. Encouraged, she wrapped him in a hug. He relaxed into her shoulder, sniffling.

"Come, I bet if Tino is sick, he'll want some cheering up from his favorite little boy." She stood up and held out her hand for him to hold.

As they walked, she glanced down at his little trusting face and felt a familiar wave of awe and fear. It was still strange to her that she was a mother—that she was *allowed* to be a mother. She didn't quite *feel* it; oftentimes she felt she was an imposter playing the part, and that at any point someone would figure it out. It had been worst during the terrible months after his birth—the long nights when she thought about climbing out of the window of their twenty-floor high-rise; the endless days of combating the voice in her head that told her her son would be better off without her, that she would be better off without him. Those first weeks of going through the motions of mothering this blob, this turnip, this warm pulsating mass that she could easily drop or crush or suffocate. It had both thrilled and terrified her that the only thing keeping this baby from death was her, a fragile dam of a woman. Her active choice to keep him alive was what kept him safe, and it was a power she did not want. For the first six months of his life, every time he began to suckle, his downy head pressed softly against her, she'd have a vision of his tiny body as a broken, bloody heap at her feet. She told no one, not even Sulan.

That was then. She no longer had to struggle to want her son; she could no longer imagine a life without him. Even so, sometimes she floated away from herself, like she did right now, to stare down at a woman she found unrecognizable. She had this thought all the time, when she lay beneath Saikeung in the bed they shared, swallowed up in luxurious pillows, or when she was being berated by her mother-in-law for not preparing Saikeung's favorite pork rib soup the right way, or when she comforted a puke-covered Samson who had thrown up in the middle of the night—who was this woman? How was it possible Zhang Suchi had become her?

They arrived at the pit where Tino was kept, and Soukei saw, to her relief, that the elephant was there. He stood by the water trough, swatting his behind with his tail, and poked at a bale of hay near his feet. If he was sick, you couldn't tell. Workers still sold buckets of carrots, turnip tops, and broccoli heads for visitors to feed him. Children still hung off the railing trying to get the elephant's attention.

"See?" Soukei said to Samson. "He's fine!"

Samson nodded, bouncing a little on his toes.

"Do you want to feed him? Shall I buy him food?" It was a pointless question, the kind you asked children in an upbeat voice even though you knew the answer. Samson had never once not wanted to feed the elephant.

They stood near the railing, their vegetables ready, waiting for a turn to feed Tino. Two older girls, who looked to be around ten or eleven, stood in front of them, leaning over the railing and waving at Tino to get his attention. One was holding a bucket of vegetables while the other munched on popcorn out of a paper bag. When the animal finally turned toward them, the girl with the bucket eagerly held out a broccoli head. Tino hovered his trunk over the vegetable but didn't touch it.

"Aren't you supposed to like this?" she asked impatiently. "Yummy yummy broccoli!"

The other girl said, "Let me try," and offered some carrots. The elephant swiped at the carrots but instead of eating them, he threw them on the ground. "Hey!" the girl cried. "That's not what you're supposed to do! You're supposed to eat this! What's wrong with you!"

The girl with the broccoli tried again. Tino curled his trunk around the broccoli, and for a moment the girl whooped with joy. But then Tino crushed it in his trunk, scattering florets on the ground. The girl started to pout. "That's not fair!" she said. "We bought this food for you and you didn't even eat it!"

The other girl threw popcorn at the elephant. "Maybe you like popcorn?" The first girl laughed and took a handful of popcorn and joined in. Little puffs of popcorn bounced off the elephant's face.

"Maami," Samson whispered, "they're being mean to Tino. We should tell them he's sick and isn't hungry."

Soukei looked around to see if any of the workers would intervene, but most weren't paying attention and the one who was seemed amused. She searched among the adults milling a bit further from the railing. Where were the girls' parents?

All of a sudden she heard a high-pitched shriek. She turned back to see one of the girls sprawled on the ground, crying. "He *hit* me!" she blubbered, nursing a skinned knee. "He took his big nose and *hit* me!"

A man pushed his way through the gathering crowd and clutched the girl's shoulders. He looked at the workers, who were converging upon the girl with apologies, and began to shout, "That creature attacked my daughter! Who is in charge here? That wild beast should be put down!"

Soukei looked beyond the flurry surrounding the girl, toward the elephant. Three workers were now herding Tino away from the railing, prodding him with a faintly sizzling pole toward the gated pen where he presumably slept at night. Her gaze landed on Tino's face, and she was startled to find Tino staring back at her. The light in his eyes was mournful yet triumphant, defiant yet resigned. For the first time, Soukei registered how unhealthy and dirty the animal looked. His skin had none of the rich leathery sheen of the wild elephants she'd seen in photographs. The flaps of his ears were thin and torn. He was gaunt despite his large size and flies plagued him. She looked back into Tino's eyes, recognizing, for a moment, something familiar. A sadness seeped into her. If not for Samson, she would never pay to see this captive creature again.

It was only when the elephant had disappeared into his prison that Soukei remembered Samson, still clutching his pail of vegetables. Had he seen the whole thing? Would he be screaming from nightmares about murderous elephant rampages tonight?

"Did that scare you?" Soukei asked, already reaching for some fumbling words of comfort. *Not all elephants. Not all zoo animals.*

"He was mad," Samson said. "Because the girls were not very nice."

"Yes, that's true," Soukei agreed.

"He can't say words. He can't say, 'Stop, leave me alone,' when people are mean to him. So he could only push her."

Soukei nodded, surprised by her son's insightfulness. Children made no sense. You could spend hours trying to convince your child that a red cup was just as good as a blue cup and they'd refuse to see the logic in that. And yet they could see the violent actions of an animal and immediately empathize with why the creature might have been provoked into them. This contradiction was one of the things that still made mothering new to her, that made *Samson* still new to her.

"But Maami, it's not nice to push people. Even if you're mad."

"No, it's not, you're right."

Samson toyed with a carrot, picking it up and putting it back in with a dull, tinny *klok*. "Maybe it's okay if someone is mean to you first?"

Soukei wondered, not for the first time, if her son was being bullied at school. One month into kindergarten, and he still hadn't made any friends and always played alone, according to his teacher. The teacher mentioned that when other children took toys from him, he capitulated easily. She wondered if he was working out if it was okay to fight back. She didn't know the right thing to tell him.

"I think—I think Tino tried nicely to show them that he didn't like what they were doing. And maybe if he had words, he would have told someone to please help him. But in the end, no one came to help him, and they were hurting him, so he could only help himself." She paused, again worried she was making a mess of things. "But if you're ever in a situation like Tino, you can tell me or the teacher, okay?"

"Maybe we should have told the girls he was sick," Samson said. "They didn't know he was sick."

"Maybe." Soukei sighed. "I don't know if that would have made a difference."

Samson seemed troubled. Soukei waited for him to say more, but he just kept playing with the vegetables in the pail. Finally, she said,

"Baobei, I think Tino went home to rest. Shall we go see some of the other animals in the park?"

She tried to drink it in, the rest of the day. The light in his eyes as he waved to her from the little train ride, the clarity of his giggles as he whirled in the teacups beside her, the sweet stickiness of his skin after he sucked down an elephant-shaped ice pop the size of his face. She had missed the first third of his life, had not loved him enough to register the joy of his first laugh, his first word, his first steps. That part of his life was lost to the fog. But now—she wanted to make up for it, to bottle up all that was precious. She hoped it wasn't too late. She hoped she could still convince him he had always been loved.

WHEN THEY RETURNED HOME IN THE AFTERNOON, Soukei immediately asked Siu Hung, their live-in amah, to draw a bath for Samson. Saikeung would dine home that night, and she didn't want him to smell the stink of animal and cotton candy on Samson's body.

While Samson bathed, she went to check in on Sulan, who had returned from her job as an assistant to a dressmaker and was resting in bed. "How was the park?" she asked. "Is Samson feeling better?"

Soukei told her everything that had happened with Tino. "I was worried it might have been too much for him. He was asking a lot of questions I didn't know how to answer."

"He's a sensitive boy, but that's what makes him perceptive and intelligent."

"Something he said made me wonder if he's being bullied. At the very least, he's not fitting in well at school. He still doesn't play with any of the other children, according to the teacher. It's not normal, right? Children his age should be making friends."

"Ai," Sulan clucked. "You worry too much. Don't you remember what you were like at around his age? You had trouble making friends, until you met Haiwen. Then you suddenly blossomed, came into yourself. Samson will grow into his own, eventually."

At Haiwen's name, Soukei felt a dull ache that, despite the years, still throbbed with heat. She had tried hard not to think of him, had pushed him into the corners of her mind. It was Sulan who still brought him up casually, as if he were just a character from the past. Of course, she didn't know that he'd been in Hong Kong, or that Soukei had once spent the night with him. It was something Soukei herself valiantly tried to forget. She wanted to forget how, for a stupid couple of days, she had thought he had appeared to save her from her life with Saikeung. Visions of that alternate life, what *could* have been, if only he hadn't been married, tormented her in those postpartum weeks. Folly and fantasy. She still burned with self-loathing when she thought of it.

"It was different for me. I was stubborn and proud enough that I convinced myself I didn't need anyone else. Samson is different. You see how interior he is. He can't even express his emotions freely."

She thought, not for the first time, of how much like Haiwen her son was—so much so that sometimes she liked to imagine he was born of her night with Haiwen, not the other terrible night. She hoped, like Haiwen, he would one day find something he loved as a way to express himself.

Sulan arched an eyebrow. "And why do you think that is? Lam Saikeung pounces on him anytime the boy shows an ounce of sadness. And then you, you're even worse. Constantly signaling to him that he should be mindful of not rubbing his father the wrong way."

"You know Saikeung's temper—"

"Ayi!" Samson came flying into the room, bounding onto Sulan's bed and launching himself into her arms. His hair was still damp and fuzzed from being towel dried and he left a powder-scented cloud of baby soap in his wake. Sulan laughed and hugged him.

"I heard you went to the amusement park today. Did you have fun?"

Samson nodded. "We went to see Tino, but he was sick and some big kids were very mean to him so he hit them. Then we went to see the monkeys and the alligator, and we rode on the teacups ride and a train ride and the carousel, where I got to ride on a camel. And I had an ice pop and a hot dog and caramel popcorn and cotton candy. Ayi, did you know that when you try to eat cotton candy, it erases in your mouth?"

"I *do* know!" Sulan said. "Cotton candy is my favorite! But come, tell me, how did you feel about the elephant hitting the girl? Was that very scary?"

Samson thought about it. "A little bit," he admitted. "But the girls were very mean so they were more scary."

"Well, did you think they deserved it then?" Soukei started to protest but Sulan glanced at her with a mischievous twinkle in her eye. She tickled Samson a little and he let out a squeal. "Maybe a small part of you was glad he hit them?"

Samson glanced guiltily at Soukei.

"You can whisper it to me," Sulan said. "Maami doesn't need to know." Giving Soukei one more glance, Samson leaned over and murmured in Sulan's ear. Ayi laughed loudly and mussed Samson's hair.

Soukei sighed impatiently. "Don't encourage him. Samson, hitting people isn't right."

Sulan hugged the boy close to her chest. "It's not right to hit people weaker than you, that's true. Or someone with less power than you. But, Samson, what's right doesn't always look the same. When someone being bullied stands up for himself, that's okay. And if you see someone bullying someone weaker than them, you *should* stand up for them, okay? Even if it's a little bit scary." Samson nodded seriously.

"But also be safe," Soukei said. "If there's a bully who is bigger than you, the best thing to do is to find the teacher."

"Is Tino a bully because he's bigger than the girls then?" Samson asked.

"No one should be bullying anyone," Soukei said at the same time that Sulan said, "But the girls aren't the ones with shackles around their feet."

Samson looked confused. Finally he turned to Sulan. "Maybe we should have helped Tino and told the girls to not be so mean and then no one would have to be a bully?"

Sulan nodded and hugged him. "Exactly," she said.

Samson fiddled his fingers. "But they seemed mean. Maybe they would yell at me or throw popcorn at me too."

Sulan poked at Samson's cheek. "The right thing to do isn't always easy."

The words rang familiar, and Soukei had a flash of Apa at the dinner table, pontificating at them. *I hope you always choose to do what is right instead of what is easy.* What would Apa have thought of her as a mother, as a woman? What failure would he have seen in her? Nothing in her life felt easy, but did that make it right? If there was a righteous path for her to take, she had never seen it clearly. And yet, here was Sulan, passing down Apa's words to her son.

"Ah, I almost forgot, I made something special for you," Sulan said. She produced a stuffed rabbit from behind her back, hand sewn with scraps of felt and silk and cotton. Samson's eyes lit up. Gingerly, he reached his arms out.

"Bunbun," he said, even though the stuffed animal looked nothing like his pet rabbit. He snuggled the toy close into his body. "Thank you, Ayi."

Sulan looked on, beaming. Soukei looked at her, and, not for the first time, wondered if Sulan would have made the better mother.

SOUKEI BATHED AND PUT ON MAKEUP IN PREPARATION for Lam Saikeung's return. She had cautioned Samson not to mention going to the amusement park to his father—"This is our little secret," she told him, even as she felt guilty for teaching her son how to lie—but still, when Lam Saikeung walked through the door, he took one look at Samson and frowned. "Your skin got darker." He looked up at Soukei. "Why does my son look like a farmer?"

Soukei bowed her head. There was no point in lying now. "He was so sad, even this morning. I didn't want him to have to go to school like that, so I took him to the amusement park to cheer him up."

Saikeung gave an exasperated cluck. "God, you coddle this boy so much! No wonder he can't get used to school! First you delay his schooling for a year because you're worried he's not ready, and now that he's actually in school, you take him out any chance you get. All this babying has made him soft. No wonder he snivels over a rabbit. At his age, I'd already seen death on the streets!"

"It's just kindergarten, it's not like he has homework—"

"They learn their letters and basic characters, don't they? What do you think I pay all that tuition for? So that he can *play* all day? You don't think things through. It's shocking, because when I first met you, I thought you were clever. But now I see that you're just as dim-witted as the rest of those bar girls."

"It was just one day—"

"Baba," Samson said, his little voice piping up. Saikeung and Soukei looked down, startled. They'd both forgotten their son was still there. "You shouldn't be so mean to Maami. You should use a nice voice, not a mean one."

Saikeung's head whipped up to look at Soukei, his face pale and furious. "Did you teach him this?"

Soukei shook her head vigorously. "He's a little boy, he doesn't know what he's saying." She grabbed Samson and pulled him behind her. "Samson, you can't talk to your baba like that. Say you're sorry."

The boy looked confused. "But Ayi said if someone is mean, we should—"

"*Ayi?* So your sister put him up to this?" Soukei was aware of her husband's tightened fists, the loud sound of his breathing.

She gave Samson a little shake. "Say you're sorry," she said in a louder, harsher voice.

"No." He said the word quietly but firmly.

"What." Saikeung's voice was dangerously low now.

"No," Samson said a little more loudly. Soukei thought of how, when Samson was around two years old, she had tried so hard to

388

excise that word from his vocabulary, but, stubbornly, he had clung to it. *Do you want milk? No! Do you want bread? No! Do you want to sleep? No! Do you want to stay awake? No! Do you want candy? No—yes.* How Saikeung had railed against her then, for not being able to control her son, even though she had heard from the other wives, who delighted in telling stories of their little ones at cocktail parties, that every child went through a phase like that. She had been afraid for Samson then, and the same fear prickled her skin now.

"Samson!" she said. "How dare you speak to your parents this way! When I tell you to say you're sorry, that's not a request! Do it!" Belatedly she realized that to a child, her voice, teetering with panic, must have sounded enraged.

A tear sprung to Samson's eye. The right one, always the right one.

Sulan rushed into the foyer, pulling Samson into her arms. "What is wrong with you," she hissed at Soukei.

Soukei remembered one time, after Samson had been particularly stubborn about eating his dinner (*No vegetables! No rice! No water! No! No! No!*), Saikeung had threatened to discipline him the way he'd been disciplined as a child. *All he needs is a good whipping and there will be no more of this nonsense.* Soukei had begged him to let her be the one to punish him instead. And she had, with Saikeung observing. She'd taken to the inside of his tiny palm with the fat end of a chopstick. Gently, she thought, as gently as she could while still making it seem real. It didn't matter. Samson's eyes had welled up in pain or fear or betrayal as he pulled his hand away. He had refused her attempts to console him once it was over.

Sulan was glaring at Saikeung.

"Don't get involved," Soukei pleaded with Sulan. She knew that

Saikeung was less likely to completely lose his temper with her sister around, but Soukei always wondered if one day, he would stop viewing Sulan as an outsider and unleash his fury upon her, possibly evict her and prevent Soukei from seeing her again.

"What nonsense have you been filling my son's head with?" Saikeung said to Sulan, his voice steely.

"I only told him to stand up to bullies," she responded calmly. "My sister said she was worried he might be dealing with bullies at school. Wouldn't you agree, Meifu, that we want Samson to stand up to bullies? Aren't you the one obsessed with him not being too weak?"

Saikeung's fists curled until his knuckles were white. "Are you calling me a bully?"

"Do you think you're a bully?"

"I let you live under my roof, eat my food, bathe in my water. This is how you repay me. This is how you both repay me."

"Don't worry, I don't plan on staying here forever. Once I have enough money saved up, I'll even pay you back."

Saikeung exhaled, releasing his fists. He ripped at his tie. "I've had a long day, I don't want to deal with you sisters." He stalked off into the bedroom.

Once he had disappeared, Sulan enveloped Samson into her body. "My little hero," she said, patting his head. "Are you okay?"

Samson nodded. He glanced at Soukei and then down at his fidgeting hands. "Maami, I'm sorry I made Baba mad at you."

Soukei's chest ached, nearly splintered. "Oh, siau noe." She held out her arms to hug him. "Maami is the one who is sorry, so sorry, for yelling at you."

"I hear Siu Hung is making your favorite red bean buns for dessert tonight," Sulan said. "Maybe you can go to the kitchen and see if she'll sneak you one before dinner."

When Samson had gone, Sulan whipped around and glared at Soukei. "*You're* supposed to protect Samson, not the other way around."

"I *am* protecting him," Soukei said, temper rising. Who did her sister think she was, barging in like that and enraging Saikeung further? Didn't she know what kind of man he was? "You have to stop telling Samson things that will only get him hurt. It's not helpful for him to think he can be a hero. He's a boy. Boys can't be heroes."

"What happened to you?" Sulan said, her voice filled with disgust. "You used to be brave. What happened to the girl with the sharp tongue who cut down the neighborhood boys who teased her? The girl who said she'd claw the face of any Japanese soldier who tried to kidnap me? Don't you think Apa would be ashamed?"

Yes, of course he would be, she thought. She'd married a rich man she did not love, like a concubine. For a moment she hated Sulan, hated how she sat easy on her pedestal. She knew—she had to know—that Soukei had married Saikeung in part *for her*. Because of her medical bills, because she lay in bed sick and weak for the better part of a year. It was Saikeung's money and connections that had helped Sulan's condition improve, enough that she could work again, could even *dream* of someday escaping this Mid-levels apartment. What had happened to Zhang Suchi? Zhang Suchi had died the moment she left Wang Haiwen sleeping in that hotel room, her last hope of running from her fate extinguished. She thought back to the envelope with the letter from Siau Zi, the one she'd ripped to shreds long ago. How tempted she was to tell Sulan: *You, too, almost married someone you did not love to save someone you did.*

"I want Samson to be *safe*," she said. Hadn't Sulan learned yet? How easy it was to lose someone, how people you believed were immovable forces in your life could vanish overnight. "If that means teaching him to swallow his pride so as not to anger his father, then so be it."

Sulan shook her head in disappointment. When she spoke again, her voice was soft. "Do you remember what I said right after Samson was born?"

It was a hazy memory to Soukei now. What she remembered was the dull, numb feeling like her body wasn't her own; the child squalling like an air raid siren; Sulan beside her bed, holding him, shushing him, because Soukei felt only terror and nausea at the sight of him.

"I told you Samson needed you. For protection, for love, for guidance. That you were his best chance at all of those things. That the two of you are on the same team." She paused. "I know you're trying to protect him. But yelling at him like this doesn't put you on the same team."

Soukei would burn down the world for Samson. That was what Sulan didn't see. Soukei knew—was enraged—that she could not protect him forever, but she had to try. Sometimes she wanted to weep with the helplessness she felt, knowing that one day she would fail. The terror of that day.

"Why does he need me, when he has you?" Soukei said with bitterness. "I'm sure you would make a much better mother."

"I'm *not* his mother," Sulan said. "And like I told your husband, I don't plan on staying here forever. I don't want to owe that man a single cent."

Soukei was seized with a new terror. She could not imagine living this life without Sulan. She could not imagine living under this roof with that man without her sister. She felt safer, knowing she wasn't alone. But also: she longed for someone to protect her. She was so tired of protecting herself.

As if reading her mind, Sulan said, "When we were little, I didn't do a good job of watching out for you, I know. You had to fend for yourself a lot. I'm sorry about that, and I tried, in our early years in Hong Kong, to make up for it. I worked hard to make as much money as I could so that we could hopefully have a better future together. I know I failed. That you've ended up protecting me. And I'm sorry, more than you can know, that doing so has been at the expense of your happiness. But, Suchi, I wish you'd find that fighting spirit again. Samson is watching. He learns from you. When you let that man push you around . . ."

"What would you have me do?" Soukei said. "This is my life. That man is who I married."

Sulan looked down. "I'm sorry." She paused. "Maybe we can—"

Soukei shook her head. "It's too late. He will never let his son go without a fight. And I can't leave without Samson."

Sulan nodded.

"Help him," her sister finally said. "Help him so he can someday help himself."

Soukei thought of her son's shy smile, his pudgy hand. His one tearful eye. And then she was thinking of the elephant's eye, baleful, resigned in captivity. She would never take Samson there again, she thought. She'd explain why. She'd tell her son what a sad place the zoo was, for keeping this noble creature against its will. For parading it around for entertainment. For not protecting it. Samson would be disappointed at first, but he would understand, because he loved the animal and would not want to partake in its suffering. She had to make sure he leaned in a different direction than his father. Her son would grow up to be a good man, an empathetic man, a man who chose right over easy every time. It was the one thing she could still do, after everything else had been stripped from her.

Sulan stood with some difficulty and went toward the kitchen, exclaiming, "Are you enjoying red bean buns without me?" and Soukei's breast ached, wondering how she would survive this life without her sister by her side.

It was ironic, really. For the first year of her son's life, she had resented how needy he was, how he only let her hold him, how he would only sleep if she carried him in her arms. She had wished then that time would move forward faster, to when he would cleave from her. But now he was his own little person. And Soukei found, with a pang, that just as Samson's world was widening to include others, her own world was shrinking. Once Sulan left, Samson would be all she had. That small, quiet, watchful human. Her entire world.

FEBRUARY 1959
Keelung

THE KNOCKING PULLED him from a dreamless sleep. It was staccato, urgent. Haiwen tried to lift his head, but the world spun. The memory of the many bottles of kaoliang liquor he and his friends had consumed to celebrate the New Year soaked into his consciousness. What time was it? The knocking grew heavier.

Haiwen stumbled out of bed, grimacing. He felt like a wet rag left to mold in a dirty basin. Although the shack he'd built for himself was tiny, the walk from the bed to the front door seemed impossibly far.

"Haiwen!" It was Lau Fu's voice, rough and urgent.

Haiwen opened the door to his friend leaning against his door frame, breathing heavily. His eyes were wild, his skin still red from the liquor. Behind him, night was fading into morning.

"Li Tsin." Lau Fu's voice was frantic. "He's dead."

"What?" The world was spinning.

"He's dead, drowned."

A fist was in Haiwen's throat, gummy and rotten. The liquor

was sour on his breath. Just a few hours ago, Li Tsin had been drunkenly singing songs with his arms draped across Haiwen's shoulder.

"He tried to steal a fisherman's boat," Lau Fu continued. "Zenpo said he tried to stop him, but Li Tsin kept shouting he was going to row back home. When the fisherman pulled out a knife, he jumped into the harbor and started swimming."

"Li Tsin can't swim," Haiwen said, his voice thick and furry.

Lau Fu clenched his eyes. "I know."

Haiwen pictured Li Tsin, his eyes that turned into crescents whenever he smiled, so he appeared extra happy, particularly when he talked about the pet pig he missed. He was the youngest of their group, the most sensitive. Their little brother.

"Zenpo jumped in after him," Lau Fu added. "But it was dark, and the current was strong . . ." He trailed off. "We'll never find the body. No fishermen will help search for someone who threatened one of their own, and you know the higher-ups won't help." He spat, wiping his mouth. "They'll forget he existed. After everything they did to him, forced him to do."

Haiwen couldn't stand anymore. He smelled alcohol emanating from each pore in his body. It was putrid. He leaned against the shoddy door frame, built out of bamboo he had cut down himself.

"What about Zenpo?"

"He's filling out paperwork at the unit office," Lau Fu said. "The fisherman demanded to file a report with other witnesses who could testify that Li Tsin was the instigator. I happened to be at the office, putting in my marriage request." He flashed a brief smile. "I wanted to be the first in the new year."

With the recent changes in marriage rules, Lau Fu had decided to marry a young Taiwanese woman pregnant with a child from a relationship she refused to talk about. "I just can't keep doing what we do, month after month, year after year," he'd said. "I have to have something or I'll never survive." He was getting old, he was a waishengren with little money. They were both making compromises.

Haiwen didn't understand how he could possibly marry when he knew he had someone waiting for him at home. He didn't comprehend the urge to put down roots in a place that was temporary.

I can't ever, Haiwen had thought. To do so would be to give up the only hope he still had. *This will never be my home.*

Hope and despair were two sides of the same coin, Haiwen now thought. Li Tsin, like Haiwen, hadn't given up hope of returning home. It was what got the boy through the bullying, the harsh work he was ordered to do, the beatings from officers. He had nothing else—because he was a forced conscript, the military never fully trusted him, and he was stuck at the bottom of the totem pole. He never had a chance of being promoted, little chance of getting married. And now, Li Tsin had died, either because hope for returning home had fled him or because he could not let go of it.

Haiwen sagged heavily against the wall. "I hope the current carries him as far as the mainland."

Lau Fu nodded. His eyes were bright and wet. "Spring Festival is always so hard."

Haiwen put a hand on Lau Fu's shoulder, and Lau Fu clasped it, each feeling for the other's solidness.

A moment later, Haiwen said, "I'm not feeling so well. I need to lie down."

"Sleep, brother," Lau Fu said.

Haiwen lay down on his thin mattress. The world spun beyond

his eyelids. An image of Li Tsin's bloated white body kept popping into his mind, mingling with sounds and images he had tried to forget: Blue-faced bodies swinging from trees. The sharp pop of a lone gunshot in the middle of the night.

The suicides had begun a couple of years ago, as soldiers had begun to despair of going home. Soldiers were cracking from the loneliness, depression, and stress. Even if they didn't kill themselves, men yelled in their sleep, hallucinating they were burning or being buried alive; they became wild and unpredictable in their confrontations with both comrades and authority. It was why Haiwen had moved from the dormitories and finally, after nine years of being in Taiwan, built his own house out of bamboo and stone several kilometers away; he'd have caught the madness if he stayed around.

Anguish spread through his chest, a thick sludge. It had been a long time since he had wept; he had gotten used to the permanent stone of grief he carried with him, a stone tears could not banish.

But now, thinking about Li Tsin, about his body floating somewhere in the vast ocean toward China, he began to cry. He had not done enough to protect him. He was filled with bitter remorse, but he understood why his friend had done it. He realized, as he choked through sobs, that in a way, he was envious.

HAIWEN WAS AWOKEN FOR THE SECOND TIME BY AN-other urgent rap on the door.

Outside, it was drizzling. Zenpo slouched in front of Haiwen's doorway, reeking of alcohol.

"Let's go," he said.

"Where are we going?"

"To the whorehouse," Zenpo said, as if Haiwen had asked a stupid question. "I need a good fuck."

"But it's the second day of the new year," Haiwen said. "Are the brothels even open?"

"Brothels are open whenever men are willing to part with their money," he said. "Just make sure to prepare a red envelope for the girls."

Haiwen looked at his friend's bloodshot eyes, at the dark circles beneath them.

"All right."

At the brothel, Zenpo purchased an hour with his favorite girl, number five, otherwise known as Hsing Hsing. "If you need a recommendation," Zenpo said as he was heading upstairs, "I suggest number seventeen or lucky number eight." As if they'd been summoned, two women appeared from behind a curtain. One seemed older, with eyes that crinkled in the corners, accompanied by a warm smile. She wore a tight blue qipao with a slit that came up to midthigh and showed off her curves. The other, clad in a sleeveless fluttering pink slip, was light limbed, with a full, round face that made her seem like an innocent farm girl. Haiwen could make out the tips of her nipples through the sheer fabric.

The brothel owner snapped his fingers at Haiwen. "Well?" he asked. "You can't just stand here. We charge for looking even if you don't touch."

While Haiwen had gone to the military brothels when he'd been stationed in the outer islands, it was never entirely *enjoyable* to him. He felt pleasure, and after orgasm, a physical sense of relief. But it was separate from his thoughts. He could never shake the feeling that he was betraying Suchi. His friends had told him he was being too sentimental, too naïve. "We all miss a sweetheart back home," they said. "But it's nice to have someone soft and warm hold you. You can even imagine it's the person you miss the most." The next time, Haiwen tried to picture it was Suchi who lay beneath him, writhing and moaning, but was so disturbed by the cognitive dissonance, he nearly lost his erection. He had never had sex with Suchi. Afterward, he held the prostitute and tried to pretend she was Suchi, but it all felt wrong. The woman was a stranger to him, just as he was to her. At that moment everything about the situation—the musky smell of sex, the woman's sticky skin, the wetness coiled between his legs—it all disgusted him.

The brothel owner was glaring at Haiwen impatiently. "Are you deaf?" The two women smiled at Haiwen, their body postures enticing, seductive, though their eyes were unreadable.

"Sorry," Haiwen mumbled, and hurried outside.

In the distance, firecrackers popped like intermittent combat fire. Haiwen's breathing quickened, and he hurried away from the noise. He found a stall nearby where he purchased a beer and some cigarettes and sat down on a low stool. Next to him a group of four middle-aged men were playing a game of liar's dice, shaking them in chipped rice bowls and flipping them over onto the table. They each peeked under their cups.

One man, a cigarette dangling from the corner of his mouth, held out three fingers, followed by two. His friend sitting opposite him, a balding man in a sleeveless shirt, shouted in Taiwanese, pointing at his friend's cup. "Khui!"

"Ah!" they all howled when they'd lifted their bowls to reveal the dice beneath. They had another rapid exchange, and while it all sounded like arguing to Haiwen, he could tell the men were good friends ribbing each other. The first man slammed some coins onto the table and pushed it toward his friend, who leaned back in his chair, triumphant.

Haiwen observed them for several minutes. They repeated the process, calling out bids and bullshit, laughing and arguing and pushing coins around. Haiwen signaled to the stall owner he wanted another beer. That was when the men noticed him. They turned and looked at him, gesturing at the dice, smiling widely, saying something he couldn't understand.

"Sorry," Haiwen said in Mandarin. Instantly, he realized his mistake. The men's smiles dropped. They shifted their bodies so they were leaning slightly away from him on their stools. "I don't speak Taiwanese," he added hastily in the local language, one of the few phrases he knew.

The men grumbled. The one who had lost earlier muttered, "Kakam'a," under his breath. The one in the sleeveless shirt cautioned that man with a shake of his head. Another, who was smoking a cigarette nervously, kept darting glances at Haiwen. Between puffs, he licked his lips.

Although Haiwen wasn't wearing military fatigues, his lack of Taiwanese, his Shanghainese-accented Mandarin—it all gave him away as a waishengren, someone who came from across the strait. He remembered the brief period he had been sent to Kaohsiung in the south, how he had had a hard time getting served at food stalls run by the locals. The nicer ones called him "o'a," a taro, while many others cursed him as "a'shanti"—mainland pig—under their breath. It was how he learned these words in Taiwanese.

"Many locals don't even see themselves as Chinese anymore," a lieutenant had once told them. "They've been brainwashed by the

Japanese for too long. They'd rather bow to the red rising sun of the Japanese Empire than salute the blue sky and white sun of the Republic's democracy. You can't trust them."

The officer had warned that, given the opportunity, the locals would rebel, riot, tear down all the military was trying to do for them. Martial law was a necessity, he said, the way boundaries are necessary for small children who can't yet be trusted to care for themselves.

Haiwen didn't understand it. He and his friends broke their backs trying to bring this island out of the dark ages of Japanese colonialism, an oppressive rule where, from what Haiwen could gather, Chinese had been considered second-class citizens. His comrades had gotten injured and even died in the process of rigging up explosives so tunnels could be dug through mountains, highways could be built, and train lines could be renewed and expanded. And yet at every turn, the locals hated them for simply existing. Didn't they see the change they were trying to bring? Didn't they fathom the ways in which their lives could be *better*?

You don't want me here? he had thought each time he walked away from another unfriendly local. *I don't want to be on this shithole island either!* Here he was, using his sweat to transform *their* home into something better, while he was unable to step foot on his, unable to make the lives of his family better in any way. They had their families, and what did he have? He was a man who, despite the house he had built with his own hands, was homeless.

The men had turned back to their game, but they were quieter and kept glancing over their hunched shoulders. Haiwen felt a pang of . . . regret perhaps, or maybe injury.

"Ei!" Haiwen called out to them. The men turned. He could see their apprehension in the unnatural tightness of their postures and wary glances. Haiwen held out his cigarettes in his palm, shaking the thin tubes loosely out of their box. "Want one?" he asked in Mandarin.

The men glanced down at his outstretched palm, then back at him. Haiwen tried to look friendly, to smile in a disarming way. One of the men, sitting closest to Haiwen, reached out, but the one in the sleeveless shirt muttered something, a warning probably, and he hesitated.

"I'll play you for these," Haiwen said in Mandarin, switching tactics. The men looked at him, uncomprehending. Haiwen pointed at the cigarettes, at the dice, and at himself. He tried to remember what the men had said when they had called out to him, what the word for *play* could be. He repeated what he could remember of the phrase, syllables mangled in his mouth.

The one in the sleeveless shirt let out a chuckle. He spoke to Haiwen in a flurry of Taiwanese. He held up a die and a coin, pointed at the cigarette.

Haiwen nodded his head vigorously.

The man consulted with his friends, then turned to Haiwen. "All right," he said in Taiwanese, which sounded close enough to Mandarin that Haiwen understood.

Haiwen scooted his stool closer to them and fanned the cigarettes out on the table. One of the men signaled to the owner of the stall, who procured another collection of dice in a bowl. They all shook the bowls, letting them rattle noisily, before they slammed them upside down on the table and peeked at their dice. The man who had lost earlier started, saying, "Tsit e liok," as he held out one finger, then six. The man with the sleeveless shirt checked his dice again and held out three fingers, then five. They gestured at Haiwen.

Haiwen studied his five dice. A five, a three, a six, two ones. He held out six fingers, then one. "Liok e tsit," he pronounced slowly, reversing the numbers the other man had said earlier. He looked around at the men's faces. They chuckled a little, and Haiwen gave an embarrassed smile, assuming his pronunciation had been off.

"Lak e it," one of the men said. He repeated himself while holding out six fingers first, then gesturing at the dice when he said "it." Haiwen realized the man was correcting him, that the numbers were different depending on if you were counting them or referring to them. It was like how "two" in Mandarin was either "er" for "the number two" or "liang" if you were saying "two things."

"Lak e it," Haiwen repeated. The men smiled, then grew serious. They stared at him intently, one nodding, another rubbing his chin, and yet another speaking to his friend under his breath.

Finally, the nervous man pointed at him, shouting, "Khui!" His face transformed into a grin.

Haiwen and the men tipped their bowls over, revealing their dice. The men stared down and laughed. The nervous man, no longer nervous, held out his hand and wiggled his fingers. Haiwen pressed two cigarettes into his hand, laughing along. "You guessed right!" The man grinned and stuck the cigarettes in his shirt pocket.

The man sitting closest to him patted him on the back and raised a short glass filled with clear liquid. Haiwen held up the glass containing his beer and clinked the bottle against the man's glass. After drinking, the man smiled and gestured at the dice. "Kesiok, kesiok."

Forty minutes later, Haiwen had lost all his cigarettes and was warm with drink. He had picked up both sets of numbers in Taiwanese, and while the men laughed at his pronunciation, they also roared appreciatively when he said them. A bright hum was running through him, a feeling he hadn't had in a long while. They were playing for petty change now, and Haiwen had called out "Khui!," sending up a loud roar of laughter and a rapid exchange of Taiwanese commentary from the men. The one Haiwen had accused of bullshitting, the man in the sleeveless shirt, was waggling a finger, a flushed grin on his face. "A'shanti," he joked.

Out of nowhere, a fist came flying into the man's cheek, sending him sprawling into the table and knocking over all the bottles. Dice scattered to the floor. Haiwen looked up, startled. Zenpo was standing over the man, his fists poised to take another hit.

"Fucking Taiwanese pig, you dare to curse my brother?"

Haiwen leapt up and tried to pull Zenpo back. "Stop!" he shouted, but Zenpo was too strong for him. He broke free of Haiwen's grasp and dove toward the man, wrestling him to the ground. The three other men were shouting. One tried to drag his friend out from under Zenpo, while another kicked Zenpo several times in the ribs. Haiwen kept pulling at Zenpo's arms. "Stop it, Zenpo, this is a misunderstanding!" He looked wildly at the other men, seeking their understanding, but any trace of friendliness was gone. The shopkeeper had also emerged, shouting in Taiwanese, then in broken Mandarin, "We don't want trouble! Leave us be!"

Haiwen tried to push his way into the fray, to pry the men apart, but he caught an elbow to his cheek, and a burst of light exploded behind his eye. He reeled back for a moment, regaining his sight in time to see Zenpo grab a bottle that had fallen to the ground, its edge broken and jagged, about to swipe at the man with the sleeveless shirt.

"No!" Haiwen shouted, launching himself at Zenpo and yanking his arm back. In that moment, one of the other men grabbed an unbroken bottle and smashed it down on Zenpo's head. Zenpo dropped to his knees heavily, stunned. Blood trickled down his forehead.

Haiwen, still holding on to Zenpo's arm, held his other palm out to the four men, who were crouching around them in a circle, breathing heavily. "Phaise, phaise," he apologized in Taiwanese. "He didn't understand," he added in Mandarin.

The men spat at the ground, shouting at them in Taiwanese. "Kan lin nia! Tshau li ma tshau tsibai!"

"Suck my cock," Zenpo cursed back in Wu. "I could report you right now and get you hauled off to where they take all you fucking Jap lovers!"

"Let's just go," Haiwen said to Zenpo, helping him to his feet. Zenpo hobbled up, but he kept shouting.

"I'm going to make sure each of you eats shit in prison!"

The men cursed back, hurling insults too indistinct for Haiwen to catch. One threw his lit cigarette at them.

"Those fucking cunts," Zenpo swore, lunging at them.

"Come on," Haiwen pleaded.

In the pedicab, Zenpo leaned against the seat with his eyes closed and teeth gritted in pain. The blood was already drying into a dark maroon on his face.

"We were just playing dice," Haiwen said after a moment. "You misunderstood the situation."

"How the hell was I supposed to know you were making friends with those hanjian? I know an insult when I hear one."

"He was joking."

Zenpo snorted. "These Taiwanese, they look down upon us rural boys. They believe they're Japanese, and like the Japanese, they believe themselves superior, even though they were no better than colonial puppets. You know, when I first came to Taiwan, I'd never seen a running faucet before. Ever! I thought it was a magic water machine. So I went to a shop and bought a faucet and when I tried to return it because it didn't work, the owner laughed at me! He laughed right in my face, called me an idiot, and wouldn't let me return it."

"These men were friendly," Haiwen said. "Once I made some effort, they—"

"Oh please, you sound as naïve as Li Tsin," Zenpo spat. "You think because you play a round of dice with those men, they'll suddenly be your friends? Let me tell you, they'll never accept us."

At the mention of Li Tsin's name, Haiwen winced.

"You weren't here in '47 like I was," Zenpo continued. "They were crazy, rioting and looting, killing a bunch of our men. I knew men's wives who had to dress in kimonos when they went to the market so they wouldn't get beat up. *Kimonos!* We barely got them under control, and even then, it took months."

Haiwen was quiet. He was thinking about the men he had been playing with, their initial fear, the surprise warmth as their faces broke into smiles. His image of them melted into Li Tsin's baby face, easily injured but also easily delighted. His chest felt stuffy. He was so tired.

Zenpo's voice was rising. "We can't go home until we root out our enemies. And our enemies aren't just across the strait. If we're to go home, we have to win this war. Don't you want to win this fucking war? Aren't you sick of this place? I am. I'm sick of it. I'd give up fucking whores forever if I could go home."

"Our enemies aren't old men playing dice," Haiwen said.

"How do you know?"

"They're just regular men."

"Everyone is just a regular man until they put a bullet in your head," Zenpo said. "It doesn't matter if they're Jap lovers or Commies—we can't make any mistakes. 'It is better to kill a thousand innocent men than to let one guilty man live.'"[14]

Haiwen had heard this saying before, had heard it floating around among certain fanatical leaders who were zealous about their quest to root out and defeat the Communists, but it shocked him to hear Zenpo parroting it.

"How can you say that?" he asked. He thought of the accounts he'd heard from soldiers who'd disguised themselves as civilians when China fell to the Communists. They whispered that the People's Liberation Army had been orderly when they "liberated" a city, that they had not looted or taken any food from the common citizens, that they had treated the people with respect and won over their hearts. Peasants had celebrated the PLA's arrival, had enlisted *because* of this. They did not need to be coerced the way Li Tsin and Zenpo had been. They were not fighting a war they wanted no part of. *How can we win against this?* Haiwen's comrades had murmured in despair when relating what they'd seen.

"Don't you think it matters if we win people's hearts and not just their bodies?" Haiwen asked Zenpo now.

"We have to be ten times as ruthless as those pigs!" Zenpo said. "If we'd defeated our enemies earlier, Li Tsin would be alive. We'd all be home by now, off this devil island. I could be fucking my own wife, playing with my kid." Angry tears streamed down Zenpo's face. "Goddammit," he said, pounding his fist into his thigh. "Why didn't that fucking fisherman just let him have the boat! Why didn't I just fucking shoot that bastard and let Li Tsin go!"

Zenpo wept next to him, loud snotty heaves that he wiped with his forearm.

The pedicab passed through several rice fields, a farm. Haiwen gazed at a calf grazing alone on the side of the road. It was drizzling but there was no farmer in sight to usher him indoors.

Zenpo's breathing slowed and his sobs subsided. Haiwen didn't dare to look at him. He heard Zenpo whisper, "We're never going home, are we?"

Haiwen thought of *home*, of the longtang, of his shikumen. He thumbed through the catalog in his mind: Suchi's laughter, clear and tinkling. His mother's radiant smile. Junjun's ruddy cheeks. His father's slicked-back hair. The hole in his chest expanded like a heartbeat, closing around a cavern. He swallowed, pushed back bile.

"I don't know," he said. In the distance, the mist rolled in along the mountains. It reminded him of a beautiful brush painting his father used to keep in his study.

"Li Tsin knew," Zenpo said. "He knew the army will never take us home."

HAIWEN WALKED INTO HIS HUT, DRIPPING FROM THE ten-minute walk from the dormitories, and went straight to the half bottle of kaoliang left over from the night before, emptying it into his belly before he crawled back into bed. There he tossed and turned, thinking about his parents, about his siblings, about Suchi.

What if Zenpo was right? What if he would never see any of them again? Wouldn't it be easier if he tried to move forward, if he did what Lau Fu did—moved on, forgot the past?

But no. He could not. Would not.

He flipped through his mind's gallery of his loved ones' faces the way he did every night to ensure he did not forget them, starting with Suchi and now ending with Li Tsin. His body was hollow with longing.

Rain leaked from the straw mat roof and plinked into a bucket he had placed in the room's center. He listened to the droplets but found it disconcerting that the rhythm was slightly off with the beating of his heart, not regular enough to be a proper syncopation. *ThumpPLINKthumpthuPLINKmpPLINK*. It agitated him, made him want to hold his breath, as if that would force his heartbeat to sync with the drips. *PLINKumpthumpPLINK*—

He was out of bed, his bare foot meeting tin with enough force his toes immediately began to throb. The bucket bounced wildly as it spilled its contents and rolled away. "Ma de!" Haiwen shouted. The water spread out over the hard mud floor, turning the ground dark. Haiwen stared at it creeping toward his feet, heaving. After a moment, he picked up a rag to wipe up the mess. He turned the bucket back over, letting it collect water anew, put on shoes, and left.

Haiwen rode his rusty bicycle out along the bumpy, gravelly roads until he was near the center of town. He had forgotten it was Spring Festival, but the rest of the world had not. The streets were crowded and cacophonous. Toddlers held sticky red sweets, older children drew pictures with chalk on the ground, elderly women taste-tested soy-roasted watermelon seeds and pickled plums from street stalls. Business owners set off strings of firecrackers in front of shops and the noise echoed throughout the alleyways; Haiwen jerked with each new series of crackles. Paper cutouts of pigs were pasted everywhere, and the air was a soup of sea salt, incense, garlic, and sulfur. Haiwen rode by the bright red temple, where people were lined up to light joss sticks and say prayers for the new year. Flanking the temple down the narrow road was the night market, most of its stalls closed, though a few diligent workers had come back to work, offering crab soup, oyster rice noodles, glutinous meatballs.

An irrational anger boiled in his gut. The last time it had been the year of the pig, he had been celebrating with his family, several months away from making the choice to join the army in his brother's stead. Why was he now alone, here? What had he done in this life or the last to deserve this?

He pedaled faster along the streets, toward the harbor, where industrial steamers dwarfed fishing boats that bobbed fragile and chary alongside them. There, he got off his bike. He stared out at the dimming horizon and wondered which of these boats was the one Li Tsin had tried to take. He scanned the waters for Li Tsin's body among the debris.

Haiwen remembered the moment he had first laid eyes on the city of Keelung as his ship had pulled in, the dread that had filled his body as he took in the jigsaw rooftops and the quaint streets. He was a city boy at heart; he missed the bustle of Shanghai, the different languages flying back and forth on the streets, the jumble of Eastern and Western cultures, and Keelung seemed too quiet for him. But when he returned to Keelung the second time, after months spent in Zhoushan and Penghu, places he'd found to be tedious backwaters, he was relieved by the sight. Keelung was no metropolis, but it offered more than rice paddies and oxen.

That was four years ago. Haiwen's relief had since given way to claustrophobia. This town, this island—all the surrounding water only served to remind him how far the borders of his home were. Taiwan was a tropical cage, and there was no way out. *Fuck defeating Communists, fuck taking back the mainland*, he thought. He was sick of the empty slogans, of the government's promises. How would they defeat the Communists when they were trapped on this tiny speck in the sea? They were supposed to be rebuilding, recuperating, fortifying their defense and enhancing their offense so they could return gloriously and defeat the Communists in a dazzling, brutal display of military awesomeness. But how could they do that when they wasted resources terrorizing locals who probably had never stepped foot outside of their own city, much less off this island to collaborate with Nationalist enemies?

Haiwen recognized the fury and desperation that drove Li Tsin to jump into the sea. Not a death wish, exactly, though Haiwen, admittedly, sometimes thought about that too. But there were moments when, on the knife-edge of despair and hope, he believed the longing that pumped through him was powerful enough to transport him home. What sort of strength does a man's love for home, for family, bestow upon him? Enough that he might fight through sickness, through injury, through thousands of meters of sea?

Haiwen tried to picture the map he had stashed somewhere in his hut, one on which he had taken a ruler and drawn a straight line from Keelung to Shanghai. Six hundred and eighty kilometers, he had calculated. Now he adjusted his body slightly to the left and closed his eyes. The salt air bit his skin.

Perhaps it had been enough for Li Tsin. Perhaps the promise of home was enough to charm limbs that had never known how to swim, and stroke after stroke he had sliced through the water, buoyed. Perhaps he was still out there now, nearly ashore, nearly home. Haiwen wanted to believe it was so.

The wind along the water was picking up, and it was beginning to drizzle again. He wiped his face with the back of his palm and rode his bike down a back street. A modest storefront advertising oyster omelets had its lights on. He ducked under the tin awning and sat down at one of the rickety tables flanking the food stand.

A middle-aged man greeted him in Taiwanese from behind the stove. Haiwen responded, "Tsit," in Taiwanese, holding up a finger and pointing it at the egg batter already bubbling on the hot metal surface. Suspicion crossed the man's face. He spoke, his voice harsh, but Haiwen didn't understand. Panic and weariness set in. He was going to be refused service again.

"Laupa!" A teenage girl, her voice slightly scolding. He hadn't noticed her; she rose from where she'd been crouched washing dishes in a bowl of soapy water. She spoke to her father, who shrugged and began to violently scrape at the egg with a spatula.

"Happy New Year!" she called out to Haiwen in Mandarin, wiping her hands on her apron and coming toward him. He realized she was older than she had first appeared, probably in her twenties. Part of Haiwen's confusion had been her hair, which she'd pulled back into two braids, a pink kerchief around her head. The other was that her eyes were unusually round and her cheeks wide and plump. But he could tell from her expression that she was older, more mature than the young girl he'd first thought she was.

"Happy New Year," he responded.

"Please excuse my father," she said fluently, surprising Haiwen. "He's not usually so rude, but ever since . . ." She put a palm to her mouth. "Sorry," she said with a short laugh. "People tell me I talk too much. Anyway, your oyster omelet will be ready soon! Would you like anything else? A bowl of flour noodle soup?"

Haiwen smiled, relieved. "Yes, that would be great."

"With pork intestines? Oysters? Both?"

"Pork intestines," he said.

The woman walked back to the stand, ladling out soup, topping it with a generous heaping of minced garlic and cilantro, and brought it to him. Haiwen drizzled some vinegar into the soup and stirred it around, watching slivers of bamboo shoots and thin noodles float through the brown liquid. He took a sip, letting its slightly sweet heartiness seep through his bones. He was suddenly ravenous, filled with a hunger he hadn't felt since the early days of the army when they had truly been starving. Before he knew it, his spoon was scraping against nearly clean porcelain.

"Tsit tng ku ku nng tng sio tu!" the young woman said as she picked up his empty bowl. "It's as if you haven't eaten for days! Luckily, your omelet is ready."

She put the oyster omelet in front of him. Green stalks of tonghao, slightly wilted, peeked through egg dotted with delicate oysters; shiny tapioca starch and pink sauce glistened on top. Haiwen separated a piece and bit into it, savoring the combination of textures and flavors.

When he was sated, he pushed the plate away and leaned back in his stool. The woman came to clear his dishes. She lingered a moment, then asked, "You're a soldier, aren't you?"

Haiwen was surprised. Few locals asked him about his work so directly.

The woman fiddled with a stray hair that had come loose from her kerchief, her cheeks flushing pink. "I assumed because, well, it's the New Year, but instead of being with family, you're eating alone." She paused. "We don't get a lot of you wandering into our shop. You all seem to stick to your canteens or stalls opened by other mainlanders. I'm impressed you even knew how to say the word *one*." She giggled. Haiwen found it amusing how easily she laughed.

"I just learned today," he admitted. "From some men I was playing dice with."

"Taiwanese men?" she asked, her eyes widening. Haiwen nodded. The woman clapped her hands, delighted. "See, I knew you weren't all bad! My father thinks you are all out to get us, but I told him he was being unfair. You seem like a normal person, not a bandit or a rapist—" Her palm flew to her mouth again. "I'm sorry, I'm being so rude, forgive me."

Haiwen shook his head quickly. "Don't worry," he said. "And you? How is your Mandarin so good?"

The girl beamed. "It's only okay," she said modestly. "I got a bit of a late start, so I've had to study hard to get rid of my accent as much as possible." She puffed out her cheeks and gave an embarrassed smile. Her girlish bashfulness charmed Haiwen. "Not everyone likes having to switch languages, but I think Mandarin sounds so refined, so pretty." She glanced back at her father, who was in the back somewhere. In a lower voice, she added, "Don't tell my father though. He thinks Taiwanese is still the best language." She rolled her eyes. "I will say, it seems more fun to curse in, though my father would kill me if I repeated some of the things he's said!"

Haiwen found himself chuckling. He thought of the insults the men had hurled at him earlier in the day. "Oh, I've heard those curses all right," he said. "They certainly sound more colorful than anything I've heard anyone say in Mandarin."

"Extra oomph behind it, right?" the woman said.

"Tell me," Haiwen asked, "what does *kakam'a* mean?"

The girl's smile faded, her eyes shifting away. "Where did you hear that?" She shook her head. "Come on, I can teach you more fun curses than that. The next time you hang out with your Taiwanese buddies, you'll fit right in!"

"You don't need to protect me," Haiwen said. "I'd just like to know what I'm being called when someone says it to me." When the girl didn't respond, he prodded her. "Come on. I promise you won't insult me. I'm sure I've been called worse."

"It means 'one who bites an orange,'" she said quietly. "Like, you know, a pig." Haiwen didn't respond immediately, and the girl bit her lip.

But Haiwen started laughing. "Well, that's certainly a creative way to refer to a pig," he said. "Very picturesque."

She looked relieved. "I guess it is? Like you can see the roast with the orange in his mouth?" She gave a nervous laugh.

Haiwen shrugged. "Mandarin is too proper, too buttoned up. It's the locals that have the most fun. Shanghainese is like that too, better curses."

"Oh, you're from Shanghai!" The girl's eyes lit up, and she bounced a little in excitement. "The magazines and movies make it seem chic and glamorous. I always imagined beautiful women in qipao and men in Western-style suits walking arm in arm down gleaming sidewalks or having coffee in European cafés. Was it really like that? You must find Keelung so boring."

Haiwen smiled. Her excitement reminded him of Suchi, how she'd exclaimed over the starlets in her magazines. "Parts of it were glamorous, I guess. But it depended on who you were and where you lived." *And where your allegiances lay*, he thought. "I lived in a very average sort of neighborhood."

"What kind of neighborhood?"

"A longtang, a community made up of row houses stuck close together so they formed alleys. Ours was one of the biggest in Shanghai. You could get lost if you didn't know where you were going."

"Wah," the woman said. "Even that sounds romantic somehow."

Haiwen thought back to the narrow lanes, how everyone knew everyone's business and could smell everyone's shit. If an old couple was fighting loudly in their house, by the next day, everyone would be gossiping about it and taking sides. In some ways it was the opposite of romantic. But it had been comforting, waking to the sound of the vendors calling out their wares, being greeted every morning by the same aunties and uncles. And it was where he had fallen in love for the first, and only, time. So he supposed it must have been romantic, in its way.

The woman's smile faltered. "Oh," she said, "I'm sorry, I've upset you. I shouldn't have asked."

"What?" Haiwen said. "No, you haven't—"

"It's just . . . your face grew so still."

He hadn't been upset. He had found those memories pleasant, had wanted to live inside of them. But perhaps this was just how it was—no memory of his childhood could ever be recalled without a sorrow so deep it could be read upon his face, even by strangers.

"Don't worry about it," he told the woman. "I like thinking about my home."

The woman broke into a wide grin, and Haiwen felt strangely pleased. It warmed him, the openness with which she smiled, the way her plump cheeks lifted so high, they almost touched the corners of her eyes. "In that case," she said, "I'd love to know more about what it was like, growing up in Shanghai."

Before Haiwen could answer, the young woman's father called to her from behind the stove, his tone harsh. She turned and responded in Taiwanese, her voice slightly impatient. Haiwen strained to understand but couldn't. As father and daughter talked loudly back and forth, Haiwen studied her. She wasn't obviously pretty, but he liked the way her features rearranged themselves into a range of genuine emotions as she talked. He had the sense that this woman, too, would be terrible at liar's dice. When she turned back to Haiwen, flashing an apologetic smile, he found himself changing his assessment—she *was* pretty.

"I better go back to help my father," she said. "But it was nice talking to you . . ."

"Wang Haiwen," Haiwen added quickly. "And what can I call you, miss?"

Did he imagine it or did a faint blush spread across her cheeks? "Tsai. Tsai Linyee."

Haiwen put down a fistful of coins, more than the meal was worth.

"That's too much!" she protested, but he shook his head.

"Happy New Year," he told her. She protested again, trying to hand some coins back to him, but he stood up and stepped away. "Really," he said. "Please."

She hesitated, then nodded. "Thank you," she said. "Then you must come back another time and have a meal on us."

Haiwen nodded, and she smiled at him, a grin that showed all

of her teeth and made her eyes crinkle at their corners. It struck
him that it had been a while since he had seen a genuine smile from
anyone.

"It's a deal," she said. From the stove, her father yelled at her
again. "Ho, Laupa!" she hollered behind her shoulder before turning
back to Haiwen. "See you next time, Wang Haiwen."

Haiwen rode toward his house in the dark, turning the conversation over in his mind. Briefly, while he'd been talking to Tsai
Linyee, he'd forgotten his grief, and this alarmed him. What if it
leaked out of his brain like the music?

He conjured up the gallery of the people he did not want to forget. He imprinted them into his memory, even as he worried that
what he knew had degraded, or worse still, was no longer accurate.
It didn't matter; what mattered was they never fade away. He cycled
through his favorite memories of his mother, his father, his brother,
his sister, Suchi, Suchi's sister, Mr. Portnoy, Mr. Reyes, his friends in
the orchestra and at school, the aunties, the uncles—letting them
sharpen his breath and saturate his senses, until they were more real,
more alive, than the people he passed by on the streets.

He would not go back to that oyster omelet stand. He could not.

MAY–SEPTEMBER 1985
Hong Kong / Los Angeles

SOUKEI PICKED UP a mango, testing it for its firmness. The smooth yellow-red skin yielded slightly beneath her fingers. She inhaled its sweet floral fragrance. "Three of these, please," she told the fruit seller. "Make sure to pick ripe ones I can eat immediately." The woman bagged the mangoes. Soukei handed her a few coins and thanked her.

The wet market was teeming with activity. Butchers stood behind slabs of glistening red pork chops, cuts of fatty belly, and knobs of pig trotters, swatting often to keep the flies away. A few rows down, red snapper and butterfish nestled in crushed ice, their scales glinting silver and coral, eyes bright in their sockets. Soukei purchased a few more fruits, vegetables, some smoked ham, two whole fish, and an entire black chicken, which she would simmer later for soup.

Saikeung often told Soukei that he didn't understand why she insisted on going to the market herself—"That's what we have Siu Fa for," he said, referring to the live-in amah they'd hired when their last amah, Siu Lai, had left. But Soukei savored her visits to the market. It wasn't just that she enjoyed browsing the produce and picking out the freshest cuts of meat; it was the energy, the amahs and housewives bumping into her with their bags laden with groceries, vendors shouting out the prices for their wares as they passed. Haggling for the best price and walking away with a deal gave Soukei a high; the minor triumph made her feel like she had value.

When she arrived at home, she directed Siu Fa on how to prep the vegetables. "I'll break down the chicken myself," she said. Siu Fa nodded and pushed up her sleeves, her bangs falling over her eyes as she bent over the daikon radish. At this angle, her skin was plump and slightly flushed, and Soukei was reminded, not for the first time, of how young she was at twenty. Siu Hung had long gone—married to a man she'd met after three years in their employ, with a baby of her own to care for. Since then, there'd been so many other amahs, young women who came into their lives for several years and cycled out. They stayed the same age while Soukei grew older, and with the years came an acclimation to their presence, the shame she'd felt in the beginning at having hired help dimming the same way her active loathing of Saikeung had. Still, there were moments like this, when the girls gave her a particular look or acted a particular way that showed their tender age, when a sense of wrongness filled her. Siu Fa was barely older than Samson, whom she picked up after as if he were a child. Would people consider it a sign of success or failure that she'd given her son a life of such privilege? But she reminded herself *she* hadn't done so—Saikeung had. If Soukei had had her choice, she and Samson would have squeezed their lives into a small, simple apartment, just the two of them.

She heard the front door slam, the squelch of sneakers on marble tile. She went out to the foyer, where her son was placing his shoes in the shoe cabinet. "You're home early," she said in Mandarin. "Don't you have practice?"

"Not today," Samson responded in English. While he understood Mandarin, he had never learned to speak it well, preferring Cantonese or, lately, English, because it was what they spoke at the pricey American school Saikeung insisted he attend. "I was just hanging out with some friends after school."

Soukei switched to English, a clumsy attempt to connect more with her son. "Last weeks before graduation. Everybody must be so sad to leave."

Samson shrugged with the indifference of a teenage boy. "I guess."

Soukei resisted the urge to reach out and brush his bangs out of his face. She could still see, hiding beneath his acne and apathy, evidence of the chubby child who had once clung to her as a toddler, who had loved making her laugh when he was in primary school. She couldn't believe he was going to college in the fall—off to the University of Southern California, which Samson had picked for its excellent tennis program.

There was a part of Soukei that was proud and excited for her son, but a bigger part of her couldn't bear to be parted from him. She loved him, fiercely. It was why, despite Saikeung's suggestion she let Siu Fa prepare all the meals, Soukei insisted on making his lunches and cooking at least one dish for dinner with her own hands, whichever was Samson's favorite. It was why she had joined the PTA at his school, though she often felt awkward around the pretty blond wives of American executives and international diplomats. For nearly nineteen years, she had shaped her entire world around him—what would she do now that he was leaving?

"Come have a snack," she said to her son. "I made yangzhi ganlu."

At this, Samson perked up and sat down at the dining table. Soukei went into the kitchen and ladled the mango sago soup into a porcelain rice bowl, sprinkling extra pomelo in, and brought it out to Samson. She sat down next to him and watched expectantly as he brought the spoon to his mouth. He grunted in approval and she grinned.

"So the weekend after your graduation, since Baba will be away again, I thought maybe we can go to Ocean Park. We haven't been there in so long."

"Ocean Park?" Samson scoffed. "That place is for little kids."

"But you used to love it so much," Soukei said, switching into Mandarin. "You used to beg me to take you whenever Baba was away."

"Yeah, when I was like eleven. Those rides are all for little kids. And the dolphins all look miserable. You know that's animal cruelty? Katie says they get depressed and try to drown themselves if they're caged for too long."

"I just thought, for old times . . ." Soukei trailed off. Ever since it had opened in 1977, Ocean Park had been her and Samson's special place, replacing Lai Chi Kok. Saikeung had never been interested in theme parks, but she and Samson had spent hours riding the log flume, getting splashed by dolphins, eating junk food Saikeung didn't approve of. It was there she got to know her son, a boy who was quiet and interior and rarely expressed himself. She'd watched him laugh with abandon on those rides, seen the shy awe spread across his face when once, chosen from the audience, he was allowed to pet a dolphin's head.

But now her son was a teenager. She fumbled at every turn, trying to find the keys to access him.

"Anyway, I can't," Samson said. "I'm going on a senior trip with my friends. We're going camping. Remember?"

She frowned. "Didn't your father say he didn't want you to go?"

Samson rolled his eyes. "Ba thinks camping is slumming it. 'I worked so hard so you can go sleep in a filthy tent like a homeless pauper?'" He mimicked Saikeung's dismissive tone, startling Soukei with his accuracy.

"Well, he probably is worried about it being dangerous. There might be wild animals or snakes in the woods and he——"

Samson pushed his finished bowl away. "God, I swear, sometimes you're worse than him," he muttered.

"What?" Soukei sat still.

"Nothing!" Samson said, his voice rising. "I'm going, and neither Ba nor you are going to stop me. I paid for the trip with the prize money I got from my last tournament. I'm using *my* money."

"I didn't say you couldn't go——"

"Then stop parroting things you know nothing about!" He stood up and slung his bag over his shoulder in a huff. "Can't you just be on my side for once?"

Soukei scrambled to her feet, her limbs taut and anxious. "I'm *always* on your side!"

"You're not," he said. "You're not even on your own side." When he slammed the door, the spoon inside the bowl rattled.

ON THE THIRD RING, SULAN PICKED UP THE PHONE.

"Tsia," Soukei said, "it's me."

"Oh, Susu," Sulan said. "It's so late there, can't sleep again?"

"En." This was a common occurrence—every time she called her sister, it was in the middle of the night, when she was sleepless and warm water or reading hadn't helped.

"Where's that husband of yours?"

"Out with clients again."

"Out, huh?" Sulan's implication was clear. Saikeung had never stopped visiting nightclubs, even after marrying Soukei. If anything, he frequented them more, given that he had invested in several, including Baak Lok Mun, which had finally flourished into an A-class spot under his eye. Soukei, on the other hand, had been forbidden by Saikeung to even associate with her former coworkers. Soukei mostly hadn't cared, but she'd felt bad about the band members, particularly Oscar and Prince, as well as Angela, Lily, and even Fai, despite her grumpy demeanor.

"I don't mind," Soukei said. "Time spent at those places means less time I have to handle him." Sulan was the only person to whom she could speak so freely. Soukei had garnered many "friends" over the years, "the taaitaai," as she called them, rich wives of Saikeung's associates who invited her to lunch at the upscale dim sum restaurant in Repulse Bay or to have high tea at the Peninsula. But the women wore her down with their fixation on the latest handbags, their love of island gossip and petty drama, the way they treated their amahs, their passive-aggressive competitiveness in comparing their children.

They were all kind to Soukei—they had to be—but she suspected they looked down upon her for her past and said unkind things when she wasn't around. After Sulan had moved to America nine years ago, she'd had nobody to confide in.

"Susu," Sulan said. Soukei could hear the hesitation in her voice. "Now that Samson will be going to college, maybe it's finally time to think about leaving him."

Soukei immediately began to reject the idea, but Sulan cut her off.

"I don't understand why you're so stubborn. You only stayed with Lam Saikeung for Samson's sake. But Samson is an adult now. So why stay?"

"This is my life," Soukei said.

"But it doesn't have to be. You could leave him."

"And do what?" Soukei asked. "Without him, I have nothing. Nothing I have is my own. My clothes, this apartment, every nice thing I have—it all belongs to Saikeung. I am a useless fifty-four-year-old woman. It's too late for me to start over."

"What about Wang Haiwen? What if—"

Soukei let out an exasperated sigh. "What? Why bring up that man again? Don't you think he's married by now, living his own life? Besides, who knows if he's even alive?"

"So he never—"

"I don't want to think about him, Tsia, please."

Sulan paused. "Then come to New York," she urged. "Come live with me."

"Don't be ridiculous," Soukei said. "As if it's so easy."

"I'll pay for your ticket, I'll help you apply for your visa. I'll protect you. I make money now. The label is doing well. It's nothing

426

close to Saikeung's riches, but I can support us." Sulan's voice grew quiet. "It's the least I can do."

Soukei didn't respond. It wasn't that simple. "How's Momo?" she asked instead. This was a wily move—Sulan always jumped at the opportunity to talk about the younger Japanese woman she lived with. Soukei still had trouble acknowledging the true nature of her sister's relationship with her business partner; it didn't make sense to her how such a thing could even be possible. That she was Japanese was even more disturbing, despite her sister's reminders that Momo had grown up in America and had suffered when she and her family had been sent to the camps by the American government. But Soukei knew her sister yearned to share more about her life with this woman, and although it made Soukei uncomfortable, she had decided to accept it as best as she could. In return, though the sisters never discussed it, Sulan understood that conversations around Momo would remain centered on her business partnership with her.

"She has such a sharp mind, Susu," Sulan said. "She's had a lot of meetings recently with the big New York department stores—Saks and Lord and Taylor and Bloomingdale's—to see if they might carry our brand. She put together such a compelling marketing strategy, ideas I never could have thought of. I'm so lucky to have her."

Soukei felt a small measure of envy for her sister, even as she admired her courage. Sulan had created the life for herself she'd always wanted, despite her condition, despite the unconventionality and unexpectedness of it. When Samson was eight, Sulan had announced her intention to move to New York to follow her dream of going into fashion design, and Soukei knew she had to help her. Together, they studied English and worked on Sulan's applications to design schools. When, after two years, Sulan was accepted into the

Fashion Institute of Technology, Soukei quietly sold some jewelry Saikeung had given her to cover Sulan's tuition. "Keep your savings for your medical fees," she had told her sister, to which Sulan had replied, "Are you kidding me? I'm going to use them to start my own label so I can pay you back!" Soukei had cried for days after Sulan's departure.

Now Sulan ran her own modestly successful brand; she had a love that made her happy; she had independence and freedom and security and a self-assuredness Soukei could not muster. It was more than Soukei had done with her entire life. Soukei thought back to Apa's high hopes for her. She had not been brave like he had asked her to be.

On the phone, Sulan talked about the business, discussing her and Momo's vision. Soukei listened, hoping the drone of her sister's voice would coax the heaviness of sleep into her eyes.

Before they said goodbye, Sulan added, "Please consider what I said. It's not too late to find your own happiness, Susu."

"I'll think about it," Soukei said, and hung up.

Alone in her and Saikeung's king-sized bed, Soukei tried to imagine leaving. The first sensation that rippled through her was intense relief, a momentary lightening of the stone that pressed against her shoulders. But that feeling was immediately replaced by a pall of fear. Sulan was wrong; it *was* too late. She was too old. This was her life, and she had to live it.

IN SEPTEMBER, SAIKEUNG BOUGHT THE THREE OF THEM first-class plane tickets to Los Angeles so they could help Samson move into college. In the six suitcases they checked, they packed several sets of silk bedding, new designer clothes Saikeung had purchased, a brand-new rice cooker and a portable hot pot, twenty pairs of shoes, and many, many Hong Kong snacks and instant noodles. Samson had insisted he didn't need all of this—"I can buy stuff when I get there, you know"—that the only items he cared to bring were his three tennis rackets, but Saikeung insisted and for once Soukei agreed.

The dorm was a shoebox, with two narrow beds and dressers on either side of the room and two desks pushed adjacent to each other on the third wall, a small window hovering between them. Soukei wondered if the dismay showed on her face as plainly as it did on Saikeung's. "This is worse than an amah's room," Saikeung muttered, but Samson rolled his eyes.

"This is college, not the Mandarin Oriental," he said. "All freshman dorms are like this."

As they were almost finished unpacking, Samson's roommate came in with his parents. He was a skinny Indian boy from New Jersey named Rohan. His father was a round-faced man with a gray mustache who shook Saikeung's and Soukei's hands vigorously while his mother, a woman with striking green eyes, beamed beside him. Samson fiddled with the zipper on his book bag, and Soukei felt a pang of protectiveness. She hadn't seen him this uncertain and nervous in a long time.

"Oh cool, you play?" Rohan asked, spying Samson's rackets on his bed.

"Yeah," Samson said, nodding. "You?"

"Just for fun. Nothing serious or nothing. Maybe we can play a couple matches."

"Yeah, that would be awesome," Samson said. Soukei felt relieved. It seemed Rohan was a nice boy.

At lunch though, Saikeung made it clear he didn't agree.

"Be careful of getting too close to that roommate of yours," he told Samson in Cantonese.

"Why?" Samson asked, biting into his sandwich. "He seems nice."

"You know how Indians are. Maybe he'll steal your things when you're not around."

"Seriously? I had Indian friends at school—"

"You don't know what I know. I deal with them a lot while doing business. They're very crafty, those Indians. Also they smell. I hope he doesn't stink up your room. Maybe you can ask for a room change. I can talk to the school if you want. If it costs a little more to move you to another room, that's okay, I'll pay for it."

"I don't want to," Samson said. "Rohan seemed cool. And he likes tennis too, so I'll have someone to play with."

"You'll have better people to play with once you make the team," Saikeung responded, his words even and tight. Alarm rose along Soukei's back. Her husband disliked being contradicted. Samson knew this. Why wouldn't he stop talking and simply agree? She lamented that he'd inherited a doubly stubborn streak from both her and Saikeung.

"I'm the one living there, not you," Samson said, his voice rising. "If I'm okay with it, what do you care?"

"Samson," Soukei said urgently.

"You might be the one living there, but I'm the one paying for you to live there! And I know what's best for you! So if I say it will be so, it will be so!" Saikeung was turning red; his voice was growing loud.

"Saikeung," Soukei said, her hand hovering over his now-curled hand. "Maybe we don't have to talk about this now, let's just eat and—"

"Quiet, woman," he snapped without looking at her. "I'm dealing with this unruly son you've raised."

"Don't talk to Ma like that," Samson said.

"I'll do what I want!" Saikeung shouted, pounding his fist down on the table. The chatter in the restaurant dimmed. She could feel other patrons' stares. Embarrassment and shame prickled her skin.

"Calm the fuck down," Samson muttered in English.

"What?" Saikeung raised a fist. "Say it again."

"Nothing," Samson replied in Cantonese.

Saikeung nodded, as if to say *I thought so*. "So it's settled," he said, his voice returning to its earlier even pitch. "You're switching rooms."

"Ci gau sin," Samson said under his breath, the curse barely audible.

"Samson," Soukei pleaded. Samson's eyes met hers. She saw the quiet rage that filled them.

"Whatever," he said in English. "What. Ever."

SAIKEUNG FLEW TO SINGAPORE THE NEXT DAY FOR A business meeting, while Soukei stayed another week to make sure Samson was settling in. Because Soukei couldn't drive, she took a taxi from the hotel to Samson's campus every day and marveled at what she saw outside her window. She had never been to America and was amazed by the wide roads, giant parking lots, infinite number of cars, and endless strip malls. Together they became tourists and visited everywhere from Venice Beach to the Chinese Theatre. It felt like the happiest week of Soukei's life.

On the last night before Soukei was due to leave, they were sharing a chocolate mousse after a nice steak meal when a troubled look crossed Samson's face.

"What's wrong, baobei?" she asked.

Samson shook his head. "It's nothing, Ma," he said.

"Come on," she urged.

"I saw Rohan today. I haven't seen him since I switched rooms. It was . . . really awkward. He sort of ignored me." He licked some mousse off his spoon, then jabbed it into the dessert. "I wish I hadn't listened to Ba. I shouldn't have given in."

"You know your father," she said. "Once he's decided on something, it will happen, whether you want it to or not. To fight him is just the more painful road toward the inevitable."

"But at least I would have, you know . . ." Samson gestured vaguely. "I don't know. Taken a stand or something. Shown him I'm not easy to push around anymore."

She shook her head. "It wouldn't have mattered."

"But it matters to me!" Samson said. "*I* would have known I tried."

Soukei thought of the many times through the years she had attempted to shield Samson from Saikeung's temper, urging him not to fight back, the times she had begged Saikeung to let her be the one who punished Samson to spare him from a beating. How sometimes—not often, but on occasion—her husband turned his unvented anger on her instead, blaming her for not raising their son well enough. A slap, an arm twist, a shove. Never anything that made her feel like her life was in danger, but hard enough that small lights exploded in her vision. It was almost worse that it happened erratically—if it happened frequently, she would have known to be on guard. Instead, every time he hurt her, she was stunned. But it was worth it to spare Samson.

"Listen to me," she said. Her voice urgent. "You just have to be obedient and do well in your studies for these four years while your father is paying for your tuition. Once you graduate, you'll get a good job and you'll never have to do anything he says again. So you have to work hard. Okay?"

Samson looked surprised. "What?"

"You never even have to talk to your father again if you don't want to. You can be free then."

Samson cocked his head. "But," he said, slowly, "if I do that, what will happen to you?"

"What does that matter?"

Samson frowned. "Maami, if I make a break with him, I won't be able to talk to you anymore. He would never let me."

Soukei shook her head. "The important thing is you do well. Then you don't owe your father anything."

Samson stared at her, and she thought she saw anger in his eyes. "How is it not important if I never get to see you again?"

"Live for yourself, baobei," she said. "That's all I want for you."

Samson stabbed at the mousse with his spoon. "Why," he breathed. "Why are you like this?"

"Like what?"

"I just wish—I want you to be—" He blew out forcefully, and Suchi realized that look of loathing—it wasn't for Saikeung, it was for her. She flinched.

"Is it so wrong for a mother to want her son to have a happy life?"

"What about you?" he asked. "What about your happy life?"

"I'm happy if you're happy."

"Why are you such a fucking martyr, Ma? Why can't you, for once, think about what you want? Do you think it does me any good that you're like this? What do *you* want?"

The words came out as angry pleas. Soukei stared at her son, at the rage that was written on his face.

"I . . ."

He stared at her. When she didn't finish her sentence, he asked her, quietly, barely audible, "Don't you *want* to leave him?"

"He's my husband," she told him, knowing this was the wrong response.

Soukei would never be able to forget the look Samson gave her then, a mixture of disappointment and disgust and sadness.

～

SOUKEI SPENT THE LAST NIGHT IN HER HOTEL ROOM unable to sleep. She pressed her face into her pillow, but she couldn't blot out Samson's expression from her mind. At four in the morning, Soukei realized why it had unnerved her so—Samson had looked just like her father.

Jittery from lack of sleep, Soukei packed her things and hailed a cab to the airport. When she arrived, she went to the ticket counter to change her flight. She found a pay phone and made two phone calls: the first to Sulan and the second to the apartment in Hong Kong.

"Can you please tell my husband I'll be staying in the United States a little while longer?" she told Siu Fa. She paused. "On second thought, don't mention that I called at all."

"Ma'am?" the girl asked. "I don't understand?"

On the flight to New York, Soukei thought about the items she regretted not bringing with her: her favorite pair of earrings, jade, which Samson had purchased for her fiftieth birthday with money he'd made tutoring; the photo albums of Samson as a child; a silk scarf she had bought herself on the anniversary of the miscarriage she'd had ten years ago; the plum qipao Sulan had given her for her sixteenth birthday, the one she had almost died in.

Those were just things, Soukei reminded herself. Things of the past. They didn't matter. Only her future did.

MARCH–APRIL 1947
Shanghai

THE NOTES WERE out of control. They spun through Haiwen's head and pushed their way through his fingertips. His bow worked furiously, his finger pads ached. But the notes taunted him, ran away, and in chasing after them, he tripped. His left hand slipped; the wrong note squealed in distress.

"Stop, stop," Mr. Reyes said. His teacher pressed his temples where his gray hair thinned. "What's going on today, hmm? Where's your head at?"

Haiwen didn't respond. He brought his violin up and started to replay the measure, but Mr. Reyes set a hand on the instrument.

"Haiwen." The trim man looked at him. "You can't attack a piece like this. The caprice cannot be *controlled*. To find the right balance, you have to listen to it."

"I'm *listening*," Haiwen said, frustrated. "I know all the notes. The tempo is just too fast, I can't keep up with it. Maybe if we slow it down—"

"You can do this," Mr. Reyes said, shaking his head. "Last week, your left-hand fingering and spiccato were coming together. This week your hands have completely stopped communicating. What has happened?"

His brother was going to join the army, that's what. Hot rage filled Haiwen when he thought of the Nationalist officer who had threatened his family. He wished he were older, bigger. But he was a scrawny kid with an instrument as his only weapon. What use was the violin?

"Maybe all of this is pointless," he said flatly.

Mr. Reyes gave an exasperated sigh. "Let's try something," he said, gesturing toward Haiwen's violin. Haiwen handed it over. Mr. Reyes took a small tool out of a nearby drawer, then loosened and removed the chin rest. "Here."

Haiwen stared at the faint chipped marks imprinted in the wood where the chin rest had been and looked up at his teacher. "How am I supposed to play like this?"

"My first violin was an old instrument that had been passed down for many decades, the only violin in my entire village. It didn't have a chin rest, so I learned to play without it. Once I had one, I learned to play the way everyone else does, but from then on I was armed with two ways of approaching a piece. It's a different technique, you'll see. It might help you with your left hand."

He gestured for Haiwen to bring the violin up.

"Don't bend your neck so much. Keep your thumb and wrist here"—Mr. Reyes adjusted Haiwen's fingers and pushed his left elbow in—"and use your hand to keep the violin in place."

The instrument felt heavy and tenuous. He didn't know how he was supposed to shift positions this way. "I'm going to drop it."

"Lower your arm, you don't need to hold it so high. Now adjust. Curve your fingers. Stretch out instead of jumping around."

Haiwen tried, but he felt clumsy. He was conscious of the instrument's weight against his wrist, of the wood slipping between his sweaty chin and shoulder. After a few bars of fumbling, he stopped. "This is like relearning the violin from scratch. I can't do something entirely new at this stage. My audition is in a month!"

"Ay, Diyos ko, don't be so stubborn. A true artist remakes themselves when faced with a challenge."

"How will it help if I'm worried about dropping my instrument?"

"Look," Mr. Reyes said. He picked up his own violin. "This is how you play the caprice with a chin rest." He played a few of the most difficult measures. "See how my hand has to completely move somewhere new each time? How much wilder it seems? I spend half my effort on ensuring I land in the right place." He took Haiwen's violin from him. "Now watch this." He played the same measures, but this time his hand curved over and stretched outward to reach the strings, with minimal shifting. "You create a home base for your hand. This gives you more control over the rest of your fingers and allows you to focus. It means *less* energy trying to control the piece and more on playing it. They say this is how Paganini himself played." He handed the violin back to Haiwen. "Try again."

Haiwen spent the rest of the lesson adapting to the awkward posture. At first it was difficult to circumvent his existing muscle memory, but soon he realized he wasn't really starting from scratch; rather, he was looking at the same thing from a new point of view. After thirty minutes, Mr. Reyes had him put the chin rest back on but keep the fingering the same as when it was off. To his astonishment, Haiwen found the portion that had given him trouble earlier was now effortless; by the third run-through, he was playing that section cleanly. Energy buzzed in his veins.

As Haiwen put his violin away, Mr. Reyes said, "It's okay to use music to express your anger. But the piece won't unspool if you force it to. Neither will your problems."

On the bike ride home, Haiwen's excitement began to ebb, replaced by dread. He knew what awaited him: his mother and sister-in-law's puffy, tear-streaked faces; Ba's taciturn demeanor; his brother's foul temper. Even Junjun was throwing tantrums more often. Haiwen wanted to close himself in his room, turn the gramophone on as loudly as possible. He wanted to practice until his fingers bled.

Several blocks from Sifo Li, he passed one of the recruitment stands that had popped up around the International Settlement. He began to pedal faster, but a soldier spied him and called out.

"Ei! You! Don't you want to help your country defeat the rebel Communists?"

Reluctant to be rude, Haiwen slowed down. "Sorry, I'm rushing home for dinner—"

"Listen, if you join, it will bring glory to your family. Everyone will know your family is patriotic."

A year or two ago—maybe even a month ago—Haiwen's heart might have been swayed by talk of patriotism. But now the word rang hollow to him—no, it angered him. What did it mean, to love his country? And furthermore, did his country love him back? He recalled a conversation he'd had with Suchi months ago, the way he'd vigorously defended the Nationalist cause, how blindly he had believed that everything Chiang Kai-shek did, he did for the betterment of all Chinese people. He could no longer muster the same fervor. Nationalists, Communists—they were all the same. Asking ordinary people to sacrifice their lives, to kill their fellow countrymen, all so their leaders could come to power.

Haiwen had understood what China was when it was under the threat of the Japanese. But now—he didn't know what patriotism meant anymore. What he wanted was a world safe and prosperous for the people he loved, for the people of Sifo Li, a world where he could play Sibelius and Suchi could sing and Haiming could raise a son and Mr. Reyes could teach. What he wanted was a future where everyone could listen to music and no one would have to starve or worry about being drafted or shot. Was that patriotism?

Maybe Haiwen did love his country. But he loved his family more.

"I'm only sixteen," he said.

The man laughed. "Guess how old I was when I joined?" he asked. Without waiting for a reply, he said, "Thirteen! I just lied about my age and no one questioned me."

"Why would you do that?" Haiwen asked.

The man tapped on a sign declaring that a soldier's rice bowl would never go empty. "When you're a farm boy who lived through the famines, the promise of never being hungry again is too good to resist." He looked Haiwen over. "But maybe that's not a problem for you." He sniffed and straightened his posture. "For everyone else, it's a matter of life and death. For you folk, war is just an inconvenience, isn't it? I keep saying it's a waste of time to try to recruit you spoiled city boys, but who's going to listen to me?"

Haiwen's face flushed with defensiveness. The accusation felt both unfair and true.

"I'm late, sorry," he mumbled.

As he rode away, he tried to shake the man's disdain from his mind. He refocused his thoughts on the caprice, conjured the peaks and valleys of the black notes on the page. He imagined each note sounding as clean as a bell, reviewed the shape and movements his fingers had to make to bring them to life. He envisioned the future version of him who could play the piece perfectly, and impatience ran through him. He wanted to be that person already. Whoever that person was, he was surely happier than Haiwen was now.

Ma greeted Haiwen as he stepped inside the courtyard. "Doudou," she said, her voice warm but tired. Over the last few weeks, the crows' feet near her eyes had deepened. "How was your lesson today?"

"Good," Haiwen said. "Mr. Reyes showed me a new technique for playing Caprice Number Five."

"Wonderful," Ma said. "You seem to be doing well under Mr. Reyes."

"I feel ready for the conservatory. If they let me in."

Ma smiled. "You'll get in, Doudou, there's no doubt about that. You've worked hard your entire life for this." She paused. "But don't forget about the other things. Your family, for instance."

Shame washed over Haiwen. She had noticed him avoiding them then, particularly Haiming. When his brother had first returned, Haiwen had stayed up nights listening to his brother's stories from being abroad. Haiming was a sophisticated stranger to him, the gestures he made and words he muttered under his breath foreign and intriguing. But recently, Haiming had been in too poor a mood to want any company. If Haiwen was honest with himself, he'd been relieved.

"The audition is coming up," Haiwen mumbled as an excuse.

"I heard you even forgot Suchi's birthday several days ago."

Longtang gossip traveled fast. The guilt Haiwen had been trying to avoid crept into his throat. He still had yet to make it up to Suchi; he wasn't sure he could. The fact that she'd been such a good sport about it made it worse.

"She's a good girl," Ma continued. "She supports your aspirations, I can tell, and that's the most I can ask for as your mother. But as—as a woman . . ." Ma paused, and a wistful look came over her eyes. "Just remember she might have dreams of her own. If you care for her, make space for those too."

She pressed something into his palm. Haiwen stared down, startled. A thin band of gold, simple and light, its braided twist its only distinctive feature. It shone brightly beneath the lamplight.

"When you're ready—if you're ready—we can talk to her parents. You know I've long considered her family. And now, more than ever, we need to keep our loved ones close."

At dinner, they ate without conversation. Until recently, they had been lucky enough to have full bowls of rice and fresh vegetables almost every day, purchased through Haiwen's father's connections. But ever since Ba's interrogation, those connections seemed to have dried up. That they still had plenty of rice stored away should have caused them all to eat gratefully. Instead, everyone in his family picked at the food with little appetite. Haiwen kept rotating the ring on his left pinkie finger, thinking about what Ma had said. Marriage to Suchi. Suchi, his wife. He tried to imagine her face when he presented her with the ring. Her joy as he slid it on. Her beautiful hand winking with the light of it. He was only sixteen, but was there any point in waiting when you couldn't picture your life with anyone else?

Junjun broke the silence.

"Someone at school said Dage is joining the army to escape a gang."

"What is this nonsense!" Ma exclaimed. "Children should not concern themselves with these things."

"Is it true?" Junjun asked. "Is that why Dage has to go away?"

"Wang Haijun," Ba warned.

"No one tells me anything," Junjun said, pouting. "You all think I'm too young, but I can handle the truth. You all said Dage was in England all this time, but how do I know he wasn't *really* in a gang—"

"We've told you everything," Ma said in an even voice. "The Nationalists are demanding one eligible son to join their ranks."

Junjun looked troubled. "Does that mean they could make Erge go too?"

"Erge is too young," Ma said. "You have to be eighteen."

"But Dage is barely Chinese! He hasn't been here for that long."

"Oh my god," Haiming breathed.

"So when will Dage leave?" Junjun asked. "How come he hasn't left already?"

"Baba needs help setting up the factories for the government. So we told them to give us a few weeks. But maybe . . ." Ma's voice trembled. "We're still trying to figure out a way so he won't have to go."

"Maybe it's okay if he does," Junjun said. "My teacher says it's an honor to fight for your country, that the men who enlist are true patriots."

"Good god!" Haiming exclaimed in English, then switched to Mandarin. "Will you shut up?"

At this, Junjun jumped up, her face red, tears filling her eyes. "Ma!"

"How can you treat your own sister this way? She's young and doesn't understand." Ma drew Junjun into her arms and smoothed her hair. "You, stop running your mouth."

Ba set his bowl down. "Can't we eat in peace?" His voice was firm.

Haiming huffed and pushed his bowl toward his wife. "Eat," he told her in English. "I'm not hungry." He stood up and went out to the courtyard to smoke. Through the French doors, Haiwen watched him pace, the orange glow of his cigarette the only point of light against his shadowy figure. Ellen ate slowly, tears trembling on her lashes. Ma tried to smile at her.

"Have more. It's good for the baby," she said, heaping vegetables on her bowl.

That night, he heard his parents' hushed murmurs through the walls. Could they bribe the officer? Officers looked the other way if you handed them a fat envelope. How much would be enough? If they sold the gramophone, the clock, the calligraphy, the paintings, her jewelry, her dresses? If they gave him his own factory?

"How can I bribe them when I insisted that I've been loyal, a true follower of the Generalissimo?" Ba said. "It would mark me a hypocrite, cast suspicion on everything else I've said."

"But surely there's someone who doesn't care that much, who would rather look the other way and make some money—"

"They despise me for being friends with a Communist. The officer who warned me in particular. I think he's lost people he cares for and this is personal to him. And since he can't punish the ones responsible, he'll settle for punishing me." He paused, his voice softer, so that Haiwen could barely hear him. "I'm so sorry to my son. That to prove my loyalty, he will suffer."

"We can't let him go," Ma said, her voice low. "They'll push him to the front lines or torture him during drills. The abductees and coerced draftees have it the worst. Can you stomach that for him?"

"I've been trying. You know I have. I've asked people with connections to higher-ups, Mr. Liao, Mr. Shen. But no one dares help me now."

"This is my fault," Ma said. "I should have figured out a way for us to live even more frugally. I just thought, Doudou and Junjun, I didn't want them to feel the pinch of the war, not when so much around them was unstable. I should have listened to you, we should have switched Doudou to a more inexpensive teacher years ago— the Filipino man, he's just as good as the Russian teacher was and it was my own closed-mindedness that couldn't accept that. And Jun- jun, I should have—"

Haiwen didn't catch whatever his mother said after that. His heart was pounding. It was because of his lessons that they had bor- rowed the money from that man who had disappeared? It was his fault, then, that his father was in this predicament. His fault that Haiming would have to go.

"No, no," his father was saying. "It's my fault. I should have known something was wrong. You were the one that warned me not to owe him too much." After a pause, he added, "Maybe I should just turn myself in. Beg them to use me instead of my son. I'm not that old, with a bit of training, I could still—"

Ma started sobbing, the cries like a muffled ghost through the walls. His father's voice turned low and tender, the way it only ever did for his mother.

"Shh. Shh. Okay, okay. I'll keep asking. Don't worry. We'll find a way. We will."

ELLEN'S PREGNANCY WAS NOT AN EASY ONE. SHE THREW up at least four times a day and hardly ate; she was thin and pale. Ma brought her medicinal broths and pickled plums and yangmei for the nausea. Haiming fretted, going through a pack of cigarettes a day, unsure of what to do for his wife, who cried when she wasn't sleeping or vomiting. They called for a doctor the day speckles of blood appeared in her vomit. The man emerged after the exam shaking his head. "She's facing a difficult pregnancy, but her nerves are making it worse. If she doesn't improve, it could put the baby in danger."

That night, after dinner, Haiwen practiced the caprice in the courtyard, while his brother paced next to him, lighting cigarette after cigarette. Haiwen was getting it. He was quickly becoming familiar with the new position; Mr. Reyes was right—having a home base for his left hand gave his fingers confidence. Haiwen lost himself in the torrent of notes, feeling the way they ran and climbed, keeping pace beside them.

When he had practiced for about two hours, he emerged from his music to find Haiming still standing in the other corner of the courtyard. He was staring into the large urn where, years ago, bright pink lotuses had once floated. Now it was filled with murky rainwater.

"It doesn't bore you, to play the same thing over and over again?" Haiming asked without looking up.

Haiwen shook his head. "It's like trying to unravel a puzzle."

"I think I'd die of frustration."

Haiwen plucked a few notes with his left finger. They sounded like rain.

"You're talented, that's for sure. I always knew you were, but to come back and hear what you can do now—" His brother shook his head. He looked up and let out a short laugh. "I really was the wrong one to take lessons."

Ma's words echoed in Haiwen's skull. If he hadn't loved music this much, they wouldn't be in this situation. He hated himself, hated his selfishness. Music was trivial, useless. He wished he despised it. He wished it would leave him forever.

"Maybe I'll quit," he told his brother.

Haiming scoffed, a hollow chuckle. "What are you talking about? Stop saying crazy things." He took a deep drag from his cigarette, blowing out the smoke in a large plume. "Listen, when I'm not around, help watch my kid, okay? Maybe even give him a violin lesson or two. I'd like it if my son were patient like you."

A lump formed in Haiwen's throat. He nodded.

"Ellen, she likes music," Haiming continued. "She likes the Western opera. I was never keen on it, but we went to see some opera once and she cried her eyes out. So I think she'd like it if our son was musical."

"Dage——" Haiwen started.

"Also, if I don't, you know, come back, Ba might ask you to take over the business. I know it's not what you want to do, so your big brother is just going to have to trouble you to do him this favor."

"Don't go," Haiwen said. "Ba would never forgive himself if something happened. I—I couldn't either. There has to be another way."

"What other way?" Haiming's voice was gentle. "Have Baba's loyalty questioned further? Wait until they seize him for interrogation again, maybe this time killing him? There is no other way."

"But if you go——" Haiwen stopped. He couldn't say it, couldn't repeat what he'd overheard Ma say about forced conscriptions.

Haiming cracked a crooked smile. "Who knows? Maybe I'll come back a decorated officer, a hero. Now, wouldn't that be something."

Haiwen couldn't smile back.

THE NEXT DAY, HAIWEN APPROACHED THE RECRUIT-
ment stand cautiously, as if getting too close would burn him. The
man was cleaning his ear with his pinkie and hardly glanced up.
"Oh, it's you."

"So no one checks," Haiwen said.

"Ei?"

"Your age. You said no one cares."

The soldier laughed. "We're so desperate, we're rounding up
countryside peasant boys whose voices haven't even cracked yet. So
no, I don't think they'll care if you say you're eighteen when you're
not." He examined his fingernail, flicked something from beneath it.
"You know, if you willingly sign up, you'll be treated better than
those farm boys we've had to conscript. Better rations, better promotion opportunities. Even the officers will look at you more favorably.
Trust me, I know." He gave Haiwen a sly smile. "Are you thinking
of enlisting?"

Haiwen said nothing. The idea had taken root overnight. Unlike
Haiwen, Haiming was *needed*. His wife needed him, his child needed
him. His father and the factories needed him. Ma had only recently
gotten him back. He was the one who shouldered the greatest responsibility and burden in their household, the man upon whom
generations depended. And who was Haiwen? He was a violinist
with a beautiful dream of playing music. Frivolous.

If someone had to go, it should be him.

"I knew it, you're a patriotic, heroic young man. Your family
will be proud." The soldier pushed the paper and pen at him. "We
can ship you out for training by tomorrow."

Haiwen looked down at the paper. He thought of what this man said. If he enlisted now, out of his own free will, he would have an easier time than Haiming. It might even be seen as a mark of loyalty, of honor, of courage.

He kicked off on his bike and fled.

For a while he wandered the perimeter of the longtang, lingering in front of stores without really seeing what they were selling. He thought of how easy it would be, to take Haiming's place. Now that he had confirmation it was possible, Haiwen's stomach churned. Could he do such a thing? *Should* he do such a thing? He thought of Haiming and his sister-in-law and their unborn baby. He thought of how he could hear the sound of his sister-in-law's muffled cries through the walls every night. They were a family. They should not be separated.

But then he thought of Suchi. Wasn't she *his* family?

Guilt crept up his spine. Family wouldn't have avoided each other for weeks, like he had with Suchi. If watching Haiming's distress should have taught him anything, it was that time with loved ones was precious.

It was time to apologize.

THE BRASS PIN SHONE IN THE WINDOW OF THE PAWN-shop, a sleek golden airplane. It was perfect, Haiwen thought, and he walked in.

"Ah, Waong Haeven," the shop owner, Mr. Li, said without smiling. "Your mother was in here just a few days ago, bullied me into giving her a good deal on some jewelry. Said she wanted something perfect for her future daughter-in-law. Funny, because if I recall correctly, it was Tsan Li'oe who . . ." The man trailed off and peered at him over the counter. "Well? Did Tsan Suji like the ring at least?"

"I—I haven't given it to her yet," Haiwen stuttered, shame and embarrassment slipping across his neck. He gestured toward the window display. "I was interested in the airplane pin." He took one of his records from his bag. A recording of Brahms's Symphony in C. "Would this cover it?"

"Another record?" Mr. Li sighed. Haiwen nodded, trying to ignore the pang in his chest as he slid the record across the counter. His records were the only things of value he had. He had pawned a Tchaikovsky several weeks earlier, in order to have enough money to cover Suchi's birthday treat from the café—a treat he had not ended up buying. But he would be using that money for her today, he thought.

Mr. Li wrote out a ticket and counted a few coins into Haiwen's hand. "These things," he grumbled as he placed the record on a low, dusty shelf next to what Haiwen recognized as the Tchaikovsky. It was hardly noticeable in the corner, and Haiwen felt a surge of gratefulness. "Nobody wants records these days. Just you wait and see. You'll come back in a few weeks and they'll still be here. You better buy them back from me then because *I* certainly won't be able to sell them."

Pin in his pocket, Haiwen biked along Fourth Road toward Suchi's longtang. He suddenly felt jittery and eager to see Suchi, to witness her pleasure at receiving his gift. He had thought a lot about what his mother had said, about keeping those you loved close, about considering what Suchi might want. He *did* care about her dreams, and he hoped this pin would make that clear; he wanted her to know he would always wait for her return when she flew away.

He had his apology ready: He was a bad boyfriend for forgetting her birthday, an even worse one for waiting over two weeks to make it up to her, and he was sorry. He had no good excuse for why, except that he'd wanted to forget everything waiting for him in the outside world, had wanted to simply focus on the thing he could control: his music. Every time he had thought of confiding in Suchi, he had felt a dread—that she might have questions for him he couldn't answer and didn't want to think about, that her family might have heard the gossip in the longtang and have sowed a seed of doubt into her mind about who his family was. Suchi's mother had never liked him; what if she had turned Suchi against him? What if Suchi no longer wanted to be associated with him?

But his mother was right: Suchi supported him, loved him unconditionally. And right now, more than anything, he wanted to lay down his troubles at her feet. To tell her about everything, how he was afraid his brother would die and it would break his family, how he feared that all of this was his fault, how he was second-guessing the point of even going to the conservatory when so much more mattered. How taking his brother's place was a possibility. How much that frightened him.

He arrived at the back door of the Zhang shikumen and was about to knock when he heard Suchi's mother's voice, loud and berating.

"I keep telling Apa you're not ready to manage the bookstore alone. But he never listens to me. You'd think, after what happened with the Waongs, he'd be a little more careful."

He heard Suchi's voice, quiet and chastised. "I was just trying to be helpful to a customer."

"Silly girl! You really don't use your brain, do you? But I suppose it's to be expected after you've been neglected by your beloved Waong Haeven for so long."

Haiwen winced at this, but Suchi's voice rose hotly. "He's just busy. He'll come when he's ready."

"Maybe he's too ashamed to show his face," her mother continued. "But perhaps it's better if he keeps his distance. If his father can be mixed up with that sort of trouble, who knows what kind of man Haeven is?"

Suchi cut in, her words simmering. "You don't know what you're talking about. Haeven is a good man and his father is innocent. If Haeven hasn't been around, it's not because he's a coward; it's because he's prioritizing his family. Because that's the kind of man he is. Someone who puts his family before everything else."

Haiwen stepped back from the door as if he'd been burned. Shame flooded his body.

Suchi was wrong. He *was* a coward. He wanted to be the man she believed he was, someone who took care of his family, someone who put them first. Someone who faced these difficulties with courage. But he wasn't that person. Suchi's mother was right: he couldn't face Suchi.

Haiwen fingered the box in his pocket and got back on his bike, his head crowded and confused, his heart fractured.

HAIWEN THREW HIMSELF INTO MUSIC. HE WENT TO lessons twice a week, to orchestra rehearsal three times a week. And every other free moment, he practiced. Haiwen tried to lose himself in Paganini. When he focused, time slowed down; his breath became even. Each bounce of his bow happened in slow motion, a graceful and light leap. In that suspended space, Haiwen felt secure and at peace. There was no world around him, no war, no impossible situations—just the bite of the string, the tension of horsehair, the pleasure of the right note vibrating beneath his hand.

But at night, Haiwen couldn't escape. He lay in bed and moved his fingers over the phantom strings on his forearm, attempting to practice, but the weight of choice crowded out the music. His mind turned to the past—memories of his earliest lessons with Mr. Portnoy, the games he and Suchi and Sulan had shared, Junjun's baby face, Ma's tender hand on his cheek—and the future, one he'd imagined so many times, a future where he and Suchi were married, where he'd become a virtuoso violinist, first chair for the Shanghai Municipal Orchestra, a future that included some blurry children and Suchi's laughter, his mother as a doting grandmother, the love, the days, the years, the growing old and gray and wrinkly with Suchi. It was his present he couldn't bear to think about, the choice before him that could result in two equally unbearable, unfathomable futures.

If he took his brother's place. If he died.

If he didn't take his brother's place. If his brother died instead.

If that happened, mightn't all the scenes from the future he dreamed of disappear? Could he be happy if his brother was gone? Could he live with himself?

He longed for Suchi. He wished he could explain to her how powerless he felt, how afraid. But he couldn't burden her with this.

Haiwen crept out of bed and retrieved the ring from his desk drawer and ran his finger along its thin band, the central twist. *She might have dreams of her own*, his mother had said. Did she still want to marry him? Did he even *deserve* her?

Several days ago, he'd asked Junjun to deliver the pin. He knew he should go himself, but he couldn't yet face her, not when he hadn't made up his mind. Still, he didn't want her to think he'd forgotten about her. He hoped she'd see the pin and understand that he supported her, that he believed in her, even if he wasn't by her side.

He was a bad boyfriend, a bad brother, a bad son. He was helpless to make the people he loved happy. But if Suchi's dreams still included him, he could still make *her* happy. He could make her a promise to love her for the rest of their lives, if she would have him.

He slipped the ring onto his pinkie. He tried to picture their future, a dazzling one filled with music and love and laughter. He squeezed his eyes shut, focusing on only those images. Suchi in a wedding dress. Suchi, singing the songs she loved. Suchi listening to him play. The visions were white and glowing, as if bathed in a too-bright spotlight.

He reached up to his forearm and commenced practicing.

HAIWEN RETURNED FROM HIS LESSON TO FIND MA SITting out in the courtyard alone, smoking a cigarette. Her pale fingers tapped the cigarette holder gently against the porcelain ashtray. She lifted her eyes to Haiwen as he closed the shikumen doors behind him. "Doudou, you're home." Her voice was resigned, sapped of energy.

Haiwen rarely saw his mother smoke anymore. She said it reminded her of a different time in her life, one that had passed, a life of opulent dance halls and adventurous travels. But here she was, whispering out smoke in delicate streams.

He put his violin down and maneuvered a stool to sit next to her. They said nothing for a while. The ember crackled against the filter as his mother inhaled.

"How's the caprice?"

"Good." At his lesson with Mr. Reyes, he had struggled through the piece two times, but on the third, he finally ran through the piece with no mistakes, at the tempo he had been aiming for. It should have been an exhilarating achievement, but Haiwen had felt empty, despite Mr. Reyes's exuberant whoops of delight.

"You'll be ready for your audition," Ma said.

Haiwen had almost forgotten. He'd learned the piece because it felt like the only thing he could control in his life. The audition no longer seemed to have anything to do with it.

"Do you want me to play it for you?" he asked.

Ma took another drag from her cigarette. "Play me the piece I like," she said. "Massenet."

As Haiwen drew out the first notes, a deep ache ran through him, pulling like a coil from his toes to his breath. He realized in all the years he had played "Meditation" before this, he had never fully understood its bittersweet longing. The melancholy, the lonesome beauty. The notes unraveled from his body, familiar yet new, and echoed through the small courtyard.

He glanced at his mother.

The cigarette had stilled between her fingers; her soft figure shuddered in her slim white qipao. It was one he'd rarely seen her wear, with a painted yellow crane that lilted from her right knee up to her upper left armpit. Her hair, permed in short, elegant waves, fell over her eyes, but he could see the glint of wetness against her pale cheeks. The white jade earrings in her lobes trembled.

For the first time, Haiwen saw how *beautiful* she was. Ever since he was young, he had heard people admire her appearance; it was something he was always dimly aware of but could never comprehend. But in that moment, he saw that she possessed a beauty that pulsed warm and rare—and what was more, he understood his mother's greatest strength was also her greatest weakness. He understood she loved him and his siblings in a way no one in this world would ever love them again—selflessly, unrelentingly, unrequitedly—and it would hurt her in the end, had probably already hurt her many times over, was hurting her at that very moment.

He knew now the selfish thing wasn't *not* telling her what he had learned from the recruitment officer. It was to tell her, to make the choice hers. The limbo she was in, the powerlessness, the indecision, the feeling she hadn't done *enough*—he knew the torment of it now. And he wanted to take it from her.

He thought of the other woman in his life—Suchi. A woman whom he had also hurt, would likely hurt again. The way his mother had pushed him to make it right with her, to consider her feelings. Because his mother understood what it meant to be a woman in this world, and she had seen how much Suchi loved him. His mother wanted Haiwen to be worthy of her.

But he could not be worthy of Suchi if he considered only himself. She deserved the type of man she believed him to be—a man who took care of his family. A man who eased the suffering of his mother. A man who saved his brother.

The music flowed out of Haiwen like breath. Tender yet resolute.

Carrying with it all he hoped to recompense his mother for. Love, remorse, gratitude, patience. A promise. He drew out the last harmonic longer than usual, until the high, gentle A became a whisper he let die into the night.

He set his violin down. His mother pressed away her tears with the back of her hand and laughed. "I'm so silly. That piece always makes me cry. You just play it so beautifully."

Haiwen stared down at his hands, where he still had the gold ring around his pinkie. His fingers were slender like his mother's but calloused on the tips from years of playing. Hers had always been soft and cool, the touch that comforted him when he was sick. How he'd longed for that touch against his forehead when he was delirious and somnambulant, longed to hear her tell him he didn't have to go to school that day, that she would stay beside him.

He would tell her after. When he had already signed the papers, when there were no more choices to be made, when there was no turning back.

For now, he reached out and took her hands into his. For now, he wouldn't go.

ABI HOPPED AROUND the kitchen while Suchi rinsed dishes. "You can't touch the cracks, Aniang, or it's bad luck for ten years," she explained as she leapt from tile to tile.

"Xiao xin," Suchi cautioned. "The floor is slippy."

"Aniang, you're stepping on the crack!" Her granddaughter stopped and tugged at her slippered feet.

"Abi, stop bothering Aniang," Samson said, coming into view.

"But she's going to have bad luck!"

"What you mean, I'm already very lucky," Suchi said. "I have you, dui ba?"

"Come on, it's time to wash up. Mommy has filled the tub with lots of bubbles."

Her granddaughter pouted. "I don't want to. I want to play with Aniang."

Samson scooped Abi up, tickling her. "I'm a giant squid, coming to kidnap you to the sea witch's lair!" Abi squealed in protest between giggles.

"Help, Aniang! Help meeee!"

Suchi glanced up at her granddaughter and smiled. "Guai, siau noe, take your bath and go sleep. Tomorrow Aniang will play with you." Shrieking laughter pealed up the stairs with her son and granddaughter.

A little while later, Samson returned alone. "She's finally down," he said, exhaling. He picked up a dish and started drying it. "Ma," he said after a moment. He dragged the word out, and she immediately tensed.

"What's wrong?" she asked, turning to look at him. "Has something terrible happened? Have you lost your job?"

He let out a small laugh. "Ma, come on, it's nothing like that! Why do you always assume the worst?"

She sniffed. "Your tone of voice. You think I can't tell when there's something wrong?"

"Everything's *fine*, Ma."

"Then?"

"Uncle Howard called my office today." He glanced at her, then continued to dry the dish in his hand. "He said he had something important to tell you, but he wasn't sure you would speak to him."

Suchi returned to washing the dishes. "I see."

Samson sighed and set the dish down. "Listen, Ma, I don't know what happened between you two during New Year's. But you told me yourself he's your oldest friend. How many of those do you have? Isn't that worth trying to mend whatever happened?"

"Nothing happened," she said, scrubbing vigorously at a pot. How could Haiwen go behind her back and call her son? The man sure had thick skin. No pride, no conscience. "Sometimes it's just like that. You meet old friends and discover all you share anymore is a common history. That's not enough to maintain a friendship."

"But—" Samson started, then stopped. "Okay, fine. Maybe you don't have to be friends with him. But he said—he said he had some information regarding your parents."

Her hands stilled, covered in soap bubbles.

"See? This could be—"

"My parents are dead."

"But don't you want to know what happened to them?"

She stared at her palms, at the white foam sliding off her fingers.

"And maybe—it's possible—"

"They're dead," Suchi repeated. She turned on the faucet; the foam burst and disappeared in a rush of water. "I don't need any other information." She turned off the faucet, dried her hands on a dish towel, and left Samson to stare after her in the kitchen.

SUCHI WAS HAPPY WITH HER LIFE THE WAY IT WAS. EV-ery morning, after Ronnie and Samson were at work, she and Nicky walked Abi to school, then came home and played games until Nicky was ready for his midday nap. While he slept, she tended to her little vegetable garden out back or watched an episode of whatever new Chinese drama was on the Chinese-language channel. In the after-noon, she prepped food for dinner and Nicky played by himself until it was time to pick Abi up from school. She fed Abi an afternoon snack while she listened to her chatter about every last detail of her day until either Samson or Ronnie came home.

She did this every weekday except for Wednesdays, when Ronnie took Nicky to a daycare in the morning and worked from home in the afternoons so she could pick Abi up herself. It was Ronnie who had insisted on this arrangement when she heard there'd been an opportunity for Suchi to sing in Coral Sunset's choir, even though Suchi had worried it would be both too much of a hassle and a waste of money.

"No, Ma, this is great! You *should* be making time to see your friends and pursue your hobbies!"

Suchi loved the choir, loved learning new music and meeting new friends, although after their argument in February, Suchi had been concerned Haiwen would show up to try to mend things. But the weeks had passed and he hadn't appeared. Suchi was relieved but also vaguely disappointed. He had given up so easily, the way he had after their fight the night before he left Shanghai, the way he had when she'd left him without a word in Hong Kong. Each time, he had let her go without any resistance. This was not a man who loved her, she thought. This was a man who only *believed* he loved her. Thank god she had not opened that door with him a third time.

～

SUCHI ARRIVED AT CORAL SUNSET TEN MINUTES BEFORE rehearsal was scheduled to begin and found Annie and Winston whispering furtively in the corner of the music room. When they saw Suchi, they waved her over.

"Have you heard?" Annie asked.

"Heard what?"

Annie shook her head sadly, and Suchi's body tightened. Had

461

something happened to someone they knew? To one of the other choir members? At their age, there was always the possibility of the worst, and it was a fear that loomed over every friendship.

Winston cut in. "Howard. Last week he got lost while driving back from 99 Ranch and couldn't find his way home. Luckily, he had that cell phone and called one of his daughters, who then called Michael, who called his son—you know, the police officer—to help find him."

Annie clucked her tongue. "It's a route he takes every week, he kept telling Michael. He had no idea how he got so lost."

Suchi's heart sank. "Has he gone to see the doctor?" she asked, trying to keep her voice steady.

Winston shook his head. "He's stubborn. He says he's fine, that he was tired. So who knows."

She had clucked in sympathy when Winston shared news of residents' dementia and Alzheimer's, but it was the half-hearted cluck of someone who was glad that condition was not hers. Yet now.

"Maybe it's just a freak occurrence," Annie said. "Who doesn't get lost on occasion?"

"Maybe," Suchi echoed. To her surprise, tears threatened the corners of her eyes.

Winston let out a loud, hearty laugh. "Aiya, why are we clucking as if the man's already dead? I'm sure it's nothing. I forget where I put my keys every day. I'll call him and remind him to do those Sudoku puzzles everyone says are good for your brain and everything will be fine."

Suchi mumbled her way through rehearsal that afternoon; she could not stop thinking about Haiwen.

HAIWEN PICKED UP ON THE FIFTH RING, DURING WHICH time Suchi had nearly hung up.

Startled by his voice, it took a moment before Suchi cleared her throat and spoke. "It's Suchi," she said.

There was a pause. She could hear the faint strains of classical music wafting through the receiver, and for a moment she was transported back to childhood, when she'd watch Haiwen listening to records with his ear pressed to the floor. The memory broke when Haiwen spoke. "Suchi." His voice was tired and careful. "I didn't know if Samson had given you my message. I—I didn't think you would call."

"I wasn't going to," she said.

"Why did you change your mind?" Haiwen asked.

She hesitated before responding. She didn't want to tell him what she'd heard from Annie and Winston. She still wasn't sure calling him was the right thing, but the possibility that something could be wrong—it had upset her, more than she cared to admit. "Samson said you had to tell me something. Something about my parents."

"Wait," he said. "First, I just want to say, about that day, I'm—"

She cut him off. "I'm only here because of my parents. That's the only reason I'm calling." She began to wonder if this had been a mistake. He was still hung up on rehashing the past. Nothing good lay in thinking about what might have been.

"All right," he said. His voice was quieter, more subdued. "No problem," he added in English.

"Good then," she said. She waited a beat for him to speak, and when he didn't, she prodded, "So what is it?"

He took a breath. "When I returned to Shanghai in 1993, Junjun mentioned my mother had been in contact with yours. In fact, it was your mother who had called my siblings to let them know my mother was dying. Otherwise, my mother had planned to hide it from them until it was too late."

Suchi could feel her blood pulsing beneath her skin. "Where was she? When was this?"

"Sifo Li. My mother had never left the old shikumen, and she and your mother crossed paths, though I don't think your mother lived there anymore. My mother passed away in 1982, so sometime around then."

Suchi swallowed the hope she had, briefly, allowed to surface. "1982. That's over twenty years ago."

"Junjun couldn't find the phone number your mother had contacted them with. And I couldn't remember your mother's name, so it wasn't easy to ask around about her, though she tried."

"Oh," she said. She pressed a fist to her sternum. Once, twenty years ago, her mother had still been alive. Perhaps that was enough, to know her mother had lived through the Communist takeover, the famine, the Cultural Revolution.

But Haiwen was still talking. "Then, out of nowhere, you reappeared in my life. And, I thought . . . well, that's why I asked you for your parents' names that one time, though I know you thought it was a bit odd."

Suchi remembered. She had playfully joked that it was disrespectful of Haiwen to think of her parents as anything besides "Tsan ayi" and "Tsan yasoh" when he'd asked, but eventually she'd told him.

"I gave that information to Junjun and Xuenong, my niece. A few weeks ago, Xuenong called me and said she had news." He paused and Suchi realized how still, how erect, she was holding herself. "Suchi, your mother is alive."

Vertigo engulfed her. She shut her eyes. She felt at any moment her careful grip on the world might loosen and she would fall into a chasm.

"Suchi? Are you still there? Did you hear what I said?"

"Yes," she said faintly.

"Your mother is alive. She lives in an elderly care home in Shanghai. Her eyesight isn't good, and she isn't always lucid, but somehow, against all odds, she's alive."

Something in her burst. As if she'd been holding her breath for so long, she had forgotten why it was so hard to breathe until the moment the air rushed in.

"Susu, are you all right?" Haiwen asked. She could hear the concern in his voice, and in her mind, she pictured the young, sweet boy who had loved her, his eyes wide with helplessness.

"I have to go," she said quickly. She replaced the cordless receiver in the cradle. Dropping her face into her palms, she sobbed.

IT WASN'T TRUE, SUCHI THOUGHT AS SHE FED NICKY mashed sweet potatoes. Haiwen's niece had made a mistake. It was another woman with M'ma's name. If M'ma had been alive this whole time, Suchi would have *known*. She would have felt it in her heart. Not just that, but the few inquiries Sulan had sent before she passed away—they would have turned up *something*.

And what about Apa? Apa would never have left M'ma alone. M'ma would never have left Apa. The two were a pair. It wasn't possible for there to be one without the other. It just wasn't possible.

Suchi's cheeks were wet. Nicky reached out with his chubby

hands, his little brow furrowed as he offered her half a rice cracker. "No cry!" he insisted, and Suchi did her best to smile and press her tears away.

At dinner, Samson commented that Suchi seemed unnaturally quiet. "Something wrong, Ma?"

"I'm just tired," she said. She caught the troubled glance her son exchanged with Ronnie. "Really, don't worry about me."

Her daughter-in-law cleared her throat. "I heard something today, from one of my friends."

Suchi tensed. Had Haiwen told others? Could news have traveled that fast?

"Uncle Howard . . . it seems he got himself into some trouble a few days ago? Did you know about this?"

"Oh, na ge." Suchi resumed eating. "I heard he was confused, mei shenme."

"Shouldn't you maybe . . . check on him?" Samson suggested in Cantonese. "You're his oldest friend, I'm sure right now he could use a friend who knows him—"

"I don't know him at all," she responded in Mandarin. "We're no longer who we were when we were kids."

When Samson spoke again, he seemed to be choosing his words carefully. "I think it must be lonely, to be the only one who knows the truth of your world. To have no one to share it with." He paused. "Maybe Uncle Howard is lonely."

AFTER DINNER, SUCHI CALLED MOMO IN NEW YORK.

"Suchi!" Momo exclaimed. Suchi smiled. She loved the woman's exuberant voice, which always sounded as if speaking to Suchi was a delightful gift. In the five years Suchi had lived with Sulan after leaving Saikeung, the Japanese woman had slowly won Suchi over. Although at first Suchi had been uncomfortable that she was moving into a two-bedroom apartment where Sulan and Momo would share *one* room, over time, Suchi understood why Sulan loved Momo so much—Momo was funny and sweet, bright and trustworthy, equally intelligent in personal and business affairs. Watching the two of them together, Suchi saw what a good team they were: how Sulan's anxiety eased around Momo's quiet steadfastness, how Momo's level-headed rationality gave Sulan's creativity room to flourish, how often the two broke into spontaneous laughter for reasons unknown to Suchi, how they implicitly *fit*. The five years spent in that apartment living with the two of them were the happiest of Suchi's adult life.

After Sulan had passed away, Suchi and Momo stayed roommates for a couple more years. They took solace in Sulan's absence together; they were the two people in this world who had loved Sulan the most, and each one's grief could only be understood by the other. Eventually, Suchi moved out to Flushing, a shorter commute to the Shanghainese restaurant where she waitressed.

After they spent fifteen minutes catching up, Suchi took a deep breath and told her she had some news.

"It's probably a mistake," Suchi said. "But my friend, he says he found our mother. She's alive."

Momo gasped. "Suchi," she said, "this is incredible. Well, of course you have to fly to Shanghai immediately."

"What? No. I'm telling you, this is a mistake, it must be."

"Why do you say that?" Momo asked. "Who would tell a lie like this? It would be cruel."

"Not on purpose," Suchi said.

"I'm sure your friend checked the facts thoroughly before handing over such big news to you." When Suchi didn't respond, Momo continued. "It's your mother. If there's even the slightest chance it might be her, how can you not go?"

For a moment, Suchi tried to picture deplaning, walking along the streets of Shanghai again, seeing her mother again. But it was wrong, all wrong. Things would have changed. The streets would not be the same. Her mother would not look the same. Suchi herself would be unrecognizable to anyone who had known her then. "It's a waste of time," she said.

Momo laughed. "Those Chang genes. So stubborn."

"Maybe when I was young," Suchi said. "I'm too old now to make such a long trip."

"Nonsense," she said. "You get around just fine! You garden and sing. You're a young seventy-six!"

"Seventy-seven now," Suchi said. "I'm not young. I feel more old every day."

"You know, it was the one thing that would have made Sulan happier than she already was. That was her one regret—not knowing what happened to your parents. If she were still alive, she'd be on the next plane out. She wouldn't hesitate. Even if there was a chance it was false, she'd find out for herself."

At her sister's name, Suchi felt a wave of grief. What Momo said was true. Tsia had never given up hope their parents were still alive and continued to search for them, but Suchi had told her it was a futile enterprise. What was the point of knowing the terrible way they might have died? she had argued, thinking, with a pang of guilt, of Siau Zi's letter. Wasn't it better to remember them as they were?

"Sulan was more brave than me," Suchi told Momo now.

"You know, Sulan used to tell me stories about what a fierce little girl you were."

"It's easy to be brave when you are young and don't know better," Suchi said.

"I think it's harder to be brave when you're young and have little control over anything," Momo said.

Suchi gave a small snort.

"Who is this friend, by the way?" Suchi could tell Momo was changing the subject for her sake, and she was grateful. "The one who found news of your mother? Is it that man at the retirement home? The one who has been wooing you?" Momo giggled, sounding like a teenager.

"No," Suchi said. "Someone from the old days. Sulan knew him. He grew up with us in Shanghai."

Momo paused. "Wang Haiwen?"

Suchi sucked the air between her teeth. So Sulan had told her. "Yes," she said.

Momo laughed, delighted. "What a wonderful coincidence!" she exclaimed. "You know, we met him once, a long time ago, before you came to live with us. I don't know if Sulan told you. He brought fabric samples to us from his company. I'm afraid Sulan was rather rude to him."

"What?"

Sulan had never mentioned it. Suchi understood why—she had snapped at her sister any time Sulan uttered Haiwen's name—but it upset her that her sister had kept such a large secret from her. If she'd known . . . *If you'd known, what?* Suchi asked herself, stopping that train of thought. Nothing. It wouldn't have made a difference.

"It's not like that," she finally said. "We are just—he's just an old friend."

"Oh," Momo said, her voice dropping in disappointment. "That's too bad."

FOR SEVERAL MORE WEEKS, SUCHI CONTINUED HER usual routine. She did not tell her family what Haiwen's niece had discovered. She wasn't sure if there was any point.

Haiwen invaded her thoughts constantly. She was remembering more and more details of their time together. A joke she had long forgotten he had told her. A tender look he had given her when she'd done something silly. It was strange how these memories she believed had been wiped clean were rising to the surface, like an underwater vault filled with photographs finally unlocked.

A few times, she picked up the phone to call Haiwen, but she never did. What good could come from a conversation? He wanted something she could not give him. He wanted a future that belonged in the past.

It was better this way, Suchi thought. Her life was stable and safe and known. She had Samson, she had Abi and Nicky. After all the decades of unrest and unease, things were good. Why upend that? Why invite new heartbreak into her life when she was finally happy?

THERE WAS A KNOCK AT SUCHI'S BEDROOM DOOR, AND Samson peeked in. "Do you have a moment?"

Suchi hurriedly covered the little notebook she'd been writing in. A few days ago, she'd seen the notebook at a stationery store and thought of how Haiwen had one like it, one he used to pencil in to-do lists and new vocabulary. She'd never kept a journal of any sort, but she decided she might try to carry one around, though so far what she had scribbled inside had been mundane, meaningless: an accounting of the bus fare and meals she purchased, a phone number here and there, a funny line or two that Abi said during the day. Suchi had been jotting down a charming story about a butterfly and a unicorn searching for cotton candy clouds that Abi had spent thirty minutes relating to Suchi with animated gestures.

"Come in," Suchi said.

"Ma," he said, settling down on the bed across from the desk where she sat. He took a deep breath. "Please don't get mad, but I called Uncle Howard today."

"Aiya, Samson—" she started, but he cut her off.

"It just seemed like you were never going to, and given everything people have been saying, I thought it would be nice to check in on him. In case you're curious, he sounded okay."

"See? I told you there's nothing wrong."

Samson shook his head. "That's not why I called him. I called because I was curious about your parents." He held up a hand before she could react. "I know, I know, you don't think there's any point. But even if you don't, I do. They're my grandparents."

Suchi flinched at the accusation in Samson's voice. He stared down at his palms and rubbed his fingers.

"He told me you'd already called him, weeks ago. That if I wished to know what he'd learned, I should ask you." He frowned. "Why didn't you tell me? Why do you have to be so damn secretive all the time? Don't I have a right to know?"

Suchi opened her mouth to defend herself, but then she caught sight of the expression on his face, the naked injury. If she squinted, he was a little boy again, eyes wide with hope. She looked away. Of course Samson was right. Her family's legacy—it was his too.

"Wang Haiwen believes he's found my mother. Or rather, his niece thinks so." She looked at her son.

After a moment, Samson reached out and squeezed her arm. The frown had vanished and he was beaming. "But Ma, this is wonderful, isn't it? Why wouldn't you share this with us?"

Suchi shook her head. "Who knows if it's even true? It's been so many years, how would you even know if—"

"Well, there's only one way to find out," Samson said.

"Not you too!" Suchi exclaimed. Heat ricocheted across her skull. "Why is everyone badgering me to go to Shanghai! I don't want to travel thousands of miles just to be made a fool of!"

"Ma, calm down," her son said, his smile disappearing. "No one's making you do anything you don't want to do. It's just, you know, you're getting older, and so is she. There might not be a lot of time left."

"And what if it is her? Wang Haiwen says she's nearly blind and is confused most of the time. She won't even recognize me!"

"She's your mother," Samson said. "Even if she doesn't remember you, isn't it worth it to see her?"

"What if she doesn't recognize me?" Suchi repeated. Her voice was high and strained. Her eyes burned. "What if I don't recognize her? What if I fly all the way over there and I *can't tell* if it's my own mother?" She could feel tears threatening her eyes. She covered her face in embarrassment.

"Oh, Ma," he said, his features softening. "None of that matters.

You know that doesn't matter." He put a hand on her arm. "Why don't you tell me about her? You never talk about them, your parents. I don't know anything about them. But I'd like to."

"I *can't*," Suchi choked out.

"But why?" Samson asked. "Don't you miss them?"

"Of *course* I miss them!"

Her voice came out louder and shriller than she intended, and Samson flinched. Suchi took a few deep breaths.

"You know, when Ayi and I first got to Hong Kong, I never stopped wishing my father would show up. I thought surely someday he would come with my mother and everything would be all right. It wouldn't be Shanghai, but we'd be together, we'd start over, we'd right our lives and we'd be happy. But as time went on, and my life became what it was . . ." She sucked on the corner of her lip and tried to blink the tears back in. "I felt relieved we had heard nothing from my father. I thought my apa, who believed I could do great things, who taught me to have courage, would be so disappointed to see what I'd become, what little I'd done with my life." She looked up at her son. "Do you see what kind of daughter I am? I *hoped* for him not to find us."

"You were young," he said. "You were doing what you had to do to survive. He would understand."

"I can't face my mother." Her voice was breathy and tight. "How can I explain who I've become, why it took me so long to find her? I've been such a coward." A sob broke through her throat, and with it tumbled the tears she'd been trying to hold back. Samson reached out again, this time his hand covering hers, stilling the violent twisting of her fingers. "I can't go," Suchi sobbed. "What can I tell her of the life I have led? I've only brought shame to our family."

"No. Ma." He squeezed her hand. "You took care of your family, just like she and your father would have. You helped your sister become a successful fashion designer. You're helping me raise Abi and Nicky into amazing people. And you gave everything up for me. You protected me, you loved me. You are the reason I ever had a chance at my own happiness. That's not nothing. That's everything."

"I didn't do anything," she gasped, shaking her head. Tears blurred Suchi's vision, slipping warm down her cheeks. She grasped at her son's fingers, clutching them.

"You were brave, Ma," her son said. "You were brave."

HAIWEN LOOKED NERVOUS. HIS THIN WHITE HAIR WAS sticking up in the back and he clutched a felt fedora in his hand. He glanced around the restaurant, not seeing her. She waved at him from her seat.

"I didn't think you would want to meet me," he said after sliding into the booth.

"The soup dumplings here are good," she said. "Let's order one basket and some stir-fried cabbage."

He nodded. She put in their order and asked for their glasses of ice water to be switched to warm water. When the waiter departed, Suchi looked at Haiwen, who sat still and straight across from her.

"I won't bite you, old man," she said wryly.

Haiwen looked alarmed. "No," he said, "I just—"

"I'm kidding," she said. "I know I've given you reason to be wary of me. I'm sorry."

"It's my fault. I overstepped last time."

"You know, I always hated when you did that," Suchi said.

"When you apologized, even for the things that weren't your fault." Her words were chiding, but she used a tender voice. She was remembering when they were children, how earnest Haiwen had always been about making it up to her when she was upset over even the smallest things. He was still the same person, she could see. Still earnest, still too much in his head. She'd been unfair to be angry at him: he hadn't changed from whom he'd once been; she was the one who had.

"Sorr—" He caught himself and sighed. He pressed a palm to the back of his head, smoothing his hair.

Suchi laughed. She filled their teacups and took a sip. "I asked you here today to thank you for finding out the information about my mother. Samson says—he talked to your niece to check some details, and it really seems it might be her."

"It was nothing," Haiwen demurred. "I just thought I'd try. If nothing had panned out, I wouldn't have said anything."

"But at least you tried." Suchi paused, fiddling with her chopstick wrapper. "Sulan wanted to find them, but I was convinced—*convinced*—there was no point to it. I told her we'd only find heartbreak."

"You were trying to protect her," he said, but Suchi shook her head.

"If only I had listened to Sulan then, we would have found my mother earlier, while Sulan was still alive, before my mother was too old to remember us. Maybe we could have brought her back to the States to live with us. Maybe—" She choked on the words. In the last few days, Suchi had felt the loss of her sister all over again, grieving that Sulan would never know what Suchi now knew. "It's my fault we didn't find her sooner."

Haiwen reached a hand out, as if to touch her, but withdrew it quickly. "No," he said. "You can't do that. You yourself told me you can't regret the past. You can only move forward. You told me that."

Suchi bit down hard on her lip, unable to meet Haiwen's eyes. She'd lived by those words. She'd spent her life not looking backward, only focused on surviving what was in front of her, pressing ahead day by day. For so many years, she'd told herself this was courage, but now the decades had passed and she found that this whole time she'd only been running away.

The waiter came, placing two warm waters in front of them. Haiwen thanked him. Suchi cupped the glass between her palms.

"You said you went back once. Tell me. What was that like?"

Haiwen sipped at his water before responding. "I won't lie to you. It was hard. Things weren't as we had left them. I felt like an outsider. My brother and sister have bitterness between them. And my parents—they're gone, and I can never make up for all the years I should have spent by their side. All of the brokenness—it sometimes feels like it's my fault. I used to go over that choice I made, the choice to leave, trying to figure out if it was truly selfless like I told myself it was at the time or if I was deluded, pretending to be a hero."

"You can't think that way."

"I know, I know." Haiwen shook his head. "We can't erase what's happened. The past is the past, and it will always stay that way. The only thing we have is the present, what's here in front of us."

Suchi thought of what they'd all been speculating about Haiwen's condition. She thought about the memories he cherished, the ones he'd spent so long holding on to, so long examining. She had never imagined that even as she tried to erase her past, there'd been someone out there who felt she was worth remembering. For all these years, Haiwen had kept everything that had been lost alive within him. Even if the rumors weren't true and Haiwen was fine, time was finite. One day all he cherished would be taken from him.

"I was wrong," she said. "Even if we can't change the past, that doesn't mean it doesn't matter. On Chuxi, I said the Susu you knew was killed off. But that's not true, not really. She still exists. You're just the only one in the world left who knows her."

Haiwen smiled at her. "And you're the only person who truly knows Doudou," he said. "That's what I came here to tell you." He sighed. "It really was my fault on New Year's, for not respecting your pain. I understand now. I'm done obsessing over the past. What matters isn't what was or what could have been. What matters is this. You knowing me. Me knowing you. That's what I want in my life."

Suchi looked at him. His face was so unlike hers, so often neutral. And yet she could read it so well, even after all these years. She knew how to read his fear and love and pride and sadness and joy. But someday, she might see his face and register only blankness. Could she bear it? Could she move forward with him in her life, knowing that was what the future might hold?

"Did I ever tell you the moment I realized I was in love with you?"

Haiwen looked surprised. He shook his head. "I don't think you have."

"It was when you came and met me at school one afternoon. It had been raining. And of course, I hadn't brought an umbrella, even though I'm sure my mother had warned me to. But then there you were. Waiting for me with an umbrella in your hand. Despite the fact that you were so often absent-minded when it came to yourself, you knew me well enough to know I wouldn't have brought one. You were the first person apart from my family to care for me like that."

Haiwen was gazing at her, and she thought she could see him trying to pull up the memory.

"I thought to myself, *This is someone who will do this for me for the rest of our lives.* And I could see all the umbrellas you would bring me, a line of them stretching into infinity, the skin of your palm on their handles becoming more creased over time, your hair turning thinner and grayer."

"Well, now I'm that man," Haiwen said, cocking a sideways smile. "I'm old and wrinkled and gray. But I didn't think to bring you an umbrella."

"But you did," Suchi said, reaching out to squeeze his hands. Haiwen said nothing, but he squeezed back, his fingers thin but solid, calloused everywhere.

THE AIRPLANE'S ENGINE HUMMED QUIETLY. SUCHI stared out the window into the dark nothingness. The map on the screen in front of her showed they were over endless ocean, heading toward the North Pole, where they would then arc back down to Shanghai in a path that Samson explained was the quickest due to the Earth's spherical shape. It had already been seven hours. Her knees were sore; she imagined her blood clotting in her joints from their being bent for so long. Soon she'd have to wake Samson so she could go to the bathroom and do the circulation exercises they kept recommending on the screen. He snored lightly next to her, slumped to one side, his head bobbing toward her. When he slept, he looked exactly as he had as a boy. Gently, she pressed his head down, letting him rest on her shoulder.

She gazed over at Haiwen, who slept with his back straight, his hands folded one on top of the other. In so many ways, he was unchanged from the boy she had fallen in love with six decades ago.

She hadn't asked him about the day he had gotten lost, or about the speculations people had about his condition. It didn't matter, she realized. Instead, she spent hours asking him what he remembered. She was hungry for memories now; she wanted to replay them over and over again with him, to recover from him all the things she had forgotten or had never known. They were both old, every day growing older. Someday he might forget her; someday she might forget him. But that was someday. Today, they still had time.

She reached out and placed her hand on top of his. His eyes opened. He smiled at her.

"Can't sleep?" he asked, his voice soft and barely audible above the engine's hum. His thumb stroked the back of her hand.

Should we call him your boyfriend now? Samson had teased. But her son didn't understand—who they were to each other, it was beyond labels. They were just them. Haiwen and Suchi.

She gazed past him, back out the window at the airplane wing's lone light.

"I was thinking about my mother," she said quietly. "A few months after you joined the army, she began lighting a red paper lantern every evening and hanging it in front of the shikumen without explanation. After a week, I asked her why she did this and she told me, *It's what mothers used to do back in my old village. For the boys who went to fight the Japanese. They didn't know if or when they'd be back, but this way, if they were on the road late at night, they could find their way home."*

She could feel Haiwen's thumb, still rubbing her hand, steadily, unwavering.

"I was heartbroken at the time, you know, and it put me in a bad temper. Just another useless, old-fashioned superstition. Still, M'ma set out the lantern every single evening without fail. When I couldn't fall asleep, I'd gaze out the window, just like this, and see the flickering red shadows and feel comforted."

Haiwen squeezed her hand. "She loved you."

Suchi nodded. Despite her mother's disapproval of Haiwen, in the end, she had wished for his safe return, if not for his own sake, then for her daughter's happiness. This quiet love was something Suchi had been too young and impatient to see. Suchi wondered now if M'ma had continued to light that lantern once the girls were gone. Maybe she kept that light burning to lead her own daughters home.

And Suchi was almost home. Or, rather, she was almost with her mother. Haiwen's niece would be waiting for them at the airport when they landed; she had promised to take them straight to the place where M'ma lived. Xuenong had warned them that while the woman had been told about Suchi's impending arrival, it was unclear how much she understood.

Suchi knew now that home wasn't a place. It wasn't moments that could be pinned down. It was people, people who shared the same ghosts as you, of folks long gone, places long disappeared. People who knew you, saw you, loved you. When those people were far-flung, your home was too. And when those people were gone, home lived on inside you.

She missed her mother. More than she had dared to let herself feel in decades. But she was excited too. Her veins trembled. She ran through all she wanted to tell her mother—about her life in Hong Kong and America, about Sulan and the business, about Samson and the kids, about finding Haiwen. She thought of all the questions she wanted to ask, questions she probably would never get the answers to, questions about Apa and their lives after the Communist take-over, about Haiwen's mother and the surprising friendship they had developed. She would apologize for taking so long to find her. Thank her for sending her away, something Suchi now understood must have been unbearably painful. There were all the memories she wanted to recount, of their lives in Sifo Li, of the little shikumen they had grown up in. She wanted to know if M'ma could still hum the songs she used to sing to the girls when they couldn't fall asleep, if she could teach Suchi how to make her famous meatballs.

She would reintroduce Haiwen to her mother, ask her, *Do you remember Waong Haeven? Your lanterns worked; we found each other again.* She thought of how it would feel, to introduce her son to her mother, to tell her, *This is your brave, strong grandson. He is idealistic like Apa and loyal like you.*

She would sit by her mother's side. She would cook her porridge and feed her until she was certain her mother was no longer hungry, or lonely, or scared.

If M'ma didn't react, if she had no answers, no questions of her own, Suchi wouldn't be disappointed. The words weren't important. What Suchi wanted most was to hold her mother's hand. To place it warm against her face. To tell her mother, *It's your daughter, Suji, returned,* and hope beyond hope her mother would recognize her.

Coda

JUNE 1982
Shanghai

P LUM RAIN FALLS in sheets upon the eaves of Sifo Li. The gutters can't keep up with the downpour; the alleys flood ankle-deep. Old patriotic posters peel from brick, the mush of their tattered messages swirling away in small eddies along with other refuse: broken bottles, dead leaves, fruit skins, chicken bones. The rooftops, many in disrepair, leak. Inside, mold crawls down the walls. Roaches skitter in from cracks and drains, taking refuge. Mosquitoes hang in the murky air.

The human residents are mostly strangers to one another, though they live as stacked neighbors. Each shikumen cleaved into boxes, entire families to a room, every door locked. In this one, a baby squalls, waking his twin. In this one, a newlywed couple makes covert love next to the husband's sleeping parents. In this one, a teenage girl studies for her exams under a flickering lamp. They all know of the old woman who has the whole shikumen to herself, have speculated with envy in their voices about whom she must be related to. But not one will think of her during this long night. They can't even remember her name.

For now, she still knows it, despite the pain and the drugs and the dreams and the sleep. She is *Ma* to her children. *Pingping* to her husband. *Waong thatha* to the other vendors. *Li Yuping* to the government officials. *Tsia* to the woman beside her, this woman, Sieu'in. A lifetime ago they were wary acquaintances, mutually disdainful of each other's backgrounds. Now Sen Sieu'in is the only friend Yuping has in the world.

But her name doesn't matter to her anymore. What matters are the other names, thick under her breath: Doudou and Susu. Haiwen and Suchi. She can see them in the courtyard, Doudou chubby cheeked, his hands playing "Meditation" perfectly, the notes drawing out like a clear wind upon sea; Suchi laughing and twirling beside him, a butterfly. They float, they fly. Beautiful, perfect, brilliant children.

Come in, you'll catch a cold, she says, for the summer rain is drawing a curtain around them, obscuring their faces. It's time to come home.

<hr>

SHE OPENS HER EYES AND SEES SIEU'IN BESIDE HER, A tired old woman in a chair. Sound fills the room, the never-ending percussion of water, a thrum, a hum, as if the entire shikumen will soon be ocean.

They're almost here, Sieu'in says. *The children.*

I know, she wants to say. I spoke to them.

She's been floating in a sea of his images: Doudou as a chubby smiling toddler; Doudou a solemn child, hair falling in his face as he practices; Doudou a quiet teenager lying on his back in the courtyard with the record player spinning beside him; Doudou's unwavering gaze at Suchi at all ages, in every room she's in, his love painfully obvious to Yuping, to everyone but himself.

In her dreams, he often comes to her as the age she saw him last, sixteen, kind and serious. She never dreams of him older, never dreams of him as a man, and she tells herself this is not because he has not made it to adulthood but because of a failure of her own imagination.

But Sieu'in continues: *You should have told them you were sick. They're your children. They deserve to know.*

Of course. Sieu'in means Mingming and Junjun. The children who are grown. She feels a pang of regret for their worry, their sorrow. But how could she have told them? She has spent so long trying to hold this family together. Her children turn to her, they rely on her, they would move mountains for her. How can she break their hearts? The job of a mother is to protect her children. Her children might never be able to forgive her for this, but surely, Sieu'in understands.

You're lucky, Sieu'in says, *to be able to have your children near you. I wish—* And in the vacuum of sound, Yuping can hear two girl-shaped holes. After a moment, Sieu'in clucks, *This weather.*

Yuping wonders: Are the children warm? Do they have somewhere to shelter? Are they wearing enough clothes, did they remember an umbrella? This is what is hardest. The not-knowing. The questions that can never be answered.

My girls loved the rain, Sieu'in says. *Suji especially. I couldn't stop her from splashing in the puddles, from running out and catching a cold. Where the rest of us saw nuisance, she saw adventure. I scolded her so many times. Perhaps I was too hard on her. Perhaps I should have allowed her her fun.*

She hears it in Sieu'in's voice. The guilt. The worry. The thing she confessed once to her, a fear: *What if they don't know how proud I was of them? What if they believe I let them go because I didn't love them?*

Gathering strength, Yuping moves her tired fingers, searching. She feels Sieu'in's hand, knobby and cold. Sieu'in is strong. She never talks about what she and her husband experienced when they'd disappeared. She will not talk about what happened to her husband at the labor camp in Anhui, how she ended up back in Shanghai alone, what she's had to do to survive, and Yuping knows not to ask. There are some memories that can never be spoken.

Yuping wants to tell Sieu'in she did her best, they both did their best. They had been given impossible choices, ones no one could be expected to make without regret. If Yuping had not let Haiwen go, it would have been Haiming whom she would have lost. If Sieu'in had not sent her daughters to Hong Kong, they would have stayed and suffered. What can a mother do but be steadfast in her love and hope?

The letter. She remembers now she must tell Sieu'in where it's hidden, stuffed between bricks of the terrace wall. When did it arrive? Weeks ago? Days? Months? Before she was too tired to walk, to talk. By then her vision was already clouding, her thoughts already muddled, but she saw the foreign stamps, and then the gold ring, impossibly, like a magic token, shook out onto the desk, and she knew.

The gold ring is loose on her forefinger now, and she tries to press it into Sieu'in's palm. She remembers when she gave it to Doudou, how earlier in the day she'd seen it in the pawnshop, simple yet elegant, and known it was perfect for Suchi. Now she slips it onto Sieu'in's finger, trying to tell her, This belongs to your daughter. This is hers. You must return it to her.

Sieu'in protests at first, saying, *Save these precious things for your children*. But then she stops. Fingers the ring. *Where did you get this?* she asks. *It looks like something I once bought for Suji, long ago.*

She nods, satisfied her friend understands, and curls her hands away from Sieu'in's attempt to return the band.

～

DOUDOU AND SUCHI ARE BIRDS ON THE WIND. THEY ARE flying toward her, branches laden with berries in their beaks. They warble a song. But the branches slip and fall. The children dive away. They are fish in this ocean, being pulled away by the current. Wait, she wants to say. Come back. She has to build a boat, a lighthouse, a siren. She has to call them home.

～

IT IS JUST HER AND SIEU'IN AGAIN. SIEU'IN, WHISPERING about the past, about Suji and Haeven. She speaks of a violin cradled in Suchi's arms the day she left. She speaks of a lantern she lit for years and years, hoping to guide them home. *I lit one tonight, but the rain*, Sieu'in says sorrowfully. *I know it's silly to hope, but one never gives up on miracles.*

Yuping remembers: They don't need miracles. They don't need lanterns. Paper, she tells Sieu'in, and after several attempts, Sieu'in finally brings her paper. She knows what she wants to dictate.

Come home. We are waiting. Nothing is your fault, if anything it's our fault, for not having protected you, for not having held you, for missing your entire life. Come home.

She says this to Sieu'in but Sieu'in doesn't understand. Write, she urges her.

Write. Write. Write.

Sieu'in, says, finally, *I never learned how to read or write.*

But that can't be possible, because the letter appears before her, written in beautiful calligraphy, careful neat characters in perfect columns down the page. She watches her own hands fold the letter, inserting it in the envelope. She puts the stamps on herself. She tracks the letter as it's carried away, out of the shikumen, out of Sifo Li, out of Shanghai, across the sea, finding its way to Haiwen.

Hurry. Hurry.

YUPING AWAKES TO HER FAMILY BY HER SIDE. SHE CAN hear her granddaughter's and grandson's quiet sobs, can feel her great-granddaughter's little hands on her arm, pulsing warm with life. Mingming calls her in a soothing voice. *Ma. Ma.* Junjun clutches her shoulder and cries into it: *Why didn't you tell us?*

She is sorry to them both. To Mingming, her eldest son. Dutiful, quick-witted Mingming, who should have inherited a textile empire, should have spent his old age retired in comfort. Mingming, who even now, after so long, grieves his wife, who can't shake the bitterness of his lot. To Junjun, her youngest. Spunky, bright Junjun, whose childhood ended too early and smiles have become rare. Junjun, who, like her, was faced with an impossible choice as a mother and now sags under the weight of what she's done. She knows they have suffered, knows they are lonely in ways she cannot fill, that a chasm lies between them she cannot bridge. Her regret is as wide as her love for them. She has failed as a mother. She has failed to protect them.

Forgive me, she tells them, but they cannot hear her, they are squabbling again, throwing barbs, placing blame. The words pierce and echo; they are haloed with the bitterness of decades-old wounds.

She wants to tell her children to stop arguing. The past doesn't matter anymore; they all did what they had to in order to live. She wants to tell them what matters most is family—it is the only thing that matters, the only way to make a home. They alone will remember Haiwen when she is gone. They alone will remember their father, and soon, her. She wants to tell them people only die when there is no one left to remember them, but if they hold each other tightly, they can keep all the ghosts of their family alive.

She is so tired. In the distance, beyond the staccato of the rain, she hears Haiwen's violin. She wishes she could hear his voice one more time. She wishes he would pause in his playing for a moment and speak to her. She wants to hear him call her *Ma*. But he is happy, right? He is healthy and eating? She wants to tell him she is waiting for him, still, and she will keep waiting for him. She can hold on until he shows up. If only she knew he was coming. Didn't he receive her letter? Isn't that why he is playing his music, to let her know he is on his way, that he hasn't forgotten her?

She calls out his name. Other voices press around her, no longer arguing, and she searches for the clear, quiet voice of her middle child, her youngest son. She hears weeping. She hears Sieu'in, firm in her ear: *Tsia, when Haeven comes, I promise I'll tell him you waited as long as you could. I promise I'll guide him to you.*

But what is Sieu'in talking about? He is almost here. She can feel it. She can hear the long, plaintive note of a violin, and it is growing louder.

Notes

1. *Shòu*, meaning "long life, longevity."

2. This famous Tang dynasty poem, whose title translates to "Home-coming" or "Returning Home," is commonly only known by its first stanza:

    I departed a youth, I return now aged
    Though my accent remains, my hair has
        thinned
    A stranger to the children that I meet
    Laughing, they ask me from where
        I come

    The second, less well-known stanza:

    Farewells were said long ago
    Familiar faces have long since gone
    Only water of the nearby Mirror Lake
    Ripples unchanged in spring breeze

3. These lyrics for Bai Guang's "Fire of Love" translate to: "Coyish glances, ebbing and flowing / Flirtatious as blossoms, tenderly as willows."

4. The Shanghainese gender-neutral third-person pronoun *yī* (伊) led Suchi to assume both her mother and the tobacco shop owner had meant "he," not "she."

5. The word for octopus in Mandarin is *zhāngyú*.

6. The lyrics translate to:

Unite, East Asian nations!
With mutual respect and independence, preventing communism together
We are the pioneers in the wilderness
We are the heroes who created civilization
Public is awakening, public is awakening, shouldering the mission
    of East Asia's revival
Cries for peace surging throughout the land
Arousing miles and miles of great progress.

Unite, East Asian nations!
Economic collaboration, cultural exchanges
We are devoted to safeguarding East Asia
We are resolute in our determination
Unafraid of hardships, unafraid of hardships, fostering the East
    Asian spirit
Bright torches have been lit, leading the peaceful new masses.

Unite, East Asian nations!
Advancing hand in hand, celebrating triumph together
We must extinguish smolders of warfare in the world

We must conquer rebellions against justice
Strive forward, strive forward, completing the East Asian
    coexistence and co-prosperity circle
Uniting six hundred million compatriots in East Asia, ushering in a
    new era in history.

7. 門當戶對 (*mén dāng hù duì*) is an idiomatic expression literally translating to "matching doors," but meaning to be well-matched in social and economic status.

8. "Main Street."

9. Sifu Li/Sifo Li.

10. *Jì* (冀) means "to hope" or "to long for."

11. Known as "Bubbling Well Road" to English speakers.

12. Baak3 Lok6 Mun4.

13. In his later years and for many years posthumously, Chiang Kai-shek was often called 蔣公 in Taiwan, a respectful honorific that approximately translates to "Lord Chiang," or sometimes 總統蔣公—"President Lord Chiang."

14. 寧可錯殺一千，不可錯放一人
Variations on this phrase have been attributed to Chiang Kai-shek, though many say it actually originated with Wang Jing-wei, who eventually betrayed his government to collude with the Japanese people during the Sino-Japanese War. Others say it dates back even further. It's hard to verify who said it first at this point, as it's a well-known expression used to justify the ruthless methods of authoritarian regimes.

Acknowledgments

～

About twenty years ago, in the wake of my grandfather's death, I became interested in the stories of the migrants who fled from China to Taiwan at the end of the Chinese Civil War. As my family was going through his things, we found a photograph of him weeping in front of his mother's grave in Shanghai, a mother he had not seen since he was nineteen years old. It was an image that I could not shake. I soon learned his story was not unique and began to search for these heartbreaking stories in Chinese-language media. What I found was an entire history of war and separation I had never been taught about in my American education.

Although I knew early on I wanted to write about this period of Chinese and Taiwanese history, I was hesitant: as I am not a historian, I wasn't sure I could bring these stories to life with the detail and accuracy that painting such a story required. Luckily for me, there are many scholars and historians who have done in-depth research on various aspects of this history, as well as first-hand accounts published by individuals. I am indebted to numerous publications for holding the answers to the many questions I had as I wrote this book.

For an overview of the Sino-Japanese War and Chinese Civil War, I turned to *Forgotten Ally* by Rana Mitter and *Civil War in China* by Suzanne Pepper. For a picture of Shanghai during wartime in particular, I am indebted to *In the Shadow of the Rising Sun* edited by Christian Henriot and Wen-hsin Yeh, *Beyond the Neon Lights* by Hanchao Lu, and *Shanghai Splendor* by Wen-hsin Yeh. *Yellow Music* by Andrew F. Jones was an incredibly fascinating and thoughtful account of the emergence of Chinese popular music at the turn of the century while *Rhapsody in Red* by Jindong Cai and Sheila Melvin gave me detailed background on the classical music scene in China during the same period. For the minutiae of daily life in Shanghai, I turned to personal biographies: *Our Story* by Rao Pingru, *Remembering Shanghai* by Claire Chao and Isabel Sun Chao, and *Shanghai Daisy* by Daisy Kwok. To bring the longtang neighborhood to life, I am grateful to *Shanghai Homes* by Jie Li and *Lilong Lives* by Jérémy Cheval. The chapters about the soldiers in Taiwan rely heavily on the scholarship of Joshua Fan in *China's Homeless Generation* as well as Mahlon Meyer's *Remembering China from Taiwan*. I am thankful to the short story collection *The Last of the Whampoa Breed* edited by Pang-yuan Chi and David Der-wei Wang, an anthology about those same soldiers. The one detail about the elephant at Lai Chi Kok is thanks to the blog of Roy Maloy (roymaloy.wordpress.com). While I had written most of this book by the time Helen Zia's *Last Boat Out of Shanghai* was published, her book helped me think more deeply about my characters and flesh them out as I went into revisions. Similarly, I am grateful to the scholarship of Dominic Meng-Hsuan Yang, whose *The Great Exodus from China* was published when I had completed drafting the novel but helped me confirm the work I was doing.

There are also many, many individual scholarly papers I consulted to confirm single details; alas, the number is so great that it would take up too much space for me to list them all here. All I can say is a great big thank-you to the many Sinologists who have published papers on China in the first half of the twentieth century.

Lastly, this book could not exist without Lung Ying-tai's 大江大海 (*Big River, Big Sea*), the first book I came across that held accounts of the ways in which the fallout of the Chinese Civil War affected individuals and families on both sides of the strait. I read most of this book digitally with a Chinese-English dictionary plug-in; I hope one day someone publishes this book in English so more of the diaspora can learn these stories.

There are also many individuals who aided me as I researched this book: Odila Schroeder, who enthusiastically engaged with my questions about Shanghai music schools in the 1940s and reviewed several early chapters. My cousin, Yiqian Yang, who patiently fielded my questions about Shanghainese terms and pronunciation for the last seven years. Chih-Yun Hsu, who shared his own father's story as a former Nationalist soldier. Patrick Cranley, Tina Kanagaratnam, and George Wang for addressing my questions on longtang communities and life in Shanghai in the early twentieth century. Clara Iwasaki for reviewing an early draft of the book for historical errors. Irene Eber for answering my questions on the Jewish section in Shanghai. Lori Feren and Rachel Siegelaub for sharing their experiences with multiple sclerosis. Rachel DeWoskin for advice on how to research in Shanghai. Tevi Eber, my sounding board for all things musical. Sofia Levchenko for answering questions I had around the mechanics of playing the violin and specific pieces. Maukuei Chang for guidance on how to approach waishengren studies in Taiwan. Joshua Fan for answering my specific questions about the Nationalist draft system. Jen Wei Ting for reviewing my Chinese names for appropriateness. Richard Peña for fielding my questions about my epigraph. Ender Terwilliger and Evan Nicoll-Johnson for engaging with my random questions on Chinese language, history, and music. All those who weighed in when I asked questions about language on social media. Thank you also to the YouTube channel of TwoSet Violin, run by Eddy Chen and Brett Yang, whose humorous violin videos were extremely educational for a nonplayer like me.

I am also grateful for the existence of the Waishengren Association, the Shanghai Jewish Refugees Museum, the 228 Memorial Museum, the Military Brothel Exhibition Hall, the Shanghai Development Exhibition Hall, the Shanghai Conservatory of Music, and many other museums and preserved sites in Shanghai and Taiwan that continue to tell these particular histories and made it possible for me to imagine stories within their spaces.

I have done my best to synthesize all the work and guidance of the aforementioned individuals and institutions, and have strived to be as accurate as possible within this book. Occasionally, in the service of storytelling, I have taken a few liberties. For instance, Sifo Li is not a real longtang that exists off Fuzhou Road but is based upon several longtang communities I visited and read about. Any other factual errors or anachronisms are my own.

Beyond the research, this book could not have been possible without a great many other individuals and organizations.

Thank you to my talented editor, Tara Singh Carlson, whose editorial vision, patience, and faith helped Haiwen and Suchi come fully alive within these pages. Thank you for taking a chance on me and for believing in this book.

To my amazing agent, Michelle Brower, who believed in my writing years before I even began work on this book. Thank you for being my biggest champion and putting up with all my neurotic emails. You are truly the best.

To the whole team at Putnam: Aranya Jain, Ivan Held, Sally Kim, Alexis Welby, Ashley McClay, Shina Patel, Katie McKee, Emily Mileham, Ryan Richardson, Lorie Pagnozzi, Jazmin Miller, Vi-An Nguyen, and Daniel Brount. Thank you for giving this book such a wonderful home.

To my team across the pond at Sceptre: Jo Dingley, Ansa Khan Khattak, Federico Andornino, Nico Parfitt, Maria Garbutt-Lucero, Natalie Chen, Kerri Logan, and Jennifer Wilson.

To the talented Allison Malecha, who shepherded Haiwen and Suchi into the hands of so many outside of the US. You are a magician. To the rest of my incredible team at Trellis Literary Management: Natalie Edwards, Danya Kukafka, Khalid McCalla, Elizabeth Pratt, and Tori Clayton.

To all my co-agents and publishing teams across the world, but particularly to Florence Rees in the UK, who found a perfect UK home for my book, and Gray Tan in Taiwan, who welcomed me into the literary community here in my second home.

To the Fulbright Association, for the time and space to research this book—the fellowship to Taiwan has changed my life in more ways than one.

To the residencies and associations that provided time, space, and funding to create this work: New Jersey State Council on the Arts, Mid Atlantic Arts Foundation, Millay Colony, Virginia Center for the Creative Arts, the Ragdale Foundation, Willapa Bay AiR, and Kimmel Harding Nelson.

To Kundiman, Asian American Writers Workshop, and VONA for not only providing me with the safe space to find myself as a writer, but also a community that has sustained me and helped me to grow. You are whom I write for.

To my family of writers, editors, and coworkers at *Hyphen* and Asian Americans for Civil Rights and Equality. It has been a privilege to hold a space for Asian Americans with you. Thank you too, to *The Rumpus* and Catapult, for making me a better editor and writer.

To Sari Botton, for publishing the essay I wrote about my grandfather that is deeply in conversation with this novel. To Catherine Chung, Matthew Salesses, Nicole Chung, and Rowan Hisayo Buchanan for publishing the short stories that were my first attempts at writing about this period; those stories made it possible for me to imagine writing a longer work.

To all of the faculty I worked with at Sarah Lawrence College, but particularly David Hollander, Nelly Reifler, and Jeffrey McDaniel— I will never be able to repay you for the impact you have had upon my writing.

To the other mentors I've had the privilege to work with throughout the years, particularly Gina Apostol, Porochista Khakpour, and M. Evelina Galang.

To my sixth grade teacher, George Penny, who nominated me for my first writing award. You were the first person to believe I had something important to say through my writing. I hope I did you proud.

To my former therapist, Dr. James Twerell. You saved my life. You believed I could write this book. I wish I could have shown it to you.

To my brilliant first readers, Juliet Grames and Erika Swyler, who, along with Jennifer Ambrose, make up the Time Traveling Circus. Thank you not just for the incisive reads, but also for the constant emotional support. To Karen McMurdo, who also provided me with critical early feedback, but more importantly, twenty-five years of friendship. To dear and talented friends Vu Tran, Matthew Salesses, Adrienne Celt, Nicole Chung, Catherine Chung, and T Kira Madden for all the publishing advice and support. Birthing a debut novel is a nerve-racking thing, but having you all to turn to has helped me survive it with grace.

To the many other friends on both sides of the world who made the writing of this book possible by making the living outside of this work something to be treasured, particularly: Jeeho Lee, Patrick Rosal, Tevi Eber, Christine Hyung-Oak Lee, Devan Goldstein, Judy Hong, Sarah Lee, Kaiwen Lin, Doreen Wang, Ing Lan Chang, Nicole Kung, Angelic Shen, Dana Liu, Peggy Wang, Hui-Yi Yen, Kathy Cheng, and Clarissa Wei. To Jasmine Ting, Jerry Chantemsin, and Connor Maley for saving my life over fifteen years ago. To 小西, 美環, Ken Lin, and my goddaughter Emma for welcoming me into your family in Taipei.

To Ernie Chang for capturing my author photo when I was thirteen weeks pregnant (and my maternity photos at thirty-four weeks!).

To the parents who helped me survive new motherhood: Adrienne Celt, Jennifer Yang, An Rong Xu, Grace Lu, and the whole New Babes Slack group.

To my BFF Eugenia Leigh. For dreaming big with me when we were baby writers and always being my person, no matter the situation. For saving me again and again. May we always be each other's loudest hypewoman.

ACKNOWLEDGMENTS

To my mother-in-law, 白沈仙桃, who watched my baby several days out of the week starting when I was three months postpartum, so that I could finally finish my revisions.

To my family for a lifetime of love and support. My grandparents, from whom I learned strength, audacity, and a capacity to dream. My aunts Lily, Cassia, and Sen. My brother, Jonathan, the first person to inhabit the stories I created. My sister, Kailene, my best friend and confidante. My father, Yen-Jo, who has always been proud of my writing despite not being much of a reader himself. And most importantly my mother, Violet, who helped me with many of the translations of verses in this book, whose love, sacrifice, and support has made all of this possible. The love I have for you is threaded throughout this book.

To my husband, Brian, who, at this very moment, is watching our child so I can write these acknowledgments, who helped me research Chinese-language sites for answers I couldn't find in English, who patiently answered all my questions about Taiwanese language and customs. I am so grateful to have a partner who fully believes in the importance of my work (despite not reading English!), who makes space for my writing, and who is as dedicated, thoughtful, and patient as you are. 我真的很愛你.

And last but not least, to my child, A. I wrote the first drafts of this book when you were just a wish, as a daughter who couldn't fathom being separated from her own mother. But as I worked on revisions with the awareness of your tiny life only a few rooms away, this book transformed into one about my love for you, a love neither time nor distance nor circumstance could ever diminish. Thank you for making my world bigger and more remarkable every day. I love you to the moon and back.